A WOUNDED
REALM

ALSO BY K. M. ASHMAN

THE INDIA SOMMERS MYSTERIES
The Dead Virgins
The Treasures of Suleiman
The Mummies of the Reich
The Tomb Builders

THE ROMAN CHRONICLES
The Fall of Britannia
The Rise of Caratacus
The Wrath of Boudicca

THE MEDIEVAL SAGAS
Blood of the Cross
In Shadows of Kings
Sword of Liberty
Ring of Steel

THE BLOOD OF KINGS
A Land Divided
A Wounded Realm

INDIVIDUAL NOVELS
Savage Eden
The Last Citadel
Vampire

AUDIO BOOKS
A Land Divided
A Wounded Realm
Blood of the Cross
The Last Citadel

Follow Kevin's blog at:

www.KMAshman.co.uk

Or contact him direct at:

Author@kmashman.co.uk

K. M. ASHMAN

THE BLOOD OF KINGS: BOOK TWO

A WOUNDED REALM

THOMAS & MERCER

This is a work of fiction. Names, characters, organizations, places, events, and incidents are either products of the author's imagination or are used fictitiously.

Published by Thomas & Mercer, Seattle

www.apub.com

Amazon, the Amazon logo, and Thomas & Mercer are trademarks of Amazon.com, Inc., or its affiliates.

ISBN-13: 9781503948433
ISBN-10: 1503948439

Cover Illustration by Alan Lynch
Cover design by Lisa Horton

Printed in the United States of America

MEDIEVAL MAP OF WALES

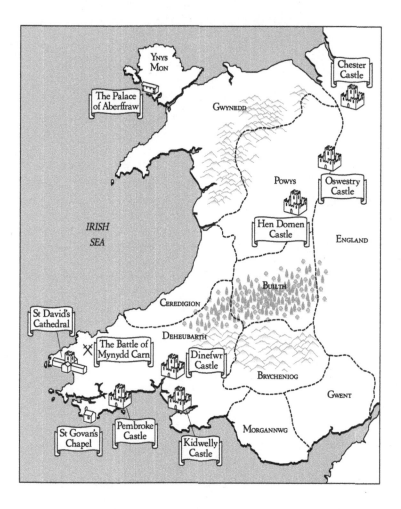

Though the borders and boundaries of early Wales were constantly changing, for the sake of our story, the above shows an approximation of where the relevant areas were at the time.

Character List

Although correct pronunciation is not really necessary to enjoy the story, for those who would rather experience the authentic way of saying the names, explanations are provided in italics.

THE HOUSE OF ABERFFRAW

Gruffydd ap Cynan: King of Gwynedd – *Gruff-ith ap Cun-nan*
Angharad ferch Owain: Married to Gruffydd – *Ang (as in hang) Harad*
Cadwallon ap Gruffydd: Oldest son of Gruffydd
Cadwaladr ap Gruffydd: Second Son of Gruffydd
Gwenllian ap Gruffydd: Daughter of Gruffydd
Adele: Angharad's maid – *Ad-Ell*

The 'll' can be difficult to pronounce in Welsh, and is formed by placing the tongue on the roof of the mouth, while expelling air past the tongue on both sides. Non-Welsh speakers sometimes struggle with this – audible representations are available online.

Cynwrig the Tall: Ally of Gruffydd – *Cun-rig*
Osian: Warrior of Gruffydd – *Osh-an*

THE HOUSE OF TEWDWR

Gwladus ferch Rhiwallon: Queen of Deheubarth – *Goo-lad-iss*
Hywel ap Rhys: Oldest son – *How-well*
Gruffydd ap Rhys: Youngest son (known as Tarw) – *Tar-oo (roll the letter 'R')*
Nesta ferch Rhys: Daughter – *Nessa or Nest-A*
Marcus Freeman: Loyal soldier of Gwladus
Dylan: Farmer – *Dill-an*
Emma: Maid of Gwladus

THE HOUSE OF POWYS

Cadwgan ap Bleddyn: Prince of Powys – *Ca-doo-gan*
Owain ap Cadwgan: Son of Cadwgan – *Ow-ain*

CHESTER CASTLE

Huw D'Avranches: Huw the Fat
Alan Beauchamp: Knight of Henry
Beatty: Innkeeper
Guy: Son of Beatty

BATTLE OF YNYS MON

Hugh of Montgomery: Second Earl of Shrewsbury
Robert of Rhuddlan: Cousin of Huw the Fat – *Ruth-lan*
Magnus Barefoot: Viking King

THE SIEGE OF PEMBROKE CASTLE

Hywel ap Goronwy: Lord of Radnor – Known as Goronwy *Gor-on-woy*
Uchtryd ap Edwin: Minor lord of Englefield – Known as Edwin
Godwin: Knight of Henry
Gerald Fitzwalter: Known as Gerald of Windsor

HEN DOMEN

Lord Belleme: Castellan of Hen Domen – *Bell-e-me*

Sir Broadwick: Knight of Henry

OTHER CHARACTERS

King William the Second: Also known as William Rufus

Henry Beauclerc: Brother of William the Second

Lord Walter Tirel: Norman Lord serving King William the Second

Arnulf of Montgomery: Norman Lord serving King William the Second

Hugh of Montgomery: Second Earl of Shrewsbury

Merriweather: Rapist

Meirion Goch: The Traitor of Mynydd Carn – *My-ree-on*

The beginning of 'Goch' is simply 'Go' but the second half is more difficult to pronounce. In Welsh, the letters 'ch' form a guttural sound at the back of the throat by drawing the tongue fully back while allowing air to escape over the top of the tongue. Non-Welsh speakers struggle with this – audible representations are available online.

PLACE NAMES

Aberffraw: *Ab-er-frow*

Brycheniog: *Brick-eye-knee-og*

Carew: *Car-rew*

Deheubarth: *Du-hi-barrth (roll the 'R')*

Dinefwr: *Din-e-foorr (roll the 'R')*

Gwynedd: *Gwin-eth*

Hen Domen: *Hen-doe-men*

Mynydd Carn: *Mun-ith Ca-rr-n (roll the 'R')*

Powys: *Pow-iss*

Ynys Mon: *Un-iss Mon*

Prologue

The year is AD 1094 and the battle of the five kings at Mynydd Carn thirteen years earlier is a fading memory in the minds of those lucky enough to have survived the bloody horrors of those few cruel days. However, the lasting impact of the battle lives on.

Three Welsh kings met their destiny on the battlefield that fateful day, three monarchs who had made a pact with the Norman invaders and sought to carve up Wales between their greedy hands. However, despite their strength and overwhelmingly large armies, they had failed to factor in two other Welsh kings who saw subservience to a Norman ruler as a price they would never pay. Loyalty to their country proved more successful than loyalty to the purse.

Gruffydd ap Cynan was in exile in Ireland having lost the crown of Gwynedd Trahern ap Caradog while Rhys ap Tewdwr, king of Deheubarth in the south, was in hiding in Saint David's Cathedral on the west coast, having been ousted from his ancestral lands by Caradog ap Gruffydd of Gwent.

Despite this, with the help of Irish mercenaries and those few free men still loyal to their respective crowns, Gruffydd and Tewdwr managed to forge an army out of the ashes of their kingdoms and marched on the three-king alliance at Mynydd Carn, determined to win back the freedom their county so deeply craved.

Against overwhelming odds, the two exiled kings emerged victorious in a war that took the lives of many, and the three conspirators who had attempted to sell Wales to the English, died at the battle, armies dispersing back to whence they came.

After the battle, Rhys ap Tewdwr returned to Deheubarth and spent the next twelve years seeking his missing son, Hywel, who, at ten years old, had been abducted by Caradog. Although he received constant reports that his son was still alive, Tewdwr eventually died at the battle of Brycheniog in AD 1093, having never found Hywel. His grieving widow, Gwladus ap Rhiwallon continued to run the estate in Tewdwr's absence along with her daughter, Nesta, vowing one day to find her missing son.

Gwladus had another son, known as Tarw, but as the sole surviving heir to the Tewdwr dynasty, Tarw's life was at risk from those who saw the south as easy pickings. Without a strong male adult to lead the family, the way was open for any pretender to the throne to march his armies into Deheubarth and even if the boy wasn't killed immediately, he could easily disappear over the ensuing months. Subsequently, Gwladus sent Tarw across the sea to Ireland for his own safety.

In the north, Gruffydd headed home to try and rebuild his shattered kingdom but made the mistake of trusting a man named Meirion Goch, who had already proven himself to be a most duplicitous man, having betrayed his own king, Trahern, at the battle of Mynydd Carn. After the battle, Meirion Goch arranged a meeting between Gruffydd and the infamous Earl of Chester, Huw the Fat, at Chester Castle. Although the welcome was initially warm, the meeting turned out to be a trap and many of Gruffydd's men were slaughtered at the banquet.

Gruffydd was taken prisoner and kept in the most squalid of conditions. For years he was moved from prison to prison, displayed at English tournaments as a pathetic king of Wales and often flogged in public to remind the people that no man, whether pauper or king, was above the reach of English law. Eventually, Gruffydd faded from the public's memory as he was incarcerated in the stone dungeon of the keep at Chester Castle. Meirion Goch pocketed the reward money from Huw the Fat and returned to Wales, quickly disappearing, safe in the knowledge that only two men knew of his treachery: Huw the Fat, who had sworn an oath of secrecy, and Gruffydd ap Cynan, the Welsh king who would soon be dead.

Across Wales, family and opponents of the fallen had moved quickly to fill the voids left by the events at Mynydd Carn, and though the new rulers did not wage war against each other, there was still suspicion between all of the Welsh kingdoms.

The Normans and their English allies combined with Flemish mercenaries to apply even more pressure along the marches on the border between England and Wales, and though there was no formal war declared between the nations, gradually vast swathes of Welsh land fell to the invaders, subsequently resulting in most of the south coming under Norman rule.

Chester

October 10th, AD 1094

The fettered prisoner struck a pitiful sight as he staggered through the narrow streets of Chester. Tangled thickets of filthy hair fell down past his shoulders, matching the matted beard hanging to his chest, his skin parchment-thin from many years of sunless captivity. The hot baths he had once taken, the servants who had shaved him, were memories from a lifetime ago.

Blood-sodden rags wrapping his feet offered scant comfort and his wrists were nought but open sores where manacles ate at his flesh. The pathetic fabric hanging from his skeletal frame was useless against the wet autumn weather, but he had learned long ago that to protest invited nothing but beatings.

But this man kept hope beating in his heart. This was the same hope that had saved his life many years earlier, and though it seemed futile, the prisoner remained defiant. Such confidence is the wont of kings.

The citizens of Chester walked quickly by, some glancing briefly at the criminal in the custody of the earl's men but most just looking down, avoiding any reason to be engaged by the riders. It was, after all, none of their business.

'You there,' called one of the guards, known as Howard, as he reined in his horse, 'is there a tavern hereabouts where a man can get a meal and lodgings?'

The passer-by nodded quickly and pointed further along the narrow street.

'Aye, my lord, turn right at the stocks and cross the bridge.'

The rider kicked his horse and continued between the daubed walls of the narrow lane. The prisoner jerked as the slack was taken up and he staggered forward, hopeful he would soon be able to rest as his captors sought food and shelter.

'That looks like the place,' said one of the soldiers.

'Aye, it will do for me,' said one of his comrades, 'a hot meal and a cot is all I ask.'

They made their way over the bridge and dismounted before the tavern walls. A young and eager boy ran out to take the horses' reins closely followed by an enormous man, red of cheek and fat of belly.

'Welcome, strangers,' said the older man, pleased at the opportunity for more custom. 'Can I be of service to you on this wet evening?'

'Indeed, you can,' said Howard. 'We seek cots for four men as well as hot food. Do you have such fayre?'

'I do,' said the man with confusion, 'but I count five.' He nodded towards the prisoner now sitting in the mud against a fence post.

'Make no account of him,' spat the soldier, 'he is nought but a filthy Welshman and as such is lower than a dog.'

'He is truly in a wretched state, what crime is he guilty of?'

'That is the business of the Earl of Chester,' came the terse reply, 'and is of no interest to you. Now, do you have this food or not? For I can easily take my coin elsewhere.'

'No, come in,' said the innkeeper hastily, 'and please forgive my impertinence, I did not realise.'

Outside, the boy took the four horses, one by one, to the stable behind the tavern. He stripped them of their saddles before wiping them down and placing a net of hay before each as well as a few hands of oats in wooden buckets. When he was done he returned to the tavern but paused to stare at the forlorn figure laying prone amongst the mud and manure.

The prisoner became aware of someone watching him and slowly opened his eyes to meet the servant's gaze. Though his body was exhausted and he felt he could barely speak, the sight of a bag of oats in the boy's hand was too good an opportunity to miss.

'What is your name, boy?' he asked, his voice no more than a hoarse whisper.

The servant remained silent.

'Your name?' said the man again. 'You do have one, I suppose, or are you nought but a wretched beggar beholden to every man?'

'I am no beggar,' answered the boy, 'for I am a working man and make my living tending the horses. I am called Tom, though some know me as Tom the Horse for I have a way with such beasts.'

'I am pleased to meet you, Tom,' said the prisoner, 'I would take your wrist but alas I am fettered.'

'I can see that,' replied Tom, 'be you a murderer?'

'I have killed many men, Tom,' replied the man, recalling the heady days of conquest and battle, 'but all in the name of a just war. So the answer is, no – I am not a murderer.'

'Then why do you lay in fetters about my feet? Surely this is the fate of the most wretched.'

The starving man stared at the small sack in the boy's hands.

'If you give me a handful of whatever is in your bag,' he replied, 'I'll tell you a story so great it rivals the tales of Arthur himself.'

Tom's eyes widened slightly. Everyone knew the stories of the great Arthur, and though Tom knew he would never reach such heights in life, it was every boy's dream to achieve knighthood.

'I cannot,' replied Tom, glancing at his sack, 'for to do so may earn me a beating.'

'Just a handful,' begged the prisoner, all pride gone at the thought of some food, 'nobody will ever know.'

'I don't know,' said the boy.

'Tom, you seem like a good man. I am not your enemy nor am I a criminal. I am a hungry soul arrested for nought but fighting for freedom, and I promise you this. A handful of oats for a starving man is a gesture more noble than the greatest of victories upon the field of battle. Grant me this boon and I swear that one day, I will repay your kindness a thousandfold.'

Tom hesitated a moment longer before digging his hands into the sack and with a furtive look around, ran forward to pour the oats into the prisoner's lap. Immediately the Welshman hid them beneath a fold in his garment and looked thankfully up at the boy.

'You have my gratitude,' he said, 'and this makes you greater than the noblest knight. One day, you can ride in my armies and be known as Tom the Kingsaver.'

'You are no king,' said Tom, laughing at the man. 'You are a mere scoundrel in custody of the true king, William Rufus.'

'I admit my appearance would state the opposite,' said the prisoner, 'but I assure you I am King Gruffydd ap Cynan of Gwynedd, incarcerated these past twelve years in the dungeons of Chester Castle. You, kind sir, have just aided a man of royal birth descended from Sigtrygg Olafssen himself.'

The boy's eyes widened in awe.

'You are descended from Silkbeard?'

'He was my grandfather.'

'Then why do you lie in fetters?'

'I was tricked by means most foul, for my comrades and I had just won a mighty battle against traitorous countrymen. When I was summoned by Huw the Fat to attend a feast in honour of my victory, we were pounced upon by a great army and thrown into the deepest dungeon.'

'Why did he not have you killed?'

'He sees me as a mere plaything to be displayed at village fayres across England. Gruffydd, the caged king, they call me and oft am I pelted with the filth of the street. Despite this I hold up my head for I have nought to be ashamed of. I am the true king of Gwynedd and one day I will retake my seat in that noble land.'

'I don't know if you tell the truth, sir,' said the boy, 'but the tale is good in the telling.' He stepped forward and dropped another handful of oats into Gruffydd's lap. 'I have to go but if I can steal some bread, perhaps I will return before the night is done.'

'Then you will be surely blessed by God,' said Gruffydd and he watched the boy disappear into the tavern before scooping the oats into his mouth.

Inside the tavern, men sat around trestle tables drinking frothing ale from leather jacks. Some had trenchers of food, ranging from bowls of meaty stew to plain bread and roasted turnip while the more affluent enjoyed fatty chunks of pork from the innkeeper's own herd of pigs.

To the rear, one man sat alone, keeping his own counsel as he mopped the last of the gravy from his bowl with a chunk of bread. Cynwrig the Tall was a trader from over the border, a tall and ungainly looking man, whose wiriness belied his natural strength. A wispy beard covered the lower half of his gaunt face while his greasy hair fell loose about the shoulders of his black leather jerkin.

Cynwrig looked up nervously. His family had traded in Chester for many years and though they were accepted by most, he knew that the fact he was Welsh made him a likely target for insults and attack from English soldiers.

The past few days had been good to Cynwrig and his purse was full of coins from the horses he had sold at market. His belly was full of cawl and eventually, he sat back to sup his ale, idly listening to the boastful talk of the men in the tavern.

'Innkeeper, more bread,' shouted one of the soldiers, 'and make sure it is served by a pretty wench, not the hog who served us earlier.'

The soldiers burst out laughing and the innkeeper's wife placed a hand on her husband's arm to stop him from responding.

'Leave it,' she said, 'we want no trouble.'

'I will not stand by and see you insulted so.'

'It matters not, their bellies are full of beer and if we raise the ire of the earl's men who knows what retribution they may seek. Leave them be for they will soon be abed.'

The innkeeper shook his head in anger but maintained his silence, knowing his wife was right. The ale was served as requested and the innkeeper came over to clear the remains of Cynwrig's meal.

'They are in high spirits,' said Cynwrig.

'That they are,' came the reply, 'but I worry, for in my experience, high spirits mixed with ale and a sense of one's own importance often turns into aggression.'

'They seem harmless enough,' said Cynwrig.

'Tell that to your countryman,' said the innkeeper, 'I doubt he would share your view.'

'My countryman?'

'Aye, they have a Welshman in fetters at the front. I suspect he could persuade you these men are not of a gentle nature.'

'And this man is a prisoner?' said Cynwrig, his brow raising with interest.

'Aye, I am assured he is a brigand of the highest order. Still, no man deserves to be treated so.'

'What do you mean?'

'He is but skin and bone and sits amongst the filth as the rain pours upon his head,' he said, shaking his head in disgust. 'My pigs are treated better.'

The innkeeper walked away to clear more tables as Cynwrig used his eating knife to prise some meat from between his teeth. To hear of a man in fetters was not unusual in Chester but the fact he was escorted by four guards suggested he was someone of importance. Huw the Fat, whose hatred of the Welsh was well known, rarely kept Welsh prisoners for long. They normally hung at the end of a rope a few hours after being caught. Cynwrig wondered what made this one different, a story he had once heard skirting around the edges of his memory.

'Do you want more ale?' asked a voice and Cynwrig looked up to see Tom holding a bucket and a ladle.

'Thank you,' said Cynwrig and he placed a copper coin on the table as the boy ladled frothing ale into his wooden tankard.

'You are wet,' said Cynwrig.

'The rain still falls,' said the boy, 'and I have had horses to sort out.'

'Those of the soldiers?'

Tom nodded.

'Did you see their prisoner?'

'I did. He is tethered to the hitching rail.'

'Tell me, Tom,' said Cynwrig, leaning forward, 'what did you make of this man?'

'He is a vagabond,' said Tom, 'and he scares me.'

'Why do you say this? Did he threaten you?'

'No, my lord, but he lays amongst the filth like a stuck pig.'

'Yet you easily cast judgement.'

'He has a silver tongue, my lord, and tried to tell me he was once the king of Gwynedd, but he fooled me not. Is there anything else?'

Cynwrig shook his head and sat back, his mind racing at the boy's words. The tale he had once heard flashed to the front of his mind – the story of a Welsh king who had disappeared into captivity after the battle of Mynydd Carn, a king named Gruffydd Ap Cynan. Surely, even if there was the faintest chance the prisoner was he, no matter how slight the likelihood, then Cynwrig owed it to his own conscience and to his country to find out.

Quietly he sipped his ale, contemplating the possibility. Years earlier, Cynwrig's father had fought against Gruffydd at Mynydd Carn under the command of Meilyr ap Rhiwallon and had been taken captive by Gruffydd's army. Meilyr was subsequently proved to be a coward when he offered the lives of his fellow prisoners in return for his own life but had been killed in disgust by one of his own men, Edward Axe-hand. Many of the Powys prisoners, including Cynwrig's father, were spared the blade and changed sides to fight on behalf of Gruffydd before being allowed to go home as free men. An unexpected gift Cynwrig's family had never forgotten.

Cynwrig quickly drained the remains of the beer in his tankard and pocketed what was left of his bread before donning his waxed cloak, and pulling the drawstring tight around his shoulders.

'Leaving so early?' asked the innkeeper, walking over to retrieve the tankard.

'Aye,' replied Cynwrig quietly. 'I thought I should take my leave before they find out my nationality.' He nodded towards the English soldiers who were well on their way to getting drunk.

'Perhaps you're right,' said the innkeeper. 'Until next time.'

Cynwrig nodded and ducked out of the door.

Outside, the rain was getting heavier, and the wind bit at Cynwrig as he hunched his shoulders and walked quickly towards the stable at the back of the tavern. Turning a corner he spotted the pathetic prisoner huddled against the wall, seeking whatever respite he could from the weather. Cynwrig looked around nervously before squatting on his haunches and shaking the man's shoulder.

Gruffydd jumped and uncurled himself from his protective ball.

'Who are you?' asked Gruffydd.

'My name is not important,' said Cynwrig, 'let's just say I am a fellow countryman. Are you hungry?'

'Always,' said Gruffydd.

Cynwrig handed over the bread and waited patiently as the man devoured it as quickly as he could.

'Do you have ale?' mumbled Gruffydd through a mouthful of bread.

'Alas no, but I have water sweetened with honey.'

Gruffydd nodded his thanks and took the leather flask to drink deeply. When he was done he handed back the flask and stared up at the stranger.

'I don't know who you are, friend, but you have my gratitude. My life is spent between such kindnesses and these days they are all too few.'

'By your state I would venture you have spent many years imprisoned,' said Cynwrig, 'and I am curious why they have you outside of a dungeon.'

'I am being transported from Bristol to Flint,' said Gruffydd, 'and suspect that once there I will finish my life at the end of a rope.'

'Why take you there when they could just as easily hang you here?'

'For in Flint it would be before the eyes of my fellow countrymen and as such, my death will be used as an example of what happens to those who defy the rule of William Rufus.'

'What people did you rule?'

'Those of Gwynedd, for I am Gruffydd ap Cynan, once king of those lands.'

Cynwrig stared at the pathetic man before him. It was hard to imagine him as anything else than a beggar.

'A fine tale for one so destitute,' he said eventually, 'but perchance the ramblings of a madman.'

'Perhaps,' said Gruffydd, 'and I cannot prove otherwise but look into my eyes, friend. Does my soul seem darkened by idiocy?'

Silence fell between them until finally, Cynwrig drew a blade and leaned towards the captive.

'What are you doing?' asked Gruffydd, recoiling.

'I am going to free you,' said Cynwrig, quickly sawing at the leather ties. 'I don't know whether you be a king or a knave but what I do know is that we share a common heritage and you seem like a sane man. Be you a brigand then I will pay the price when I meet my maker, but if you speak true, then I am repaying a debt.'

'What debt?'

'The life of my father,' said Cynwrig sawing at the tethers, 'but we have little time and I will explain as we go.'

Gruffydd gasped in disbelief.

'Do you have horses?' he asked as Cynwrig pulled him to his feet.

'I do, but outside of the town. Can you run?'

'Alas, my feet are but shreds of skin.'

'Then I will carry you,' said Cynwrig. He bent over and lifted Gruffydd onto his shoulder, surprised at how little the man weighed. Within moments Cynwrig the Tall was running through the darkness, carrying the King of Gwynedd to freedom.

Ireland

Though only thirteen years old, Gruffydd ap Rhys was already maturing into a strong fighter, as was to be expected of the son of a king. He took to his training each day with renewed vigour and as he struck the wooden dummies with all his might, he thought of his father, Rhys ap Tewdwr, taking strength from his memory, for though the training often tired him to the core, he was determined to become the best warrior he could be in order to avenge his father's death.

As long as he could remember, the ways of the warrior had been a daily lesson within the wards of his family's castle but since the terrible events of the previous year, the security of his life had been shattered. The Normans had taken his father's head at the battle of Brycheniog, along with those of his two half-brothers.

Knowing her youngest son was probably destined to share a similar fate, his mother petitioned King Murcat of Dublin to take Rhys into his protection and though Murcat gladly agreed, Nesta, his older sister, stayed with their mother in Deheubarth.

Since he had been in Ireland, Gruffydd ap Rhys, or Tarw as he was more commonly known, had been schooled in the arts of warfare by the warriors of Murcat's army as well as in the ways of court etiquette by those closer to the king. Subsequently, he was growing into a fine young man, already bearing a hidden passion to return to Wales and free his father's people from tyranny.

One afternoon, during a particularly tiring bout of training, Tarw was interrupted by a servant calling out for him.

'My lord, King Murcat wishes to see you.'

Tarw paused at his work before wiping the sweat from his half-naked body, donning a tunic and running to the Irish king's quarters. He knocked on the door before peering inside and seeing the king standing with his back to the fire.

'Tarw, come in,' said red-faced Murcat.

The boy approached and knelt before the man who had treated him like a son.

'Stand, boy,' said Murcat, 'such gestures are for the eyes of the court, between us there will always be equality as befits two kings.'

'I am no king, my lord.'

'Not yet, perhaps, but the rights are yours by birth and one day you will ride across Deheubarth at the head of an army ten thousand strong. Perhaps, on that day, I will kneel before you.'

'No matter what my fate, my lord, I will always be proud to bend my knee before you.'

'Nonsense,' said Murcat, 'come, share a flask of ale with me and tell me how went your day.'

'The training goes well,' said Tarw, 'though truth be told, I find the larger shield cumbersome in the fight. I prefer the smaller round version.'

'Ultimately you will use what makes you comfortable,' said Murcat, 'but in your training it is important you experience all weapons from broadsword to mace, for who knows what you will find in your hands upon the field of battle?'

'I understand,' said Tarw. He took a sip of ale and stared at the king, wondering why he had been summoned.

'Tarw,' said Murcat with a heavy sigh, 'I have today received dispatches from your country and I bid you steel yourself for some upsetting news.'

'My heart is already hardened from the deaths of my brothers and father,' said Tarw, 'so issue the news, my lord, you can wound me no more than I am now.'

'Tarw,' responded the king, 'I have been informed that your sister has been taken into custody by William Rufus and sent to London as a ward of his court.'

'What would the English king want of my sister?' asked Tarw, bewildered by the news.

'Who knows the mind of an English king?' said Murcat. 'Since William the Bastard died and Rufus ascended to the throne, his decisions have been as wild and varied as the wind. Perhaps he sees her as a threat?'

'I don't see why, my sister has no inclination towards regaining the throne of my father, and besides, I am the heir to the Tewdwr dynasty, not her.'

'That may be so, but don't forget, she shares the same bloodline as you and is descended directly from Hywel Dda. She is already twenty-one yet still unwed. Should she marry and have a son, your kinsmen could see him as the true king of Wales and rally behind his name. By taking her into his custody, Rufus has denied the Welsh that possibility.'

Tarw's eyes widened with anger.

'If he harms a single hair on her head I swear he will feel my blade between his shoulders, king or no king.'

'Cool your anger, Tarw,' responded Murcat, 'your enemy is in London, not Ireland. Anyway, I doubt your sister is in danger for her death could raise the ire of your countrymen and Rufus can't risk that. I suspect she will be trained in the ways of the English court and perhaps married off to a suitable English noble.'

'She would never do that,' growled Tarw, 'she would spit in the face of any Englishman seeking her hand.'

'And since when have women had any say in who they wed?' asked Murcat.

'You don't know Nesta,' said Tarw, recalling the many fights he and his sister had shared as children, 'she looks like an angel and fights like a wildcat.' He smiled wryly. Although he worried for his sister, of all the people he knew, she would be able to look after herself.

'Perhaps so, but this is the king of England we are talking about, he will suffer no such tantrums. He would have her beaten unto a whisker of her life should she rebel. No, I suspect her life will now be planned out before her.'

'To serve the English is a fate worse than the most awful death,' said Tarw quietly.

'Perhaps, but see the good that comes out of this, at least she is alive. The last thing you want is to lose another sibling, especially after the deaths of your brothers.'

'I have another brother.'

'Ah yes, the missing Hywel, but, my boy, nobody has seen him since the year you were born. Surely you do not think he is still alive? Do not set your heart upon ever seeing him again, for though it pains me to say, it is unlikely he has survived being held hostage for this long.'

'I will not believe it until I hear someone say that they saw him killed,' said Tarw, his voice trembling, 'for many was the night I overheard my father recount rumours from travellers who told of a captured prince deep in the dungeons of an English castle. He searched for years but though Hywel was never found, the stories persisted and one day, I swear on my father's grave, I will find him.'

Murcat sighed and stared at the boy.

'You are a stubborn young man, Tarw,' he said, 'but I admire your spirit.'

For a while, Tarw allowed his mind to slip back to the time when he was a young boy. The many days he spent hunting alongside his father in the forests of Deheubarth and the long winter evenings before the fire in the main hall, wrapped in the protective arms of his mother.

'Tarw,' interrupted Murcat, 'you do understand what is happening here?'

'Yes,' said Tarw, 'but what news of my mother?'

'She is to travel with Nesta as her chaperone. Your lands at both Carew and Dinefwr are to be stewarded by a man going by the name of Marcus Freeman. Do you know of him?'

Tarw thought back, remembering the times the Welsh nobleman had rode alongside his father as his trusted man and had been responsible for bringing the reinforcements to the battle of Mynydd Carn just in time to avoid a disastrous defeat. Subsequently, he had gone on to fight alongside Tewdwr in many other conflicts until the king fell at the battle of Brycheniog.

'Aye, I do,' he said eventually. 'He was a loyal kinsman to my father and has since proved a trustworthy steward to my mother.'

'Then your family's lands are in good hands until she returns.'

Tarw nodded and silence fell between them.

'There is something on your mind,' said Murcat eventually. 'Out with it.'

'My lord,' replied Tarw after a few moments, 'I have spent much time recently thinking about my father. My heart is heavy and I yearn to avenge him.'

'It is to be expected,' said the king. 'It is a terrible thing that he died, Tarw, but you can take comfort in the knowledge that his death was honourable. Knowing him the way I did, I am sure he was happy with the manner with which he met his fate. To die in the stirrups is a noble end for men such as us and if he was given the choice, I know he would have preferred that death, than go to his god an old man.'

'I appreciate your words,' said Tarw, 'but I know his heart was heavy through not finding my brother and I cannot feel anything but guilt to think while my father spent every waking moment seeking Hywel, I was hidden away here like a frightened sheep, doing nothing to aid his quest.'

'Now you listen here,' said Murcat. 'The responsibilities of kingship are vast, something you will learn in time, and to place one of his sons in a place of safety was not something your father would have undertaken lightly. It was his duty to ensure the Tewdwr line goes on and to do that he had to ensure one of his sons lived long enough to marry. The fact that you have spent so long away from your family is indeed regrettable but as long as the wars in your country continue to spill royal blood, the safest place for you is here with me. He knew it, I know it and in your heart, you know it.'

'I just wish I could have spent more time with him.'

'It is a great shame, for he was a good man. I knew him for most of my life, Tarw, and though the matters of kingship kept us apart for many seasons, when we shared ale it was as if we were the closest of brothers.'

'One day,' growled Tarw, 'I will return to Deheubarth and wrest what was once ours from the grip of the English, if necessary by force of steel.'

'It is a future I thought you would seek once you come of age but that day is many years away. For now you should concentrate on becoming the best man you can be. Bide your time, Tarw and learn the ways of the warrior. When you are ready, I will allow you to return to Wales with my blessing, but I would be dishonouring your father's name to let you go sooner. Pay heed to your instructors and when the time is right, I promise you will return to Deheubarth a match for any man in the use of arms.'

'I understand,' said Tarw, grasping the king's wrists, 'and you have my gratitude.'

'Then you had better get back to your training. There is a long path ahead of you, Tarw, a path that does not get easier but one day you will wear your father's crown, of that I am certain.'

Hen Domen Castle

A hundred leagues away, across the Irish Sea on the border between Wales and England, Hen Domen Castle echoed with the sound of a garrison practising their skills at arms. All around the bailey, men paired off and fought with training swords, carrying out the drills that could well keep them alive in the godforsaken country that hated their very presence. Archers manned the palisade, firing arrow after arrow at straw-filled dummies arranged like a besieging army before the castle walls while dozens of servants ran back and forth, retrieving the arrows and transporting them by the basketful back up to the palisade. In the distance, lancers charged targets placed at either end of the cleared ground before the castle and local farmers had been brought in to clear and burn any new undergrowth that had started to reoccupy the important open approaches.

Steel clashed on steel and as sergeants shouted their commands, a scruffy urchin scurried up to the kitchen carrying a wooden slop bucket. The small kitchen smelled of roast pork, wood smoke and sweat as two cooks worked hard to prepare the one hot meal a day the castellan demanded for his garrison of fifty men.

Sir Broadwick, an English knight in the service of Hugh Montgomery, was known as a hard taskmaster, and was very aware that a well-fed garrison meant strong soldiers when it came to conflict. To that end, the kitchens were tasked with preparing a daily cauldron of meaty soup to be dispensed at noon every day, straight after the training sessions. This meant that the afternoons were usually quiet and though a midday assault from any Welsh rebels was unlikely, the lookouts were doubled during such times and the gates locked. Broadwick was nothing if not a cautious man.

The boy waited patiently at the door, knowing that any interruption risked the ire of the cooks and that was something he didn't want.

'Are we ready?' roared a voice from across the kitchen.

'Aye,' replied another, 'send it out.'

Four servants walked quickly over to the cauldron each carrying two wooden buckets. One of the cooks used a giant ladle suspended by a chain to scoop out the potage and fill the two buckets of the first man.

'Next,' snapped the cook, impatiently, as he wiped the sweat from his face with the sleeve of his tunic, 'come on, I have more work to do.'

The first two buckets were quickly replaced with two more and as the servants carried the hot food out of the door and down the steps to the bailey, another followed with a basket of freshly baked bread.

'One bowl each,' shouted the cook as the kitchen emptied, 'and no more. Any left can go back into the pot for tomorrow.'

For a few moments the kitchen fell silent and the cook sat on a stone bench to catch his breath, for although the worst was over, he knew his work was still not done.

'How long for the pork?' asked a voice from across the kitchen.

'Almost done, Master Steward,' replied the cook, wiping more sweat from his brow, 'it will be ready by the time the master returns.'

'Make sure it is,' said the steward, 'for today his mood is most foul.'

'I noticed,' said the cook, 'but why he can't eat potage like everyone else is beyond me.'

'Such is the life of the privileged,' said the steward. 'The common man is sustained by soup while the rich get steaks.'

The cook stood up and walked over to the smaller fireplace where a young girl was religiously turning a spit.

'I hope you've been basting this pig as you've been shown,' growled the cook, 'because if the master complains his meat is dry, I swear you'll be on this spit instead of a pig come the morrow.'

The girl nodded quickly, indicating the almost empty pot of goose fat.

'Yes, Master Cook,' she said, her eyes wide with fear at the prospect of being roasted alive.

'Good,' said the cook, 'now get out of my way.'

The girl got up from the stool and stood in a corner as the cook sliced a piece of flesh from the piglet.

'It's done,' he shouted through a mouthful of pork, 'you can set the master's tray.' He straightened up and turned around, but stopped short as he spied the boy in the kitchen doorway.

'Who are you?' he shouted, 'and what are you doing in my kitchen?'

The boy took a step backward in fear.

'Well, speak up or I'll have the skin off your back before sundown.'

'Master Cook,' stuttered the boy eventually, 'My name is Simon. I have been taken on by the jailer not two days past and have been sent by Master Berian to beg slops from your kitchens. He says the prisoners haven't eaten for two days.'

'*Slops!*' roared the cook. 'There is no such thing as slops between these walls, boy. All food is used and little goes to waste so tell that useless master of yours that unless he learns some manners, his prisoners will have to go without. Now get out.'

Simon took another step backward but the steward called out before he could leave.

'Wait!'

The boy looked at the second man, expecting another tirade but the steward was more reasonable.

'When did you say they were last fed?'

'The day before yesterday, my lord, and Master Berian has been tasked with using them to collect firewood on the morrow. He fears they will be too weak to work.'

'Come in,' said the steward, 'we will see what we can find.'

Simon followed the steward into the kitchen, his mouth watering at the wonderful aroma of roast pig. As he passed the cook, the man lunged towards him in a mock attack and laughed aloud as the boy fell into a table.

'Leave him alone,' said the steward, 'he is just doing his job, no different to you or me.'

'Bloody prisoners,' mumbled the cook, returning to the piglet, 'I'd let them starve if it was my decision, or better still, let them dance at the end of a rope.'

'Well, luckily it's not your decision,' said the steward, 'and besides, they do the work that others around here would fear to encounter.' He walked to the furthest table followed by the boy. 'Here,' he said, pointing to a pile of turnip tops and cabbage cores, 'fill your bucket with those and here's something to add a bit of taste.' He reached below the table and retrieved the bones of two rabbits complete with heads. 'There's not much meat on them,' he said, tossing the carcasses into the urchin's bucket, 'but the brains are still in the skulls and the bones should give a bit of flavour. It's not much but it should keep them going for a day or two.'

'Thank you, my lord,' said Simon, lifting the bucket with both hands. 'My master will be very grateful.'

'What about you?' asked the steward. 'What do you eat?'

'I have what is left on my master's plate after he has finished.'

'I expect that is not much, seeing how much fat the jailer has about his waist. Are you hungry?'

The boy nodded silently.

The steward looked around and picked up half a loaf of bread.

'Here,' he said, 'eat that while you are here.' He looked across at the cook and called out. 'Master Cook, cut me a slice of that pork and bring it over to the boy. I can see his bones through his skin.'

'You are going to give a servant the master's meat?' gasped the cook, the astonishment clear in his voice. 'He will have your hide from your back.'

'Only if he finds out,' said the steward, 'and if he does, I will know where it came from. Besides, he won't miss one more slice, you seem to be doing it some damage yourself.'

The cook grudgingly cut a slice of pork and threw it over to land on the table.

'Don't you go thinking this will be a regular thing, boy,' he said, 'we have no time for the likes of you around here.'

The boy picked up the pork and ran to a corner before sitting down and stuffing the meat into his mouth.

'Slow down,' said the steward, 'nobody is going to take it away from you.'

Simon stared back silently and after the meat was gone, followed it with the bread and some ale from a mug given to him by the steward. Never had he dined so well and his stomach soon hurt from the quantity of food. Several minutes later he stood and picked up his bucket.

'Finished?' asked the steward from the table.

'Yes, my lord.'

'Good, then you had better be going. Berian will be wondering where you are.'

'Yes, my lord,' said the boy as he scurried across the kitchen, giving the cook a wide berth.

'One more thing, Simon,' said the steward before the boy left, 'the meat is our secret, understood?'

'Yes, my lord,' said Simon, 'may the angels bless you.'

'Be gone,' shouted the cook and the boy ran from the kitchen with a smile on his face.

'What did you get?' snarled the duty guard a few minutes later.

'Some vegetables and a couple of rabbit heads,' said the boy, holding out the bucket. Berian glanced into the bucket but seeing nothing worth taking, nodded towards the pot hanging over the fire.

'Chuck it in,' he said, 'and watch over it so the water don't boil away. I'm gonna get some sleep. If anyone comes, tell them I'm up at the keep doing something.'

'Doing what?'

'I don't know, anything. Just make sure they don't find me sleeping, understood?'

'Yes, my lord,' said the boy and he watched the hunched man retire to the small room that served as his quarters. The boy carefully added all the ingredients to the pot and watched it boil, carefully stirring it occasionally to stop it from burning. By now, the food he had enjoyed in the kitchens was taking its toll, and warmed by the embers of the fire, Simon was soon fast asleep on the guardroom floor.

'Wake up, you scoundrel!' shouted Berian, kicking Simon hard in the small of his back. 'How long have you been sleeping?'

'Just a few moments,' gasped the boy, pushing himself out of boot range.

'A few moments,' shouted Berian, 'then how is the fire nearly out?'

Simon looked in horror at the few remaining embers, knowing he must have been asleep for longer than he thought.

'And this soup,' continued Berian, 'it's burned.'

'Perhaps it's not as bad as it smells,' stuttered Simon with panic in his voice.

'Just get out of my way,' snarled the guard and reached for the metal poker to rake the remaining embers back into life. 'Well, don't just stand there,' he shouted again, 'make yourself useful.'

'What do you want me to do?'

The jailer glanced at the pot of spoiled soup.

'Take that to the prisoners,' he said, 'and make sure you tell them it was you that burned it.'

'Yes, my lord,' gasped the boy and he lifted the handle of the pot before leaving the room.

'And don't think I'll forget about this,' shouted Berian as he left, 'there'll be a price to pay, I can assure you that.'

Simon left the guardroom and crossed the bailey. He pushed open the door and saw another guard sat on a stool outside the prisoners' cell.

'What do you want?' asked the guard.

'I have food for the prisoners.'

The guard stood up and looked into the pot, his nose wrinkling at the foul smell.

'It stinks,' he said, 'what is it?'

'Rabbit head stew, but it's a bit burned.'

'Still too good for the likes of them,' said the guard, nodding towards the cell. He stood up and approached the doorway. 'Follow me.' He opened the door and the boy could see a barred gate on the inside. Beyond that, was a tiny room full of bedraggled prisoners, most huddled together to garner some warmth. The stench of human filth was horrendous and the boy's hand flew to his nose in an effort to ease the stink. The guard's head spun sideways in a similar effort and his face screwed up in disgust.

'Oh, sweet Jesus,' he cursed, 'what's that stink?'

One of the men looked up. He seemed much older than the rest. His eyes were sunk deep into his skull and his teeth were blackened like burned tree stumps.

'It's him over there,' said the old man, nodding to where a naked man lay curled up on the floor. 'Died three nights ago, he did, and your comrades saw fit to leave him here.'

'Where're his clothes?' whispered Simon.

The old man didn't answer, but his fingers unconsciously rubbed at the rotting jerkin about his own shoulders. In the corner, another prisoner sat alone, his head resting on his knees. Simon gasped as the prisoner slowly lifted his head and stared deep into his soul, his sunken eyes piercing like the sharpest knife.

'Stand back,' said the guard drawing his sword. 'The boy's got some food but if there's any funny stuff when I open the gate, I swear you'll all be dead before you reach the door.' The men nearest the gate pushed themselves back towards the wall as the guard produced a key. 'Now sit on your hands.'

The prisoners did as they were told as Simon turned his gaze towards them. Never had he seen men in such a state. Their bodies were adorned by rotting rags and their limbs were almost as thin as the cadavers he often saw swinging from the hanging tree. Every one had a tangled beard reaching down past his chest and all were covered in the filth of captivity.

The gate swung open and the guard pushed the pot through with his foot before slamming it shut and securing the lock. The boy expected a mad rush but was surprised when nobody moved.

'There's your food,' he said, 'don't you want it?'

'Of course we want it,' said the old man looking over at him, 'but if you think we are going to give you the satisfaction of fighting between ourselves for the sake of some slops, you are sadly mistaken.'

A younger man struggled to his feet and walked across to pick up the pot before returning to the line of prisoners against the far wall. The first man nodded and the younger man scooped a handful of food in his own mouth before passing it on. When it reached the corner, the lone prisoner took his share before handing the pot back, all the time his eyes never leaving those of the young boy outside the bars.

'Bring the pot over here,' ordered the guard when the pot was empty, 'or there'll be no water.'

The young man placed the pot against the gate and waited as the guard ladled water from a nearby barrel through the bars.

'Can you spare no more?' asked the young prisoner. 'Our mouths are like dust, such is our thirst.'

'It's all you're getting, so stop your moaning,' said the guard, and he turned to leave. 'Come on, boy, let's go.'

Simon didn't move, as he was transfixed by the stare from the lone prisoner in the corner.

'I said, let's go,' snapped the guard, cuffing the boy around the head, causing him to fall away from the gate.

'What about the dead man?' asked Simon, getting to his feet. 'Surely we have to bury him?'

'We'll sort him out tomorrow,' said the guard, slamming the door, 'he's going nowhere.'

'My lord,' said Simon as they walked back to the guard room, 'who was the man with the icy stare?'

'The one in the corner?'

'Aye, he said nothing the full time we were there, yet his eyes cut into me like a blade.'

'Take no heed of him,' said the guard, 'he's just a madman.'

'Where is he from?'

'I don't know, he has been here far longer than anyone I know.'

'Has anyone asked him?'

'On many occasions.'

'What does he say?'

'He doesn't say much but when he does, it's something about being a prince of Deheubarth. Like I said, he's nothing but a madman.'

Simon followed the guard out of the cells, confused. He had heard many stories about madmen and they were all depicted as raving beasts. The last thing he would have expected was to see one who thought he was a prince, especially one with a tear running down his cheek.

London

June 11th, AD 1095

Nesta ferch Rhys was a mere child of eight when her brother had disappeared during the war of the five kings, and she had seen more than her fair share of bloodshed. Though not many knew, she had even taken a man's life before she had reached the age of nine when her beloved mother's life had been in danger, and she knew that if necessary, she would do the same again. Since then she had suffered alongside her family during the endless searching for Hywel and watched hopelessly as the strain of the search eventually took its toll on her father's health. When he had been killed at the battle of Brycheniog, she could not help but wonder whether the outcome would have been different had he been stronger in body and in mind.

Since the battle at Mynydd Carn, Nesta had discarded the innocence of childhood and quickly grown into a strong young woman, passionate about her heritage yet obstinate when it came to the accepted rituals of life that were part of being a princess. Many courtiers came to Dinefwr, asking her father for permission to court his daughter but Nesta was nothing if not resilient and steadfastly turned them all down, knowing deep inside that she was destined for greater things.

However, the protection she had taken for granted had disappeared when her father had died. The original treaty between Rhys ap Tewdwr and William the Bastard became invalid, and seeing an opportunity to expand its reach into South Wales, the English Crown immediately sent its forces into Deheubarth and northward along the coast to Pembroke.

Gwladus had complained bitterly, petitioning the king repeatedly, but as her army was relatively small and she had little influence, Rufus paid her no heed. Within a year, most of Deheubarth lay under English rule. Despite this, and in an effort to keep her allies quiet, Rufus allowed Gwladus to keep her castles at Dinefwr and Carew as well as enough lands to sustain her household, providing she offered no succour to the rebels rallying against him in mid and north Wales.

At first, Gwladus accepted the new way of things but soon it became clear that more than English eyes were cast in the direction of Deheubarth. Welsh nobles and rebels alike all took an interest in the kingdom without a king and soon, realising that Nesta in particular could become a figurehead around which a rebellion could grow, William Rufus decided it was too great a risk to leave such a prize in the hands of two women. Striking in the dead of night, a column of soldiers spirited Nesta away from Dinefwr, along with her mother, and took them to the Palace of Westminster in London.

After an initial period of stubbornness, Nesta realised there was no point in fighting against the inevitable and settled down into daily court life. The Palace of Westminster, once graced by no less than Edward the Confessor himself, was a sumptuous residence and more than suitable for any monarch. Westminster was spectacular. Its huge stone walls and beautifully designed tapestries put all other buildings to shame, and when she saw she even had her own sumptuously decorated quarters, the captivity became a little easier to take.

Nesta's presence at the Palace of Westminster caused the English court more than a little worry. Her outstanding beauty made her a potential wife for any of the king's nobles but her loyalty to Wales and fiery temper meant few had the mettle to take her on. Indeed, whenever she was introduced to a would-be suitor, she lost no time in belittling them with insults and promises that if they laid a single hand upon her, she would kill them while they slept. Many men kept their distance, not needing the trouble such a woman merited and though her stance earned her the anger of those close to the king, she steadfastly stuck to her position that she would only marry a noble of Welsh birth with lands within her homeland.

Gwladus, too, soon settled into court life. The loss of her husband in Brycheniog had taken its toll on her appearance and she had aged visibly in the year since his death. Her fair hair was braided and tied back under the dyed linen veil upon her head and a dark blue dress hung low to her ankles. She had grieved for her husband for many months and only the fact that she chaperoned Nesta at the castle gave her the strength to go on.

The rooms at the palace were warm and dry while the food was flavoursome and plentiful. Slowly, as the pain of Tewdwr's death eased, Gwladus's strength returned and for the past few months she had been strong enough to share her daughter's walks.

'The day is warm upon the skin,' said Nesta, as they walked, her arm linked through that of her mother.

'It is,' said Gwladus, 'and brings back fine memories of our walks in Dinefwr.'

'The river was cleaner there,' said Nesta, 'this one stinks like a cess pit.'

'The result of so many people living along its banks,' said Gwladus. 'Never have I seen so many people living in one place.'

'I hate it here,' said Nesta passionately, 'and would return home in a heartbeat.' This was not a new conversation but no matter how many times Gwladus offered her daughter comfort, Nesta remained angry.

'Nesta, the times are changing and though I too long to return to the fields and forests of your youth, I suspect you are safer here, at least until the rebellion settles down. Since your father's death, the south of Wales has been overrun with William's forces and they build strongholds right across our country. I fear the days of freedom are disappearing and it is only a matter of time before our country is annexed.'

Nesta's eyes flashed as she turned to her mother.

'If I had my way, I would ride alongside those brave men and help drive the invaders out.'

'Perhaps you would,' replied Gwladus, 'but you are here and you should make it work. Why don't you grant audience to some of those nobles who send their interest? Who knows, there may be one or two who cause your heart to beat a little faster.'

'I am not interested,' said Nesta, 'and what's more, I hate the fact that I am on the receiving end of choices made for me. Why can't I choose who I want? Am I not royal born?'

'Come, Nesta, do not be naïve. It is exactly because of that reason we don't enjoy the luxury of free choice,' said Gwladus. 'Your station could mean the difference of life or death for many men, for with the right marriage, allegiances are formed and wars avoided. Make no mistake, if your father was alive you would probably already be married to a man of his choice.'

'But he isn't alive,' said Nesta, 'and I resent any other man, be he English or Norman born assuming that privilege. I will decide when I am ready and not a moment sooner.'

'Well.' Gwladus sighed. 'I hope that day is in the near future for if not, I suspect the king will sell you off to a minor noble, whether you like it or not.'

'We will see about that when the day comes,' said Nesta as they reached the end of the path.

'So,' said Gwladus as they retraced their footsteps, 'I suppose you will be going to the banquet tonight?'

'I have an invitation.' Nesta sighed. 'But if it is yet again for me to be paraded before withered old men desperate for a younger wife, I think I may feign illness and stay away.'

'I hear Gerald of Windsor will be there,' said Gwladus, 'I believe he is to be given a reward for his continued victories against the rebels in Powys.'

'Even more reason to stay away,' said Nesta. 'Why would I celebrate the successes of someone who sheds the blood of those I call kinsmen?'

'*Nesta*,' snapped Gwladus sharply, causing the girl to stop. 'This nonsense has to come to an end sooner or later. The politics of men are above the likes of you and me, and even though they fight the men of our homeland you have to realise it is a situation out of our control. This Gerald is young, handsome and is a favourite of the king, even though he be English born. At least you would be back in Wales and perchance you could have a calming effect on him, perhaps even softening the severity of his rule. You would be a lady within your own manor in the lands of your youth. Surely such a prospect is worth considering?'

'Mother, I realise you are worried about me,' said Nesta, 'but you do so needlessly. I know I have to choose soon and rest assured I will, but whether that is in the next few hours or the next few months, only God knows. Please stop upsetting yourself with worry for my future, it will take care of itself.'

'At least come along tonight,' said Gwladus, 'if only for my sake. It will not be the same without you there.'

Nesta smiled. 'If it means so much to you then I will – but on condition you don't try to wed me off to every man in the room.'

'If that is what is needed, then I promise,' said Gwladus and they continued their journey back towards the castle. For a few moments there was a comfortable silence before Gwladus spoke again. 'Though I do hear that Gerald of Windsor is very fair of face.'

'*Mother*,' scolded Nesta, playfully pinching the skin on Gwladus' arm. 'Will you never cease?'

'No, sweet child,' responded Gwladus with a laugh of her own, 'probably not.'

That evening, Nesta and her mother entered the grand dining hall and stood behind their seats opposite each other, as befitted their station. The other ladies present also took their respective places as they waited for the men to arrive. Every second seat was empty, waiting for a male occupant, for when the feast started the mixture of men and women would be equally balanced, an arrangement conducive to a pleasant atmosphere.

Despite her earlier indifference, Nesta was secretly intrigued as to who she would find on either side of her, and despite frowning at her mother she was actually looking forward to the evening's proceedings.

The master of ceremonies announced the entrance of the men and a column of knights, lords and nobles entered the room before taking up the places between the ladies. Everyone sat down as they waited patiently for the king to arrive and Nesta took the opportunity to glance discreetly at the men next to her, pleasantly surprised to find both were equally young and neither had a face worthy of nightmares.

'My lords, ladies and gentlemen,' announced the herald within moments, 'please be upstanding for his royal highness, King

William the Second, by the grace of God, King of England and Duke of Normandy.'

Everyone took to their feet, and as the heralds blew a fanfare the king entered followed by his family and those nobles who were his closest advisors. As soon as he was seated, the rest of the invited guests followed his lead and within moments, a band of minstrels filled the air with delightful music.

Servants emerged from the doorways carrying silver decanters of wine and set about charging the beautifully engraved goblets while platters of copper and pewter were laid in front of each guest. Soon the hall took on a hum of conversation as people began to introduce themselves. Nesta found herself sat alone, staring across the table at her mother as each man alongside her introduced themselves to the woman on their far sides.

Gwladus caught her daughter's glance and smiled encouragingly, much to Nesta's annoyance, and she was about to make an amusing gesture when the man to her left spoke for the first time.

'My lady,' he said, inclining his head slightly, 'please forgive me, I do not believe I have had the pleasure of your company before this night.'

'Nothing to forgive, sir,' replied Nesta cordially, 'my name is Nesta ferch Rhys, daughter of King Rhys ap Tewdwr.'

The man hesitated momentarily before speaking again.

'And would that be King Tewdwr of Deheubarth?'

'I know of no other, but alas he was killed at the battle of Brycheniog.'

'Ah,' said the young man, his smile faltering, 'then I am afraid fate has played a cruel trick upon us both this night and I hesitate to introduce myself.'

'What situation prevents your introduction? Surely this is a night for merriment and, despite our obvious differences in nationhood, perhaps we can put them aside for one evening.'

'In normal circumstances I would agree,' said the man, 'but I am honour-bound to declare myself. My name is Frederick De Bois, knight of Normandy.'

'Well, I am very pleased to meet you,' said Nesta holding out her hand, 'let us be friends for at least one night.'

'My lady,' said Frederick, 'I'm afraid you misunderstand. I am a knight of William and recently fought under the command of Bernard de Neufmarché in Wales.'

Nesta withheld a gasp at the sound of the familiar name and though she maintained her smile, it was false and cold.

'Pray tell,' she said through gritted teeth, 'which conflict?'

'My lady, I am sorry but I have to tell you that it was at the battle of Brycheniog.'

Nesta's blood ran cold for whether it was deliberate or by chance, she was sat next to a man who had fought against her father on the day he and her two half-brothers had been killed.

'I'm sorry,' whispered the man, the anguish clear upon his face, but it was all Nesta could do to stop herself screaming and lashing out at his face. She swallowed hard, wondering how she could escape the room without causing embarrassment but before she could do anything, a light tap came upon her shoulder and a gentler voice broke the awkward moment.

'My lady,' said the voice, 'if you would be so kind, please allow me to introduce myself.'

Slowly she turned around and stared unseeingly at the man sat on her opposite side.

'My lady,' he said again, taking her hand, 'I am Gerald Fitzwalter of Windsor, first knight of William's forces in Wales.'

'I . . . I . . .' started Nesta but she was lost for words; sitting between a man who may have played a part in her father's death and a knight responsible for the siege of her entire country was too much to bear.

'My lady, are you all right?' asked Gerald, seeing the panic on Nesta's face. But she simply stared back, her eyes unseeing as her mind slipped away, seeking the relative safety of nothingness.

The sounds of voices seemed leagues away as Nesta's consciousness struggled to the surface. She felt a cold cloth on her forehead and slowly she opened her eyes to stare into the face of Gwladus.

'There you are,' said her mother gently, 'for a moment we were a bit worried.'

'What happened?' asked Nesta, realising that she was no longer at the feast.

'You fainted, my love,' said Gwladus, 'it seems the excitement was too much for you.'

'I fainted at the banquet?'

'You did, and this kind gentleman carried you into these chambers to recover.'

'Hello, Nesta,' said the man, his face appearing above that of Gwladus, 'please forgive me for laying hands uninvited upon your person, but I thought you may be a bit more comfortable out here, the heat was rather oppressive in the hall.'

'Thank you,' said Nesta, as her mind started to clear, 'you were the man sitting to my right.'

'I was, and in case you don't remember, my name is Gerald Fitzwalter, more commonly known as Gerald of Windsor.'

'I remember,' said Nesta, 'overlord of William's army in Wales.'

'I am indeed but please do not take it as a slight against your proud nation for I am a mere soldier doing what is instructed by my king. Your country is a wild and beautiful land, and already it has captured my heart as the place where I would see out my life.'

Nesta pushed herself up into a sitting position and accepted a cup of honeyed water from her mother. She looked up at the knight at her side, taking in his appearance. His hair was fair and his eyes a deep blue like none she had ever seen before. His features were strong and a scar on his right cheek spoke of a life of conflict in the service of the king. Despite the disfigurement, Nesta realised he was a naturally attractive man.

'Pretty words, my lord,' she replied after taking a sip of water, 'yet you wage war against those who have lived there for generations.'

'Such is the way of the world, my lady, but trust me when I say that I bear arms only against those who threaten me or my men. But come, if you feel well enough, perhaps we can continue this conversation in more comfortable circumstances.'

Nesta got to her feet aided by Gerald and her mother. They helped her to a seat against the wall and Gerald sat next to her, handing over the cup of water. Nesta sipped gratefully.

'Will you be all right, dear?' asked Gwladus. 'I should return and make our apologies.'

Nesta stared at the man at her side. The fact that he was an enemy of her countrymen meant she did not anticipate any great pleasure in his company. But there was something about his manner that suggested it would not be the worst experience of her life. Besides, most of the guests were enemies of Wales.

'You go back, Mother,' said Nesta, 'I will return in a few moments.'

'Are you sure?'

'Of course. If this gentleman is half the man his manner claims he is, then I have reason to believe he will ensure my safety in your absence.'

'Then I will leave you in his capable hands,' said Gwladus. She turned to leave the chamber, a hint of a knowing smile around her mouth.

'So,' said Nesta, turning to Gerald, 'if you are indeed responsible for waging war upon my people, what brings you to London?'

'First of all,' said Gerald, 'I am not responsible for waging war, the responsibility for that lies with the king. I am, however, responsible for carrying out policies and actions on his behalf. Contrary to popular belief, we do not ride through your beautiful country slaughtering the innocents. Our weapons are drawn only in self-defence against men of war but unfortunately, the Welsh are a proud people and men-at-arms are quick to seek conflict. In such circumstances, am I not entitled to defend my own life and the lives of my men?'

'But the land belongs to them,' said Nesta feeling her anger rise, 'and if you stayed whence you came then there would be no bloodshed.'

'Nesta,' said Gerald, 'the forces of William, be they English, Norman or Flemish are simply a different target. The Welsh princes have spent generations fighting each other to no avail. Father fights son and brother fights brother. That is the way it is and the way it has always been. Surely you can see that if there was one king, whether he be Welsh or English, at the head of all nations, then this bloodshed would end and men could get on with their lives without fear of invasion or slaughter?'

'Spoken like a true invader,' said Nesta, the disdain clear upon her face.

'Perhaps so.' Gerald inclined his head. 'But that depends on which side your allegiance sits. One man's invader is another man's liberator.'

'Even if you believe in what you say,' said Nesta, 'surely you can see that it would leave a bitter taste in any Welshman's mouth to bend a knee to English rule?'

'Nobody expects anything different to what you do now,' said Gerald. 'The serfs will still be beholden to great families like your own so will know no different.'

'But our taxes and such will be payable to the English Crown. Surely you can understand how bitter that will be?'

'So William's treasury gets bigger, but in return you get the full power of royal justice against any who break the king's laws. Is that such a bad thing? Is not peace and prosperity a worthwhile outcome in return for those very lords who oppress their own people being brought to heel?'

'My father never treated his people unfairly yet he and my brothers were cut down at Brycheniog,' Nesta said quietly, a lump forming in her throat.

'I am very sorry to hear that,' said Gerald, 'but alas, when situations have deteriorated so much that swords are drawn then common sense disappears as bloodlust rises. We are all guilty of such things, even your father, but such is the way of men. I would rather hold the dove of peace than the sword of justice but if the latter is needed, then I will wield it with every fibre of my being.'

At his words, Nesta looked up at the young noble, noticing for the first time his kind eyes. He smiled at her. Quickly she realised she was staring and looked away.

'I am feeling much better now,' she said clearing her throat, 'perhaps we should return.'

'Only if you are sure,' said Gerald.

'I am fine,' said Nesta, standing up. Please escort me back to the hall.'

Gerald also got to his feet and offered her his arm.

'Would you please do me the honour?' he asked.

Nesta hesitated but as she was still a little unsure of her balance, slipped her arm though his.

Nesta and Gerald of Windsor re-joined the banquet but though Gerald returned to his original place at the table, Nesta was invited to sit next to her mother for the remainder of the evening.

Eventually, the meal was finished and the entertainment came to a close. Many of the guests left the banquet hall and retired to other rooms to mingle while Gwladus took the opportunity to walk across the hall to engage one of the few ladies at court she called a friend.

Nesta sat back and looked around the hall. She had attended similar banquets on several occasions in the past but they never failed to impress her. The decor was wonderful, the food exquisite and the atmosphere one of grace and privilege. It was a different world to the one where she had grown up and certainly far more civilised. Yet despite this, she would leave it in a heartbeat for the chance to breathe in the fire smoke in the hall of Dinefwr Castle.

For a few moments she allowed herself the luxury of remembering the many days where she had ridden hard through the forests of Dinefwr, hunting the deer alongside her father's nobles, as good as any man in the saddle. The noise from the room faded as she remembered the sweet rain upon her face and the sea breeze blowing through her hair. Even the simplest of pleasures like drinking straight from crystal clear streams, or eating berries from a bush, now seemed like a magical dream and so very, very far away.

'Are you well, my lady?' asked a voice nervously, and Nesta returned to reality with a jolt.

Beside her stood Gerald of Windsor holding a goblet of wine in each hand.

'I am fine, thank you,' said Nesta, sitting up straight and turning her head away so he couldn't see the redness in her cheeks.

'Are you sure? If you feel faint again I can bring your mother.'

'That won't be necessary,' she said, glancing up at him, 'I was just remembering . . . something.'

'Dreaming of home?' asked Gerald.

Nesta's brows lifted slightly and she smiled in acknowledgement at his perceptiveness.

'Actually, I was,' said Nesta, 'that's very astute of you.'

'I often do the same,' said Gerald. He paused before adding, 'may I join you?'

Nesta nodded gently and Gerald sat in her mother's seat, placing one of the goblets before her.

'I took the liberty of bringing you some wine,' he said. He leaned forward to whisper in her ear. 'Don't tell anyone but it's from the king's cellar. I risked my very life to steal a few drops from his personal decanter. Quite divine if I may say so.'

'You stole wine for me?' said Nesta with a sarcastic smile.

'Well, initially both goblets were for me,' said Gerald, 'but now I am next to you, courtesy demands I share. Of course, if you don't want it . . .' He made a show of reaching for the second goblet but was stopped by Nesta's hand on his wrist.

'No, I accept your gift,' she said, 'how could I refuse such a noble gesture? It's not often a man risks his head to bring me a drink.'

For a moment both fell silent until Gerald glanced down at Nesta's hand still on his wrist.

'Oh heavens,' gasped Nesta, removing her hand, 'I'm so sorry.'

'Not at all,' said Gerald, 'it was quite pleasant. Anyway, let us not waste time on the niceties of court life, let's drink and savour the results of my ill-gotten gains.' He picked up the goblet and lifting it to his lips, proposed a toast. 'To Wales.'

Nesta stifled a laugh and picked up her own goblet.

'What's so funny?' asked Gerald.

'I don't know,' said Nesta with a smile, 'but if this wine is half as sweet as the honeyed drivel dripping off that silver tongue of yours, then I expect to be quite sick before this night is out.'

For a moment Gerald stared at Nesta until a few seconds later, both burst into laughter.

For the next hour or so, Nesta enjoyed the company of Gerald of Windsor and gradually relaxed into his company. Together they talked of Wales and Nesta's life growing up in a Welsh castle yet both were careful to avoid the obvious political differences that would only cast a cloud on the evening. Eventually she realised that though he wouldn't have been her first choice of companion, and despite their different stance on her home country, she found his company agreeable and mildly entertaining so wasn't surprised when she felt a pang of disappointment as her mother returned, her face flushed with excitement.

'Nesta,' she said, 'you must come quickly.'

'Mother, can't you see I am busy?' replied the young woman.

'Indeed,' said Gwladus,' but this is important. The king himself is holding audience and has agreed to meet you.' She turned to Gerald. 'Sir, would you mind if I tear her away for a few moments, opportunities like this are few and far between for people such as us.'

'Of course,' said Gerald, 'please go ahead. I'll be right here when you return.'

Gwladus took the arm of her daughter and led her through to a side room where the king was chatting, surrounded by a circle of young women, each transfixed by his every word. Gwladus eased her way through to the front of the circle and made eye contact with the king.

'Ah, there you are,' said William, 'please, step forward so I can see you both properly.'

The line of women parted to allow mother and daughter through and both curtsied before the king.

'My lord,' said Gwladus, 'my name is Gwladus ferch Rhiwallon, wife of King Rhys ap Tewdwr of Deheubarth.'

'I am delighted to meet you,' said the king, 'and please accept my condolences for the loss of your husband and sons.'

Gwladus nodded gently in acknowledgement but did not answer.

'And who is this?' asked William, turning his attention to Nesta.

'This is my daughter, Nesta ferch Rhys,' said Gwladus, 'currently unattached and a ward of your court.'

'Of course,' said William, 'I have heard many stories about this one, and may I say, not all complimentary.'

The gathered women giggled at the veiled insult and Nesta felt her cheeks burning once again. All eyes turned to her, expecting a response and the room fell quiet as she struggled to find something to say.

'Actually,' said a voice from across the room, rescuing her from her predicament, 'I find such spirit in a woman extremely attractive and so much better than the giggling sycophancy that many ladies display these days, don't you agree?'

'It has its merits,' answered the king eventually, looking across to the man who had interrupted his conversation. The other man smiled and lowered his head slightly in a semblance of a bow.

Suddenly disinterested, William turned away to talk to somebody at his side. Nesta breathed a sigh of relief and as she glanced over to thank her rescuer, the man raised his goblet in a parody of a toast. Nesta was overwhelmed, not just by his generosity in rescuing her from an awkward situation but also by his striking good looks. Unlike the other men in the room who wore their hair short, this noble had brown hair that fell immaculately about his shoulders and a neatly trimmed beard that somehow served to enhance his attractive, almost feminine features. His clothes were embroidered with gold thread and he was obviously a man of high importance around the court of King William.

'Thank you,' she mouthed silently and received a wink in return but before they could share any conversation, the man was ushered away by his seconds. Gwladus stared after the rapidly disappearing man before turning back to face her daughter.

'Well, you certainly made a good impression on him,' she said.

'Just as well,' said Nesta, 'for I was embarrassed beyond measure. Mother, why do you insist on doing these things to me?'

'I admit it did not turn out the way I expected,' said Gwladus, 'but we must take every opportunity presented if we are to survive in this cruel world.'

'I told you, I'm not interested,' hissed Nesta.

Gwladus stared at Nesta with anger on her face before taking her arm and dragging her out into a corridor.

'Now you listen to me, young lady,' she said, 'we are two women without husbands in the middle of a war that has already robbed us of so much. Our lands are diminished, our armies dispersed and we have little money to speak of. I have lost a husband and two sons to this war and another lies incarcerated in some unknown dungeon. My only other child resides in Ireland being brought up by strangers while you, Nesta, are surrounded by royalty and wealth. You, out of all of us, have the chance to rebuild a life worth living yet you continue to throw every opportunity back in the faces of those trying to help. Your childhood is over, Nesta, and it is time you grew up.'

'Don't you think I miss them?' hissed Nesta. 'Don't you realise that I too cry myself to sleep at night thinking about my brothers and father? You are not the only one to mourn, Mother, I loved them just as much as you.' Tears appeared in her eyes and Gwladus took her daughter into her arms.

'I know, child,' she said, 'and they loved you too but it is precisely for that reason you should take whatever opportunity life lays before you. They would not want you to struggle in life, not knowing where your future lies. If they were here now they would be agreeing with me, looking for the best possible match in order for you to be safe and comfortable. Don't you see? I go on so because I love you and want what's best.'

Nesta nodded and wiped her eyes.

'I know,' she said, 'and I am sorry for being such an ungrateful daughter.'

Gwladus held her again.

'Don't be silly, it has been a long night and we are both tired. Why don't we make our apologies and retire to our quarters?'

Nesta nodded and smiled weakly.

'I'd like that,' she said and after linking her arm through that of her mother, both women left the banquet to make their way back to their rooms.

The following morning the palace was a hive of activity. Messengers ran to and fro and it soon became apparent that something serious was afoot. Nesta and Gwladus wandered the passages trying to find out what they could, but to no avail; none of their associates seemed to know anything and those that did, weren't saying and were avoiding eye contact wherever possible. Finally, the mother and daughter left the court and made their way out into the gardens, glad to get away from the drama. But they hadn't gone far when they saw a group of men deep in conversation.

'Isn't that Gerald of Windsor?' asked Gwladus. 'That nice young man from last night.'

'I believe it is,' said Nesta. She paused and stared over at the man before making a decision.

'Wait here,' she said, 'I have an idea.'

Before her mother could stop her, Nesta walked over to the group of men and coughed politely to make her presence known. All four men looked over and Gerald's face lit up in recognition.

'Lady Nesta,' he said, 'a very good day to you.'

'And to you,' replied Nesta. 'I was wondering if you could spare me a few moments of your time.'

'Of course,' replied Gerald. He turned to his comrades. 'Please excuse me, I will return shortly.'

'Make haste,' said one of the men, 'for our steeds await.'

Gerald nodded and joined Nesta to walk over to a nearby tree.

'You look well this morning,' said Gerald, 'I trust the illness that afflicted you has cleared away?'

'It has,' said Nesta, 'thanks to you.'

'I did nothing, Lady Nesta, except enjoy your company.'

'On the contrary, sir, you looked after me when I was unwell and for that I am eternally grateful.'

'I did nothing that any other man wouldn't do. Did you find the evening agreeable?'

'Surprisingly, yes. The company was most pleasant, as was that wine.'

'Shhh,' said Gerald looking around in mock fear, 'I hear they seek the thief as we speak.'

'Well, they will not learn his identity from me,' said Nesta with a smile. 'After an embarrassing start, the evening turned out to be most pleasant.'

'I am gratified,' said Gerald with a slight nod, 'though I am bound to say I was disappointed you did not return after your audience with the king. Did I offend you in some way?'

'Of course not, and that is why I wanted to speak to you, to apologise for my unannounced departure and to thank you for your most courteous attention.'

'The pleasure was all mine,' said Gerald and he kissed Nesta's hand.

'So,' said Nesta, 'is it possible our paths may cross again some-time soon?'

Gerald's face dropped and he stared at the young woman with dismay.

'Oh, I'm sorry,' said Nesta, 'I have obviously been too forward and have embarrassed you. Please forgive me.' She turned to walk away but Gerald called out after her.

'My lady,' he said, 'of course you have not embarrassed me and there is nothing I would love more but alas your timing is unfortunate for I have to ride away this very day.'

'To where?' asked Nesta, turning back around.

'I am not supposed to say,' said Gerald looking around, 'but if you promise not to repeat it, I will share my destination.'

'I have nobody in these walls that I call a close friend except my mother,' said Nesta, 'anything you say is safe with me.'

'Then let me explain,' said Gerald. 'News arrived at the palace last night that the Welsh rebellion has taken a new turn. As you may know, Gruffydd ap Cynan escaped from captivity a few years ago and has been using Ireland as a base to campaign down the Welsh coast. In reality this is a minor problem but it is rumoured that he has now allied himself with the rebel Cadwgan ap Bleddyn and seeks the return of Gwynedd to his rule. If this is indeed the case then it is a completely different situation and needs addressing.'

Nesta paused, recognising the name of the king who had fought alongside her father at Mynydd Carn all those years earlier.

'What are you going to do?' she asked eventually.

'William intends marching into Wales to put down the rebellion before it has a chance of spreading. I have to ride today to muster those men already in Wales in case the rebel army descends upon them before it can be crushed.' He paused and stared at her in silence for a few moments. 'Nesta,' he said eventually, 'I know these are your countrymen we are talking about but I have no choice in this matter. I have to go and serve my king and hope that you can see beyond the immediate heartache that is the outcome of all wars. If so, and if you see even the slightest ember of the way my heart already burns for you, then perhaps, when this is done, you will see fit to receive me as a suitor. Do you think such a thing may be possible?'

Nesta thought for a few moments considering the news. Apart from nationality she had no affiliation with Gruffydd, and Cadwgan had been one of her father's sworn enemies, twice attacking her homeland of Deheubarth in her lifetime. Despite them being fellow countrymen, she owed neither any allegiance and besides, her mother had been right – it was time to grow up.

'Yes, Gerald,' she said with a smile, 'not only is that possible, I will look forward to your return.'

This time it was Gerald's turn to smile.

'In that case I will not spare the horses and be back before you know it. Fare ye well, beautiful lady.' He bent and took her hand before kissing it gently. 'Until we meet again.'

Nesta blushed slightly but before she could respond, Gerald turned and ran back to his comrades.

'What was all that about?' asked Gwladus when Nesta returned.

'You wondered what was going on in the palace, well now we know.'

'You just asked him?'

'I did, and he was very honest in his answers. The king is going to war, Mother, he's marching into Wales within days.'

Gwladus caught her breath before taking her daughter's hand and leading her back towards their quarters.

'Mother, what are you doing?' gasped Nesta. 'You're hurting me.'

'There is no time to lose, Nesta, I need to know exactly what he said. Now come, we will return to our rooms and you will recount the conversation, every word.' The two women continued along the path but just as they were about to enter the gate, a knight of William stepped out and stopped them in their tracks.

'Stop right there, ladies,' he said, 'there have been developments.'

'Out of my way,' said Gwladus, 'we are residents of the palace.'

'Not any more, you're not,' said the soldier. 'Lady Nesta, I have been instructed to escort you to the castle at Windsor without delay. I have a cart waiting, or you can have a horse, if you so prefer.'

'Windsor?' said Nesta. 'But our rooms are here.'

'I know not the politics, my lady, only that you are denied access and will be transferred to Windsor immediately.'

'This is nonsense,' said Gwladus, 'all her things are in her rooms, let us pass.'

'Her possessions will be transferred by the morning, but alas you, my lady, will not pass through this gate today, nor any other day.'

'I am a queen in my own right,' snapped Gwladus, 'and want to see the king. Send him word immediately.'

'Lady.' The guard sighed. 'This is by the king's command. Now I suggest the lady Nesta comes peacefully or I will have her dragged like a common criminal. I also suggest you seek lodgings for yourself while there is still light, the king has graciously issued you a purse.' He threw a small leather pouch on the floor at Gwladus' feet.

'What do you mean?' asked Gwladus slowly. 'Surely I am to accompany my daughter?'

'Alas not, the instruction is for her only.'

'I'm not going anywhere without my mother,' started Nesta and grabbed Gwladus' arm.

'I was afraid it would come to this.' The guard sighed. 'I tried to be kind, now I have to do it the hard way.'

With a flick of his hand he gave a signal and two men ran from behind the gate to grab Nesta. The young woman screamed and tried to fight but the men were experienced soldiers and dragged her through the gate to a waiting cart. Gwladus tried to follow but the knight pushed her back and she went sprawling into the mud.

'Don't be silly,' said the knight, 'this has already gone far enough. Take the purse and find lodgings before you are arrested and tried as an enemy spy.'

'Is that what this is about?' gasped Gwladus. 'The fact that we are Welsh?'

'Like I said, lady, I know not the politics but I guess that in the circumstances, your nationality doesn't help. Now, be gone or I will bring the dogs.'

Gwladus picked up the purse and walked backward away from the gate, her head spinning with how fast the situation was changing.

'Nesta,' she called over the guard's head, 'be strong. I will travel to Windsor as soon as I can. Don't worry, I will be there soon.' With that she turned and walked towards the bridge over the Thames, fully aware that despite her promises, she had no idea what she was going to do.

Windsor Castle

June 15th, AD 1095

Nesta sat alone in a locked room within a wooden keep. Two lonely and confusing days had passed and still she was no closer to understanding the forces that had brought her here, or where her mother was. The door was locked from the outside, as it had been since her arrival, and her chest of clothes sat in the corner. The castle consisted of a wooden palisade surrounding a very large bailey and unlike most of the other castles she had seen, contained two keeps, one of which was on the higher ground within the castle's perimeter. Nesta knew she was in the lower keep but apart from that, knew very little else.

She had arrived in darkness and though she had fought and protested throughout the whole journey, her resistance was pointless and she was pushed into the room with naught but the clothes she stood in. Since then her captors had brought food and drink and made up the fire but had steadfastly refused to discuss her predicament. Finally, she had given up shouting and considered her situation.

Nesta was fully aware that prisoners of royal birth were often incarcerated for many years by some kings but that was usually in cells or dungeons. If this was indeed a similar predicament, then her cell was at least comfortable – though she knew that to attempt escape was futile.

A single window allowed the entry of sunlight but was far too high for her to contemplate escape. The room, though comfortable, was quite sparse. A large bed at one end of the room was accompanied by a single chair and a table upon which she ate her meals, while a rug dominated the floor. A fire burned in the hearth, for which she was grateful, and several candles lit the gloomy room, illuminating the many tapestries hanging on the walls.

Nesta felt tired and frightened. Being locked up was hard enough but not knowing what was happening was even worse. She flopped down on the bed for what seemed the hundredth time and tried to sleep but was soon jerked back awake by the sound of a key being turned. She jumped to her feet and faced the door, determined to give whoever was there a piece of her mind.

The door swung open, and to her surprise the guard entered closely followed by a woman and several servants. The first two brought a large bowl and towelling while the next two carried a bucket of steaming water between them. The last servants carried a pile of clothing each and laid it all out upon the bed.

'What's this?' said Nesta, looking around as the servants poured the hot water into the bowl.

'My lady,' said the maid, obviously in charge of the others, 'his majesty, Prince Henry, brother of King William the Second and son of William the Conqueror, invites you to dine with him in his quarters.'

'Prince *Henry* lives here?'

'On occasion. Currently he resides within these walls and specifically requested your presence this evening.'

'Is that the reason I have been brought here?' asked Nesta indignantly. 'Just to sit at the table of a foreign noble I have never met?'

'I have no idea what you are talking about,' said the woman, 'and only know I have been sent here to help you prepare. The servants will wash you and there is a selection of clothing upon the bed, most of which should fit you well. Once we are done, I will escort you to the royal chambers where you will meet Prince Henry and share his fayre.'

'And what if I refuse?'

'That is entirely your choice but I suspect you will stay incarcerated within these four walls until such time that the prince would enjoy your company.'

Nesta's first thought was to create a scene but realising there may be an opportunity to ask the prince about her mother, she finally nodded her agreement.

'So be it,' she said haughtily, 'but dismiss your servants, I am more than capable of dressing myself.'

'As you wish,' said the maid with a slight bow. 'If you need anything, just knock on your door and the guard will notify me. I will be on the next floor down and can be here in moments.'

'Thank you,' said Nesta and she watched the woman leave, before flinching at the sound of the lock being thrown once again.

Two hours later Nesta sat on her bed, waiting to be summoned. Sure enough, the maid came back and made Nesta stand as she walked around her, inspecting her dress and her hair.

'Give me the brush,' she said quietly and Nesta waited patiently as the woman brushed Nesta's long, raven-black hair. 'That's better,' said the maid eventually, 'now put this on. We will do your hair again when we reach the other keep.' She handed over a parcel wrapped in plain linen.

'What's this?' asked Nesta.

'Open it and you will see.'

Nesta unwrapped the parcel and held up a midnight-black cape, embroidered with trimming of the deepest red. The hood was edged with fox fur and the whole thing was lined with silk.

'Oh my,' she gasped, 'it is beautiful.'

'It is yours, my lady, a gift from Henry himself.'

'A gift, for me? Why would he do that?'

'I do not know the minds of royalty, my lady, though suspect he may be enamoured of you.'

'What is your name?' asked Nesta.

'The servants call me Lady Carla,' said the woman, 'for my mother is of Italian descent, but I am no lady, being the daughter of a humble groom.'

'May I call you Carla?'

'Of course.'

'Then let me say this, Carla, if your master thinks he can buy his way into my affections with a simple gift then he is very much mistaken. I have been treated abysmally and know not where my mother is. That is the only reason I will tolerate this tyrant, to better our circumstances.'

'I heard you had spirit, my lady, and can see the gossipers did not lie. I am sure your dinner will be eventful, for the prince is also of strong character.'

'We will see,' said Nesta, donning the cape. 'Now lead the way, Carla, let's get this over with.'

When they reached the upper keep, the guards outside the imposing door made Nesta remove her hood so they could see who she was. Satisfied she was no threat, they let her in and both she and Carla made their way up the stairway to the upper rooms. Finally,

Carla showed her into a side room where she produced the brush and proceeded to redo Nesta's hair.

'Satisfied now?' asked Nesta eventually.

'You want to look your best, my lady,' said Carla, 'for this is the second most powerful man in Britannia.'

'Titles do not impress me, Carla.'

'Perhaps not, but consider this. If you make him happy then perhaps he would be more enamoured to help you with your mother.'

'A point well made,' said Nesta, 'so I will try to stop myself removing his eyes with my nails.'

Nesta watched as Carla unsuccessfully stifled a giggle but before she could utter a word, the door opened and a male servant appeared.

'His Highness will see you now,' he announced and stood to one side as Nesta crossed the floor.

'My lady,' said Carla, just before she left the room.

'Yes, Carla?' said Nesta turning around.

'Just . . . be careful,' she said and before Nesta could answer, she pushed past to walk down the stairs.

Nesta stepped through the double doors and was immediately hit by the warmth inside the room. A fire roared in the hearth and hundreds of candles sat in decorative holders all around the walls. She thought her own quarters were comfortable, but in comparison, they were a hovel. Carpets covered the floor from wall to wall and rich tapestries, glowing in colour, depicted hunting scenes from royal life. In the middle of the room, a table was set up covered with a white linen cloth and set out with platters of highly polished silver. The goblets seemed to be of gold, and bowls of fruit like she had never seen before lay between the only two place settings present. The doors closed behind her and she looked around, seeking her host – but he was nowhere to be seen. She wandered around the room, examining the opulence on display.

'See anything you like?' asked a voice and she spun around to stare at the man who had emerged from a side chamber.

'*You*,' she stuttered, 'what are you doing here, I mean . . . are you . . .'

'Yet again you seem lost for words,' said the man, 'so let me make this easy for you. Yes, I am the same man who rescued you from embarrassment at the king's banquet a few days ago, and just to clear up any confusion, my name is Henry Beauclerc, and yes, I am the king's brother.'

'I had no idea,' whispered Nesta, 'you should have said.'

'If I remember correctly, there was no time for discourse for I was whisked away on matters of the court and by the time I had returned, you had gone.'

'Yes, I remember,' said Nesta, 'my mother and I retired for the night.'

'Understandable,' said Henry, 'still, no harm done. Why don't we be seated and we can get to know each other a little better?'

Nesta made her way over to the table and one of the servants pulled back a chair for her to sit.

'Thank you,' said Nesta, sitting down and straightening her dress.

'Would you like some wine?' asked Henry.

'Just a little, thank you.'

They waited for the servant to finish pouring before raising their goblets.

'To you,' said Henry.

Nesta laughed. 'I'm not going to toast myself so may I suggest, the house of Tewdwr?'

Henry paused and stared at Nesta. Her suggestion bordered on the verge of contempt but she returned his gaze, her eyes sparkling with defiance. Finally, he smiled and raised his goblet once again.

'The house of Tewdwr,' he replied, inclining his head as he joined Nesta in drinking to the king's enemy.

'So,' said Henry, replacing his goblet on the table, 'I would imagine you have many questions.'

'I do indeed,' said Nesta, replacing her own goblet, 'and though I do not wish to spoil what promises to be an interesting evening, perhaps it would be better to get the more unpleasant ones out of the way before we start.'

'I agree,' said the prince, 'so ask your questions, Lady Nesta, and perhaps you may end up seeing that I am not the tyrant you think I am.'

'My first question, my lord, is very simple. Why am I being held here against my will? I have committed no crime yet you have abducted my person and locked me away like a common criminal.'

'The question is indeed very simple,' replied Henry, nodding towards the servants to start serving the meal, 'yet the answer is quite complex. First of all, you are not seen as a criminal, merely a guest of the king. Indeed, once the current situation in Wales settles down, you are seen as a potentially important ally to the Crown.'

'What makes you say that?'

'You are a princess of Deheubarth, Nesta, and a very attractive one at that. The king is fully aware that your family name commands a lot of respect in the south of your country and as such, hopes that one day, when you marry, you will be open to treaties between our countries. To that end, he ensures you are treated well and has even instructed our command in Deheubarth to hold back from destroying your castles.'

'If I am truly not a prisoner, as you suggest,' said Nesta, 'why am I locked in my room?'

'Ah yes, an unfortunate situation but a necessary one. The reason for that is simple, Lady Nesta, and one which I am sure you will understand.'

'Please continue.'

'As you are aware, the political situation has changed in Wales and as such, my brother is forced to undertake a campaign to sub-due some rebellion that seems to have flared up near the marches.'

'You talk of Cadwgan?'

'Indeed. Do you know of him?'

'I do. A surly man with no manners yet one with a fire in his heart that burns for his country.'

'Similar to yours, I would venture.'

'Yes, my heart burns for my homeland but I am no murderer. A statement that cannot be similarly made on behalf of Cadwgan.'

'Ah yes, I seem to remember a report that he once campaigned against your father.'

'Twice,' said Nesta, 'yet was defeated on both occasions.'

'So you hold no allegiance to him?'

'No, yet I am closer to his politics than I am to those of your brother.'

'And therein lies the problem,' said Henry.

'I don't understand.'

'The thing is,' continued the prince, 'William is about to set out on a campaign against this rebel and has the full support of the English nobles at his back. Already the corridors of Westminster echo with excitement at the thought of a new campaign. However, even though you are not directly linked to this Cadwgan, the ladies of the court only see the fact that you are Welsh and your presence, along with your mother's, will kindle fear and conspiracy. If not against the king, then certainly against you.'

'So you brought me here for my own safety?'

'That is one reason, but I have to admit, your constant ridiculing of the suitors brought before you was becoming an embarrassment to the king, and as such it was decided a while ago to move you here.'

'And my mother?'

'Alas your mother holds little importance to the king.'

'Why?'

'Because she has lived her life and will give birth to no more sons to rise against us. You, however, are a different thing altogether. You are seen as a powerful potential wife for any man strong enough to take you on; you could bear many sons. To William, that makes you either a dangerous enemy or a powerful ally. He just can't decide which.'

'Even so, that doesn't explain why he kicked an old woman out into the muck of London.'

'He had to do something for the benefit of the court. Too many people already whisper he treats you two better than some of his own. It was a gesture, no more. But fear not, she was given a healthy purse. Your mother will come to no harm.'

'The words come easy to you, my lord, yet I fear the reality may be different. She is a Welsh queen in an English city at a time when there could be war between the two countries. Even if we end up enemies, surely chivalry demands that a royal foe is treated with respect and dignity.'

'Granted,' said Henry, 'but alas the decision was not mine.'

'Perhaps it was not yours at the time, but your allowance of the situation to proceed unchecked does you no favours. I beseech thee, my lord, if there is anything you can do to find out if she is alive, then show me you are a man greater than your brother, crown or no crown.'

Nesta picked up her goblet and sipped at her wine as Henry stared at her in amusement. Finally, he beckoned to a nearby man-servant to come over, and after whispering something in his ear, dismissed him immediately before turning back to face Nesta.

'I can promise nothing,' he said, 'but will see what I can do. Now, shall we eat?'

Nesta gave him the semblance of a smile and sat back as one of the servants placed slices of roast swan upon her plate.

'One more thing, my lord,' she said as the servant stepped away.

Henry replaced his knife on the table and smiled, somewhat impatiently.

'Yes?'

'You said I am seen as a nuisance at court. If that is the case, why don't you just send me back to Wales?'

'Because, Lady Nesta, you are a princess of Deheubarth and even though you are a woman, you could potentially become a figurehead of the rebellion.'

'Both you and I know that will never happen,' said Nesta, 'but even though I am here, the Tewdwr dynasty will continue.'

'I suppose you talk of your brother in Ireland?'

'I do.'

'It is a fair point but we are comfortable that he will never raise a sword against us.'

'Why not?'

'Because of you,' said Henry.

Realisation dawned in her eyes as the truth of the matter was finally revealed. She was a hostage against her brother reviving the seat of Tewdwr. Though the fact in itself was not unsuspected, it finally dawned on her that as long as her brother was still alive, she would never be allowed home.

'Nesta,' said Henry quietly, 'if you don't mind, I am rather hungry. Perhaps for one evening we can forget the politics of nations and just enjoy each other's company.' He nodded towards her plate and gave her a gentle smile. 'Besides, your swan is getting cold.'

Despite Henry's revelation, Nesta turned her attention to the meal. At first the conversation was somewhat one-sided as Henry tried to engage her in conversation, but gradually his gentle charm relaxed her and she found herself beginning to enjoy his company.

'Was the meal to your liking?' asked Henry as the servants took away the platters.

'It was most agreeable,' said Nesta. 'Thank you.'

'Say nothing of it,' said Henry, 'the pleasure was all mine. Shall we take a more comfortable seat?' He indicated the two sumptuous chairs near the fire.

Nesta nodded silently and made her way over to sit opposite him.

'So,' said Henry after one of the servants had recharged their goblets, 'why don't you tell me something of yourself?'

'I believe you know all there is to know,' said Nesta.

'On the contrary,' said Henry, 'I was aware there was a feisty Welsh princess detained at Westminster but I have to admit, I took no great interest and now you sit beside me, I find you are nothing like I imagined.'

'And what exactly did you imagine?' asked Nesta.

'Oh I don't know, some scantily clad wench with wild hair and the manners of a tavern girl.'

Nesta stifled a laugh. 'Is that how you really see us?' she asked.

'No, not really.' Henry smiled. 'Though I have to admit your manner and personality far exceed what I have been told about the Welsh. I expected an opinionated vixen at the very least, yet here

I am engaged in conversation with a beautiful lady as charming as any I have met at the court of William.'

'We are not savages, sir,' said Nesta, 'our royal lines go back hundreds of years and though you come from across the sea, our nations have traded for generations.'

'Indeed, and that is why I had such an inaccurate picture. Our barons report a wild land with wilder people.'

'Perhaps they see the other side of my people,' said Nesta, 'the side that fights fiercely when confronted with invasion and the destruction of everything their ancestors worked towards.'

'Of course,' said Henry, 'and I am wrong to make assumptions, so perhaps, for the rest of the evening you could enlighten me as to the real nature of your country and your people.'

For a few moments Nesta sat back and stared at the king's brother. Although she was under no illusions – he was a master at making people feel at ease in his presence – his interest seemed genuine and soon they were engaged in conversation about the country she loved. Henry allowed her to speak freely, smiling at her undoubted passion as she regaled him with the stories of her youth and soon, any underlying tension eased away as they gradually relaxed further into each other's company.

For a few hours, the troubles of the world seemed a lifetime away for Nesta and as the evening came to a close she slowly realised that despite her initial reluctance and expectations, Henry had actually been charming company. So much so, that when it was time to leave, she found herself slightly disappointed that the evening had come to an end.

Finally, after saying her goodbyes, she walked back across the bailey alongside Carla and though she initially kept her thoughts to herself, her heart raced as if she had run a thousand leagues.

The king's brother was everything she had ever hoped to find in a man – handsome, courteous and amusing, yet strong in character and with a repartee that kept the evening fresh and interesting. The fact that he was a member of the Norman royal family seemed irrelevant and even if he had been the poorest soul, her heart would have raced just as quickly.

'Was your evening enjoyable?' asked Carla as they walked into the lower keep.

'Indeed it was,' said Nesta, 'for in a time of war and politics, Henry was a breath of fresh air.'

'It is true he has a way with words,' replied Carla, 'and it is said he can charm the birds from the trees with his oratory.'

'I think it was more than that,' said Nesta, 'we seemed to have a connection. I know that tonight will probably never be repeated but even if I never see the man again, I will treasure the experience for what it was.'

'Well,' said Carla as they reached the door of Nesta's rooms, 'you just be careful, my lady, many others have walked this path before you and have ended up no more than a conquest for his reputation.'

'I know what I am doing, Carla,' said Nesta, 'but thank you for your concern. Now, if you will excuse me, I am looking forward to my bed.'

'Of course,' said Carla. 'Good night, Lady Nesta.' The woman turned away but as she disappeared down the stairs, Nesta noticed something had changed: the guards had gone. In addition, the key that had been located in the outside of the door was now on the inside, enabling her to decide who came in. Nesta smiled at the gesture of trust, obviously sent from Henry. Though there were undoubtedly guards upon the main gates, she was no longer a prisoner in her own rooms.

The night was a sleepless one for Nesta as her mind spun in turmoil at the conflict within her. She had sworn not to fall for the charms of any man unless it was on her own terms, yet here she was, contemplating that which was surely impossible. Finally, she fell asleep and for the first time in what seemed an age, was comfortable enough to feel as if she was home. Subsequently, it was difficult to focus when she was woken by repeated knocking. She stumbled from her bed across the room before standing at the locked door, stretching her arms as she tried to shake off the tiredness.

'Who is it?' she asked after a particularly deep yawn.

'My lady, it's Carla,' said the voice. 'I come with a gift from Lord Henry.'

'Another gift?' said Nesta. 'Is he usually this generous?'

'Only to those he holds particular affection for,' said Carla.

'Give me a few minutes,' said Nesta, 'and I will get myself dressed.'

'My lady, I suggest you open the door immediately for this gift will not wait.'

Nesta's interest piqued and she unlocked the door.

'As you wish,' she said eventually, 'but I warn you, I do not look the best when freshly risen from my bed— *Mother!*' she cried, pushing the door open fully and throwing her arms around Gwladus's neck.

Gwladus caught her breath, not expecting such a response, but within moments she disentangled herself from Nesta's grip.

'Nesta,' she said, 'I am quite overwhelmed, but let us at least seek the sanctuary of privacy before displaying our emotions before the castle staff.'

'Oh don't worry about Carla.' Nesta laughed. 'She is lovely.'

'Still, I don't think it is appropriate.'

'Come in,' said Nesta excitedly. She turned to the maid. 'Carla, I don't know how you did it, but thank you so much.'

'My contribution was one of information only,' said Carla. 'The decision to send out couriers to find your mother belongs entirely to Lord Henry.'

'Then will you pass on my gratitude and promise I will visit him later to thank him in person?'

'He is not in the castle today or tomorrow,' said Carla, 'but has asked that I request your company three days hence, to go riding with him in the forests of Kent. I am to relay your response by messenger the very second I receive it.'

Nesta paused and then smiled gently at the servant.

'Well, please tell him I will be delighted to join him.'

Carla returned the smile and curtsied before turning to leave the keep. Behind her she heard the door shut and the joyful laughter as mother and daughter were reunited.

'What has happened?' squealed Nesta. 'Where have you been?'

'On quite an adventure,' replied Gwladus, sinking onto Nesta's unmade bed. 'I wandered the streets of London for half a night and eventually ended up staying in the back room of an inn, an experience I wish never to repeat. The activities of certain ladies were rather loud, I have to say, and I piled up every stick of furniture against the door lest someone thought I was a working girl.'

Nesta's hand flew to her mouth to stop the laugh escaping.

'It's not funny, Nesta, the following morning the landlord offered me a job as a skivvy. I mean, do I look like a wench?'

This time there was no stopping Nesta and she burst out laughing as she threw her arms around Gwladus.

'Oh, Mother,' she said, 'I know it must have been horrible but I am just relieved you are safe.'

'I am fine,' said Gwladus, disentangling herself once more, 'a bit shaken but unhurt. More importantly, how have *you* been? It's been three days since I saw you last and to be truthful, you look dreadful.'

Nesta's hand went up to her messy hair and she laughed again.

'Take no notice, I was fast asleep when you came and have had no time to see about my appearance. Be seated while I make myself presentable and after that, you can tell me about your adventure.'

As she got dressed, a maid knocked on the door and brought in a bowl of boiled goose eggs along with some bread and cheese and a flask of warm honeyed water.

'Ah, breakfast,' said Nesta, pinning up her hair.

'It's nearer midday than breakfast time,' said Gwladus, 'but still, come and eat something. I need to explain why I am here.'

'I though Henry had sought you out?'

'He did, but luckily he knew where I was for I have made petition at these gates these past two days.'

'And you weren't allowed to enter?'

'The guards at the gate were most courteous, yet diligent in their task. Anyway, the thing is I am here now and just wanted to make sure you were well before . . .' She hesitated.

'Before what?' asked Nesta.

'Before I return to Wales.'

Nesta stared at her mother in shock. 'What?' she gasped.

'Nesta,' said Gwladus, 'I am returning to Wales and will be leaving tomorrow.'

'But why?' asked Nesta, in shock. 'I don't understand.'

'The situation has changed, Nesta, and though it took my expulsion from Westminster to realise it, I now know my place is back in Deheubarth. Your father may be dead, but I am still queen, and as such have duties to uphold.'

'But you said Marcus Freeman is looking after the estates.'

'He is but he is getting old and can only do so much. My place is there, Nesta. Our people need me.'

'Then I will come with you,' gasped Nesta, her voice rising as the reality of the situation sunk in. 'I will petition the king and request release immediately.'

'Nesta,' said Gwladus quietly, 'we both know he will not allow you to leave, at least not yet.'

'I will ask Henry to speak on my behalf,' said Nesta, pacing back and forth. 'I will get down on bended knee if needed and beg my release, I will—'

'Nesta,' said her mother sharply, 'enough. I hate this as much as you but the reality is you have to stay here. I, on the other hand, am needed back in Wales and though it breaks my heart to leave you, it is for the best.'

Nesta stopped her pacing and stared at her mother. Despite her strength and resolve, the thought of being left behind made the tears well up behind her eyes.

'Please,' she whispered, trying desperately not to cry, 'don't leave me. I need you here.'

Gwladus quickly closed the gap between them and threw her arms around her daughter.

'Nesta,' she whispered, 'my sweet, sweet child. I am so sorry to tell you like this but there was no easy way.'

'But why?' asked Nesta, pushing her mother away as her tears began to flow. 'You have been with me all this time, why desert me now? What have I done that is so bad?'

'Nesta, you have done nothing,' gasped Gwladus, reaching out to her again, 'you are still my wonderful daughter, and a more precious child no woman can ever wish to have. But you are a grown woman now, and we both have burdens to bear. Over the past year my eyes have been clouded with majesty while my heart was dulled with grief. I couldn't face life without your father so refused to allow myself thoughts of home. However, these past few days have provided clarity in my mind. You have a future here, Nesta, and once the rebellion ends, who knows – it could be at the side of a noble. I, on the other hand, cling to your skirt ribbons like a younger sister. You are settled now and have turned into a strong young woman. You no longer need me at your side, Nesta, I have to return home.'

'But where will you go? Deheubarth is under Norman control.'

'Indeed it is but we still hold lands in our name and Marcus has ensured both castles have been maintained in good order.'

Nesta stared at her mother, the hurt clear in her eyes.

'Oh, Nesta.' Gwladus sighed. 'Please don't look at me like that. You know I have never been made welcome in the English court but made myself busy seeking suitors on your behalf. To be truthful, I see now it was naught but a useful diversion while I grieved but I am a queen of Deheubarth and as such, should be in that kingdom leading our people. Your father would have expected no less.'

'So what will become of me?'

'You will be fine. I have had a long conversation with the castellan this very morning and he assures me that Henry means you no ill. I am going to return home and intend leaving at first light tomorrow. The purse given to me by William is more than enough to cover my expenses and when I reach Dinefwr, I will take over the estate from Marcus.

'Please let me come with you,' begged Nesta, her voice breaking.

'Tell me honestly,' said Gwladus, taking her daughter's hand, 'do you feel at risk here or do you feel safe behind these palisades?'

'I am safe, of course, but . . .'

'Then it is better that you stay here, if only for my sake. Wales is a wild and lawless place at the moment, and Cadwgan's rebellion spreads across the country like wildfire. You must stay here until the situation has eased and when we know where our future lies, I will send word to you. Perhaps by then, William will be of kinder disposition and allow you to return home.'

Nesta stared at her mother but offered no more argument. She knew Gwladus was right, but like so many times before she just wished that she had not been born a princess. The burdens of station were sometimes too heavy to bear.

'What if I never see you again?'

'Oh you will, my darling,' said Gwladus taking her daughter in her arms again, 'I promise you, once this mess is all over then we will be reunited in Dinefwr and who knows, we may even have Hywel and Tarw at our sides.'

'I do hope so, said Nesta.

Quietly and for several moments, the women held each other tightly, remembering the many hardships they had each endured since Nesta was a child. Finally, Gwladus eased her daughter away and after wiping the tears from her daughter's eyes, picked up the hairbrush from the table.

'Anyway,' she said, 'I have a full day to spend with you. Let me make some sense of that hair and perhaps we can take a walk.'

'I'd like that,' said Nesta, and she sat down in the chair to let her mother do her hair, as on hundreds of occasions before.

As she brushed Nesta's hair, Gwladus comforted her daughter with tales from years before.

'Remember that banquet when you and Hywel crept down to see what the noise was about?'

'I do,' said Nesta with a smile, 'the noise was horrendous.'

'Oh yes!' Gwladus laughed. 'One man had drunk another's ale, if I recall correctly.'

'I thought they were going to kill each other,' said Nesta, enjoying the rhythm of the brush in her hair.

'And what about those walks along the sands?' said Gwladus. 'I think they were my favourite times. When you and your brother would make my heart stop by swimming out of your depth.'

'You always were a worrier,' said Nesta, and for a while they both fell silent, alone with their thoughts, until Nesta spoke again.

'Do you know my favourite memories?' she asked quietly.

'Tell me,' said Gwladus.

'The winters,' said Nesta. 'Playing in the snow and helping the staff carry firewood from the stores. We would be allowed to stay up late by the fire and eat cawl straight from the pot. After that, Hywel and I would cuddle on father's lap as he told us the stories of Arthur. Remember?'

For a second, the hairbrush stopped and Nesta turned to see tears rolling down her mother's face.

'Oh, Mother,' she said, standing up quickly. 'Are you all right?' She threw her arms around Gwladus and held her tightly; this time it was her mother's turn to break down.

'I miss them, Nesta,' sobbed Gwladus eventually. 'I miss them all so much.'

Nesta knew that nothing she could say would make it better so both women just held each other tightly, waiting for the pain to go away.

Several hours later, Nesta stood at the fire, watching her mother gather her things.

'Do you have lodgings tonight?' she asked.

'Yes, the local bishop has kindly offered me rooms at his house and Henry's men will ensure I get there safely. Tomorrow I join a column heading into Wales but will part company with them in Powys. Don't worry about me, Nesta, in Wales your father's name still carries some weight and the house of Tewdwr is still revered by many nobles.'

'I will miss you,' said Nesta as her mother donned her cloak.

'And I will miss you,' said Gwladus, hugging her daughter tightly, 'but I'm sure that before this year is out the war will be over and we can once more walk arm in arm through the fields of Deheubarth.'

Nesta smiled and kissed her mother before leading her out of the keep and down to the gate.

'Be strong, Nesta,' said Gwladus as they paused before the palisade. 'I will think of you every day until next we meet but until then, you have my love and my blessings.'

'Goodbye, Mother,' said Nesta as Gwladus passed through the gate. 'I love you.'

Gwladus waved and disappeared into the night along with the four soldiers appointed as her bodyguard.

'See you soon,' said Nesta quietly, more for her own comfort than anything else. But she was wrong, for it would be a very, very long time before she once more set eyes upon her mother.

The Village of Dinefwr

May 26th, AD 1096

The innkeeper walked around the tavern, using a broom to sweep any spilled ale into a trough that ran along one wall of the room. A few men remained, nursing their tankards despite the dawn being already upon them. The innkeeper sighed as he negotiated their feet. He would have thrown them out had they not been some of his best customers. Times were hard and he needed all the trade he could get. One man, lying along a bench near the fire, was unknown to him but had spent a pretty penny getting gloriously drunk the previous evening.

The innkeeper paused and looked down on the sleeping man. By the look on the outsider's face, he was certainly no stranger to hardship. His face was weathered and haggard while a set of three deep scars ran down one cheek, each standing out clearly against the man's yellowing skin. His hair was thinning and what was left was tangled in a mess that had seen neither comb nor soap for many a year.

The innkeeper wrinkled his nose at the man's stench, for though the tavern was the haunt of strong men, the smell of honest sweat was distinctly different from the stench of neglect. He knew he would have to wake him up and ask him to leave – the stranger had caused some petty arguments the previous evening, and he couldn't leave his daughter, Bethan, to deal with such a man on her own.

'Wake up, stranger,' he said, shaking the man's shoulder, 'it is time to leave.'

'Leave me alone,' mumbled the man as he rolled over to face the back of the bench, pulling his cape closer around him.

'The tavern is closing,' said the innkeeper, 'and you must take your leave.' When there was no response, the landlord shook his shoulder again.

'Do you hear me, stranger? The tavern is closed, you have to go.'

Without warning the man shot up and pushed the innkeeper back against the wall.

'I told you to leave me alone,' he hissed, 'I paid good coin for ale and a bench so why don't you keep your side of the bargain and let me sleep?'

'I have,' said the innkeeper, staring into the dangerous man's eyes, 'but dawn is upon us and we have to sort out the inn. Now, why don't you just leave quietly before you are hurt?'

The stranger produced a knife and held it against the landlord's throat. 'And what makes you think there is any chance that I may get hurt?'

'This does,' said a voice behind him and the stranger felt the press of cold steel against the back of his neck. He froze, knowing he had been bettered and slowly lowered his blade.

'What is your name, stranger?' asked the voice.

'Merriweather,' came the strained reply.

'Well, Master Merriweather, I suggest you drop your blade or die where you stand.'

For a few seconds there was no movement but when the pressure increased on the blade, the knife clattered to the floor.

'I'm going to step back now,' said the voice, 'and let you leave, but don't even think about trying something stupid, there are another three blades at your back.'

The pressure eased and Merriweather turned to stare at the others still in the tavern. Each had a blade of some sort in his hand and the attacker knew there was nothing he could do.

'Get out,' said the nearest man, 'and don't ever come to this place again.'

'No man has the right to tell me where I can or cannot go,' growled Merriweather.

'Perhaps not, but if your ugly face is seen here again, then we can't be held responsible for your safety. These are troubled times, Master Merriweather, and oft men disappear without trace. It would be such a shame if the same fate happened to you.'

'I paid for ale, a bed and a morning meal,' growled Merriweather, 'and my coin is as good as any.'

'Ale you've had aplenty, the bench was your bed and –' the man picked up a crust of stale bread left over from the previous evening – 'here is your meal. Now get out, for my temper wears thin.'

'What about my knife?'

'Consider it compensation for threatening the life of our landlord. Now, I won't tell you again, get out!'

Outside the tavern, Merriweather pulled his cape tighter around him and wandered towards the village square. People from all around the area were already busy setting up carts and stalls for the weekly market and he knew he could probably get some hot potage from one of the vendors, or if he was lucky, some warmed ale. As he went he passed a wagon carrying a mountain of woollen fleeces, returning the stare from an old man driving the horse team.

'Do you have a problem?' sneered Merriweather.

'No,' said the old man slowly, 'my apologies, I thought I knew you for a moment.'

'Well, I don't know you,' said Merriweather, 'so I suggest you keep your own business and I will be getting on with mine.'

'Of course,' said the old man, 'my apologies.'

Merriweather cleared his throat before spitting on the ground and after one more threatening glance, continued his walk towards the market.

'Who was that, Dylan?' asked the old man's wife beside him.

'Just someone I thought I knew,' he replied, 'but it seems I am mistaken. Come, we should make haste.' He flicked the horses' reins and continued along the road, glancing only briefly back at the man.

The rest of the morning saw the market in full swing as people came from miles around to barter their wares. Farmers sold live animals to butchers and each other, while bakers filled trestle tables with loaves and pastries. Brewers sold flasks of ale to man and woman alike – a popular drink due to the risk of drinking contaminated water – and dressmakers sat upon blankets, carefully sewing unfinished garments of plain linen. Pie makers were always popular, especially when the pies were still hot from the stone ovens, and already a few men stood waiting patiently at a table, anticipating the delivery of the first batch.

'Cerys,' said the old man, once their fleeces had been unloaded, 'why don't you go and get something for us to break our fast. My belly is in need of a gift and if rumour is correct, the pie maker of Dinefwr stands alongside the best in the region.'

'You and your pies!' His wife laughed. 'I sometimes wonder which you love more – pastries or me.'

'Don't risk an answer from me, woman.' replied Dylan with a smile, 'for you may not like the judgement given!'

Cerys laughed again and flicked her shawl at him before making her way through the growing crowd.

Half an hour later, Dylan sat on a wall eating his pie as he waited for the auction to start. Cerys swept the back of their cart in preparation for the supplies she anticipated buying with the money earned from the sale of the fleeces.

'There he is again,' said Dylan, between mouthfuls.

'Who?' asked Cerys from behind.

'That man from the tavern earlier; I'm sure I know him from somewhere.'

Cerys stared over at the man, now skulking between stalls with a mug of ale in his fist.

'I don't know him,' said Cerys. 'Anyway, why are you so concerned?'

'I'm not, it's just that I have a nagging feeling of unease, as if he has wronged me in the past.'

'If he had, I'm sure you would have told me,' replied Cerys.

Dylan took another bite of his pie before washing it down with a swig of water from his leather flask. Despite his wife's assurances Dylan still felt uneasy and he watched closely as the man negotiated the market. It was obvious the scoundrel was up to no good, and Dylan wasn't surprised when he picked up a leg of cooked chicken when a stallholder was looking elsewhere. Dylan was about to call out and alert the stallholder when a dog leapt from beneath the table and went for the leg of the thief.

Merriweather jumped back and kicked out at the chained dog before turning and facing the angry stallholder.

'I assume you are going to pay for that meat,' said the owner.

Merriweather made a show of inspecting the chicken leg before handing it over.

'Nah, looks a bit rotten to me,' he said, 'you can keep it.' He turned and walked away, giving the dog a wide berth as the stall owner returned the chicken leg to the table.

Dylan stared at the back of the would-be thief, the light of recognition dawning in his eyes.

'It can't be,' he said quietly, 'after all these years . . .'

'What was that, dear?' asked Cerys.

Dylan looked up at his wife on the cart, remembering an oath of silence he had taken many years earlier.

'Nothing to worry about, my love, it's just that I recognise that man from years ago, just a good-for-nothing wastrel from my past.'

'Then steer away from him,' said Cerys climbing down from the cart, 'we don't need any trouble.'

'Of course,' said Dylan, placing the last of his pie in his mouth. But although his wife was content with his answer, he knew he couldn't let it go – there was something he had to do.

The day went well for Cerys and Dylan. Their fleeces all sold and they filled their cart with sacks of grain and seed for the new planting. Cerys bought a roll of linen to make them both some new clothes and Dylan had an axe head repaired at the blacksmith. Midday came and went and as the stallholders started to pack away their wares, Dylan led the horses and the cart back through Dinefwr. As they neared the edge of the village, he stopped outside the tavern and tied the reins to a hitching post.

'Dylan, since when have you frequented taverns?' asked Cerys from her seat upon the cart.

'I'm not going to drink, my love, I just need to find out something.'

'Find out what?' asked Cerys. But it was too late – Dylan had already ducked inside.

The tavern was warm and lively and though it was quite dark inside, enough light was provided by the fire and dozens of candles around the walls. Men sat on benches on either side of long trestle tables, quaffing their foaming tankards while others picked at platters of meat and cheese or slurped from wooden bowls of hot, nourishing cawl.

Dylan made his way to an empty seat in the corner and caught the eye of a serving woman.

'Can I get you something, stranger?' she asked, wiping the dregs of spilled ale from the upturned cask serving as a table.

'I'll have one of those,' said Dylan pointing at the drink on a nearby table.

'That will be a copper coin,' said the girl, holding out her hand. Dylan fished out his purse and pressed a coin into her hand.

'I wonder if you could perhaps help me,' he said, 'I am looking for a man.'

'Aren't we all?' She laughed with a screech.

'No,' corrected the farmer, looking around nervously, 'there was a man in here this very morn and I was wondering if you knew where he was?'

'Many men come in here, dear,' said the girl, 'but they all look the same to me after a while.'

'Not this one,' said Dylan, 'he looks very shifty and has three marks running from here to here.' He dragged his own fingers down his face, indicating the location of the man's scars.

The girl's smile faded and she straightened up.

'Oh, him,' she said, 'yes, he was here and a more unpleasant soul you could never wish to meet.'

'What makes him so vile?' asked Dylan.

'Well, for one thing he stank,' said the girl, 'and after several ales, tried it on with most of the girls in here. Now I am no shrinking flower, my friend, but even I have my standards and no amount of money would encourage me to lift my skirts to someone like him. Besides, by the end of the night he was blind drunk and claimed some stuff that had most of our customers seething with anger.'

'What was that?' Dylan asked quickly.

'Well,' said the woman leaning forward so as not to be overheard, 'he claimed to have bedded our exiled queen, Gwladus ferch Rhiwallon.'

Dylan caught his breath as he realised his suspicions had been correct. The dog attacking Merriweather in the market had brought his memories flooding back and Dylan had recalled how, many years earlier, his own dog had chased away a scoundrel after Dylan found him raping a woman. If this was the same man, then it was possible he would soon spread his story amongst the people of Dinefwr and the queen's reputation would be in ruins.

'Do you know his name?' he asked.

'Is he a friend of yours?' replied the girl. 'For if so, I would keep it to yourself. He made a few enemies while he was here.'

'No,' said Dylan, 'he is no comrade of mine, but I need to know his name. Do you have it?'

'As a matter of fact I do, for there was a fight this very morning and he said his name was Merriweather.'

'Merriweather,' repeated Dylan. 'I don't suppose you know where he is from?'

'Alas I don't,' said the girl, 'and nor do I want to. An unpleasant sort he was and I don't want to see him back here. Now, let's get you that ale.'

She walked to the back of the room and handed the penny over to the landlord. The man stirred the open cask with his ladle before lifting it out and pouring the ale into a waiting wooden tankard. The girl returned to the table but was surprised to find it empty – the stranger had gone.

Outside, Dylan flicked the reins and urged the horses forward.

'Well,' said Cerys, 'did you find out what it was you wanted to know?'

'Aye,' said Dylan, 'that I did.'

The Forests of Gwynedd

August 25th, AD 1096

Three months later, a young boy peered around the flap of his father's command tent deep in the mountains of North Wales.

'Father,' he said simply, 'they have returned.'

Cadwgan ap Bleddyn, Prince of Powys and leader of the Welsh rebellion, followed his son from the tent and over to where a group of men sat astride their steaming horses. Water skins were passed around and it was obvious they had ridden hard. As leader of the Welsh rebels, Cadwgan had located his command tent deep in the forests of Mid Wales, away from the scouts and spies of the English. But even though he was a rebel, he maintained the appearance of a prince and kept himself well groomed, as befitting of a royal position. His black hair was kept to shoulder length and his beard was well trimmed – unlike the men now before him who were unkempt from the weather and many hard days' riding.

'Richard,' said Cadwgan, addressing one of his lieutenants. 'How went your journey?'

'My lord,' said Richard, wiping some honeyed water from his beard, 'the passage was hard and I return with mixed news. Though Gruffydd ap Cynan is agreeable to your proposal and welcomes the opportunity to share the campaign, he is still struck down by the rigours caused by his captivity and reluctantly has to hold back until his strength is regained. I have a letter from him explaining the situation.'

'A shame,' said Cadwgan, 'he would have made a valuable ally against Huw the Fat.'

'I'm sure he will yet ride at your side,' continued Richard, 'but in the meantime, we have to manage with what men we have.'

'We will see,' said Cadwgan, 'but while we wait there may be others to share our burden. Place your horses in the hands of the squires and join me in my tent. I will have meat and ale brought to soothe your bones.'

'A prospect most welcome, my lord,' said Richard, and he slid from the horse before handing over the reins to a nearby boy. He retrieved a leather bag from the saddle and followed Cadwgan through the trees towards his campaign tent.

'Please,' said Cadwgan, when every man was present, 'make yourselves at home. My squires will tend to your armour.'

Richard and his men discarded their cloaks followed by their chainmail. Several squires took the garments away for drying while the men stood near the fire to dry out their wet jerkins.

Cadwgan waited patiently as they sorted themselves out, fully aware that the trip from Ireland was known for its danger and hardships, not least the sea crossing. Eventually, the messengers had dried enough to take their place at the table and Cadwgan joined them, embracing the familiar smell of damp riding leathers.

Servants entered with trenchers of hot mutton, and soon Richard and his men were eating meat and quaffing ale from leather skins as if they were never to taste it again.

'Your men have a thirst about them,' said Cadwgan.

'The road was long, my lord,' said Richard, 'and the sea journey more difficult than anticipated.'

'Surely it is no more than two days to Ireland with a fair wind?'

'Aye, but oft the waves were higher than the bows and I regret to say my stomach now lays at the bottom of the sea, as do the stomachs of all my men.'

Cadwgan laughed and raised his tankard of ale towards his lieutenant.

'You have always said you are no sailor, Richard. Anyway, to business – where is this scroll you speak of?'

Richard placed his eating knife on the table and reached for the leather bag at his feet. He handed over the sealed scroll before resuming his meal. Cadwgan broke the seal and read the document silently before placing it to one side and sitting back thoughtfully.

'You seem troubled, my lord,' said Richard.

'Not troubled, Richard, but there is much to do.'

'Can I be of help?'

'Ordinarily, yes – but you are just returned from a difficult journey and have earned a rest.'

'There is no such thing as rest for a soldier in times of war. Just tell me what you want and I will get it done.'

'In that case, I have a task I would entrust to few others.'

Richard put down his tankard and wiped the froth from his moustache with the back of his hand.

'Name it, my lord.'

'I want you to gather a patrol of best men and prepare to ride with the dawn. Gruffydd may have declined our proposals for an alliance due to illness, but there is another who is ready to move as we speak. Take a message to him and request his presence as soon as possible.'

'Who is this man?' asked Richard.

'Hywel ap Goronwy.'

'The Lord of Radnor is joining our cause?'

'He is. He too suffers from the attention of the Marcher lords and has sent word that he will ride at our side. As will Uchtryd ap Edwin.'

'An exciting prospect,' said Richard, 'but may I counsel caution?'

'Speak your mind, Richard.'

'The reputation of Goronwy goes before him like a vanguard. However, the pedigree of Edwin may not be so pure.'

'In what way?'

'I have heard he is a man of limited intellect and is sometimes a burden to his allies. It is only due to the reputation of his father that he retains his cantref. If we are to engage these men, then perhaps we should test their mettle before deploying them in any place of strategic importance.'

'Noted,' said Cadwgan, 'but my invitation remains. It will take them a few days to arrive, so in the meantime I will decide a suitable target and witness their value from afar.' He turned to his son. 'Owain, you will join Richard upon this task, it is about time you witnessed the ways of warfare at first hand. Leave us now and see to your equipment and your horse.'

'Aye, Father,' said Owain, and he ran from the tent.

'The boy is growing up fast,' said Richard between mouthfuls of meat.

'That he is,' said Cadwgan, 'and each day brings a new worry, for he is a fiery brand with no thought of danger.'

'Are not all such boys the same?'

'Perhaps so, but Owain gives me concern. He acts before thought and many times I have had to pay reparations for damage done on his behalf.'

'Really?' Richard laughed. 'What possible damage could a boy do that causes you so much anxiety?'

'He sees himself as a man already and craves battle. I have denied him the opportunity for there is much yet for him to learn.

In frustration he has gathered a group of like-minded young men about him and seeks adventure of a different kind. Every few days I am faced with a fresh claim for compensation from a farmer or trader who has experienced their youthful zest. It seems that he favours livestock as target practice and the company of maidens to make the evenings shorter.'

'I am impressed!' Richard laughed. 'To have an interest in women at such a young age is an admirable trait.'

'Like I said, he is a boy beyond his years. Mark my words, one day he is going to lay trouble untold at my door.'

'Let the boy enjoy his life, my lord, heaven knows it can be short enough. No man knows the span of his days so let him live while he can.'

'Aye, that is also my whim, but anyway, enough of domestic affairs, tell me of your journey to Ireland.'

Across the Irish Sea, Gruffydd ap Cynan slept soundly on a couch in the solar, the room the family used for sleeping and relaxing. Deep yellow flames glowed lazily from between slow-burning logs, casting shadows around the room as Angharad sat back in her chair, gazing lovingly at her husband. Even now, after more than a year, she still couldn't believe he had returned home after so much time in captivity.

Since he had returned, she had spent almost every day at his side, helping him to recover after all the torturous years as a captive of Huw the Fat. There seemed not a pinch of muscle on his skeletal frame and sometimes she thought he wouldn't make it but despite this, she persevered and watched him slowly improve, gaining a little strength each day.

At first, exercise was out of the question and it was all he could do to walk himself to the garderobe to see to his toilet. But within months, the rich meals carefully prepared by the kitchen staff under the watchful eye of his wife, slowly added flesh to his bones. Despite her husband's weakened state, God had seen fit to bless them with their first child within a year of Gruffydd's return, and they named him Cadwaladr.

Cadwaladr was fast asleep in the cot made by the estate carpenter and only stirred slightly when a knock came upon the solar door. Angharad checked that neither of the two at slumber had been woken before going to the door and lifting the latch.

'Adele,' she said quietly, 'is everything all right?'

'No, my lady,' said Adele, 'will you come with me?'

Angharad glanced back before going through the door and closing it quietly. Adele was already halfway down the corridor and Angharad walked quickly, trying to catch up with her.

'What's the problem?' asked Angharad, turning into the buttery.

'You are the problem, my lady,' said Adele, 'you are going to make yourself ill if you're not careful. Now sit down and forget your worries, if only for a few moments.'

Angharad looked at the small table Adele had set for her. A platter of roast pork and cheese sat alongside a freshly baked loaf and a bowl of butter. A jug of warmed wine sat invitingly alongside the food. Angharad sighed in appreciation.

'Adele,' she said, 'what would I do without you?'

'Oh, probably starve yourself,' replied Adele. 'Now eat something and relax for a few moments. I've asked one of the chambermaids to stand outside the solar in case Cadwaladr wakes up.'

'You are truly a treasure,' said Angharad. 'Come, sit with me and share the fayre.'

'I have already eaten,' said Adele, 'but would enjoy a sip of wine if the invitation extends that far.'

'Of course it does; come, bring another beaker and sit awhile.'

Adele did as she was bid and filled both cups.

'*Hmmm*,' said Angharad, 'the pork is still warm.'

'Freshly cooked for tomorrow's table,' said Adele. 'I had to steal a few slices when the cook left the kitchen for a moment. He will be livid when he sees the beast has already seen the attentions of a carving knife.'

Angharad laughed. 'Why is it that cooks are always so cantankerous?'

'It has surely always been the way.' Adele sighed. 'And I suspect it will always be so.'

Angharad picked at the meat and smiled at Adele. Adele had served her loyally for many years, and Angharad felt that the other woman was closer to being a friend than a servant.

'My lady,' said Adele gently, 'you look like you have the woes of Ireland upon your shoulders. Pray tell – what worries you so?'

Angharad put her cutting knife down and looked at her friend.

'How long have I known you, Adele?' she asked.

'Far longer than you deserve.' Adele smiled, with a hint of mischief in her eye.

'I agree,' said Angharad, 'and if it wasn't for you I don't know how I would ever have survived those years without Gruffydd. But survive them we did and I thought I could never be happier when he appeared on our doorstep.'

'My lady, you make it sound like the happiness will be short-lived.'

'Alas, I feel it might be. The master is still weak but already he plans on taking the fight back to Wales.'

Adele stared and shook her head in disbelief.

'My lady,' she said, 'forgive me for being rude, but sometimes I think your husband is blind to what lies beneath his very nose. He has lived through a hell he had no right to survive, was chased across

Wales when he was barely alive, and crossed the Irish Sea hidden amongst a cargo of pigs meant for the slaughterhouse. You would think that he would recognise God's compassion and settle down to raise his new family in peace.'

'I agree,' said Angharad, 'yet I think it is not to be. Already he has received representations from Cadwgan ap Bleddyn and conspires to join the rebellion as soon as he is able.'

'Men and cursed wars,' said Adele. 'Why can't they see they are not the answer? Why they can't just settle for a roof, a platter of food and a family's love, is beyond the likes of me.'

'Me also,' said Angharad. 'We are lucky enough to have this house, a parcel of land and an income from the king of Dublin, but always Gruffydd wishes to return to Wales. I fear he will not rest until he sets foot on home soil. My heart bleeds for him, it really does, and he has tried to repossess Aberffraw so often it makes me weep, but this time I feel it will be the death of him.'

'Well –' Adele sighed – 'there is no way of knowing the future, my lady, perhaps this time the good Lord will reward his persistence with victory.'

'I hope so,' said Angharad, 'I really hope so.' She picked up her cup and after a silent toast towards her friend, drank the remainder of the wine before resuming her meal.

The following day, Gruffydd was out of bed and already dressed by the time Angharad awoke. She glanced down at the crib and was surprised to see her son was also gone.

Quickly, she got out of bed and ran to the window but saw no sign of her husband. Hearing the door ease inward she turned in relief but saw it was only Adele, bring her warm water with which to bathe.

'Adele,' she said starting forward, 'please tell me you have taken Cadwaladr to be dressed.'

'Fret not, my lady, for the child is already dressed and has been fed by the nurse maid.'

'Oh,' said Angharad. 'And my husband, do you know his whereabouts?'

'Indeed,' said Adele, 'he has taken his son to get some fresh Irish air.'

'Really?' asked Angharad in surprise. 'Do you know where they are?'

'The last I heard they were heading for the stables,' said Adele, 'I believe the king is going to introduce your son to his first horse.'

'*What?*' gasped Angharad. 'The boy is not yet able to walk, how can he be expected to ride?'

'I wouldn't worry,' said Adele, 'he may be a stupid man when it comes to kingship but his heart is good when it comes to his son.'

'Nevertheless!' Angharad laughed at the other woman's bluntness. 'Help me dress for I would join them as soon as I can.'

Half an hour later, Angharad and Adele walked through the stables and out into the training yard.

'Dermot,' asked Angharad, 'have you seen the king?'

'Aye, my lady,' said the stable hand, 'he is beyond the stable wall showing Master Cadwaladr his horse.'

The two women walked quickly but as they turned the corner, Angharad suddenly held her hand up and both women stopped dead in their tracks, transfixed by the beauty of the scene before them. Gruffydd was sat on a low wall holding Cadwaladr on his lap while in front of them, a foal no more than a few weeks old stretched his head downward to sniff at the child's face. The foal's mother was eating oats from a nearby wooden bucket and completely unperturbed at the attention of Gruffydd and the baby, so when Angharad slowly approached, it did little more than raise its head to check the newcomer wasn't a danger.

'My love,' said Angharad gently, as Gruffydd acknowledged her presence, 'you had me concerned for a while.'

'Really?' said Gruffydd as a particularly loud giggle from the child made the foal prance a few paces away. 'Why is that?'

'Because when I awoke, neither of you were to be seen.'

'Is a man not allowed to spend time with his own son?'

'Of course you are, it's just that you have spent so little time with him, this was . . .' she paused for a few moments, seeking the right word, '*unexpected*.'

'You are right,' said Gruffydd, 'I have been found wanting as a father. For too long I have nursed grudges instead of my child but hopefully those days are gone.'

'In what way?'

'Every day I feel myself getting a little stronger than the day before. My gait gets longer and I am no more out of breath after the first flight of stairs. I now realise I am a very lucky man and have been given a second chance by God, so while I am here, I aim to spend at least a portion of every day with my son.'

Angharad smiled gently as she looked lovingly at her husband. Though he was still gaunt from his sufferings, he was nowhere near the skeletal ex-prisoner that had returned over a year earlier. Many of the scabs had fallen off and most of the sores healed after careful attention by physicians. His long matted hair had been shaven off soon after his arrival and had now grown back to resemble the carefully tended style he had worn as a younger man – although his eyes seemed deeper set than they had ever been.

'It is good to hear,' she said eventually, reaching up to gently touch the ridge of his oft-broken nose. 'And am I to hope that your ambition will be a casualty of this new-found realisation?'

'If you are asking if I intend relinquishing any dreams of retaking Ynys Mon, alas no. However, I will not be carrying out any assault until I am fully recovered and have an army capable of achieving victory. Be that in a few months or a few years, it will be when it will be. In the meantime, I intend to spend as much time as possible with you and my child.'

Angharad smiled. For a few moments she had thought he had decided to give up on his dreams of returning to Gwynedd. Although it wasn't quite as good news as she had hoped, it did at least mean he would be staying with her for considerably longer than she had imagined. She sat beside her husband and looked him in the eye.

'If that is indeed the case, my love, then there is something you should know. You will not be spending time with your child.'

'I don't understand,' said Gruffydd, 'why would you deny me this right?'

'Oh, I'm not denying you anything,' said Angharad, with a mischievous twinkle in her eye. 'You just have your information wrong. What you will be doing, darling husband, is spending time with your children.'

Gruffydd stared at her for a moment, unsure what she meant. But gradually his eyes lowered and he stared at her stomach before returning his gaze to her face.

'Do you mean . . .?'

'Yes,' said Angharad, 'I am carrying your second child, my love. You are going to be a father again.'

Gruffydd was lost for words and looked around in desperation.

'Adele,' he said, seeing the servant grinning by the stable,' come here quickly, take Cadwaladr from my arms so I can embrace my wife.'

Adele did as she was bid and moments later, Gruffydd held his wife tightly, hardly believing how truly blessed he was.

'I will make you proud of me, my love,' he whispered, 'you and our children. I swear by all that is holy, one day we will all enjoy the privileges to which we were born.'

Pembroke Castle

October 17th, AD 1096

As part of King William's campaign into Wales, Gerald of Windsor had ridden through the south of Wales as part of a larger force, tasked with securing the shipping port of Pembroke. Quickly they captured and occupied the old wooden fortress dominating the town, before fortifying its poor defences with new palisades supported by swiftly erected buttresses. Within a month, the stockade was solid enough to resist any moderate attack, and happy his men were as safe as they could be, Gerald and a hundred men consolidated the garrison while the rest of the army, under the command of Arnulf of Montgomery, marched northward in an effort to link up with King William in Gwynedd.

The next few weeks were relatively uneventful in the fortress, for though the town hated the thought of the English so close at hand, there was nothing they could do against the well-armed garrison. It was a typically quiet night when Gerald looked out across the palisade alongside Sir Godwin of Bristol, his second in command.

Godwin was a stocky man, grizzled in both manner and appearance, having worked his way up from humble origins. His shaved head was in stark contrast to the magnificent beard that hung down to his chest and though he was brutal in combat, his advice was often the first sought by Gerald.

'It is a quiet night, my lord,' said Godwin quietly.

'Aye it is,' said Gerald. 'Let's hope it stays that way.'

'I'd wager the taverns of Windsor are full just about now.'

'No doubt,' said Gerald, 'and the ale flowing freely.'

'Forget the ale,' said Godwin, 'I would settle for watered wine as long as it was served by a willing wench.'

Gerald laughed. 'It seems you think of nothing else these days, my friend.'

'It has been a long time since I laid alongside any woman,' said Godwin, 'do you not also miss their company?'

'Indeed, though these days there is only one woman who occupies my thoughts.'

'You talk of the Welsh princess?'

'Aye, I do.' Gerald smiled to himself. Nesta had occupied his mind since the day they had met.

'But surely you have only met her once?'

'I have met her twice, Godwin. Her beauty is enthralling yet there is something quite different in her manner that sets her apart from other ladies of the court.'

'And what is that?'

Gerald thought for a while before replying.

'Fire,' he said eventually, 'a flame in her heart that defies any man's attempts to control her spirit.'

'So you see her as a challenge?'

'No, I don't. Just as it is a stupid man who breaks a spirited horse, then I believe I would be no less stupid to try and douse that fire.'

'So what do you envisage?'

'When this is done, I will visit her and try to win her affection by genuine means. Although we met only fleetingly, I'm sure there was something between us.'

'I hope you are right, my lord,' said Godwin, 'for I have never seen you as love-struck as you are now.'

Gerald punched his comrade in the arm. 'Nothing wrong in seeking a wife, Godwin,' he said, 'especially one as spirited and beautiful as Nesta.'

The two men fell silent again as they stared down to the distant town.

'How much longer do you think we will be stationed here?' asked Godwin eventually.

'A few months,' said Gerald. 'When Arnulf meets up with the king, I expect they'll send a relieving force back down the coast and allow us to return to London. By then the rebellion will be broken and a much smaller force can operate from this castle.'

'Castle?' snorted Godwin. 'It is no more than a pile of earth with a few sharpened stakes. These Welsh have no idea how to build a fortress.'

'It is not the castle that is attractive,' replied Gerald, 'but the location. Pembroke is the coastal gateway into Wales and whoever controls the port controls the west coast. The harbour offers safe anchorage for ships and any forces stationed here can quickly strike in any direction at a moment's notice. Until then we must make the most of what we have.'

The two men looked down into the nearby town of Pembroke. Chinks of candlelight leaked from closed shutters on the many homes, each amplified by the complete darkness of the autumn night. A dog barked in the distance, breaking the silence that seemed to seep into the soldiers' very bones.

'Godwin,' said Gerald eventually, 'have you noticed anything about this night?'

'Not really, why?'

'Don't you think it is a bit quiet?'

'I suppose so, but why is that a problem?'

'I don't know, it just feels a bit unnatural.'

'Perhaps there be spirits abroad?'

'I believe in no spirits apart from the Spirit of Christ,' said Gerald, looking nervously over the palisade.

'Silence is always preferable to the madness of battle.'

'I agree, but listen again. There is something missing.'

Godwin paused and stared towards the town.

'The taverns are silent,' said Godwin eventually. 'Other nights the revelry makes my blood race with jealousy.'

'Indeed,' said Gerald, 'and though the silence is welcome, why would the taverns have their doors closed to customers?' Before Godwin could answer, Gerald turned and snapped. 'What is the state of the men?'

'A quarter are on sentry duty while the rest sleep, my lord. Standard defence tactics.'

'Wake the rest up,' said Gerald. 'I have a bad feeling in my bones; something isn't right.'

'As you wish, my lord.'

'And stock up the arrow baskets around the palisade walls. If something should happen, our archers should not be found wanting.'

'Aye, my lord,' said Godwin, as he descended the ladder to see to his duties. But before he had crossed the bailey, a cry rang out through the night.

Gerald's head spun to stare towards the sentry post a few paces away and witnessed the silhouette of one of his men falling from the wall, an arrow lodged deep in his chest. He paused for only a second before running towards the gatehouse, an action that saved his life as an arrow thudded into the timber wall behind him.

'*Alarm!*' he screamed. '*Every man to arms, we are under attack!*'

Beyond the palisade, Hywel ap Goronwy pushed his wildly unkempt hair back from his face and spat on the ground before roaring his commands towards his waiting army. After many weeks, Prince Cadwgan had finally given Goronwy the chance to prove the mettle of his men and the opportunity to destroy the English garrison was an opportunity he could not miss. The silence of the night was ripped apart as his warriors burst from the undergrowth and stormed towards the flimsy defences. Their roars of defiance filled the air, accompanying the hundreds of arrows already flying unseen through the night sky. All along the treeline, archers removed lids from fire pots and tipped glowing embers onto pre-prepared piles of kindling. Small flames were quickly fed with sheep's wool and within minutes, trails of fire lit up the night sky as flaming arrows thudded into the palisade and beyond.

'*Ladders!*' screamed Goronwy. 'Before they have time to reorganise.'

Men ran from the undergrowth carrying siege ladders, and within moments the thuds of timber on timber mixed with battle cries as the Welsh besiegers sought to better the outer defences.

Within the fortress, men ran around in disarray as the seriousness of the assault became apparent.

'*Every man to the defences!*' roared Gerald. 'Their men are already upon us.'

'My lord,' shouted Godwin, 'our archers are not yet fully armed.'

'Forget the arrows, there is no time. Every man to take a blade whether he be knight or knave and repel those already scaling the walls.'

'Aye, my lord,' shouted Godwin and turned to the confused defenders in the bailey. '*You heard him,*' he roared, 'get to the palisade and use everything you have to keep them off the walls.'

Men ran up the earthen bank on the inner side of the palisade, grabbing whatever they could as weapons.

Gerald tore along the bank, seeing those men who had reacted quicker than others already engaged in mortal combat. Drawing his blade he ran to the nearest fight and waded into the fray, smashing a man's collarbone with a swipe from his blade before piercing another's chest as he appeared over the palisade.

The enemy already over the wall fought like madmen, their faces blackened with soot and their eyes as wild as demons. Furiously, the defenders fought for their lives and though many attackers fell screaming to their deaths, the fight was even. Within moments Godwin's reinforcement joined those at the palisades and any enemy already within the fortress was quickly dispatched, their bodies being hurled back over the palisade to knock down those still climbing the siege ladders.

'*Spread out,*' shouted Gerald, 'and make sure our rear walls are defended, this may be a feint.'

The battle wore on through the night as the Welsh tested different parts of the defensive wall. Time and time again, Gerald's men ran to different areas, each time fighting furiously to repel the enemy. Men fought and died in bloody confrontations, often without chance of support as the defenders were stretched to the limit. Behind them, many of the supply carts were ablaze and any tents that had already been erected were no more than ashes, victims of the constant hail of fire arrows from the trees outside the castle.

Eventually the pressure eased and the defenders gasped in relief as the attackers retreated to the safety of the forest.

Godwin appeared on the ramparts, sweat pouring from beneath his helm to mingle with the blood upon his face.

'My lord,' he gasped, dropping down to sit beside his exhausted commander, 'it seems they have been bettered and the night is ours.'

'If it is, my friend, then it is a fortuitous outcome we do not deserve.'

'On the contrary, the men fought bravely and should be commended.'

'I do not doubt the mettle of our men,' replied Gerald, 'but curse myself for allowing this situation to occur without adequate preparation. I allowed complacency to be our bedfellow and forgot we are deep amongst enemy territory. These ramparts should have been manned with twice the number of men, and our focus these past few days should have been on denying any enemy the luxury of cover. That treeline should have been cut back until it was at least out of arrow range; now they have shelter from which to attack us at their whim.'

'Let them come,' growled Godwin. 'We have repelled them once and will do so again. If they think they better us with pointless attacks, they will be sadly mistaken. Already the ramparts are being stocked with spare weapons from the carts and by the time the dawn comes, every man will be equipped with chainmail and sharpened steel. We will not be found wanting again, my lord, trust me.'

'Good,' said Gerald. He looked at his friend. 'You are wounded,' he said, seeing the pinkness of bleeding flesh running down one of Godwin's cheeks.

'A glancing blow only,' said Godwin holding his hand to his face, 'but his aim should have been better. Now there is one less Welshman for us to worry about.'

'Nevertheless, have it washed and sewn.'

'I will, but for now it will have to wait, we need every man upon the ramparts.'

Gerald nodded and leaned back against the palisade.

'You look exhausted,' said Godwin, 'close your eyes for a while, I will oversee the defences.'

'I don't think sleep will come to me in the circumstances,' said Gerald, 'but a few minutes' rest will be good. Task the same to the rest of the men. Nobody is to leave their station but every other man to grab a few moments' sleep if they can.'

'Aye, my lord,' said Godwin but before he had even walked a few paces away, a shout echoed through the night.

'*To arms, they come again.*'

———— ⁓ ————

For several days, the Welsh kept up the pressure on the castle's defences and though men were no longer thrown indiscriminately at the walls, the constant probing, even in isolated areas, meant that the defenders got little, if any, rest. Gerald and his men took it in turns to snatch whatever rest they could and the supplies were rationed in case the siege lasted for longer than a few days. It was during one such rest period that Gerald found himself being shaken awake by one of the guards.

'My lord, they are coming again.'

Gerald rolled from beneath the cart where he had sought a few moments sleep and pulled himself to his feet.

'Full attack?' he asked as he shook the sleep from his mind.

'No, my lord,' said the guard, 'another probe, though this time on the eastern wall.'

'It seems these devils never rest,' said Gerald, tightening his sword belt.

'They know they stand little chance of breaching the wall,' said the guard, 'yet keep the pressure on our defences. Our archers have picked off many, yet still they come. I'm not sure what they hope to achieve.'

'Really?' said Gerald. 'Then let me enlighten you. Whoever their commander is must know we have limited supplies and the cordon he has set up around the castle ensures we will receive no relief any time soon. Winter is almost upon us and he knows we can't hold out much longer. Where is Sir Godwin?'

'Already on the ramparts, my lord.'

Gerald nodded and ran across the bailey to join his number two. The attack was brief yet ferocious and again, many Welsh attackers lost their lives in the most brutal of fashions. Within the hour, the assault eased off and the night fell quiet once again, with only taunts from the distant forest edge breaking the silence of the night.

'Let's hope that's the last one for tonight,' said Godwin, sliding down to sit with his back against the palisade. 'I don't think we can last much longer. The men are on the point of breaking.

'How look the supplies?' asked Gerald.

'Four hogs and a barrel of oats,' said Godwin. 'With a little luck we can last another week but after that, we will have to seek terms.'

'This fortress is of too much strategic importance,' said Gerald, 'and before we abandon it to the Welsh, we will try everything in our armoury to deny it to the enemy.'

'There is nothing left, my lord. We already use the enemy arrows collected from their earlier onslaughts; our only strengths are the walls and the men behind them.

'On the contrary,' said Gerald, 'we have cunning and we have our lives.' He paused for a few moments before turning to his right-hand man. 'Tell me,' he said, 'I understand the archer, John of London, was killed in last night's skirmish.'

'Aye,' came the reply, 'that he was. He was a good man, as loyal as they come.'

'I know,' said Gerald, 'but before this siege is over, there may still be a part for him to play. Come with me, Godwin, I have an idea.'

———

Down in the forest, Goronwy and his second in command, Uchtryd ap Edwin, stood in the shadows, staring up at the wooden walls of the outer palisade.

'Their stubbornness frustrates me beyond reason,' said Goronwy, 'we outnumber them in horse, archers and men-at-arms, yet despite everything we throw at them, we are repelled at every juncture.'

'We need more men,' said Edwin, 'to assault all four walls at the same time. Do this and we will secure a breach in no time.'

'I agree, but alas, Cadwgan has sent word he cannot commit any more men as William Rufus is close upon his trail and every man may be needed for the confrontation. All we can do is wait and hope that Rufus turns away and heads back to England. If so, Cadwgan will send reinforcements with all haste.'

'That may be too late,' said Edwin, 'winter is upon us and we have little left in the way of supplies. Our men are disheartened and wish to return to their families before the snow falls. Many talk of leaving in the night.'

'I know,' said Goronwy, 'yet we are close, Edwin, I can feel it in my bones. The English must be running short of supplies and it is only a matter of time until the hunger cuts their bellies as sure as any sword. Another week or so and the flag of truce will be hung from the palisade, I am sure of it. A few more days, Edwin, that's all I ask.'

'I'll see what I can do,' said Edwin, 'but can't promise anything. We have lost many men already and those that are left see no end to this siege. Ten days and that's it, you can stay here with your men if you want, but after that I will lead mine eastward to prepare for winter.'

'Ten days should be enough,' said Goronwy. 'I suspect they are down to their last supplies and short of eating their dead, must be on the point of starvation.'

The following night, Godwin and Gerald walked amongst a group of twenty well-armed knights, each undergoing final checks as they prepared to ride out from the castle walls.

'Are you sure about this?' asked Godwin.

'Trust me,' said Gerald, 'I know it sounds drastic but if this works, it could end the siege within days.'

Godwin looked at the men. Each was gaunt through hunger but all had volunteered for the mission, desperate to break the monotony of life under siege.

'You know what to do,' said Gerald turning to the armed men, 'once the gate is open, you are to charge the enemy lines on the east side, as if trying to assault their command tents. Do what damage you can but risk not your lives, this attack is not about conquest but diversion.'

'Can I ask to what end, my lord?' asked one of the knights.

'Alas not, lest you be captured, but rest in the knowledge that this task is important if we are to successfully defend the fortress. Now, if you are ready, there is no time to waste. As soon as the gates are open, spare not the horses. Stretch every sinew to fall amongst them like devils, but before they have chance to muster their defences, turn away and retreat to the safety of these walls. Is that clear?'

'Aye, my lord,' said the knight.

'Then let's get it done and may God go with you.' Gerald turned and walked over to the gates. The extra poles had already been removed and four men prepared to pull them open. He looked up at the sentries on the parapet. 'All clear?'

'All clear, my lord,' said the guard.

Gerald took a deep breath.

'In that case, there's no point in waiting any longer: open the gates.'

With a command from Godwin, the gates swung inward just enough to allow the horsemen to pass through in a double column and within moments, all twenty were thundering through the darkness towards the distant treeline.

'Shut the gates,' shouted Gerald, 'all archers to the parapet to cover their return.'

'My lord, there are few arrows left,' said Godwin. 'Our fletcher makes new from the castle timbers but they are of poor quality.'

'I care not,' said Gerald, 'use what you have to bring our men back alive.'

'So be it,' said Godwin, and he gave the necessary commands.

As the front of the castle burst into life, Gerald ran over to the rear of the fort and into one of the stables. Two horses stood quietly in the far stall, accompanied by a nervous-looking squire.

'Are you ready?' asked Gerald as he entered.

'I am, my lord, but still don't understand the point of my quest.'

'All you need to do is exactly as we discussed,' said Gerald. 'Once the fight starts to the east, any enemy attention will be drawn that way and you can slip out quietly without being seen. Take your time, stay in the low ground and you should be fine. Once past their lines, you know what to do.'

The boy looked up at the silent passenger tied onto the second horse and gulped nervously.

'Yes, my lord.'

'Good. Make sure the place chosen is near to the road and will be quickly found.'

'Aye, my lord. Once the package is delivered, I will return as quickly as I can.'

'No, Iain, once you have done the deed, ride as hard as you can southward and seek Carmarthen Castle. The castellan there will give you shelter until this thing is over.'

'But my place is at your side.'

'I know, and should I survive these next few days, you will once more be my squire. But if I fall, the castellan at Carmarthen will ensure you are appointed to a good knight.' Gerald paused as he saw the fear in the boy's eyes. 'Iain, what you are about to do could save the lives of hundreds of men, not just today but in the future. Take heart and be the man you hope to one day become. If this comes off, and we all escape with our lives, I will send representation to Rufus telling him of your bravery.'

The boy's eyes widened at the prospect and without another word he mounted his horse.

'I will do everything I can to secure a favourable outcome, my lord,' he said once he was secure in the saddle, 'even unto death.'

'I know you will,' said Gerald, 'now we must get you from this place before it is too late.' He opened the far door of the stables and led the way to the single postern in the rear wall. The sentry above indicated that it was all clear and another guard opened the gate.

'Be brave, Iain,' said Gerald.

'I will, my lord,' said the boy and he rode out into the darkness, leading the second horse behind him.

Once the boy had gone, Gerald walked back to the eastern wall and climbed up to the ramparts. In the distance he could hear men screaming as the sounds of the surprise attack drifted up the slopes.

'It looks like they have caught them off guard,' said Godwin as Gerald approached.

'It seems so,' said Gerald, discarding his cloak, 'but I am under no false illusions, twenty men cannot win us a victory on their own. I just hope our casualties are minimal.'

He turned to see men carrying wicker baskets up the slopes to the ramparts.

'Is that the meat?'

'Aye, my lord, it is,' said Godwin, 'the last of the pigs were slaughtered this afternoon and butchered into joints as requested. They are fresh from the fires.'

'Good, share them out amongst the men on the ramparts but tell them not to eat any on pain of punishment.'

'Are you sure about this, my lord?' asked Gerald. 'Our men are starving.'

'I understand your reluctance,' said Gerald, 'but a few days will make no difference. We need to do this in order to underpin my main plan.'

'If this is what you wish then it will be done,' said Godwin, 'though to be honest, I see no merit in it at all.'

'Trust me, my friend,' said Gerald, 'all will be revealed in good time.' He made a silent prayer, hoping he was right.

Down in the forests, the lead knight, Sir Thomas of Shrewsbury, realised they could do no more. Many of the enemy lay dead or dying, and in the confusion Welshmen ran like frightened sheep through the darkness. The attack had gone as planned and only one man had fallen to an enemy blade. Now it was time to regroup as had been agreed.

A horn echoed through the night and every horseman turned to rendezvous at a nearby stream junction.

'Is everyone here?' shouted Thomas, trying to count the heads.

'Only Wallace has fallen,' came the reply, 'a pike severed his head from his shoulders.'

'There is nothing we can do for him now,' said Thomas, 'our task is complete. It is time to return.'

'Wait,' shouted a voice, 'the enemy is in disarray. The route to the harbour lays clear and I saw several boats laying at anchor. Why don't we just ride on and make our escape?'

'*What?*' gasped Thomas. 'Are you talking about desertion?'

'I am no coward, my lord, and will fight any man upon the field of battle but this is a lost cause. The castle is nothing more than a wooden box, there is no food left and we face an enemy that disappears into the night. Put me before a foe and I will fight to my last breath but I refuse to starve to death or be taken prisoner by those beneath me. I for one will not be returning to Gerald and aim to leave this place tonight.'

'You talk of treachery,' snarled Thomas and drew his sword, but two other men rode their horses between the arguing knights.

'Stay your hand, Thomas,' said one of the men, 'for he only says what many of us already think. Our lives and honour are forfeit if we stay in such a place and I too would rather live to fight another day than stay here and die needlessly. If that makes you think me a coward then so be it but the man speaks true. I will ride with him and implore you join us.'

'I will never leave a comrade in need,' spat Thomas, 'no matter how dire the circumstance. That is our creed, Sir Martin, the title of knight carries a code of honour as well you know.'

'I agree, but nowhere does our code say we should die needlessly in a lost cause. Ride with us, Sir Thomas, and we will plead our case before the king.'

Thomas stared at the men, knowing they had to make a decision soon before the enemy regrouped.

'How many of you feel this way?' he asked.

Several horses rode over to stand behind Sir Martin, leaving only Thomas and three others.

'And you are all of a similar mind?'

'Aye,' said several voices, confirming their choice.

'Then so be it. I deplore your decision but no blades will be raised against each other this night. Do what you will but be it known that one day we will meet again and when we do, there will be no such generosity shown.'

Sir Martin nodded and as one, fifteen knights turned to ride towards the harbour, leaving Thomas and three others behind him.

'My lord,' said one of the knights, 'the enemy have regrouped and advance upon the castle.'

'Then let us return,' said Thomas quietly, 'and do whatever our duties demand, but I swear this before God and before you three good men, before I die, there will be a reckoning for this night.'

***

'*After them*,' roared Goronwy in a rage, 'how dare they have the gall to bring the offensive to me. We are greater than them in number and strength and yet they test my patience to the limit. Throw every man against the wall and tear the castle from beneath them.'

'My lord, we just don't have the strength for such an action,' shouted one of his sergeants.

'I care not,' he replied. 'I will not allow them to slink away like thieves in the night, fire the walls and bring the ladders.'

'My lord—' called the sergeant.

'*Do as I command*,' shouted Goronwy, 'or suffer the consequences.'

After a few moments' pause, the sergeant turned to his men and relayed the order.

'You heard our lord, to arms and have at the castle walls with everything we have.'

For a few minutes, men ran around gathering the ladders and weapons before mustering in their sections. Soon the forest edge was lined with what was left of the Welsh army.

'Ready?' shouted Goronwy, 'men of Wales – *advance!*'

'*Here they come*,' shouted a sentry, 'stand to the walls.'

Four of Gerald's bravest men swung the gate inward and watched in silence as the remaining knights thundered through before sliding from their mounts.

'*Close the gates*,' roared Thomas, 'the enemy are hot on our heels.'

'Where are the rest?' shouted Gerald. 'Surely not all have fallen?'

'I wish that they had,' replied Thomas, 'for to our shame they have taken the opportunity to desert.'

'Why would they do that?' gasped Gerald.

'No time to explain, my lord,' said the knight, 'the Welsh are close behind us.' He ran up the bank and onto the parapet, organising the men as they spread out behind the palisade.

'*All men to the walls*,' shouted Gerald, 'repel them with everything you have.'

Within moments the Welsh fell upon the castle, using everything they could to gain entry. Brushwood was piled against the palisade but the constant wet weather over the previous few weeks meant it burned slowly and was easily extinguished by water and soil from the defences. Some attackers managed to breach the walls but were soon put to the sword by Gerald's knights before having their ladders pushed away by archers bearing long poles designed for just such a task.

'My lord,' gasped Godwin, appearing at Gerald's side, 'we have no more arrows.'

'They don't know that,' said Gerald, hurling a boulder down onto some men below, 'and think the lack of archer volleys are simply because we are busy fighting the assault. Keep the men at it, Godwin, the tide turns in our favour.'

Sure enough, the siege ladders against the walls all fell away as the assault faltered and the Welsh retreated a hundred paces to reorganise.

'Put those fires out,' shouted Godwin to the defenders, and he watched as buckets of water were poured from the parapets to extinguish the flames.

Gerald stared at the silent enemy and saw the opportunity he had been waiting for.

'Listen to me,' he hissed to the men either side of him. 'Watch what I do and follow my lead.' He turned to Godwin. 'When this starts, tell the men to laugh as if they are having a good time.'

'But why?'

'Just do it, Godwin, we may not have this opportunity again.' Without waiting for a reply Gerald stood up in full view of the enemy.

'*Goronwy*!' he shouted through the fire-lit darkness. 'Call that an assault? Why, we could repel you all day at that rate. In fact, the only damage you have done is to my evening entertainment.'

'I will make you eat your words, Englishman,' shouted Goronwy.

'Well that would be good, for you interfered with our feasting.'

'Cease your wittering, Englishman,' shouted Goronwy, 'for you face hardened Welshmen before you. Such taunts fall on deaf ears.'

'Really? Well you all look a bit cold and hungry, why don't we share our fayre with you?' He bent down and grabbed a roast leg of pork before hurling it over the wall towards the enemy. 'There,' he shouted, 'with my compliments; in fact, have some more.'

Responding to his signal, the other men reached into the baskets of roast pork and started to throw them over the walls.

'Laugh,' hissed Godwin, running along the parapet, 'laugh damn you, we want them to think we are in good heart.'

'We are starving, my lord,' replied one of the defenders, 'yet throw good meat to feed the enemy.'

'Do as you are told, man,' snapped Godwin, 'there is method in this madness.'

The parapets rang with laughter as men hurled the roast joints towards the enemy until eventually the baskets were empty.

'Go on, Goronwy,' shouted Gerald, 'tell your men to collect the meat – you have my word we will withhold our arrows.'

Down in the enemy lines the exhausted attackers stared in disbelief at the bounty thrown before them and some men ran forward to grab what they could.

'*Leave it!*' roared Goronwy – but it was too late; men ran from all directions to gather the meat.

'Let them feast, Goronwy,' shouted Gerald from the palisade, 'the Lord knows they have earned it. If you need more, just ask, for we have plenty to spare.' Again laughter rang across the clearing and in a fit of rage, Goronwy stormed back towards his command tent, closely followed by Edwin.

'*What are these games he plays?*' shouted Goronwy, throwing his helmet across the tent. 'He is besieged with no way out yet he mocks me in front of my men with gifts of meat. Is there no end to this man's arrogance?'

'You have to admit he knows how to raise your ire,' said Edwin.

'He may play games now,' growled Goronwy, 'but it is I who will have the last laugh. I will keep him there until he begs to be allowed to surrender, even if it takes all winter.'

'My lord, we do not have the supplies to maintain such a siege,' said Edwin.

'Neither does he!' shouted Goronwy. 'You didn't fall for that display of nonsense regarding the meat, did you? That was purely for our sakes so our men would fear he is well supplied and we would withdraw.'

'I don't agree,' said Edwin, 'what commander worth his salt would give the last of his food to the enemy if they were starving, and what of the attack from their horsemen? They had nothing to gain yet rode amongst our lines with impunity. No, that man is confident of victory and I say we should withdraw while the weather is fair.'

'We are not withdrawing, Edwin,' snarled Goronwy, 'we agreed ten more days. Give me those and I swear I will have that man's head upon a spear.'

'I don't know,' said Edwin, 'the men's morale is already low and they fight for a mouthful of roasted pork. How can we hope to control them now?'

'Withdraw them to the forest,' said Goronwy, 'and I will address them in the morning.'

'So be it,' said Edwin. He left the tent as Goronwy retrieved a flask of ale. It was going to be a long night.

A few leagues away, Iain, Gerald's squire, dismounted from his horse and tied the reins to a tree before untying the second horse and leading it further along the path. The body of the dead archer was still slumped over the horse's back and though the forest was full of dangers, Iain was more concerned with delivering his macabre package than avoiding brigands or rebels. The dawn was almost upon him when he finally reached his destination and he stopped to stare at the lodge at the side of the road. There was probably a high footfall along the road and a good chance that archer's body would soon be found.

Iain turned to the corpse and cut the binds, letting the body fall to the floor. He took a Welsh arrow from his belt, and after pausing to gather his courage raised the arrow high before driving it downward into the back of the dead archer's neck. The shaft smashed through the dead man's spine and out through his throat.

As the archer had been dead for two days, there was no fresh blood, so Iain drew his knife and dragged the blade along his own flesh to open a wound, spreading the blood around the base of the arrow. Finally, he took a satchel from around his own neck and placed it carefully beneath the tunic of the archer.

With his task finished, he retreated into the trees and ran back the way he had come before climbing astride his horse and galloping south to find Carmarthen Castle. His job was done.

***

The following day brought fresh problems for the Welsh. And Gerald's defenders took to taunting them from the security of their palisade. All the day through, men took it in turns to throw insults over to the treeline where the Welsh sentries sought shelter from the biting sea wind. Edwin had spent most of the day persuading groups of men to stay with the siege, repeating Goronwy's promise that the siege would soon be at an end and the surrender of the English was mere days away. Though a few men decided to leave, overall the majority promised to stay a few more days and huddled beneath their cloaks as they sat around the campfires.

'Well?' said Goronwy, when Edwin returned to the command tent.

'A few days, but no more,' replied Edwin.

'Trust me,' said Goronwy, 'it's all we need. The man is bluffing and I believe he and his men are in dire straits.'

'I hope you are right,' said Edwin, 'for the mood of our men is the lowest I have ever seen.'

'It will all be worth it, Edwin,' said Goronwy. 'We cannot let them establish a foothold here in Pembroke – the dock is too strategic to the west coast.'

'I understand the importance,' said Edwin, 'but there is only so much a man can take. Our own men starve and freeze with no sign of the enemy weakening. You can't blame them for feeling disheartened.'

'I understand,' said Goronwy. 'Now, let's muster the men ready for an assault.'

'Are you not listening to me?' asked Edwin in exasperation. 'It was all I could do to persuade them to stay. If you think those that stay are about to throw themselves against that damned palisade yet again then you are sadly mistaken.'

'I am the commander here,' shouted Goronwy, 'and they will do as I say or feel my wrath.'

'*Listen to me!*' replied Edwin. 'They will not do it. Force their hand and they will ride from here within the hour. Just be grateful that they will continue the siege, else this is over.

'*No!*' roared Goronwy. '*You* listen to *me*—' But before he could continue a man burst through the flap of the tent and stared at the two arguing warlords.

'What is it?' snapped Goronwy.

'My lord,' said the soldier, 'there have been developments.'

'Spit it out, man,' said Edwin.

'My lord,' said the soldier, 'a rider has arrived in camp, sent on urgent errand from the Bishop of St David.'

'And?'

'Apparently one of the bishop's servants came across a dead body this morning a few leagues hence. He was on the road northward but it seems he was felled and robbed by a brigand.'

'Why is this of interest to us?'

'Because though his purse was empty, there was a message still within his satchel, a scroll addressed to none other than Arnulf of Montgomery himself.'

'What did it say?' asked Edwin quietly.

'Read it for yourself,' said the guard, holding up the parchment. 'It's not good.'

Edwin reached out but before he could take the scroll, Goronwy snatched it from the soldier's hand and walked away as he read the contents.

'What does it say?' asked Edwin eventually.

'Nothing of importance,' said Goronwy crumpling up the scroll.

'What does it say, Goronwy?' asked Edwin again.

'It is another trick,' shouted Goronwy, 'the man plays games with us.'

Without warning Edwin lashed out and punched Goronwy, causing him to crash across the table and onto the floor. Edwin reached for the discarded scroll as Goronwy stormed to his feet, looking for his blade – but the guard drew his own sword and held it against the warlord's throat.

'Leave it,' he said, 'he needs to know.'

Edwin flattened out the crumpled document and read the words out loud.

My lord Arnulf,

I hope this message finds you in good health. As promised, we have secured the fortress at Pembroke and though we have seen some resistance from the Welsh rebels, I have seen nothing that causes me concern. Your extra knights managed to gain access via the postern without being discovered and the garrison is in good health. With regard to the promised supplies, I lose no sleep over the lateness of the column as we are still well stocked and can last at least three months with our existing stores. Worry not about our fate for we are in hearty mood and welcome the attentions of the Welsh on a daily basis if only to relieve the boredom. Give my respects to our king.

Your servant,
Gerald Fitzwalter of Windsor

Edwin looked up at the guard.

'Can this be confirmed as genuine?' he asked.

'My lord, the scroll was secured with the seal of Gerald himself. It is genuine.'

'Leave us,' said Edwin and as the guard left, he turned to face Goronwy.

'It is a trick,' growled Goronwy. 'Don't you think all this is a very fortunate coincidence? It is nothing but a ploy to get us to leave.'

'There is no talking to you,' said Edwin quietly. 'Your army falls apart around you, hurting from cold and hunger. Many are already dead from pointless assaults against a fortress well manned with English knights and yet you cling to your dream of conquest. It is over, Goronwy, I am taking my men home.'

'If you leave now,' shouted Goronwy, 'I cannot maintain the siege, you have to stay a few more days.'

'*Don't you understand?*' roared Edwin. 'It is over, Goronwy. We tried our best but came up short. This battle is over and we have lost. I'm going to muster my men and ride out before it gets dark.'

As Edwin left the tent, Goronwy sat back in the chair and stared into space, his heart drained of any emotion. Eventually, one of his servants entered and stood before him.

'My lord,' said the servant quietly, 'is there anything I can get you?'

The warlord looked up at him and stared for a long while before answering.

'Yes, Jonas,' he said, 'pass word to today's captain of the guard. Tell him to attend me with all haste.'

'Yes, my lord,' said the servant and he turned to go.

'And Jonas,' added Goronwy, the defeat clear upon his face.

'Yes, my lord?'

'Pack your supplies, we're going home.'

The following morning, every man in the castle stood behind the palisade walls, staring down to the treeline. The air was silent except for the calls of circling crows as they sought out any dead yet unburied. All eyes stared at the returning patrol of twenty knights as they galloped back to the castle.

'Open the gates,' called Gerald, and as the giant doors creaked inward the column galloped through before turning to face the men upon the battlements.

'Well?' said Gerald, descending from the ramparts.

The lead rider removed his helmet and pushed the sweat-soaked hair back from his face before answering.

'You were right, my lord,' said the knight, 'the forests are empty, the Welsh have gone. The siege is over.'

As an almighty roar of celebration filled the air, Gerald turned and stared at the smiling man at his side.

'You did it,' said Godwin, 'your subterfuge won the day and saved every man here. Well done, my lord, well done.'

He held out his arm and as each man took the wrist of the other, many of the garrison clambered down the buttresses to gather around their master.

'Silence,' shouted Gerald eventually. He waited as the excited talking died away.

'Fellow warriors,' said Gerald eventually, 'this is a special day and your heroism will echo down the ages. Every man here should feel proud of themselves and I will personally see that each is suitably rewarded.' Holding his hand up to silence the cheer, he continued. 'Yes, there is cause for celebration, but now is not the time. First we will tend to our wounded and bury our dead. We will say prayers to God, beseeching he takes our comrades' souls unto heaven. After that, we need to find food and to that end I seek volunteers to sally forth amongst the farms and villages.' He turned to Godwin. 'My friend, can I entrust you to lead this task?'

'It will be my honour, my lord.'

'Good. Care will be needed for we are strangers in a foreign land but I expect little defiance. Tread lightly and pay for what you take, but leave nobody hungry for on that route lies defiance.'

'Understood.'

'The rest of us will take a well-earned rest,' continued Gerald. 'A few hours, no more. When we are refreshed, we will set about repairing our defences and ensuring such a siege is not possible again. Over the next few months the walls will be made higher and thicker. The armoury will be stocked with arrows until it is solid with willow. Blades will be sharpened and food stores will be stocked to bursting point. Ownership of this castle was hard earned, my friends, and now we have control over it, we will never let it go.'

Cheering broke out again and as the sergeants started to bark out their commands, Gerald and Godwin walked slowly across the bailey.

'My lord,' said Godwin as they walked, 'I have a confession to make.'

'Forget it,' said Gerald, 'today is about successes not failures.'

'Nevertheless, I need to unload my burden.'

Gerald stopped and looked at his friend. 'Go on.'

'I have to admit,' said Godwin, 'I thought your ploys futile and you had cost the lives of every man here.'

Gerald stared at Godwin before slapping him on the shoulder.

'Well,' said Gerald, 'if that is the extent of your confession then you are truly a pious man.'

'You do not resent me for showing so little trust in your judgement?'

'Why should I resent you, my friend, when I worried about exactly the same thing? Now come, I think there may be half a flask of ale at the back of my tent.'

Several leagues away, the last of the Welsh columns crested a hill and descended into the valleys on the other side, leaving two men behind them on the ridge. For an age they looked back the way they had come, staring at the tiny speck they knew was the fortress at Pembroke.

'I had him, Edwin,' said Goronwy quietly, 'I know I did. A few more days and victory would have been ours.'

'You may be right,' said Edwin turning back to the road, 'but alas the circumstances dictated otherwise. Let it go, Goronwy, it is time to go home.'

Three months later, William Rufus summoned Gerald of Windsor to London to bestow recognition for his heroic actions. The ceremony was impressive and his deeds were lauded by all present but despite this, his mind was on other things and as soon as the opportunity arose, he rode hard from Westminster to reach his destination before it got dark.

Finally, he and his three comrades saw the outer palisade of Windsor Castle and they reined in their horses to stare at the impressive fortress.

'It seems Henry is in residence,' said Godwin.

'It does,' said Gerald, seeing the colours of the prince flying high above the upper keep.

'Do you think he will let you see her?' asked Godwin.

'Why not?' said Gerald. 'Since William has returned from Wales, the country lies in relative peace and I see no reason for Henry to hold Nesta prisoner any longer. Hopefully he will release her into my custody.'

'There is only one way to find out,' said Godwin, 'and that is to ask.'

'Then what are we waiting for?' said Gerald and all four men rode up to the gates of the castle.

'Hold and state your business,' demanded one of the pikemen on the gate.

'I am Sir Gerald of Windsor,' said Gerald, 'and I seek audience with Henry.'

'Have you made arrangements? For the king's brother is a busy man.'

'I have not, but am favoured by William himself. I ask that I be granted audience on short notice. Send word to the prince on my behalf.'

The guard spoke to another soldier and within moments, a servant could be seen running up the hill towards the upper tower.

'My lord,' said the guard, 'I cannot grant you access to the bailey yet, but if you and your men wish to wait within the gatehouse, you will be made welcome. We have a good fire in the hearth and potage to warm your bellies. Prince Henry is not known for his urgency in responding to such matters.'

'Thank you,' said Gerald, 'that will be much appreciated.' The four men tied their horses to a hitching rail and entered the wooden gatehouse. Each man discarded his cloak and enjoyed the welcome glow while drinking heated ale with their fellow soldiers. For the next hour or so, the visitors answered questions about the war in Wales but eventually Gerald got bored and wandered to the steps on the inside of the tower.

'Where do these go?' he asked.

'Just to the gatehouse battlements,' said the guard.

'Can I go up?'

'Of course.'

'Then I will get some air,' said Gerald, 'this room is very warm.' He turned and climbed the stairs, emerging onto a wide platform overlooking the gate and moat. Another sentry greeted him from an alcove providing cover from the biting wind.

'Who are you?' asked the guard, levelling his spear.

'Relax,' said Gerald, 'just a visitor waiting for audience with Henry. Your comrades have given me and my fellows shelter while we wait.'

The sentry replaced his spear in the upright position and blew on his hands.

'So why do you not warm yourself by the fire?' he asked.

'It's a bit too warm down there,' said Gerald, 'I just need some fresh air.' He looked out over the town of Windsor and the seemingly never-ending maze of streets. Hundreds of smoke trails wound upward from thatched roofs, evidence of so many people seeking comfort away from winter's breath but apart from that, there was little sign of life.

'How long have you been waiting?' asked the guard.

'Since about noon,' said Gerald. 'It seems your master will not be rushed for anyone.'

'That is a true statement,' said the guard, 'however, I suspect your wait will soon be over.' He nodded towards the lower keep where the door was open and a man swathed in a black cloak emerged into the snow.

'Is that Henry?' asked Gerald.

'It is,' said the guard, 'and it looks like his afternoon has gone particularly well.' He followed the statement with a laugh but before Gerald could say anything, another figure appeared in the doorway, though staying out of the bitter wind.

'Is that Nesta ferch Rhys?' asked Gerald, recognising the woman's long black hair.

'It is,' said the guard, 'do you know her?'

'I do,' said Gerald, 'why is she free to roam? I thought she was a prisoner of Henry.'

'She was,' said the guard joining Gerald to stare over the bailey towards the lower keep, 'but it seems Henry took a liking to her and they have been lovers for months.'

Gerald's heart fell as the words sunk in and he stared forlornly across the bailey.

'Are you sure?' he asked eventually.

'It is no secret,' said the guard, 'and Henry often stays the night with Nesta. It is said if she wasn't of Welsh descent, he would consider her for a wife but alas, nobody can choose their own birth.'

'No,' said Gerald quietly, and as if to confirm his worst fears, in the distance, Henry took Nesta in his arms, kissing her deeply before she stepped back inside and closed the door of the keep.

'See what I mean?' said the guard. 'If that was a kiss of friendship then I need more friends like her.' He laughed at his own joke and turned towards Gerald – but the knight had already left.

'Come,' said Gerald as he reached the bottom of the stairway, 'we will wait no more.'

'But I thought—' started Godwin.

'We are going,' snapped Gerald, 'there is nothing here for us. Gather your things and have the horses brought around. We leave for Wales immediately.'

Dublin

October 12th, AD 1098

Angharad sat on a blanket contentedly watching her three young children play upon the grass. Cadwaladr, her first son by Gruffydd, was now three years old; his younger brother Cadwallon was two; and the newest addition to the family was a beautiful baby girl by the name of Gwenllian. She had been born the previous year and was just starting to walk.

The past few years had been difficult for Angharad. Gruffydd's recovery had been slow and at first he had played little part in the rebellion in Wales, preferring to spend the time with his growing family. But ever since Gerald of Windsor had managed to break the siege at Pembroke Castle two years earlier, her husband had taken a far keener interest in the affairs of the country he called home. Gruffydd was itching to become more involved and Angharad recognised the signs already.

'My lady,' said a voice, 'I thought the children may want some refreshment after all this running around.'

Angharad broke from her reverie to see her oldest servant – and closest friend, despite their differences in station – standing nearby with a tray of sweet meats and a jug of honeyed water.

'Thank you, Adele,' said Angharad, patting the blanket. 'Come, sit alongside me.'

Adele did as she was bid and smiled over towards the children.

'It seems Cadwallon is getting the better of Cadwaladr,' said Adele, 'despite him being the smaller.'

'Let not his size fool you,' replied Angharad, 'for his heart makes up for any difference in age. I believe he will be a fearless warrior one day, though it has to be said, I suspect his older brother yields advantage due to love rather than fear.'

'I agree,' said Adele, 'for they enjoy the true love that brotherhood brings. Let them enjoy it while they can, for politics have a way of souring relations between kin as they grow older.'

'These boys will never set blade against each other,' said Angharad, 'I will never allow it. Besides, they share a love for their sister such as I have never seen before.'

Both women looked over to where Gwenllian was toddling in the wake of her brothers, dragging a twig behind her in an unconscious parody of the wooden swords that held the boys' attention.

Gwenllian was not yet a year old and already strong enough to stumble around the grass in clumsy pursuit of her brothers. Her fair hair mirrored that of her mother and fell below her ears in natural curls, framing a pretty face with piercing blue eyes. Though she was still a baby, her personality already hinted at an iron will and she managed to get her own way in many things.

'She is truly a beautiful child,' said Adele.

'She is, yet I fear she is going to be trouble,' said Angharad, 'I can just see it in her eyes.'

As if she had heard the women, Gwenllian stopped in her tracks and stared over towards them. Both women burst into laughter and were rewarded when Gwenllian responded with a cheeky grin and an outburst of giggles.

'She makes my heart melt,' said Adele, 'she surely does.'

'As she does mine.' Angharad laughed, wiping tears of mirth from her eyes. 'But she makes me worry so.'

'In what way?'

'Oh, I know I fret about things beyond my control,' said Angharad, 'but the future is so uncertain, I feel I am exposing her to a lifetime of strife.'

'My lady, she is the daughter of a king and you are safe here in Ireland. With forethought, she will live a full and fruitful life and by the look of her, even at this tender age, I will wager there will be princes fighting wars to claim her hand, such is her beauty.'

'Ah, but therein lies the problem. I want no man fighting over her for that way lies the road to tragedy. At the moment we may be in Ireland, but where will we be next month or the month after that? I love my husband dearly, Adele, but if he is successful in his cause then we could be back in Ynys Mon before the year is out.'

'Is that not what you desire?'

'With all my heart but Wales is a dangerous place at the moment. William Rufus wages war on the rebels, Huw the Fat seeks out my husband with a passion and even the Welsh princes fight amongst themselves for the lands of their fathers. What is to become of my beautiful daughter if she is brought up in such circumstances? My dreams already fill with worry and I fear I will be doing her an injustice if I was to subject her to such things.'

'Can I be so bold as to make a suggestion, my lady?'

'Of course,' Angharad said, slipping her arm through Adele's.

'Then I would suggest that nobody knows what will happen in a few years or even a few days from now. Anything can happen before she is of an age to wed. Wales may even have a unifying king and if that man be Gruffydd, then she can have the choice of all men. Put aside your worry until that time, for nothing you can do now will change the path God has in mind for her. Anyway, it seems to me she will be well able to look after herself.'

Angharad followed Adele's gaze and saw Gwenllian in a struggle with one of the boys for ownership of a discarded wooden sword. Both pulled an opposite end but when the little girl started screaming at him, Cadwaladr knew he was beaten and relinquished ownership.

'Do you know what?' Angharad laughed as Gwenllian wandered off with her prize. 'I think you may be right.'

The Island of Ynys Mon

April 13th, AD 1099

Six months later, Hugh Montgomery sat at a trestle table within his campaign tent, picking at the remnants of the feast upon his trencher. Though the occasion was relaxed, and his chainmail discarded, he was still adorned in quality black-leather armour in case of any call to arms from the camp guards. Opposite him sat Robert of Rhuddlan, cousin of Huw the Fat of Chester, and the officer in command of the joint forces. He was similarly attired though wore a tabard and belted dagger over his armour.

For the last three weeks, the armies of both men had made their way across north Wales and invaded the island of Ynys Mon, wresting it from the hands of the rebellious Welshman Cadwgan ap Bleddyn. The fighting had been as bloody as the worst battles, with little quarter from both sides, but finally the English emerged victorious and after four long years of Welsh rebellion, the strategic island was once more in the hands of the English crown.

Montgomery was ecstatic and announced two days of feasting for his nobles while allowing his men to run unrestrained across the island, indulging in the actions due to the victors in all such wars.

Reports of rape and murder were dismissed with a wave of the hand as he and his court enjoyed the spoils of the victory.

'So, Robert,' said Montgomery, 'what lies before you now?'

'I will return to Chester,' said Robert, 'and give a full report to Huw D'Avranches though I suspect he already knows of our success, such is the extent of his informers.'

'I hear he is fatter than ever.' Montgomery laughed.

'Indeed – he is a sight to behold and struggles to walk such is his size. But disrespect him at your peril for his reach is long and his temper short. Many men who have borne him insult have been found dead in their beds the following morning.'

'Especially if of Welsh birth?'

'Indeed. He has a hatred for any this side of the border, fuelled even more by the continued freedom of Gruffydd ap Cynan.'

'I was surprised Gruffydd was not here to face us,' said Montgomery. 'Our spies in Ireland reported he was petitioning anyone of like mind to join him in supporting Cadwgan's forces here on Ynys Mon. Luckily for us it seems his pleas fell on deaf ears for if he had managed to raise an army then I suspect our victory may not have been so straightforward.'

Robert laughed and stared at Montgomery with surprise. 'Why do you say that? He has been no threat since Mynydd Carn.'

'Come, Robert – any man who can survive twelve years in captivity will always be a threat,' replied Montgomery, 'and Huw the Fat was furious when he found out about his escape.'

'I heard he was rescued by a band of brigands a hundred strong.'

'Surely you did not believe such nonsense?'

'I had no reason not to. Why, were events different than those described?'

'Robert,' said Montgomery handing his tankard to a wench for refilling, 'Gruffydd was stolen away from his captors by a single man, a young Welshman by the name of Cynwrig the Tall.'

'One man against all those guards? He must have been a formidable opponent.'

'On the contrary, there was no fight for the guards were all drunk in a nearby tavern.'

'And they left nobody on watch?'

'Not a single one. Suffice to say, Huw the Fat was enraged and had the guards killed in the most awful way. In addition, he sought out the family of Cynwrig the Tall and had them all hung in front of their kinsmen.'

'What about Cynwrig?'

'He was never caught and we suspect he campaigns alongside Gruffydd. Huw the Fat was very clever – by spreading the rumour of an ambush, he secured the help of William Rufus. Our king was reluctant to offer extra support for Huw's continued campaign against the Welsh but when he heard about this supposed enemy action, he used it as an excuse to launch his first invasion.'

'From what I can understand that campaign was naught but an exercise in politics for not a sword was drawn in anger.'

'It's true there were no confrontations but a man can only fight an enemy that stands before him. William Rufus campaigned for many months across the north but Cadwgan and his forces hid amongst the mountains until the king returned whence he came.'

'Yet last year, he stood and fought?'

'Indeed, and though his influence is still a thorn in the side of the king, by taking this island today, the campaign has severed the head from the snake. Rufus may already be back on his way to London, my friend, but make no mistake: this victory is as great as they come. Without Ynys Mon, the campaign would have been deemed a failure. Today we have taken the homeland of Gruffydd himself and probably ensured peace for at least a generation.' Montgomery leaned forward and carved a cheek from the hog's head upon the table. 'So,' he continued, 'have you received the final head count from the marshals?'

'Twenty-three dead; twice that wounded. A good result, for the enemy dead lie in their hundreds. It would seem the lack of a figurehead left them without direction and their opposition was found wanting. I was almost disappointed to find there were no cavalry or even a serious threat from men-at-arms. Still, the victory is the important thing and we can report back that Ynys Mon is once more subject to the rule of William.'

'I'll drink to that,' said Montgomery, and both men drained their tankards. The rest of the night they joined their fellow nobles in drinking and eating, and in violating enemy women captured from the villages on the island. Little did they know that twenty miles away, the steady dip of oars propelled a fleet of six ships towards the island, manned with some of the most feared fighters of the time and commanded by no other than the Viking King of Norway himself – Magnus Barefoot.

The Viking king stood bare-chested in the bows of his ship, the sea breeze stirring the blood in his veins. His long fair hair was tied back from his face and the sides of his head shaved down to the scalp. Tattoos ran down one side of his head from brow to shoulder and continued down across his chest to his belt line. His skin was covered with countless scars – some received in battle but most the result of the many trials of combat enjoyed by him and his men as means of passing the time between battles.

The crossing had been uneventful and at last the island was before them.

'My lord,' said a voice quietly, 'the lookout reports the sound of waves upon the shore.'

Magnus nodded and bent to pick up his helmet from the deck of the ship. 'Have our archers man the rails,' he said. He stared hard into the mist. Somewhere amongst its cloak lay the island of Ynys Mon and though he knew of its importance both as a fertile producer of crops and as a strategic outpost to control the northern half of Wales, his interest lay only in what had been agreed during negotiations in Ireland.

'Well?' said another voice behind him. 'It looks like we made it.'

Magnus turned and looked at Gruffydd ap Cynan. The exiled king had petitioned Magnus in Dublin to regain the island on his behalf, and though Magnus rarely fought under the flag of another, the potential to have a beholden ally on the western coast of Britannia was too good an opportunity to ignore. Subsequently, they had agreed terms and the Norwegian fleet now crept along the Welsh shore, waiting for the mist to disperse before landing.

'The shore is but an arrow's flight away,' replied Magnus, 'but we will wait until the mist lifts its cloak.'

'I thought the mist would aid you in the approach.'

'It will, but it is a double-edged sword for we could be sailing into a strong English encampment and no matter how big the advantage of surprise, a well-organised force could reform and counter-attack. No, we will choose the time and place of the landing with consideration. Are your men ready?'

'They are. We have been too long from these shores and they strain to be unleashed against the English.'

'A hundred men does not an army make, Gruffydd.'

'No, but with your five hundred alongside us and another five hundred Irish mercenaries, I guarantee we will emerge victorious. My men were brought up on this island, Magnus, and know every path through every wood. You just get us there and we will do the rest.'

Magnus could hear the emotion behind Gruffydd's words – though the army was small he hoped that their passion would help guarantee victory.

'We will see soon enough, Welshman,' replied Magnus, looking up. 'The sun lifts her skirts as we speak.'

———⏑———

Hugh Montgomery was still fast asleep when one of his officers called him from outside the tent.

'Who's there?' he replied.

'My lord, I have disturbing news from those on watch at the shore.'

Montgomery was instantly awake and jumped to his feet.

'Give me a moment,' he said. He looked down at the sleeping wench in his bed. For a captured enemy she had been surprisingly eager to please him in the night but nevertheless, he cursed the ale for letting her stay. Such people had a habit of slitting the throats of their sleeping captors, given half a chance. He shoved her shoulder to wake her before turning to seek his leggings.

'My lord,' she groaned, 'the day is yet early.'

'I have business to attend,' he said, 'get dressed and get out.'

The woman took a few seconds to wake before coming to her senses.

'My lord,' she asked nervously, 'I suppose you don't want to see me again?'

'You suppose right,' said Montgomery, 'but your company was most welcome. Here –' he tossed over a coin – 'it was well earned.'

The woman looked at the coin on the sheepskin covers. 'I am no whore,' she said.

'Whore or not, just take it and leave before I throw you out.'

Despite her disdain, she picked up the coin and after pulling her dress over her head, ducked out of the tent. Montgomery donned his jerkin and summoned the messenger still outside.

'Enter!'

A chainmail-clad soldier ducked into the tent and stood before him. He did not wait for formalities.

'My lord, the watch reports the sounds of boats off the eastern shore.'

'Be they fishing boats?'

'I think not, my lord. Fishermen would be making a lot more noise and seldom travel in fleets.'

'Why do you not have more definite news for me?'

'The morning mist lies heavy on the sea and though that will soon lift, I thought it wise to inform you early in case it is a threat.'

'Alert the men,' growled Montgomery, 'and have my horse prepared immediately. We will see what it is that raises the concern of battle-hardened men.'

The English army mustered at the edge of the eastern shore, most of them worse for wear from two days of celebration. Many more were scattered across the island, still enjoying the fruits of their victory but those who could be found assembled into ranks as they waited for Montgomery to arrive. Eventually he appeared and rode in front of his command, peering out through the rapidly disappearing mist.

'Robert,' he called, seeing his friend at the head of the Chester infantry, 'you too heard the concerns?'

'Aye, that I did and thought it better to prepare for the worst rather than hope it was hearsay.'

'A sentiment shared,' said Montgomery, as he looked across the ranks of his army.

'I estimate we are about at half strength but have sent messengers to all the local villages to raise the alarm. With luck we should have the full compliment by evening, bar a few. I just hope these reports are a mistake and we sallied forth for no more than a keen fisherman.'

'As do I,' said Robert, 'but whatever the reason, I feel we are about to find out.' He pointed out to sea and for a few seconds, Montgomery saw no change but as the mist finally dissipated, the sight of six Norwegian fighting ships brought a chill to his bones.

A murmur rippled through the ranks of soldiers waiting in the chilled morning air. The ships were similar to the Viking longboats feared by so many but were much larger. Rows of multicoloured shields were fastened to the rails and the serpentine-carved head of a sea snake coiled backward as if poised to strike.

'Knarrs,' said Montgomery quietly.

'Knarrs?' asked Robert, riding up alongside him.

'Viking cargo ships,' said Montgomery, 'but oft used to convey warriors. There will be many men on board.'

'Perhaps they have come to trade.'

'I think not, the shields tell a different story. Stand to your men, Robert, I think we will soon come under attack.' He turned away and called out to the ranks of soldiers. 'Men of England, to arms. Sergeants, take the archers to the shore. I know not if these strangers mean us harm but it is good to show we are ready to repel them if needed.'

The shouts of the sergeants pierced the morning air as they called the ranks to task. Within moments the men were donning whatever spare protection they carried ranging from gambesons to chainmail shirts. Helmets were untied from packs and soon the army was ready to move. As a body they marched down to the shore and spread out facing the stationary ships.

'Archers to the fore!' shouted Montgomery.

The ranks opened for the bowmen to come through and each planted their arrows in the soft ground before them.

'String your bows,' called Montgomery, 'and await my command. If they deem to take this shore without parley they will be met with willow and steel.'

Every soldier stared out in silence, each nervous about what may lay before them for though they were battle hardened, the skills and brutality of the Norsemen were well known and not one of the English relished the chance to meet them in battle.

Magnus and Gruffydd stared at the men lining up on the shore.

'Do you recognise the standards?' asked Magnus.

'One is Hugh Montgomery while the other bears the flag of Rhuddlan,' said Gruffydd. 'A banner subservient to Huw the Fat.'

'I am glad to know those I face,' said Magnus, 'in the meantime, we will wait.'

'I grow tired of waiting,' said Gruffydd, 'why do we not sail in and attack them head on?'

'A glorious idea but one doomed to fail,' said Magnus. 'They have deployed archers close to the shore and though we do not fear death, to fall with no hope of victory is not honourable. We will hold position and judge the mettle of this Hugh Montgomery. Perhaps he will retire but worry not, whatever his plans, we will meet this man in combat before the sun sets.'

For the next few hours the Norwegian fleet sailed back and forth along the bay, though never coming within arrow shot of the defending army.

'What game do you think he plays?' asked Robert, on the shore.

'I think he is taking note of our strengths and weaknesses,' said Montgomery. 'Those ships will hold about five hundred men in total unless there are horses aboard. That number is less than half ours so he knows he has to pick his time and place carefully if he is to have any chance of success.'

'Do you fear them?'

'I respect them for they are formidable warriors, but I do not fear them. Our own men are well blooded and will match them with courage. In addition, all those late to the muster have been gathered in the vale behind us and this fleet will have no knowledge of their strength. If we are attacked, their addition will ensure the enemy is outnumbered three to one and that will suffice.'

Back on the knarr, Magnus Barefoot had seen enough.

'Olaf,' he called, 'take us in to hailing distance. Let's see if these men have the sense they were born with.'

'Why hail them?' asked Gruffydd. 'They are invaders in my lands and deserve to feel the wrath of our blades.'

'Sometimes words are mightier than the sword,' said Magnus, 'but fret not – if they refuse to cede the island then they will soon see the error of their judgement.'

The oars dipped into the sea and the boat turned towards the land, closely followed by the rest of the fleet.

'My lord, the ships are turning,' shouted one of the soldiers, 'they're heading this way.'

Montgomery turned to see the enemy heading for the shore.

'Shield wall,' he shouted, 'archers, prepare arrows!'

The ranks of his army took the necessary steps as Montgomery mounted his horse. Digging in his spurs, he rode along the front of the ranks, encouraging each man as he went.

'Do not lose this battle before a blow is struck,' he shouted, 'for if your heart is already filled with fear then we are lost. These Norsemen are flesh and bone like you and I. The tales that precede them are naught but boasts of old men and though they are known as good fighters, forget not that most of their conquests were against cathedrals and villages. Seldom have they come against a trained army such as you, and those that have were often found wanting.'

The men cheered in support with many banging their weapons against their shields.

'You men,' continued Montgomery, 'have already struck fear into the best the Welsh have to offer and have ridden the breadth of this country, without equal. The sound of your marching footsteps strike fear into the stoutest hearts and you have taken Ynys Mon from beneath the feet of their princes. Remember this, for you are the equal of these men and soon they will learn a painful lesson.'

By now the men's blood had risen and they roared their support, screaming insults across the shallow water to the oncoming ships. Montgomery smiled inwardly. To raise the ire of an army was the most important job of any commander, for to fight without fire in your heart was to end on the wrong side of a defeat. As the men raised the volume of their challenges, he spurred his horse to race back and forth across the front of their ranks.

'Archers,' he roared as the water splashed up from the hooves of his galloping horse, 'target the lead boat. Upon my command, ready . . . *loose!*'

The air filled with arrows and the English army stared in expectation as hundreds fell about the ship.

'It seems they are in no mood to parley.' Magnus laughed from beneath his shield.

'I told you so,' said Gruffydd. 'Their arrogance is beyond belief and they see all men as inferior.'

'Then let's show them what others are capable of,' said Magnus, and as soon as the hail of arrows eased, he jumped up to call to his men.

'String bows,' he called, 'and let them see they play with us at their peril.'

All along the ships the shout was repeated and within seconds the air filled with Viking arrows, each tipped with a sharpened bodkin capable of piercing the strongest of chainmail. Any men caught unawares on the shore fell to the hail of death but most sought protection beneath their own shields. For several minutes, each army exchanged volleys of arrows and though some men fell, neither side gained much of an advantage.

'Enough distraction,' roared Magnus, 'give the signal to beach the boats, it is time to test their mettle.'

Backs bent to the oars and within moments the ships ploughed forward, powered by men who had grown up in such circumstances. The Viking archers doubled their rate of fire, seeking not individual targets but keeping up the pressure to disrupt the enemy lines as the ships neared the shore.

Montgomery cantered his horse along the defending lines encouraging his men.

'*Here they come!*' he roared. 'We will meet them head on amongst the surf while they lack organisation.' He drew his sword and held it high. 'Take heart, men of England – be true to your comrades and follow my lead.'

As the ships neared the shore, Montgomery peered over the edge of his shield and could see the bloodlust in the faces of the Vikings. Above the noise of his own army, he could hear the rhythmic beating of the enemy's weapons against the hulls of the ships, a sound that had sent fear into the hearts of men for hundreds of years.

'*Let them come, men!*' he roared. 'But fear not for this is a day that—'

His rallying call went unfinished as his head flew sharply backward and he fell slowly from his horse, an arrow protruding from his eye.

Silence fell upon the ranks as each man stared in confusion at the twitching body of their commander. Within seconds their nerve started to break and they looked around in fear, seeking guidance from their sergeants.

Up on the slopes, Robert of Rhuddlan looked on in horror as the bows of the ships beached on the shingle, their speed and force driving them high onto dry ground. Immediately, the occupants poured over the sides into the surf and ran forward a few paces before lining up to present a shield wall towards the defenders.

Robert was at a loss. It was too late to get down to take command and he knew that without coordination, the irregular soldiers would lack cohesion and the ranks would fail. With lead in his heart he realised there was nothing he could do and the front lines of the army were on their own. He turned his horse and galloped back into the vale, knowing his only chance was to muster the cavalry and strike before the battle was over.

Magnus Barefoot stood behind his men, his magnificent beard hanging low to his chest. In one hand he held a small round shield while the other wielded his trademark battleaxe. He had seen Montgomery fall and knew it was an advantage he could only have dreamed of, for these people were mainly peasants brought in to fight the battles of the nobles, while his own men had learned the way of war from an early age. He also knew that without leadership the enemy would be lambs before wolves.

He pushed through to the front and stared at the enemy lines. The shouts of the sergeants echoed across the shore as they tried to regain the discipline of their command but it was too late, the sight of Montgomery being killed was too much and within moments, some of the defenders broke ranks to run back towards the perceived safety of the dunes at their backs. More followed and soon confusion reigned as fighting broke out between some of the defenders, desperate to escape the imminent Viking onslaught.

This was the moment Magnus had waited for and he looked over at the Welsh lines formed up on his left flank, headed by Gruffydd ap Cynan.

'Well,' roared Magnus, 'this is what we came for. Welshman, what are you waiting for?'

Gruffydd grinned and drew his own sword. 'Our homeland lies before us, men,' he responded, 'let us wash it clean with English blood.'

With an almighty roar, the Welsh exiles charged across the shore to meet the defending English. Magnus and his own men shouted their battle cries and joined Gruffydd in the assault.

Within moments they crashed into the Englishmen, but rather than meet a solid line of steel, the enemy ranks were loose and uncoordinated. Immediately, the Vikings made inroads and the defenders were torn apart by the ferocity of the assault. From then on, the enemy was doomed and as they fought desperately for their lives, Gruffydd's Welsh infantry fell upon their weaker flanks, rolling up the enemy defences with ease. The result was inevitable and knowing the battle was lost, the English broke ranks, an action as catastrophic as it was stupid.

Up on the hill, Robert of Rhuddlan had returned with his cavalry, but he soon realised the hopelessness of the situation, and that to commit more men to the fray would only result in further English losses. The battle was lost and the occupation of Ynys Mon short-lived. He would gather whatever survivors he could and along with the rest of the army still waiting back in the vale, retreat to the straits as fast as possible, all the time hoping the Norsemen failed to follow.

Decision made, he wheeled his horse and galloped back the way he had come, the screams of his dying fellows still ringing in his ears.

Down on the beach, Gruffydd looked across to Magnus, taking in the gruesome sight. The Viking leader stood legs apart with one hand holding his bloodied axe skyward. In the other hand, he held the head of one of the defenders, the blood still pouring from the severed neck as the Norseman roared out his battle cry.

'Magnus,' shouted Gruffydd, sheathing his sword, 'the day is ours, call off the men.'

For a second there was no reply but slowly the chieftain turned and gazed unseeingly into the eyes of the Welsh king.

Gruffydd caught his breath, hardly recognising the man who had sailed with him from Ireland. The Viking's features were contorted with rage and his mouth dripped with blood where he had torn apart an opponent's throat. His eyes possessed a manic stare and the berserker bloodlust was obviously still upon him.

'What did you say?' growled Magnus eventually.

'The battle is won, there is no point in continuing the slaughter.'

Magnus' eyes narrowed as he considered the request. 'Are these men not your enemy?'

'They are,' started Gruffydd, 'but—'

'Have they not invaded your lands and killed your kinsmen?'

'Yes, but—'

'And did we not make a pact that my men would rid these lands of their stench on your behalf?'

'We did—'

'Then hold your insults, Welshman, and let us do what it is we do best for if I deny my men the killing, they may well seek it elsewhere, perhaps amongst the ranks of your own.'

Without waiting for an answer, he discarded the head and stepped over the body before racing towards a skirmish involving several of his men against a group of determined defenders.

Gruffydd watched him go and although the Welsh king was himself a feared warrior, he had never seen any man fight as did the Norsemen. The brutality was unrelenting and every man who stood against them was cut down without mercy. Soon the sounds of battle fell away, but were immediately replaced with the roars of Viking victory.

***

Gulls and crows paraded along the edge of the dunes finding rich pickings of warm, bloodied flesh as Gruffydd mustered his men to count the cost of the casualties sustained.

'Twenty of our own dead, my lord,' said one of his sergeants, 'and as many wounded. Three won't see the day out.'

'And the Irish mercenaries?'

'Ten won't see another dawn. Their fellows are taking them back to the ships as we speak.'

Gruffydd nodded silently. In the circumstances it was a small price to pay. He looked across to the Norsemen. Already they were building fires for their own dead while others were rolling barrels of ale down gangplanks for the funerary celebrations. They were indeed a strange people and absolutely fearless in warfare. He hoped he would never have to meet them on opposite ends of a battlefield.

As he watched, Magnus Barefoot approached, his blood-spattered face now calmer in the aftermath of the fight.

'The fight went well, Welshman,' said Magnus, 'the gods will feast in our name this night.'

'I'm sure they will,' said Gruffydd, 'and you have our gratitude.'

'Gratitude does not weigh down a man's purse,' replied Magnus, 'at least not on the day of the fight.' He looked around. 'Some of my men already drink in the halls of Valhalla as we speak, each of them dead in your name, but they died an honourable death with a blade in their hand and I envy their glorious end. However, make no mistake – I will hold you to the oaths we shared across the sea and will expect them to be fulfilled.'

'My word is my bond, Magnus,' replied Gruffydd. 'One year from now send a ship to these shores and the first payment will be waiting. In addition, any ship bearing your banner will be granted safe harbour in my kingdom for as long as I live.'

Magnus grunted and looked towards the far hill where the remnants of the enemy were disappearing over the brow.

'Many make their escape, Welshman, but we will hunt them down until the last have fed the soil with their blood or have fled across the straits to the mainland. But that is a task for the morrow. First we will honour our dead and drink to the gods.'

'I thought your men were Christian souls?'

'Some are and some still follow the old gods, but either way, it is good to have many such options, don't you think?'

'There is but one god, Magnus, and he is all-powerful.'

'Was it the Christian god who lay this English army before us like lambs to the slaughter, Welshman?'

'It was his will.'

'And what about the arrow that felled their leader before an axe had been thrown, surely it was guided by the hand of Thor?'

'Everything in this life is at the whim of the Lord God, Magnus, and you would do well to remember such a thing.'

'Perhaps so, Welshman,' said Magnus, 'but I am a pragmatic man and will leave my final decision in such matters until my death is imminent. Now, I must go and honour my fallen brothers. Tomorrow we will cleanse your lands alongside you but today we feast. Go and say your prayers to your one god, Welshman while we celebrate ours with wine, fire and blood.'

Windsor Castle

July 6th, AD 1100

After Gwladus had left Windsor, Nesta had gradually allowed herself to become closer to Henry and soon began to live the life of a favoured courtesan at the Castle. Despite her Welsh loyalties, over the following six months she had fallen in love with the king's brother, and although she knew she could never be Henry's wife, he had given her a beautiful house where she enjoyed every privilege she could imagine, short of being a queen. Though she missed her mother and Wales, she had become content with her life. Her household staff were many, she enjoyed favoured seating at all court functions at Westminster and even the king himself talked to her on a friendly level, knowing how important she was to his brother. She spent her days running Henry's affairs at home and though he was often away, many nights he shared her bed as the lovers they had become. It was on one such night when Nesta woke from a fitful sleep to see the king's brother staring out of the window into a stormy night sky.

'Henry,' she said quietly, 'does something bother you?'

Henry turned and smiled at the woman he loved.

'No, my sweet,' he said, 'I just can't sleep. Close your eyes and I will join you presently.'

Despite his request, Nesta rose and, tying a nightgown around herself, joined Henry at the window. She stood behind him and wrapped her hands around his chest, holding her lover tightly within her embrace.

'I will not sleep knowing something plays on your mind,' she said. 'Share your concerns, my love, and perhaps I can offer clarity from a distance.'

'Alas, these concerns are not for sharing, Nesta, for they are the burdens of royalty.' He turned to face her in the darkened room, lit only by the ornate fire pots glowing red in each corner. 'Nesta, you know I love you more than any other woman alive.'

'So you say.' Nesta smiled mischievously.

'I am being serious,' said Henry, 'and it is important that you know that.'

'Of course I know it,' said Nesta, taking his hand, 'and would have departed this place long since had I thought differently.'

'You also know that if I could, then I would make you my wife without hesitation.'

'That is a subject that perhaps we should avoid, my love, for I see no reason we cannot be joined.'

'You know why,' said Henry, 'my brother would never allow it.'

'Your brother will not live for ever,' said Nesta, 'and should you outlive him, then one day I can truly sit at your side.'

'Perhaps,' said Henry, and he once more stared out over the darkness of Windsor. 'Nesta,' he said eventually, releasing himself from her embrace, 'I have to go. I have promised to meet my brother in the New Forest two days hence and share the hunt.'

'It does not take two days to reach the lodges.'

'I know, but there is some other business I have to attend to on the way, so I would benefit from an early start.'

'And what business would this be?' she asked, gazing into his eyes.

'Just the business of men, Nesta, but worry not, I will return in a few days and arrange some quality time together.'

Henry turned and gently brushed a lock of her hair from her forehead.

'You are a special woman, my love,' he said. 'And I am lucky to have you.'

'Yes, you are,' said Nesta with a smile and she tiptoed up to kiss him on the lips. 'Be safe, my love, I will count the breaths until you return.'

Henry smiled and after another lingering kiss, left her alone in her bedchamber. An hour later she heard his horse trotting across the courtyard and she looked out of the window, catching his eye as he rode out between the gatehouses with a patrol of his personal bodyguards.

Two days later, Henry sat astride his horse alongside many of the royal household in the village of Brockenhurst in the New Forest, an area of woodland favoured by the king. Beaters with dogs had already been sent out on a circuitous journey into the forest to scare the deer herds towards the king's party. Everyone drank hot ale to take the chill from their bones.

'An interesting flavour, brother,' said Henry, as the riders waited for the signal to start.

'Indeed,' said Rufus, 'the kitchens have added eastern spices to provide a kick.'

'Well, I hope we are as successful in the hunt,' said Henry, 'for the result is as hot as the devil's hearth.'

'Both men sipped on their ale, until Rufus spied a noble standing alone to one side.'

'Isn't that Lord Tirel?' asked the king, 'I thought he was abed with an illness.'

'He looks fine to me,' said Henry.

'I am pleased,' said the king, 'for it provides me with an opportunity to have some fun. Come, let us see if he is agreeable.' He turned to a nearby squire. 'Bring me the package attached to my saddle.'

As the squire ran to the nearby horse, the king and his brother approached the nobleman standing alone to one side.

'Lord Tirel,' said the king, 'a very good morning to you.'

'And to you, my lord,' responded Tirel.

'Are you well? I heard you were indisposed only a few days ago.'

'Indeed I was, sire,' said Tirel, 'but angels have surely smiled upon me for I would have been sorely disappointed to miss this day.'

'Well, I am happy you are here for your reputation as a bowman precedes you and I would have sport with your prowess.'

'I'm not sure what you mean, sire,' said Tirel.

The king turned to the returned squire who handed him a leather wrap.

'This was a gift from my father when I was a young man,' said Rufus, turning back around and undoing the strap. 'It contains six arrows from the finest fletcher in France. It is said that even the blindest man with poorest bow would hit their target if these be their shafts. Of course, I hold no time for such foolishness but as there is a wager as to who brings down the first stag, should I be the victor then there would be many cries of witchcraft and sorcery amongst my retinue.'

Several voices raised in laughter from the king's nearby courtiers.

'Quite right too.' Henry laughed. 'For you need no help from bewitched arrows, brother, your aim is truer than any man here.'

'Nevertheless,' announced Rufus, 'I will not be accused of unfair advantage. Walter Tirel, you are an archer of great note and I say to you: to the good archers, the good arrows.'

He handed three of the arrows to Tirel, who examined them closely. They were as light as a feather yet carved with tiny images of prey animals wrapped around the shaft. The bodkins were made of silver and the pure white feathers were from the wings of a snow goose.

'They are indeed beautiful,' said Tirel, 'but I cannot accept, sire; they are gifts from William himself.'

'Nonsense,' said Rufus, 'I have been anticipating this hunt for many days but seek fair competition. Accept the gift, Lord Tirel, and do the best you possibly can to outhunt me. Drop the first stag and ten pounds of silver will be yours.'

The group gasped at the generosity and turned to face the noble. 'And if I lose?' asked Tirel.

'There will be no comeback,' said Rufus jovially, 'except for my constant teasing for many years to come.' He laughed out loud at his own joke, as did his followers. 'So, what say you?' asked Rufus when the laughter had died down. 'Do we have a wager?'

Tirel glanced at Henry before turning his attention to the king. 'Aye, my lord, we do.'

'Excellent,' shouted Rufus. He turned to find the hunt master. 'Lord Grayling, if there is nothing else, we are ready to begin.'

'Aye, my lord,' came the reply, and to the sounds of horns echoing across the misty fields, King William Rufus led his party into the New Forest.

* * *

The morning's hunt was unsuccessful, with only a boar brought down and when they finally stopped to eat at midday, conversation was muted. Spirits rose only when the news came in they had all been waiting for.

'Sire,' shouted Lord Grayling, 'there is talk of a ten-point stag less than a league from here.'

'Excellent,' said Rufus, throwing his tankard to one side, 'call off the dogs lest they scare him away.'

'The dogs are already secured, sire,' said Grayling, 'and I have taken the liberty of refreshing your mount and, indeed, that of Lord Tirel.'

The king looked over to Tirel and grinned.

'Well, here we go, my friend, you and me against the beast. Let the better man blood his arrows first. Ready?'

'As ready as I ever will be, sire,' said Tirel, 'lead the way.'

Both men exited the tent and climbed astride their horses.

'Follow with a cart,' shouted Rufus, 'but stay a while back so as not to spook the beast.'

'Aye, sire,' said Grayling, and the whole hunting party watched as the king and Lord Tirel galloped in the direction the hunt master had indicated.

'My money is on the king,' Grayling announced to Henry, as they disappeared into the distance. 'I have never seen him bettered in such a competition; your father tutored him well.'

'We will see,' said Henry, before turning around and calling out. 'Mount up,' he shouted, 'and bring forth the carts. Whoever the victor, I suspect we will have a carcass to butcher before nightfall.'

Rufus and Tirel both rode the same way, sharing any sign of the stag with each other before coming across fresh spoor near a stream.

'Still warm,' whispered Tirel, seeing the steam rise from the animal's faeces. 'It can't be far from here.'

'Then let us each go our own way, my friend,' replied the king quietly, 'and may God guide the arrows of the better man.'

Tirel nodded and crossed the stream to head for the high ground while Rufus followed the footprints downstream. For what seemed like an age he crept slowly until finally he gently pushed some branches to one side and saw the prize before him, a beautiful ten-point stag in the prime of his life. The animal was grazing peacefully on the lush vegetation at the side of the stream, and looked up only briefly when Rufus snapped a tiny twig beneath his boot. The king froze, hoping the stag hadn't seen him, holding his breath until the animal resumed feeding. Slowly, Rufus placed his arrows on the ground, keeping one in his hand to load his bow. He notched the shaft onto the bowstring and lifted the weapon up to take aim. Gradually, he slowed his breathing, steadying the shake that crept to his fingers, knowing his grasp must be solid to ensure a straight flight. Out of the corner of his eye he saw a movement and cursed silently as he saw Tirel also notch his bow across the other side of the clearing.

'*What are you doing, you stupid man?*' he hissed under his breath, as Tirel broke cover and stepped into the clearing. '*You will scare the beast.*'

Sure enough, the stag looked up in fright and with a single bound, cleared the stream to run directly at the king's hidden position. For a second Rufus froze, as the giant animal raced towards him, but he quickly recovered his poise and raised his bow again to take aim.

Across the clearing, Tirel had already drawn his bow and as the beast bounded towards the king, the archer let his arrow fly. The shaft sped fast and true through the air but though it found a target, it was not deer blood that ran down the shaft – it was human.

Rufus gasped in pain and fell back amongst the bracken, Tirel's arrow sticking out of his chest.

'My lord!' shouted Tirel as he ran across the clearing. 'I did not see you in the foliage.' He dropped to his knees beside the king and examined the wound. 'Oh, sweet Jesus, what have I done?'

'Your approach was all wrong,' gasped the king, 'you were upwind of the prey and there was no way you could have dropped him from there.'

'My heart is heavy with my choice, my king,' said Tirel, 'but I cannot take back the shaft. Ease your thoughts and if you require, I will take your confession on behalf of the church.'

'There is no need of confession,' gasped William, 'for I feel the arrow has lodged short of my heart. The pain is great but if I can survive until the cart arrives, perhaps the apothecaries can yet save my life.'

'Sire, let me take your confession,' begged Tirel with tears streaming down his face, 'lest the carts are late and you are denied entry into the kingdom of heaven.'

'Tirel, trust me, I cannot move but the wound is not mortal. I already hear the cart in the distance and will soon be in safe hands. Worry not, for I know your part in this was an accident. You will not be held accountable.'

'Alas I will,' sobbed Tirel, 'and will surely lose my head as must all men who take the life of a king.'

'I am not dead yet, Tirel, now call the cart before it is too late.'

Tirel's shoulders shook as the tears ran down his face to drip onto the king.

'Tirel, call the cart,' gasped the king again, 'quickly, man, lest it passes us by.'

'My lord, forgive me,' sobbed Tirel, and he lifted his hand to grasp the shaft sticking out of the king's chest.

'Tirel, what are you doing?' gasped Rufus. 'Stop it or you will—'

Before he could continue, Tirel gritted his teeth and drove the arrow deeper into the chest of the king, piercing his heart with the silver bodkin.

Rufus's eyes widened and though he opened his mouth to cry out, all that emerged was a gasp of excruciating pain.

'My lord, forgive me,' sobbed Tirel as he stood up to back away from the thicket, leaving on the ground the body of the dead king.

'My lord,' shouted Grayling for the tenth time. 'King William, where are you?'

'He must be around here somewhere,' said Henry, 'for I clearly heard him cry out only a few moments ago. Tell the men to spread out, he may be injured.'

The rest of William's hunting party formed a line and walked towards the stream. Several minutes later, a voice cried out in alarm and everyone ran over to find Grayling cradling the king's body.

'Mother of Christ,' whispered Henry, and all present formed the shape of the cross on their chests.

'Is he all right?' asked one of the nobles, jumping from his horse.

Grayling simply shook his head and looked up. 'My lord,' he said quietly with tears running down his face, 'I fear the king is dead.' He looked over to Henry still sat upon his horse. 'Long live the king!'

Henry stared down at the body of his brother held in Grayling's arms. The beautiful arrow shaft protruding from the king's chest shone in the afternoon sun, as if mocking the horror that was the death of a monarch.

'My lord,' said Grayling quietly, 'do you wish to say a prayer over your brother?'

Henry didn't answer. His face was ashen at the sight of the dead king and his heart raced at the implications.

'Who is responsible for this?' he asked simply.

'There can only be one man,' said Grayling, 'and that is Lord Tirel.'

'Where is he?'

'There is no sign of him, sire, but he is a loyal and faithful servant of William. Surely this is nothing more than a tragic accident.'

'If this is so,' said Henry, 'then he will not be found responsible. However, I would hear the tale from his own mouth.' He turned to one of the sergeants. 'You there, gather your men and find Tirel. Once he is in your custody, bring him to me in Windsor. The rest of you, secure your mounts for a long ride – you are coming with me.'

'Sire,' said Grayling, 'what about your brother?'

'See that his body gets to Winchester,' said Henry.

'But surely you wish to say your goodbyes?'

'It is too late for that, Lord Grayling, for his soul already speeds its way to heaven.' Henry tugged the reins to turn the horse but before he left Grayling called out once more.

'Sire, you are next in line to the throne and we have already lost one monarch this day. Where are you going?'

'I am returning to London with all haste,' said Henry, 'but have to call in at the hunting lodge first. Take my brother to Winchester and once he is laid out in the cathedral, I will attend him there.' He turned his horse and accompanied by five men, galloped back along the forest track.

Within hours, Henry was back at the lodge and as his men sought fresh horses, he took the opportunity to walk into the nearby trees. Bending over he placed a purse of silver beneath a log and after looking around to see he had not been observed, returned to the lodge where the staff were already mourning his brother. He did not wait to see whether Tirel arrived to claim payment – he had to get to London as soon as possible. There was a treasury to secure.

Windsor Castle

July 21st, AD 1100

Nesta stood in the window of her quarters at Windsor, staring out at the hive of activity in the bailey below. Henry had arrived earlier in the day and though he had to take care of some urgent business, he had sent a message to say he would attend her in the early evening. Nesta hadn't seen Henry since the day he had gone hunting with his brother and had spent the last two weeks worrying about him. A knock came on the door and Carla entered the room.

'My lady,' she said quietly, 'he is here.'

'Thank you, Carla,' said Nesta turning around. 'I am ready.'

Carla stood to one side as Nesta straightened her dress and walked to the centre of the room to wait. Moments later the door eased open and Henry entered. Carla took his cloak and retired from the room, leaving them both alone. For a few moments, each stared at the other in silence, until Nesta lowered herself to the floor in a perfect curtsey.

'Your Majesty,' she said with her head lowered, 'welcome to my humble home.'

'Nesta,' said Henry, his face screwed up in confusion, 'what are you doing?'

'Greeting my king as is my duty,' said Nesta, still not making eye contact.

'Nesta, stand up,' said Henry.

'As you wish, Majesty.'

'Nesta,' said Henry, 'stop this foolery and greet me the way you have done a hundred times before.'

'If this is what you command, my lord.'

'Nesta,' shouted Henry, 'enough nonsense. Why are you being like this? Am I not the same man who left your bed not two weeks since?'

'No, Majesty, you are not,' said Nesta. 'You left as a brother to William but have come back a king in your own right. The two positions are worlds apart.'

'The stations may be different but the man beneath this crown remains the same,' replied Henry.

'Is he?' asked Nesta. 'For the man I knew would have stood beside me at his brother's funeral. He would have invited me to his own coronation or at the very least would have sent a message explaining what was happening.'

'Is that what this is all about, Nesta – the fact that all this happened in your absence?'

'I was not absent, Henry,' said Nesta. 'I was right here all along, almost beside myself with worry about what had become of you. All I had was rumour and hearsay about what was happening and I did not know what to believe.'

'That is why I am here now, Nesta,' said Henry, 'to offer the explanation you deserve.'

'Two weeks later?'

'I know it is not ideal but it is the best I could achieve. You have to understand that there was much to do and though you were on my mind, matters of state kept me away. Now most have been concluded, I can at last pay you some attention.'

'I know not why you bother,' snapped Nesta. 'If I am that much of an embarrassment that I do not warrant even a pew at your coronation, then you may as well just send me home, out of your way.'

'*Nesta!*' roared Henry, slamming his fist onto an adjacent table. 'Enough.'

Nesta stepped backward, shocked at the display of violence.

'Now you listen to me,' shouted Henry. 'I came here with affection in my heart and intentions to make good my shortcomings but you are making it very difficult. Now sit down and listen to me lest I walk through that door for the last time and you never see me again.'

Visibly shaken, Nesta sat in one of the two seats before the fire while Henry took the other.

'Forgive my outburst.' Henry sighed. 'But I ask you to listen to me. When the king was killed, there was no time to lose. My older brother, Robert, long nursed a claim to the throne of England and if I had not acted quickly, he would now be ruling our country. I rode to Winchester Castle as fast as I dared and secured the treasury before spending a whole day arguing with the clergy regarding my right to the title. Luckily, the nobles backed my claim, but with the archbishops of York and Canterbury not available, we had to make do with the bishop of London and convene a coronation as quickly as possible. If we had wasted any more time, then Robert could have returned from crusade within weeks and pursued his challenge as the older son, and if that had happened, the country would have been plunged into a civil war. I could not allow that to happen, Nesta, so had to move quickly. But, unfortunately, during the chaos, I found no time to keep you abreast of events. I am sorry, but that is the way it is. Yes, I love you, but you have to understand, these are momentous times and sometimes, despite your upset, my life does not revolve around you.'

Nesta stared at Henry in shock. She had never heard him so angry or so forthright but through her distress, she knew he was right. She coughed gently to clear her throat before speaking.

'I understand, my lord,' she said.

'Nesta, in the privacy of your chamber or indeed mine, please refrain from formal titles, for it creates a barrier difficult to surmount.'

'Thank you,' said Nesta, before continuing. 'In the circumstances, I accept the explanation and beg forgiveness for my outburst but you have to understand that I was hurt and frightened. A simple note would have sufficed.'

'You are right,' said Henry, 'and I condemn myself for neglecting to organise such a small but important gesture. Please forgive me.'

Nesta smiled and held out her hand. 'Already forgotten,' she said.

Henry kissed her hand and stood to seek the wine jug already sat upon the table.

'So,' said Nesta, 'now you are a king, how does it feel?'

'Like the weight of a nation has been draped across my shoulders,' said Henry, pouring two goblets of wine.

'As indeed it has,' said Nesta, joining him at the table, 'but what about Robert?'

'What about him?'

'Is he not still a risk? After all, he is the older brother, what if he challenges your claim?'

'He cannot,' said Henry, 'for I was born to the purple and successfully argued my point at Winchester.'

'Born to the purple?'

'It means I was born to a ruling king while Robert was born before my father took the throne. By accepting my argument, the barons support my claim and should Robert challenge the throne, he takes on the whole of England.'

'So your kingship is secure?'

'It is.'

'Then perhaps this calls for a toast,' said Nesta and raised her glass. 'To my lover, King Henry the First.

Henry sipped his wine before replacing the glass on the table and taking Nesta in his arms. He kissed her deeply and led her over to her immaculately made bed.

'Come,' he said, 'for despite my folly in excluding you from matters of court, you were always in my thoughts at night.'

'Is that all I mean to you?' Nesta laughed as he threw her on the bed. 'Nothing but relief to your royal desires?'

'You know better than that,' said Henry kissing her neck, 'but I have to admit, other women pale in comparison to my feisty Welsh vixen.'

'So they should,' gasped Nesta as he started to disrobe her, 'for with you there is nothing held back.'

'Nor should there be,' whispered Henry. 'But enough talking, there are more important things to address. Look to your king, Nesta, for this night I need you more than I ever have done before.'

The following morning, they sat at the table within Nesta's chambers. The room was quiet and Henry seemed overly focused on the piece of fish that formed his meal.

'Henry,' said Nesta, 'something concerns you.'

Henry looked up at the beautiful raven-haired woman before him. Never had he loved any woman as he did this one but he knew he was about to break her heart. He pushed the platter away and washed his hands in the finger bowl before wiping his hands on a napkin and turning to the servant.

'Leave us,' he said quietly.

When they were once more alone he sat back in his chair and lifted his gaze towards the woman he loved, staring deep into her soul.

Nesta gazed back patiently, knowing full well that he would speak when he was ready.

'Nesta,' he said eventually. 'Never have I known any person, alive or dead, that causes my heart to both ache and bound with joy as much as you do. I love you more than life itself and these past few years have been the happiest I have known.'

'And mine,' said Nesta with a smile.

'The times we have shared,' said Henry, 'will be the last thought on my mind when I leave this life, for never will they be bettered. Yet all this time, we have been living a lie.'

Nesta's face dropped slightly and she sipped her honeyed water before looking back up at him.

'In what way?'

'Many were the nights when we talked of sharing our life together, Nesta, and I longed for such a union just as much as you. Together we condemned the king for disallowing our union but at least we were together in private.'

'We were,' said Nesta, 'but now you are king, you can change that rule and put us together as God intended.'

Henry looked away and took a deep breath before returning his gaze to Nesta. 'I can't,' he said quietly, 'the clergy won't allow it.'

Nesta stared at the king with confusion.

'What do you mean the clergy won't allow it? Are you the king or not? Because where I am from, the king makes the laws, not some holy men who feed off the backs of the poor.'

'I agree,' said Henry, 'and in different circumstances I would have taken that road, but alas it is not so simple. To secure the throne I needed the support of the clergy, and to get that I needed the barons on my side. This was a difficult situation and I had to concede to some conditions before they agreed to offer me their support.'

'What conditions?'

'Peace on our northern borders,' said Henry.

'Now I am confused,' said Nesta, 'how does peace in the north have any effect on whether you and I get married?'

Henry looked down at the floor in silence.

'Henry,' said Nesta, 'please, I am waiting for an explanation.'

'Because in order to secure an alliance with our northern allies,' said Henry, looking back up, 'I am to marry the Princess Matilda.'

Nesta stared at Henry in horror as his words sunk in.

'Who is Matilda?' she asked eventually.

'She is the daughter of King Malcolm of Scotland.'

'But I don't understand,' said Nesta, 'I may not live the life of a queen but even I know Malcom died many years ago.'

'Indeed he did, but there still exists many family ties and the union will provide a link by which peace can be secured.'

Nesta sat back in her chair, aghast at the revelation.

'When is this union to take place?' she asked quietly.

'Within months,' said Henry, 'and the clergy have already sent for her.'

'Where is she?'

'In Romsey Abbey in Southampton.'

'She is a nun?' gasped Nesta. 'But surely that is against the laws of God.'

'She is no nun, Nesta, but was sent there for education by her aunt.'

Nesta got up and walked around the room.

'You knew of this last night,' she said, 'before you took me to my bed.'

'Yes but—'

'So all the time you were telling me that you loved me, another woman lay in your thoughts?'

'No, Nesta,' said the king, 'you were and are the only woman to occupy my mind. The marriage is one of convenience only.'

'Convenient for whom?' shouted Nesta. 'For you, for her, for the church? Because it is certainly not convenient to me.'

'*For the country*,' roared Henry, storming to his feet. 'In the name of God, woman, can't you see I am as hurt as you in this affair? Of course I would rather have you at my side but I had no choice in this matter. It was agree to this or lose the crown.' He slumped back down in his chair and looked over at Nesta.

'So where does this leave me?' she asked quietly. 'Am I to be thrown out as I once was by your brother?'

'Of course not,' said Henry. 'This is your home and you can stay here as long as you want. In fact, I can't see why this situation need change. I won't be able to stay here often but I can visit.'

'You want me to stay here?' said Nesta in a lowered tone. 'Waiting for the occasional visit whilst most nights you sleep alongside your queen?'

'I know it's not ideal,' said Henry, 'but at least we can still share what we have.'

'So you want me to be your mistress?' said Nesta. 'Available at your call to satisfy your lustful needs while this Matilda reaps the benefits.'

'It is not unusual for a king to have mistresses, Nesta, surely even you must know that.'

'I do,' said Nesta, 'but I thought you were different. I thought we had something special.'

'And we do,' said Henry, 'and that is why I do not want it to end. Yes, this marriage is unavoidable, but the love we two have for each other should not be abandoned for a simple matter of state.' He stared at Nesta for a long while before speaking again. 'I have to go back to Westminster,' he said eventually, 'but will return tomorrow evening. Perhaps you can have your decision by then.'

Nesta simply nodded and when Henry walked over to kiss her goodbye, she offered him only her cheek.

'Until tomorrow,' said the king, and he left Nesta alone to fight the deluge of heartbroken tears welling up behind her eyes.

The following day was the longest that Nesta could remember. The choices before her were difficult but finally she made her decision, and after bathing and taking her evening meal, she dressed in her best gown to await the king. Eventually he arrived and after handing his horse over to the grooms, headed straight to Nesta's house in the grounds of the castle.

Nesta stood to greet him as he closed the door. They stared at each other in silence. Finally, Henry broke the silence and spoke gently.

'Nesta,' he said, 'as promised, I have returned for your decision. Whatever path you decide, I promise you my lifelong love, whether it is by my side or not, so, if I may be so rude, please share your mind for my heart yearns to know whether it is to be broken or not.'

'Henry,' said Nesta with a sigh. 'I have fought this decision every moment since you left and in the end, it was obvious I was fooling myself. The matters of kingship are greater than I and I was a fool to think I could keep you to myself. I know this now, so I will treasure the few years we had. I pride myself in being as independent as circumstances allow and vowed I would never be beholden to any man, but that was before I met you. Nobody has touched my heart as you have and I have invested too much to just walk away now. I will stay, my king, and if you so desire, will happily be your mistress.'

Henry smiled and stepped forward but Nesta stopped him with a raised hand.

'But,' she continued, 'there are conditions.'

'Only you would dare impose conditions on a king,' said Henry with a smile. 'What chains would you place around your monarch's neck?'

'Only one,' said Nesta. 'I will happily be your mistress and take what time you can spare. I will not, however, hide amongst the shadows as a guilty secret. If you want me as much as you say you do, then it must be with the full knowledge of your wife-to-be.'

'What are you saying?' asked Henry.

'I am saying that my position must be made known to Matilda, in every sense. I will never embarrass her with my presence at any function she attends and will keep myself to the realms of Windsor; however, it is important she knows of me. If you promise me this, then we can proceed together.'

'It is quite a boon you ask,' said Henry. 'I am not yet wed, but you want me to tell my would-be wife that I will often sleep with another.'

'You said that kings are known for infidelity, and if this is indeed the case, as the daughter of a king herself she will understand the situation.'

'Yes, but to rub it in her face before the vows are made is a little harsh.'

'You said she was an orphan and this union is for the greater good of two countries, is that correct?'

'It is,' said Henry.

'Then trust me,' said Nesta, 'she will not call off the union. A woman without prospects will never forgo the attentions of a king, just because he has interests in another.'

'How do you know that?' asked Henry.

'Because, that is exactly the situation I have been in these past two days. If Matilda and I can share the quandary you have set upon the both of us, then we can equally share the bounty.'

Henry stared at Nesta before nodding and holding out his hands.

'You are a very special woman, Nesta ferch Rhys,' he said eventually, 'and if that is the toll that must be paid, then so be it.'

'Thank you,' said Nesta, 'now if you don't mind, I am feeling a little emotional and seek my own company. When the task is done, let me know and I swear we will not talk of this again.'

Henry nodded and smiled.

'I understand,' he said, 'and will do as you ask. Fret not, my love, for though this is the end of one era, another awaits before us.' Without another word, he turned and left the room, passing Carla on the stairs.

The servant entered Nesta's quarters and saw her mistress on the verge of tears.

'Is there anything I can get you, my lady?' she asked quietly.

'Yes, Carla,' said Nesta as the tears started to flow, 'bring me a new heart for this one is torn in two.'

The Island of Ynys Mon

August 7th, AD 1100

Gruffydd stood upon the hill, surveying his lands, with Cynwrig the Tall. The past few months had been brutal but with the aid of Cadwgan's rebels and the forces of Magnus Barefoot's Vikings, not only had they driven the invaders from Ynys Mon but also from most of the northern half of Wales.

'My lord,' said Cynwrig, nodding towards the main track leading down to the palace ruins. 'It seems they may have enjoyed a better passage than we thought.'

Gruffydd looked the way Cynwrig indicated and saw the long-anticipated wagon train from Ireland. A column of mounted Irish mercenaries flanked the six wagons rocking along the uneven track – a strong force but one that was needed in such dangerous times.

'This is a great day, Cynwrig,' said Gruffydd with a smile, 'for today is the first time my family has occupied Aberffraw in many a year.'

Angharad handed Gwenllian and Cadwallon down to Adele, who placed them on a grassy bank at the side of the muddy track.

'I can do it myself,' said Cadwaladr, shunning his mother's offer of help and she watched nervously as her oldest son climbed clumsily from the wagon.

'He is a child of five who thinks he is ten,' said Adele from the bank.

'Indeed,' said Angharad, 'but they need to learn and as long as they are not in danger, then we will suffer the knocks and bruises together.' As if reinforcing his mother's words, Cadwaladr fell from the last rung of the ladder into the mud.

'Cadwaladr.' Angharad sighed. 'You are now all muddy. What will your father think when he sees you?'

'I will think my little boy is already turning into a man,' boomed a voice.

Angharad turned to see her husband slide from his horse.

'Father,' shouted Cadwaladr and escaped his mother's clutches to run to Gruffydd.

The king swung the boy into the air; an action quickly repeated with his other two children as they too joined the father they hadn't seen for many months.

'Whoa!' Gruffydd laughed, entangled within his children's arms. 'I have been captured yet again.' For several minutes he listened to his children's excited chatter until eventually, after a nod from Angharad, Adele relieved him of each child, ably aided by Cynwrig.

'Come,' said Adele, when they were once more upon the floor, 'let's go and explore.'

When the children had left, Gruffydd turned to his long-suffering wife and gave her a warming smile.

'Hello, my love,' he said, 'welcome home.'

For the next hour or so, Gruffydd walked Angharad around the site, explaining what was happening regarding the repairs. The palace had been burned to the ground and though its replacement was only half built, the carpenters had already constructed a temporary house for the royal family. The walls were formed from vertical logs with each joint packed with mud and straw to keep out the sea winds while the roof was thatched and swept down almost to the floor. In comparison to the stone building under construction, their temporary home was quite small yet it still comprised of a small hall for daily life and several bedchambers for the royal family and servants.

'Actually,' said Angharad as she stood in the centre of the hall, 'when I read your letter regarding this place, I had my doubts but now I am here, it's better than I had hoped.'

'And it's only temporary,' said Gruffydd. 'A year from now the new palace will be complete and you will have a home fit for a queen.'

'Will you not build a castle?'

'Castles I have aplenty,' said Gruffydd, 'but this will be our home. Yes, there will be a palisade, but the building itself will be made of stone, with a slate roof. We will have arrow loops at low level but any windows will be on the higher levels and protected by stout shutters. Our home will be as strong as any castle, my love, but should there be a need to use such a place then there are others in Gwynedd that will suit. So no, I will not build a keep here, this place will be a centre of trade, discourse and family.'

'It sounds idyllic,' said Angharad, 'and an ideal place to bring up our four children.'

'Three children,' corrected Gruffydd.

'Four,' said Angharad, 'a springtime baby next year.'

'You are with child again?' gasped Gruffydd.

'I am.' Angharad laughed. 'For it seems that every time you come to visit me in Ireland, you leave more than just a memory.'

'This is wonderful news,' said Gruffydd, 'my kingdom is restored, our palace is being rebuilt and now another child to add to our family.'

'It has been a long time coming, my love,' said Angharad, 'but at least it now seems like we have a future.'

'Indeed we do,' said Gruffydd, 'and one in which we can bring up our family safely.'

'How can you be so sure?' asked Angharad, voicing the fears that had plagued her ever since Gruffydd had become more active in the rebellion. 'Is it not the case that we could be attacked at any minute?'

'It seems not,' said Gruffydd, 'for since the death of William Rufus, there has been a warming in the relations between Wales and England. Henry has a lot on his plate settling into the role of monarch, and has sent representations to all the Welsh kings, myself included, seeking a cessation in hostilities from all parties. Only yesterday his messengers left this place with my agreement and it seems that all the Marcher lords have withdrawn their forces back to their strongholds.'

'What terms does he command?'

'None that I can see as yet.'

'There will be terms, I can assure you that.'

'Of course, but until they are drawn up, the only agreement is that both sides sheath their swords. I have no doubt the terms demanded will benefit the English Crown more than us but by that time we will be in a far better position to negotiate.'

'So it is not yet over?'

'We are in a better position than for many years,' said Gruffydd. 'Anyway, why are we discussing politics before you have even unpacked? Let's get you settled into the house. There has been a deer on the spit since this morning and I have had the kitchen staff fill tubs of hot water to wash the dirt of the road from your beautiful skin. Retire to your room, my love, and I will have the servants bring you what you need.'

'What about the children?'

'Fret not for I have a longing to hear their laughter and once I have done chasing them around the manor, I promise they will be worn out. With a hot meal inside them, I'm sure they'll sleep until dawn, leaving us time to be alone.'

'Then I will take advantage of this respite,' she replied, 'no matter how fleeting, for the journey has taken my strength and it will be good to bathe in hot water.'

Gruffydd kissed his wife on the cheek.

'Go, I will wake you when we are ready to eat.' He watched her disappear through a door in the far wall before leaving the building and striding out to find his children.

'Defend yourself, heathens,' shouted Cynwrig, waving one of the toy swords in the air, 'for I am a hideous ogre and love to eat the children of kings.' With an almighty roar he jumped down from a wall and chased the squealing children around the garden. Adele laughed at their antics, touched to see the children happy again after such a long journey. Gruffydd walked up beside her and she turned to curtsey.

'My lord,' she said in greeting.

'Adele,' said Gruffydd, 'it is good to see you again. I thought you were to stay in Ireland?'

'It was going to be that way, my lord, but alas my husband died several months ago – he fell from his horse. I have no other family so when Lady Angharad invited me along, I was only too happy to accept. That is of course, if you are agreeable.'

'My condolences about your husband, Adele,' he replied, 'and as for whether I am agreeable or not, I think it is one of the best things she has done. She sees you as a friend, rather than a servant and truth be told, I am sometimes quite envious of the trust between you.'

'You underestimate her love for you, my lord,' said Adele, 'and no matter what advice I may give her, she always knows her own mind.'

'And have you ever advised her to leave me?' asked Gruffydd with a twinkle in his eye.

'On many, many occasions, my lord,' said Adele with a wicked smile.

Gruffydd smiled back and looked over at his children.

'They seem happy,' he said.

'They are wonderful children,' said Adele, 'but will benefit from spending time with their father.'

'A father who perhaps needs some lessons in how to play,' said Gruffydd thoughtfully, as he watched Cynwrig pretend to die upon the grass.

'It's not that hard,' said Adele with a smile, 'all you need is one of these.'

Gruffydd looked down at Adele's hand and with a smile he took the toy sword.

'Truly, a weapon fit for a king,' he said, and turning away from the servant, strode out into the garden, holding the wooden sword above his head.

'I am King Gruffydd of Gwynedd,' he roared across the gardens, 'and I have been told there is an ogre to be slain.'

The children squealed in delight as their father joined the fray and as battle ensued, Adele left the games to walk back to the manor.

Early the following morning, Gruffydd walked out of the manor and sat on a bench alongside the stable to watch the sun come up. Inside he could hear the sounds of a horse being prepared and soon a man emerged leading his steed behind him.

'My lord,' said Cynwrig, as the king stood up, 'I am surprised to see you here.'

'I just wanted to say my goodbyes, Cynwrig,' said Gruffydd, 'and to pass on my gratitude for everything you have done for me and my family.'

'Your gratitude is not needed, my lord, for I go forth of my own free will.'

'I know, but there is a home here for you for as long as you need.'

'I appreciate that, my lord but recently my mind has been awash with which path my life should take. Now you are settled in Aberffraw I feel it is time to decide my future. Whether it is here at your side or elsewhere, I don't know but by seeking my own company, I feel the right path will be revealed.'

'Is your heart truly set?'

'It is.'

'Then I will not hold you back.' Gruffydd held out a leather purse. 'Take this,' he said, 'it will make your journey easier.'

'Thank you,' said Cynwrig. 'I will take my leave now but if God is by my side, I will be back within a year.'

'Make sure you are,' said Gruffydd, 'for I saw the way Adele was looking at you over our meal last night and I suspect there were not a few glances returned in similar vein.'

Cynwrig smiled.

'And that is why I must go now,' he said, 'for if matters of the heart were to delay me then I fear I would never go.'

'Be safe, Cynwrig the Tall,' said Gruffydd, as he watched the man who had saved his life ride to an almost certain death.

The following few months were busy ones at Aberffraw as the work on rebuilding the palace continued apace. Angharad grew into her role as queen as her pregnancy advanced and as the pressures of war eased away, the people across North Wales settled down to repair their own homes and concentrate on rebuilding their lives. Winter was surprisingly mild and Gruffydd shared his time between running his affairs at Aberffraw and visiting neighbouring nobles in a never-ending circle of treaties and agreements, each designed to mutually protect every participant from any future aggression from the English.

The frost was still upon the ground when Gruffydd sent a message to all the landowners in Gwynedd asking them to attend him at the hall in Aberffraw. Over the period of two days, more than a hundred nobles turned up, each being housed in the new manor hall or in the temporary village of tents in the palace grounds.

'Honoured guests,' said Gruffydd after the meal had ended, 'first of all, can I again extend my gratitude for your attendance this day. I know you have much to do but thought it only reasonable that I speak to each of you face to face.'

The hall fell quiet as he continued.

'These past few years have been hard for all of us and there is not one man here that has not lost men or property in the fight against the English. I know that all those present strongly resent the fact they are now poorer after the attentions of the Marcher lords but I say this. If every man here had put up the resistance of Cadwgan ap Bleddyn and his sons, then perhaps this war would not have lasted as long as it did.'

A murmur of dissent rippled around the room.

'I feel the wind of annoyance at my words,' said Gruffydd, 'it would seem that perhaps they strike too close to home for comfort.'

'What are you saying?' asked a voice.

'What I am saying,' said Gruffydd, 'is that it is time for truth. I invited you here today as the king of Gwynedd. For many years I have held this station, but during that time I was either incarcerated in an English dungeon or sailing between my home and Ireland, often fighting the invaders with minimal resources. Much of that, as well as many of your own hardships, could have been avoided if we had stuck together.' He looked around the room. 'It pains me to say,' he continued, 'but while most men here focussed on looking after their own interests, some even making private agreements with the English to ease their winters, others were suffering the cold and hunger whilst taking the fight to the enemy. It is those men who should be feted by our minstrels and bards, for their struggles have brought this peace about, not favourable agreements signed behind closed doors.'

'My lord,' said a voice sounding from the rear as a man stood. 'As you are aware, I have already offered you my support and indeed, as Prince Cadwgan can attest, many of my kinsmen died at the siege of Pembroke Castle.'

Prince Cadwgan nodded in acknowledgement of Goronwy's assault.

'However,' continued Goronwy, 'that conflict was on the other side of the country and undertaken under the veil of secrecy. The families of those men live deep in the shadow of the English Marchers and if news of even the slightest transgression fell upon English ears, it would result in an armed force seeking retribution.'

'I understand you face the greater risk,' said Gruffydd, 'and your exploits in Pembroke have not gone unnoticed. However, you are the exception and there are others here who make no contribution to the struggle against the English. That, my friend, has to be addressed.'

'Some of us can barely feed our cantrefs,' called a voice. 'How can we be expected to raise an army?'

'I ask no man to take on an unfair burden,' replied Gruffydd, 'but there are other ways to support those on the front line. A bag of oats would feed a horse for a week; a chicken would feed two men for a day. All I am saying is that in such times, those who take the fight to the enemy should be able to rely on the support of their fellow countrymen.'

'Your comments are noted, my lord,' said Goronwy, 'but with respect, the war is now over, so short of administering a very public admonishment to those of us who live in the gaze of the English, what exactly is your point?'

'My point is this, Lord Goronwy. It is no secret that the English Crown covets our lands and seeks any opportunity to push westward. For many years they have pressed all those along the border, your lands included, and what do we do? We fight amongst ourselves like children while the English pick us off one by one. How many of our men have survived English arrows only to eventually fall at the end of one fired by a Welshman? For too long we have fought each other while the English look on, ready to step in if opportunity beckons. If we had only united under one banner, we could probably have matched them on the field.'

'We can never match the strength of the English army head on,' said Goronwy.

'Not on an open battlefield, perhaps, but there are other things to consider – advantages that bring us to more than their equal.'

'What things?'

'Our landscape for one,' said Gruffydd, 'the mountains and the forests. The grain fields of Ynys Mon and the hidden farms in the countless valleys across the country. Put these alongside our weather and it is a fortress as formidable as any castle.'

'Mountains do not win wars,' said Goronwy.

'No, people do, and that is why I asked you here. I propose to maintain an army big enough to withstand any of the Marcher lords' garrisons should they decide to march westward. This force, upon confirmation, will immediately ride to the aid of any manor needing their help within days. They will be well trained, well horsed and a match for anything the English have.'

'How many?' asked Goronwy.

'The numbers can be agreed but I anticipate about a hundred.'

'A hundred horsemen against ten thousand Englishmen will be as effective as a single fly against a horse.'

'Against the whole English army, I agree,' said Gruffydd, 'but that is not how things are going to happen.'

'How can you be so sure?'

'Because I have agreed terms with Henry.'

The reaction among the men was immediate.

'What terms?' shouted a number of men. 'We knew nothing of this!'

'He has agreed to grant me recognised kingship over the whole of Gwynedd and Meirionnydd. In return, I have assured him that we will withhold any unprovoked attacks on the Marcher lords or any English column going about their business in the south.'

'You had no right to agree terms on our behalf,' shouted another dissenter.

'*I had every right*,' roared Gruffydd. 'For I am king of Gwynedd and saw no other man lifting a finger to sort out this mess.'

He looked around at the shocked men.

'While many of you were asleep in your beds, Cadwgan, Goronwy and I fought the English, often outnumbered and with hunger in our bellies. Our victories were few but what we earned was the enemy's respect and that respect was what I brought to the table with Henry. For the first time in years, we have peace in North Wales and a chance to let our children grow without fear of injury.'

'If that is the case, then why do you want this mobile force?' asked Goronwy.

'Because the Marcher lords, believe it or not, are not legally beholden to promises made to Henry.'

'Not beholden to their king?' asked a voice. 'How can that be?

'Because Henry's father, William the Bastard, gave them freedom of rule along their western borders and it is written into their own laws that the Marcher lords are free to engage the Welsh as they see fit. I asked Henry to repeal that law but he is unable to do so. Therefore, although we are safe from Henry's army, the Marcher lords still present a risk.'

The men in the room talked amongst themselves for a while until finally, Goronwy spoke again.

'Assuming we decide to support you in this venture, what do you want from us?'

'The burden is light,' said Gruffydd. 'Each lord is to supply one man and one horse along with all the supplies needed to sustain them for one year – this agreement to be renewed on an annual basis.'

'What if they are killed?'

'Men often die in the defence of their country,' said Gruffydd, 'that is the nature of things. Ask only for volunteers and ensure they are not wed. I also recommend they are of sound mind and can ride a horse.'

'And this is your plan to defend Wales against the attentions of the English?'

'Not long-term, it has to be said, but it will give us time to rebuild our kingdom whilst free from the attentions of the Marcher lords.'

Conversation broke out amongst the men again as each discussed the merits of the plan. Finally, a man stood and waited for silence before he spoke.

'My lord, you have been a wonderful host and last night's reception was, shall we say, interesting.' Many men laughed at the memory of the ale-fuelled revelries but fell quiet again as the well-respected man continued. 'However, I have business to attend back on my lands and cannot afford to wait around here any longer. You have made your request clear and if we go down the path of examining every minute detail then I fear we will still be here next winter. Therefore, I will pledge my support for this plan and will ensure you have a worthy man, strong and true, before this month is out. Now, if you will forgive me, I will take my leave.'

'Thank you, Lord Green,' said Gruffydd, and the nobleman left the hall.

'As you know, I will match Lord Green's commitments,' said Cadwgan standing up, 'and offer my services as well as four experienced sergeants-in-arms to lead the force.'

'A generous offer,' said Gruffydd, 'and one well received.'

'I will send a man,' shouted another voice.

'As will I,' called another.

Soon, the majority of the lords present had met the commitment and, happy that agreement had been reached, Gruffydd called the assembly to a close, saying his goodbyes as each man left the hall to head back to their own lands. Finally, Gruffydd returned into the hall to find one man remaining.

'Lord Goronwy,' said Gruffydd, picking up an ale jug, 'I did not see a commitment from you?'

'That is because I did not make one,' said Goronwy, 'and cannot until I return to my manor.'

'Why not?' asked Gruffydd.

'I lost a lot of men at Pembroke, my lord,' said Goronwy, 'and it is all I can manage to keep starvation from the doors of the village. One man can make all the difference if we are to enjoy a successful planting.'

'Agreed, but why not pledge the value instead? Surely you have sufficient coin left in your treasury?'

'A little,' said Goronwy, 'but I will have to check with my steward before I can commit to your noble cause.'

'You surprise me, Lord Goronwy,' said Gruffydd, 'for I thought every noble would be abreast of his own financial circumstances.'

'Ordinarily that would indeed be the case,' said Goronwy, 'but these last few years I have had a man in my employ who has a way with money second to none. In his hands it seems to stretch further than you would have thought possible and I now leave all matters of finance to him.'

'He sounds like a valuable asset,' said Gruffydd.

'He is indeed and I am lucky to have found him.'

'Where does he hail from?'

'Funnily enough, he is a Gwynedd man; you may know of him. His name is Meirion Goch.'

Gruffydd's tankard stopped halfway to his mouth and he turned to stare at the noble.

'Do you know of him?' asked Goronwy.

Gruffydd thought furiously. Meirion Goch was the man who had betrayed him to Huw the Fat all those years earlier. Despite many discreet enquiries across the country, Gruffydd had failed to find out his whereabouts. But now he had resurfaced, it was better to feign indifference lest he disappeared again before the king had chance to exact his revenge.

'I think I may have heard the name,' said Gruffydd casually, 'but can't say I know the man. Anyway,' he said quickly, seizing the opportunity to change the subject, 'we digress. I understand your problem, Lord Goronwy, so can I suggest three months' leave to settle your affairs? After that time, perhaps we can meet again.'

'Thank you, my lord,' said Goronwy with a slight bow, 'your understanding is welcome. Until we meet again.'

'Travel safely, Lord Goronwy,' said Gruffydd as he watched the man leave the hall. But though his demeanour was calm, Gruffydd's heart raced within his chest. At last, after twenty years, it seemed that the man responsible for his incarceration was within his reach.

Chester

May 2nd, AD 1101

Cynwrig the Tall walked his horse through the streets of Chester, surprised at the changes that had been made to the town in the last twenty years. New houses had been added and the population had increased beyond the town boundaries. In the distance he could see the walls of Chester Castle, now totally rebuilt in stone, and the flag above the keep told him that the castellan was in residence.

It was a sobering moment, realising Huw the Fat was almost in hailing distance. The earl had ordered the death of Cynwrig's family six years earlier as retribution for his part in Gruffydd's escape and since then, Cynwrig had dreamed of this moment.

The years since his parents, wife and children had been hanged in the market square of their village had been long for Cynwrig, but the pain was just as raw. At first he had berated himself repeatedly, blaming himself for their deaths, and if it hadn't been for Gruffydd and his seconds, he would have sought revenge without thinking and probably died having got nowhere near the earl. However, the advice was to bide his time until his name was naught but a distant memory to Huw the Fat and the opportunities for retribution would thus be easier. Revenge was a dish better served cold.

Since leaving Gwynedd the previous autumn, Cynwrig had travelled the length of Wales, earning his keep as a farmhand before moving on as each job ended. During this time, his thoughts returned to the fate of his family at the hand of Huw the Fat and finally, as winter came to a close he decided the path he needed to take. Decision made, he crossed the border and headed south to the port of Bristol. Once there he had sought out contacts that he had gained years earlier as a trader and though many had already moved on or died, he finally found one man he recognised. Eventually, the man had finished work for the day and after carefully sounding the merchant out, Cynwrig had been supplied with the substance he required, costing him half of the purse given to him by Gruffydd. Once his business had been completed, he headed north once more and finally arrived in Chester.

He headed towards the castle but stopped outside a tavern a few hundred paces from the perimeter wall.

'Good day to you, stranger,' said a man emptying a bucket into the road. 'You are new around here. Can I be of assistance?'

'Yes, I think you can,' said Cynwrig. 'I am looking for a room for a few nights. Do you take travellers?'

'Of course,' said the man, 'and you are in luck. I have a room out the back for a very reasonable rate. It's nothing fancy but it is dry and enjoys the warmth of the fireplace on the other side of the wall. You'll find few better in these parts.'

'It sounds good,' said Cynwrig, 'can I see it?'

'Of course. Follow me.'

Ten minutes later, Cynwrig had stabled his horse and carried his pack into the inn. The room was basic but clean and more than adequate for his purposes. After he had unpacked his few things he made his way through to the public room, already being populated by workers from the local farms.

'Ale?' asked the landlord, Beatty, as Cynwrig entered.

'Aye,' said Cynwrig.

'I will have the serving girl bring it over. Do you want something to eat?'

'What is on offer?'

'Workers' fayre,' said the landlord. 'Simple but honest food. Take a seat and I will have it brought out.'

'Thank you,' said Cynwrig. He sat at a trestle table near the fire. His drink arrived in moments and soon he had a plate of hot pork with onions and turnips along with a pot of gravy made from pork fat and water.

'A feast fit for a king,' said Cynwrig as Beatty placed a hand of dark rye bread alongside his plate.

'Ha, I'm not sure about that,' said Beatty, 'for as a young man I worked in the kitchens of the earl's castle and if his meals are anything to go by, then this is a mere morsel compared to the tables of the rich.'

'Perhaps so, but for a man with a hunger as great as mine, then this meal is as good as any feast.'

'Then I will allow you to enjoy it in peace,' said Beatty. 'If you want more ale, just call out.'

'Thank you, I will,' said Cynwrig as he set about his food. When he was done, he sat back and downed the rest of his ale before holding up his hand to request another. Beatty acknowledged the gesture and after filling two tankards, came across to Cynwrig's table.

'Do you mind if I join you?' asked Beatty.

'Of course not,' said Cynwrig as a serving girl took away his platter.

Beatty placed both tankards on the table and drank deeply of his own before letting out a satisfied belch and looking across at Cynwrig.

'So,' he said, 'you are not from around here?'

'No, I am Powys-born though I used to trade here many years ago as a young man.'

'I would not remember,' said Beatty, 'for I am from Worcester and came here ten years ago.'

'Do you own this tavern?' asked Cynwrig.

'Own?' Beatty laughed with a sneer. 'Of course not. It is a very profitable business and as such, has been sequestered by the earl. All such businesses are soon absorbed into his estate and the tenants paid a pittance to run them on his behalf.'

'Do you talk about Huw D'Avranches?'

'Aye, Huw the Fat,' replied Beatty, 'and a more suitable name no man could ever have. His girth exceeds the width of that barrel and it is said his day consists of little more than counting his income from the taxes he imposes and eating whatever his kitchens place before him.'

'A sad state of affairs,' said Cynwrig.

'Indeed,' replied Beatty and picking up his tankard, he drank it dry before calling out to the serving girl.

'Two more ales over here.'

'I am fine with what I have,' said Cynwrig.

'Nonsense,' said Beatty, 'the night is young and I would enjoy hearing tales from a stranger. Worry not about coin for the ale is free.'

'Surely you will get in trouble for such generosity?'

'The earl will never know,' said Beatty, 'besides, I worry not about any retribution he may bring, for I am not long for this world.'

'Why do you say that?'

'I have an affliction within me,' said Beatty as the serving girl ladled fresh ale into their tankards from a wooden bucket, 'a lump within my chest that grows by the day. The apothecary says he has seen such a thing before and it is a matter of months before it ends my life.'

'Can he not give you potions?'

'He has given me plenty of potions,' said Beatty, 'and a pretty penny they cost too. I have also been bled to within a whisker of my life, yet nothing he has done has any effect. Finally, I told him to stay away for the few pennies I have left will be left to my daughter.'

'You are married?'

'Alas, my wife died, but her sister brings up the child on a farm outside of Chester. I send what I can but it is barely enough to keep her fed. I fear for her future, friend, for when I am gone she will be open to the whims of the world.'

'Does she not have a dowry?'

'A dowry?' Beatty laughed. 'She is the daughter of an old soldier who now drinks himself stupid in a tavern owned by a cruel earl. Who would have a dowry in such circumstances?'

'So how long do you think you've got?' asked Cynwrig.

'That trickster who sold me false hope reckons no more than a month and in this statement, I think he is actually correct.'

'Why?'

'For I already feel the tendrils of the growth creeping around my heart. Few are the days when I can get out of my bed without pain and even then I need to sample the earl's ale to deaden the ache.'

'I don't know what to say,' said Cynwrig.

'There is nothing to say,' said Beatty. 'My life may soon be over, but at least I know that death sharpens his scythe as we speak. Many men do not have the luxury of knowing their days are done.'

'True,' said Cynwrig, and he lifted up his refilled tankard. 'I may not have met you before, Beatty, but allow me to propose a toast. To your past life and the journey ahead.'

'Ha!' Beatty laughed and picked up his tankard. 'My life may not have been so grand but the journey before me will be interesting if nothing else.' He drained his tankard and signalled for more before turning back to Cynwrig.

'So,' he said, 'enough about me, tell me of yourself. You say you are a Welshman yet have come here without fear. Surely you know that Huw the Fat resents your race with a passion?'

'I do, but I am here to conclude some unfinished business.'

'And what business would that be?'

'It will have to stay with me at the moment for to reveal it could cost me my life.'

Beatty took another drink from his tankard but his eyes did not leave those of Cynwrig.

'You have me intrigued,' he said eventually, 'any business that could cause a man to lose his life must sit far past the legalities of our masters.'

'I cannot share it with you,' said Cynwrig, 'except to say it is within the walls of the castle. I aim to stay here a few days and then beg audience with the earl.'

'Ha.' Beatty chuckled. 'Good luck with that. Huw the Fat keeps his doors closed against all petitions these days and grants audience only to the rich and the noble. You my friend, are neither.'

'How do you know?'

'Because,' said Beatty, 'your garb is that of a working man and you eat in a common tavern. If you'd have had money, you would be in the manor with sheepskin as covers and a wench to warm your bed.'

'I have money,' said Cynwrig quietly, 'and may be willing to part with some towards your daughter's dowry. That is, of course, if you are interested in making an agreement.'

For the first time, Beatty put down his tankard.

'Continue,' he said.

'From our discourse so far, I assume you are no great supporter of the earl,' suggested Cynwrig.

'That is no secret,' said Beatty, 'for most men around here hate him with a fiery passion. Mine is as hot as any.'

'Then I have a proposal for you,' said Cynwrig, looking around. 'You say you are not long for this life and fear for the future of your daughter.' He opened the collar of his tunic to show the landlord a leather purse around his neck. 'This purse contains a hundred coins,' he said, 'enough to marry your daughter to a tradesman. If you agree to help me in my quest, it is yours.'

For a few moments there was silence before Beatty answered. 'And if we fail?'

'Then the money will be no good to me for I will lay alongside you in a common grave, but at least your daughter's future will be secure.'

'What do I have to do?' asked Beatty.

'It's very simple,' said Cynwrig, 'I need you to get me into the castle.'

———

'Impossible!' said Beatty when their tankards had been refilled again.

'Didn't you just tell me you once worked in the kitchens there?'

'I did, but that was many years ago.'

'Nevertheless, you know the passages and the weak points.'

'My friend,' said Beatty, 'since I worked there the castle has been rebuilt. Where I once worked behind palisades of timber, they now work behind walls of stone as thick as a horse is long. I have no idea what lies behind the outer walls.'

'But surely there is a way to gain entry? There has to be.'

'There may be,' said Beatty, 'but I will have to seek guidance.'

'From where?'

I know someone who works in the kitchens. He leaves the castle once a month to visit his sister. He usually calls in on his return and shares an ale with me. If anyone knows, then he will.'

'When he is next due?'

'A few days from now, though there is no guarantee he will show.'

'Is he trustworthy?'

'He should be,' said Beatty, 'he is my son!'

Dinefwr Castle

May 16th, AD 1101

In the south of Wales, a widowed queen sat in the lonely hall of her family castle, threading a needle by the light of several candles. A servant sat opposite her, washing the platters they had used for their meal in a wooden tub. A fire burned in the far wall and though Gwladus wasn't destitute, the life of a ruling queen was far in the past. Eventually, she sat back with a sigh and rubbed her eyes.

'My lady, leave that,' said the servant, 'I will do it when I finish these.'

'Nonsense,' said Gwladus, 'the concentration does me good. Besides, the hall will look a bit brighter when this tapestry is finished. I'll get the village carpenter to make a frame and we will place it on the wall above the fire.'

The servant smiled. Gwladus had been doing the tapestry for over a year and though she worked on it almost every night, the hunting scene it was supposed to portray was far from evident.

'Then at least let me thread the needle,' said the servant.

'Thank you, Emma,' said Gwladus. She put the needle to one side before looking around the room, deep in thought.

'Do you remember when these halls were full of life?' She sighed.

'Alas, my lady, I was only a young girl when your husband last graced this place and did not attend such occasions.'

'Of course you were,' said Gwladus, 'how foolish of me. Well, let me describe them to you. First of all, there was always a great roaring fire in that fireplace, not the paltry few embers we have now, and one boy had the task of keeping it banked high at all times. This draughty hall, believe it or not, was always warm, even in winter and there was always something going on. During the day, the ladies of the castle embroidered or painted; well, at least that's what the men thought we did! Mostly we shared stories about the failings of our husbands.'

The servant smiled at the queen's recollection. 'Were there banquets?' she asked.

'Often,' said Gwladus, smiling, 'and we hosted many kings over the years. But my favourite times were when the snow lay heavy on the ground and my husband's men managed to catch a deer or a boar. Often we were snowed in and rather than cut up the carcass in the kitchens, we would spitroast the beast in that very fireplace and sit around the tables listening to the stories of the knights.' She sighed. 'Alas, those days have long gone.'

'Perhaps one day they will return,' said Emma hopefully.

Gwladus just smiled sadly. For a while they chatted but were interrupted when a knock came at the door and Marcus Freeman walked in from the cold.

'My lady,' said Marcus, 'there is a man at the gates asking for audience.'

'What does he want?'

'He said he has business for your ears only and requested I give you this.' He handed over a tiny parcel wrapped in linen.

Gwladus opened the parcel and gazed down at the exquisite necklace within.

'That is beautiful, said Emma with a sigh. 'Perhaps he is a suitor, come to whisk you away to a life of riches.'

Gwladus didn't answer, just stared down at the necklace, fighting the terrible memories that came flooding back.

'My lady, said Emma, 'are you all right?'

The queen was visibly shaken at the sight of the necklace and once again ignored Emma as she looked up at Marcus.

'Did he give a name?' she asked quietly.

'He did, my lady. He said his name was Dylan, a farmer from the west coast.'

Gwladus gasped as her suspicions were confirmed and her hand shot out to steady herself on the back of a chair.

'My lady!' exclaimed Emma. She stepped forward to help support the visibly shocked queen.

'Let him in, Marcus,' said Gwladus eventually, her hands shaking, 'he is welcome at our hearth.'

'As you wish,' said Marcus with a slight bow, and he left the hall.

Emma helped Gwladus to a chair and knelt in front of her, her face filled with concern.

'My lady,' she said, 'what has caused you to feel so? Who is this knave who has such a terrible effect upon you?'

'He is no knave,' said Gwladus, 'on the contrary, twenty years ago, this man saved my life.'

'But if that is so, why do you seem so upset?'

'Because he brings with him memories of an act so heinous, I have banished it from my mind in fear of madness.'

'What act can be so terrible that it has this effect after so long a time?'

Gwladus looked at the girl who had become not just her maid but her closest confidante. For a moment she considered sharing her story but knew she did not have the strength to say the words after so many years of silence.

'It is a terrible tale, Emma,' said the queen, 'and perhaps one day I may share it. But today is not that day. Now, please ensure we make this man as welcome as we can. He once helped me greatly and I consider him a friend.'

'Of course,' said Emma standing up, wondering what had happened to affect her queen so much. 'As long as you are all right.'

'I will be fine,' said the queen, 'now, let us greet our guest properly.'

A few moments later, Marcus escorted a rain-soaked man into the hall, before returning to his duties.

'My lady,' said the man, as he knelt before the queen, 'it has been a long time.'

'Get to your feet, Dylan,' said Gwladus gently, 'you are amongst friends.'

'You will always be my queen,' said Dylan, standing up, 'and the queen of many others in Deheubarth.' He paused and looked around at Emma replacing the bar across the doors. 'Majesty, I have come with news for your ears only and request a private audience.'

'Of course,' said Gwladus, 'and we will talk soon enough, but first come to the fire and warm your bones. Our table may be lean but our hospitality is warm.'

'Thank you, my queen,' said Dylan, and he walked over to the flames.

'Emma, please prepare some food and drink for our guest.'

'Will bread and cheese suffice?' asked Emma.

'That will be fine,' said Dylan. He sat in an offered chair near the fire. For a while he made small talk with the queen as they watched Emma toast the bread. Finally, she served it covered with melted cheese and the two women waited as Dylan enjoyed his humble meal. When he finished, Emma took the platter away and replaced it with a tankard of ale.

'Thank you, Emma,' said Gwladus, 'please give us some privacy. I will call you if required.'

'Of course,' said the girl, and she left the room.

'So,' said Gwladus, turning to Dylan, 'it seems you have come a long way to discuss something you swore would never pass your lips again.'

'Indeed,' said Dylan, 'and I have kept that oath for many years but I have news that needs to be shared with you.

'Then share it, Master Dylan, for my ears hunger for that which makes an old man travel halfway across a kingdom.'

'My lady,' said Dylan. 'A few years ago, I came across the man who committed that hideous crime upon your person. At first I wasn't sure if it was him so asked questions amongst the taverns of Kidwelly and Pembroke and soon found out it was indeed the same man.'

'But why, Master Dylan. What did you hope to achieve?'

'My apologies, my lady, but despite my promise to you, the knowledge of his hideous crime still lays upon me like the heaviest manacles and knowing that he still lived amongst your people with impunity, kept me awake at night. At first it was sadness but that soon grew to anger and if it wasn't for the fact my wife was ailing, I would have taken it upon myself to seek retribution on your behalf.'

'That was a noble thought, but would have been foolish,' said the queen.'

'I realised that and the thought of my wife suffering her last years without me there to protect her, should I have fallen, ultimately stayed my hand. By the time you returned to Dinefwr, he had disappeared once more so I maintained my silence.'

'Do you know where he went?'

'I heard he had travelled north and thought that would be the last I saw of him. Alas, I was wrong and I have found out that the knave returned to Kidwelly a few weeks ago.'

Gwladus's face fell and she turned to stare into the fire. It was as she expected, and the memories of the day she had been raped came flooding to the fore.

'Why would this interest me after all this time?' she asked eventually. 'It happened a long time ago.'

'These were also my thoughts,' said Dylan, 'but I thought you should know the varlet lives not five leagues from this very spot and has a loose tongue.'

'What do you mean?'

'Already there are rumours that he sells his story in return for free ale and though many men turn away from his foul mouth, there are some who listen with interest. Especially when he claims to be the father of your son.'

'*What?*' gasped Gwladus. 'But Tarw was born months earlier.'

'Dates have no meaning for this man,' said Dylan, 'and he alters his tale to say that not only did it happen a year earlier, but you participated willingly in return for coin.'

'But surely no man would believe such a lie.'

'Ordinarily no, but his trick is to carry the Bible and swear an oath upon it that he once lay with you. Oh, he is careful with his words and during his oath does not refer to the question of willingness, but by then the tale is told and there are some that believe his words. Surely we must do something, for this man besmirches your honour.'

'It is not my honour that worries me, Master Dylan,' said Gwladus, 'but the fact that he is claiming to be the father of my son. If this rumour is allowed to continue then when Tarw returns from Ireland, as one day he surely will, his claim to the throne of Deheubarth could be challenged.'

'Then we cannot allow this rogue to spew his lies a moment longer. He must be stopped.'

'Tell me,' she said, 'do you think he will listen to reason?'

'Do you?' responded Dylan. 'The man is a rapist and a brigand. He does whatever he has to do to survive.'

'What about if we paid him to keep his mouth shut?'

'Once he has been fed, he will be back for more. This man is the lowest of the low and will stop at nothing to feed his greed.'

'So how do we go about stopping his bile?' asked Gwladus, already knowing the answer.

'He has to be killed, my lady, there is no other option.'

'You talk of murder,' said Gwladus.

'I talk of justice,' said Dylan, 'a suitable punishment for raping a queen and seeking to undermine a nation. I suggest you assemble a squad of armed men as soon as possible and send them to administer justice on your behalf.'

'No,' replied Gwladus sharply, 'we cannot involve anyone else. You and I are still the only ones who know about his crime and that is the way it must stay. Sending men to kill someone without trial will raise too many questions and the truth may come out. For Tarw's sake, I cannot allow that to happen. Whatever we decide to do, we must do it alone.'

'Then I am at a loss as to what we can do.'

Gwladus thought for a few moments before speaking again.

'Where does he lay his head at night?'

'Alas, he dwells within a nest of vipers but is oft seen amongst the taverns of Kidwelly. He is known for his formidable temper and most step out of his path when he nears.'

'Can he be bettered?'

'By a younger man, perhaps, someone trained at arms. If I thought I could emerge the victor then I would gladly challenge him on your behalf but my bones are now weak and my eyes weaker still.'

'I appreciate your offer,' she said, 'but know not what you can do to help.'

'My lady,' said Dylan, 'the night is yet young, our bellies are full and there is a fire in the hearth. I'm sure that between us, we can think of something before this night is through.'

'Will not your wife be worried for you?' asked Gwladus.

'Alas, she died a while back.'

'I am sorry to hear that, Master Dylan. And what about your farm?'

'It became too much for me to manage. I now live in lodgings near Kidwelly and look after a few pigs to make a living.'

'Will they not need your attention?'

'I have made arrangements, my queen, so have a few days. If there is anything I can do, then my arm is yours.'

'So be it,' said Gwladus. 'Let us scour our minds to see if there is a path to be trod, otherwise I fear the Tewdwr dynasty may come to a sad end.'

For the following few hours, queen and farmer – two people who would never normally have had a conversation – exchanged ideas, as equals, about what they could do to stop the damaging rumours. Finally, they agreed on a plan and though it was dangerous, it was the best they could do.

'That's it, then,' said Gwladus as she stood up to leave. 'I will retire to my bed and then start making the necessary preparations on the morrow. Give me five days from now and then set the plan in motion.' She picked up a bell on the table and rang it gently. 'Emma will make up a bed for you in one of the side chambers and we will speak again in the morning. Good night, Master Dylan, and you have my eternal gratitude for bringing this situation to my attention.'

'There is no pleasure in such a task, my lady,' said Dylan, 'but you will always be my queen.'

Gwladus smiled and left the hall as Emma appeared with an armful of furs.

'There is a spare bed through that far door,' she said, 'will these suffice?'

'They will be fine,' said Dylan, 'just leave them here.'

'If there is nothing else, then I too will retire,' said Emma. 'Have a good night, Master Dylan.'

'Thank you,' said Dylan.

'Oh, there is one more thing,' said Emma turning to face the farmer. 'The queen asked me to return this to you. She said it belongs to your family.'

Dylan looked at the necklace in the servant's hand. With a tight-lipped smile, he picked up the priceless jewellery and held it up to the light of a nearby candle.

'For now,' he said, 'but soon I hope to gift it back to its rightful owner,' and with a grim smile, he placed the necklace into his pocket.

Back in Chester, two weeks had passed before Beatty's son arrived. The resemblance was striking and though Cynwrig had never met the boy before, it was obvious as soon as he entered the tavern.

'Guy,' said Beatty placing a tray of used tankards back on a table as the boy entered the room, 'welcome home.'

'Father,' said Guy, 'I regret the lateness of the hour but alas the river has washed away the bridge and I had to come the way of Longman's ford.'

'I heard about the bridge,' said Beatty, 'but don't fret about things outside your control, you are here now and that is what's important. Do you hunger?'

'No, but my thirst is great.'

'When do you have to be back at the castle?'

'On the morrow.'

'Then take a seat and remove your cloak. I have a barrel freshly brewed and crying out for sampling. This is my friend, Cynwrig. You two get to know each other while I sort out the drinks.'

Guy sat opposite Cynwrig and nodded in greeting.

'Good to meet you, Master Guy,' said Cynwrig, 'your father has told me much about you these past two days.'

'You are staying here at the tavern?'

'I am,' said Cynwrig, 'for I have business to attend; business, I may add, that I hope you will help me bring to fruition.'

'I am intrigued,' said Guy, 'but unless the venture includes preparing a meal then I fear perhaps you may have the wrong man.'

'On the contrary,' said Cynwrig, 'from what your father says, I suspect you will do very well. At least, that is, if you want to become a wealthy man.'

Guy stared at Cynwrig with interest. 'Why do I suspect that whatever it is you have in mind, there may be danger involved?'

'Life is dangerous in general,' said Cynwrig, 'but your father returns with the ale, let us settle into the evening and all will be revealed.'

For the next hour or so the three men relaxed beside the fire, drinking ale and telling stories. As the evening progressed, Cynwrig got to like the young man and felt that he could be trusted. Finally, he leaned forward and spoke in hushed tones.

'So,' he said, 'to business. From the flavour of your conversation I understand you are not loyal to the earl.'

'Loyal,' scoffed Guy. 'On the contrary, my heart is as cold to him as to the wolves in the forest. Indeed, I trust the wolves more.'

'So if I was to offer you a chance to steal something from him, would you be agreeable?'

'It depends,' said Guy.

'On what.'

'How much would be the pay for such a venture for a start?'

'That's easy,' said Cynwrig and he withdrew the leather purse from within his tunic, placing it on the table before them.

'What's that?' asked Guy without losing eye contact.

'Silver coins,' said Cynwrig, 'more than an honest man could earn in half a lifetime. Upon completion of the task, this purse they are yours to do with as you wish, half for you and half for your father.'

Guy glanced at Beatty.

'You are aware of this?'

'I am,' said Beatty, 'and am happy to continue on those terms. However, as you are the one who will carry most of the risk, I am happy to accept one third and only do that so I can provide your sister with a dowry. The rest is yours to set yourself up in business somewhere else, somewhere safe.'

'What about you?' asked Guy.

Beatty glanced at Cynwrig before turning back to his son.

'I will be fine here,' he said.

'Beatty,' said Cynwrig quietly, 'tell him. Your son is a man and needs to know the truth.'

'What are you not telling me?' asked Guy.

Beatty hesitated again before taking a drink from his tankard and looking his son in the eye.

'Guy,' he said, 'I am dying and probably will not see the next full moon.'

Guy sat back in his chair in silence. Over the next few minutes, his father explained about his illness and his worries for the future for both his daughter and Guy. Finally, he too sat back and looked at his son.

'So that's it,' said Beatty. 'As you can see, my part in this carries no risk at all as whatever happens, I will be dead in weeks. You, however, have all your life before you and can turn down this offer with no comeback. You can carry on in the kitchens if you so require but should the task be acceptable to you, then you will be a rich man and your sister's future will be assured.'

Guy looked between Beatty and Cynwrig.

'The prize is indeed a great one,' he said eventually, 'and my heart aches at the thought of losing you, Father. But if it is your time to go to the Lord, and if I accept the challenge, then I could use some of the money for a proper headstone.'

'Worry not about a stone, Guy,' said Beatty, 'for once I am gone I will have no use for such adornments. No, I will rest easier knowing you and your sister have a future. All we need is for you to say yes to the task.'

Guy turned to face Cynwrig.

'You say I have to steal something from the earl?'

'You do.'

'You do realise that the earl's chambers are guarded with many men-at-arms?'

'So I gather, but what I want from him can be accessed from the kitchens.'

'The kitchens are open to many workers,' said Guy, 'what could I possibly steal there that would warrant your purse?'

Cynwrig glanced at Beatty before producing another package, this time a small earthenware bottle. He placed it on the table beside the purse of silver.

'What's that?' asked Guy.

'Hemlock,' said Cynwrig eventually, 'brewed to its most potent form.' He looked up and gazed deep into Guy's eyes. 'What I want you to steal, Guy, is a life. I want you to help me kill Huw the Fat.'

The Dock at Pembroke

May 20th, AD 1101

On the west coast of Wales, another tavern was busy with those men lucky enough to have freedom to drink ale. This one, however, was no place for boys, or those of a weak character. The Dead Dog Tavern was situated near the dock in the town of Pembroke and was nothing more than a drinking den frequented by sailors and thugs. The local sheriff often brought around his men-at-arms to find any brigands rumoured to frequent the tavern, but not before sending a subtle message to the landlord announcing his proposed visit. That way, his job was made easier as only the drunkest were available for arrest and the sheriff usually left with a prisoner or two, along with a nice pocketful of coins and a belly full of meat and ale. It was better that way for even though most of the ruffians escaped the sheriff's reach, at least they were kept to one corner of the dock and did not wander into the taverns of the greater town.

On this night, the tavern was particularly busy for two trading ships had just docked and as always, the sailors had coin to spend and lusts to fulfil. The tavern was full of men hoping to cut a deal or win at games of chance while outside, several women hung around in the gloom, waiting for the custom they knew would inevitably come their way.

Inside, the noise was raucous as men argued and bartered over nothing. Tests of strength broke out between the crews of two ships while other men watched with interest as money changed hands freely. One such man sat quietly in the corner with his cloak still wrapped around him, minding his own business amongst the furore. Yet his eyes were alive, flicking back and forth, seeking the man he had come for.

'Another ale?' asked the landlord, making the stranger jump in alarm.

'No, I am fine,' said Dylan, placing his hand over his tankard.

'I said, *another ale*,' growled the landlord, 'for you have been nursing that one longer than a mother does a baby. This is a business so if you're not drinking, get out. There are many here to take your place.'

Dylan removed his hand from over his tankard.

'Another ale sounds fine,' he said quietly.

'I knew it would,' said the landlord, pouring the ale from a jug. 'That will be another penny. What are you anyway, some sort of priest?'

'Yes,' said Dylan quickly, realising he had been unwittingly given a perfect cover story, 'sort of. I am undergoing training and have come to the port to purchase cloth on behalf of the monks at the cathedral.'

'Well you be careful, priest,' said the landlord, 'for this is no place for meek men. I suggest you drink up and then get lost before the fighting starts. Now, where's that penny?'

Dylan paid the price and sat back into the shadows, trying to make himself look as insignificant as possible. For what seemed an age he sipped on his ale until finally a man entered and walked over to an empty seat at an upturned barrel. Dylan tried not to stare but he had to be certain. For several minutes the newcomer talked to some other men before passing something over the table and standing to leave. As he turned, Dylan saw three vivid scars on the man's face.

Pulling his cloak tighter, Dylan followed the scarred man out of the tavern and through the dark streets towards the town but had not gone more than a few hundred paces before he lost sight of him in the darkness. He quickened his pace but it was no good, his quarry had disappeared. Dejected, he turned to leave, only to find himself face to face with the scarred man, holding a knife level with his face.

'Who are you stranger?' growled the man. 'And why are you following me? Answer with haste or my blade will take your eyes.'

'Please,' gasped Dylan, 'hold your anger, I offer no threat to you; indeed, I come bearing an opportunity to make you a rich man.'

'Keep talking,' said the man.

'Am I correct in saying you are the man known as Merriweather?'

'How do you know my name?' snapped the man, pushing Dylan against the wall.

'Please,' gasped Dylan again, 'listen to me. I was given your name by a rogue in the tavern in Dinefwr a few months ago. I do not know his name but he said only you could help me with a situation I find myself in.'

'What situation?' asked Merriweather.

'I am in possession of certain items of great value,' said Dylan, 'but they do not belong to me.'

'What items?'

'Jewellery, gold coins, that sort of thing. Items that have untold value yet cannot be sold at market without eyebrows being raised and awkward questions being asked.'

'And you want to sell them to me?'

'Perhaps, or I thought you would be able to sell them elsewhere and perhaps take a commission. If, of course, that's the sort of thing you do.'

Merriweather looked around the darkened street and moved in closer.

'Perhaps I do, perhaps I don't. It all depends on who's asking.'

'I am a simple farmer, sir,' said Dylan, 'but my stock died and my crops wither in the fields. I am taxed beyond my means and need money to survive. Selling these valuables are the only way I have to feed my family.'

'What are these valuables exactly?' asked Merriweather, 'and how did they come to be in your possession?'

'They are what's left of a hoard hidden by one of the kings killed at Mynydd Carn. I came across them not far from here hidden in a copse. I didn't know what to do with them so hid them in a safe place until I decided what to do.'

'The battle of the five kings took place over twenty years ago.'

'I know, but I came across it about ten years since. Like I said, my mind was shocked by so much wealth and I am ashamed to say, my greed got the better of me. Over the years I dipped into the hoard until all the pennies were gone. I even spent the silver pennies but I know that if I was to try and trade the jewels it would get me hanged.'

'I don't believe you,' said Merriweather.

'I can prove it,' said Dylan.

'How?'

Dylan reached beneath his tunic and pulled out a leather wrap. He opened the folds and revealed the queen's necklace he had shown to Gwladus days earlier. Merriweather's eyes opened in surprise and he took the necklace from Dylan, holding it up towards the light of the moon.

Dylan held his breath. This was probably the most dangerous part of the plan for if Merriweather recognised the necklace, he may realise it was a trap. He stared at the brigand as the necklace spun in the moonlight.

'It looks, familiar,' said Merriweather, 'perchance I have seen one similar before. Tell me,' he continued, looking up at Dylan, 'what's to stop me sticking you right now and just taking the necklace anyway?'

'Nothing,' said Dylan, 'but if you do, you will never know the location of the rest. There is much more where that came from including about a hundred gold coins. Kill me and they will lay for ever where they are hid, never to be found.'

Merriweather stared at Dylan before placing the necklace within his own tunic.

'Let's just say I am interested,' he said eventually, 'who else knows of this hoard?'

'Just you and me.'

'And you say it is not far from here?'

'If we leave in the morning we can be there by nightfall tomorrow.'

'And what sort of deal do you want?'

'A fair share,' said Dylan. 'I am not a greedy man and know you will incur risk in bartering the jewellery to those who can afford it so all I ask is half of what you get.'

'Half,' sneered Merriweather, his scarred face catching the moonlight. 'Without me that stuff holds no more value than pretty glass. I will give you a third and no more. Agree to that and we have an agreement; any more and I leave right now and the deal is off.'

'But what about my necklace?'

'Call it incurred costs for the benefit of this audience.'

Dylan gulped but hesitated before answering. He knew he had Merriweather interested but to agree too quickly may raise his suspicions.

'The deal is harsh,' he said quietly.

'Take it or leave it,' said Merriweather, 'but make haste for there is a very pretty neck I intend to hang this trinket around before this night is done. One third, no more.'

Dylan made a show of internal anguish before finally agreeing the deal.

'You have me at a disadvantage,' he said eventually, 'for my need is great, I will take a third.'

'Good,' said Merriweather, 'meet me here mid-morning on the morrow but let me warn you, if this is trickery, then your throat will feel my blade before you have time to blink. Understood?'

'Understood,' said Dylan and he watched the brigand disappear into the night.

Chester Castle

May 21st, AD 1101

A few days after he had met Cynwrig for the first time, Guy Beatty sat astride one of two horses pulling a cart towards the palisade. As usual, a tired-looking soldier stepped out to block the path as they neared the gate.

'Hold there,' said the guard, his spear held level in a half-hearted gesture of defiance. 'Who are you and what business are you about?'

'Your eyes are getting old, my friend,' said Guy quietly. 'I have been gone only a few days and yet you do not recognise the source of the extra ale when such things are rationed.'

The soldier approached the cart quickly.

'Keep your voice down,' he hissed, looking around nervously, 'you never know who is listening.'

'Worry not,' said Guy with a quiet laugh, 'I suspect the sergeants are all still drunk in their beds and as for D'Avranches, he doesn't see daylight these days until the sun is already high.'

'That may be the case,' said the soldier, 'but people have a way of finding out such things. Anyway, what are you doing here so early?'

'I have a delivery for the castle on behalf of my father. He suffers an illness and asked me to deliver this cart on his behalf.'

'What goods do you have?' asked the soldier, his neck stretching to peer over the sides.

'Twelve casks of ale and ten sacks of grain.'

'I was expecting no such cart on my watch.'

'No, it was due in a few days. But like I said, my father is ill and won't be able to deliver it himself. As I was due back today I said I would bring it.'

'I should check with the cook,' said the soldier.

'Fine,' said Guy, 'but stand well back for he is a berserker when aroused from his sleep. Trust me, I have been on the receiving end of his wrath more than once.'

'I have heard such things,' said the soldier as he climbed up on the cart wheel to peer at the goods. As Guy had said, there were twelve casks of ale and towards the front, ten sacks of grain stacked on top of the first six barrels.

'If you prefer, I could take them back,' said Guy, 'but that will make me late for the baking and I don't know when my father will be able to bring the ale, such is his illness.'

'No,' decided the soldier, 'go on through, but it will cost you an extra pastry from that oven of yours.'

'Ha, thinking of your belly as usual,' said Guy. 'Leave it to me, my friend, I will leave one in the usual place at sundown.'

The soldier smiled in anticipation and stepped aside as Guy urged the horses forward. Within moments, Guy was in the bailey and after tethering the horses to a hitching rail, climbed aboard the back of the cart to move one cask to one side.

'Hurry,' he said quietly as the hidden passenger looked up at him from beneath the sacks of grain.

Cynwrig jumped down and pulled his cloak about him.

'What now?' he hissed.

'I'll pass the word to the servants in the kitchens and then we will all return here to empty the cart. When we do, pick up a sack and join the back of the group.'

'Won't they realise there is an extra pair of hands?'

'Cynwrig, the world of a kitchen servant consists of beatings and the occasional meal. They have no interest in who works alongside them, for the faces change almost on a daily basis. They are more worried about surviving than checking who is helping them in the dark.'

'So how are you allowed out?'

'I am a master baker,' said Guy, 'and as such enjoy certain privileges. Anyway, enough chatter. Lose yourself in the shadows, I will return shortly.'

———

It was over an hour before Guy returned along with eight other servants, freshly roused from their beds. Voices mumbled quietly as they unloaded the carts and before long, the men split into twos to carry the casks up to the keep. Cynwrig took his chance and stepped into the line behind Guy, lifting a sack of grain onto his shoulder. Moments later he was climbing the steps toward the tower atop the central mound and looked at the ground as he passed the guards on the reinforced door. He followed the rest of the servants into the store room and dropped the sack alongside the others before heading back to the doorway but before he stepped out, Guy grabbed his shoulder and directed him into a side room.

'Wait here,' he hissed, and Cynwrig hid himself behind a crate in a darkened corner.

For the next hour or so the activity increased as the castle's kitchens came alive. Fires were stoked and water placed in giant pots to boil ready for the garrison's meals. The sounds of unsuspecting chickens in their cages filled the air, unaware of the fate about to befall them while two servants dragged a squealing piglet to the butcher's table in another room.

Cynwrig stayed hidden until Guy returned and, taking advantage of the activity, the baker led him through the kitchen to another side room.

'Just do as the others do,' he whispered, leading Cynwrig to a large oaken table.

'This is Bryn,' announced Guy to the two flour-covered women in the room, 'he has been taken on for a few days' work. Show him what to do.'

'I knew nothing of this,' said the older woman.

'You said you wanted help,' replied Guy, 'here it is. Do you want him to stay or not? For there is always plenty of other work that needs doing.'

'No, he can stay,' said the woman and pointed to a pile of iron bread tins. 'Take those to the sluice and wash them out. Make sure they are clean, mind, or you will feel the sharp end of my tongue.'

Cynwrig glanced at Guy before doing what he was told.

'Work hard,' snapped Guy, 'and there may be some cawl for you at midday. But if I have reports of laziness, you will be thrown out quicker than you came in.'

Cynwrig threw Guy a sarcastic smile as the baker left before returning to his task.

Back in Deheubarth, both Dylan and Merriweather had met up as agreed and rode through the afternoon before finally reaching their destination in the early evening. Dylan reined in his horse and stared towards the sea before them.

'So, where is this chapel?' asked Merriweather, seeing no buildings on the cliff edge dropping away from him.

'Down that path, built into the face of the cliff,' replied Dylan.

'Lead the way,' said Merriweather.

Dylan stepped onto the worn path leading down to the rocky beach. Within minutes they turned a corner and saw Saint Govan's Chapel nestling against the rocks.

'Interesting,' said Merriweather, 'is it not used?'

'No. In the past monks used it as a retreat but it was soon forgotten and fell into the state you see before you. Now only birds and goats use it as a shelter.'

'And the treasures are in there?'

'They are. It was the safest place I could think of.'

'A good choice,' said Merriweather. He looked down at the sand at his feet. 'It seems you may be telling the truth for there is no sign of anyone else passing this way recently.'

'Come on,' said Dylan, 'let's get this over with.' He led the way over to the chapel and pushed the door open. Merriweather followed him into the gloom and looked around with interest.

'The roof seems sound,' he said, 'and there is fresh water. This could make a good hideout.'

'It may be remote,' said Dylan, 'but it is still a place of worship. God would frown upon this place being used by brigands.'

'Let me worry about what God thinks,' said Merriweather. 'Now, where are the baubles?'

'Over here,' said Dylan and he made his way into the darkest corner. He lifted a slab and reaching beneath, retrieved a small casket still dirty from the earth.

'Open it,' said Merriweather excitedly.

Dylan lifted the lid and reached in.

'Here it is,' he said and with a sudden movement threw the contents into Merriweather's face.

⌣

At first, Merriweather just took a step backward in shock as his face was covered with a white powder, but he quickly recovered his senses and glared at the farmer now cowering in the furthest shadows.

'*I warned you not to try to fool me*,' roared Merriweather. Drawing his knife, he stepped towards Dylan. He hadn't gone even a few steps when he suddenly stopped and his hands flew to his face in agony.

'*Aaarggh!*' he screamed. 'My eyes! What have you done?'

With his fingers clawing at his face, Merriweather stumbled around the darkened room, falling against the walls as he screamed in agony.

'Water! For the love of God, get me water,' he shouted.

But Dylan just stared in horror. He knew the powder would burn the brigand – that was the whole point – but he wasn't expecting such agony. Silently, he watched as the quicklime burned into Merriweather's eyeballs, dissolving the soft tissue in a maelstrom of unlimited pain.

The brigand found the trickle of water that ran through a hole in the wall and scooped it as fast as he could onto his face, but to no effect – the damage was done. His eyes were dissolving in their sockets.

In desperation, Merriweather stumbled around the room, swinging wildly with his blade while still screaming in agony. Crashing into the door, he realised where he was but rather than running out, he slammed the door into place and turned around to face blindly into the room.

Despite the darkness, the limited light seeping through the narrow window openings meant Dylan could just about see his desperate victim. Blood and mucus ran down Merriweather's face and saliva hung from his frothing mouth as he stared unseeingly into the darkness.

'You may have tricked me, old man,' gasped Merriweather, 'but I swear I'll kill you, eyes or no eyes.'

Staggering forward with both arms outstretched, he started making his way around the wall. Dylan pushed himself further into the alcove but the noise from the movement gave away his position. Merriweather's head spun to face the noise and he moved quickly to ensure he blocked any route to the door behind him.

'There you are,' hissed Merriweather, tightening the grip on his knife. He stepped forward again and Dylan kicked out, making contact with his attacker's knee but despite the roar of pain, the brigand fell forward onto the old man. Even in his wounded state Merriweather was more than a match for Dylan and though he had lost the knife in the fall, his hands reached out to close around the old man's throat.

His grip tightened and despite his struggles, Dylan started to lose consciousness, knowing that this was it, he was dying.

Suddenly, the pressure eased and Dylan opened his eyes to stare up at the surprised look on Merriweather's face. Below his attacker's chin he could see the glint of cold steel, bloodied but still visible in the gloom where a blade had emerged from his throat. Behind Merriweather, Dylan could see the contorted face of Gwladus, still holding the hilt of the knife with both hands and as he watched, Gwladus pulled the knife back out before plunging it immediately between Merriweather's shoulder blades. Even as he fell to the floor, Gwladus repeated the action, driving the blade over and over again into the brigand's corpse. Finally, it seemed that all the strength left her and she broke down, sobbing uncontrollably as she released the shame she had carried since the day Merriweather had raped her twenty years earlier.

⌣

Several hours later, Gwladus and Dylan stood on the cliff above the chapel watching the waves splashing against Merriweather's discarded corpse. They were both quiet as they wrestled with their own demons, but finally, Dylan broke the silence.

'My lady,' he said, 'I'm afraid I do not have your necklace. He must have used it on one of his whores last night.'

'It matters not,' said Gwladus, 'it is a small price to pay.' She turned to look towards the horses several hundred paces away, being looked after by Emma. 'The girl has no knowledge of what happened down there,' she continued, 'and I must ask that this is yet another secret we keep between us.'

'My lips are for ever sealed, my queen,' he replied.

'To the grave?'

'To the grave,' he confirmed.

'One more thing,' said Gwladus, 'never let this become a burden on your soul. Your conscience is clear. It was my hand that took that man's life, not yours.'

'There was no murder carried out this day,' said Dylan, 'but justice. I believe that man to have been responsible for more evil than we will ever know.'

Gwladus nodded silently but still stared down at the disappearing corpse.

'Then it is over,' she said eventually. 'Let us put it from our minds and never again speak of this day. Where does your path lead, Master Dylan?'

'I have no path, my lady,' said Dylan, 'and simply survive from day to day as I wait to join my wife in heaven.'

'Then you must return to Dinefwr with me. There is always a place for an honest and trustworthy man.'

'I'd like that,' said Dylan.

'Then it is agreed,' said Gwladus. 'Come, it is time to go home.'

Chester Castle

May 21st, AD 1101

Cynwrig had been kept busy in the bakery all day and his arms ached from the effort. He was no swordsman, preferring to spend time with the priests and the apothecaries, and subsequently the kneading of the dough drew on muscles rarely used. By the time the morning rush was over, his undershirt was drenched with sweat and the fat women laughed at his obvious discomfort.

'Here,' said one eventually, placing a bowl of broth and a hand of hot bread on one of the cluttered tables. 'You've worked hard and need to keep up your strength.'

'Thanks,' said Cynwrig, sitting on one of the benches, 'I never knew making bread was such hard work.'

'You get used to it,' said the woman, placing a jug of honeyed ale alongside the food. 'Get it down you, there is plenty to do this afternoon. That pig needs to be roasted and I think you are going to be at the spit.'

'At least I get to sit down.'

'You do, but if you think you are hot now, wait until you're near that fire.' The other woman laughed at the crestfallen look on Cynwrig's face.

'Don't you fret,' said the first woman, 'just keep a jug of ale at your side and you'll be fine.'

Cynwrig finished his food, looking up as Guy joined him at the table with his own bowl.

'It looks like you've had a busy morning,' said Guy dipping his bread into the broth.

'Those women know how to work,' whispered Cynwrig. 'I thought we had come here to kill Huw the Fat, not me. When do we make our move?'

'Keep your voice down,' hissed Guy, looking around the kitchen, 'I'm waiting for the right opportunity. D'Avranches is a careful man and to rush it now would invite disaster.'

'What do you propose?'

'The earl loves his food and is fond of roast meat with bread when the day is on the wane.'

'But that is hours away!' said Cynwrig.

'I know, but he has already eaten and until he summons his evening meal there is nothing we can do.'

'What do you mean?'

'Sometimes he favours chicken while other times he chooses pork. Until his platter is decided we cannot administer the poison. Even then it will be difficult as the cook personally prepares the meat and carries it to his room.'

'We can pour it into his wine.'

'That may be easier but it is not poured until the meal is ready.'

'Can we not poison the jug?'

'Others may drink from the same vessel and these people are my friends. No, it has to be directly into his goblet.'

'What do you propose?'

'I'm not sure but if no other opportunity presents itself, I will create a diversion and you see if you can deliver the poison. That's the best we can hope for at the moment, just stay alert and seize whatever opportunity arises.'

'So be it,' said Cynwrig as he finished mopping up the last of the broth from his bowl.

'On your feet, young man,' snapped the old woman coming back to the table, 'there's a pig to roast.'

'Young man,' said Cynwrig getting to his feet, 'it's been a few years since someone called me that.' With a last glance towards Guy, Cynwrig followed the old woman to the fireplace and sat on the stool at one end of the spit.

'Here's your ale,' said the woman, handing him a jug, 'just call out when you need a refill, but don't go getting so drunk that you can't see the beast burning. There's nothing the master hates more than burnt pig.'

For the next few hours, Cynwrig turned the spit, waiting for Guy to come back, his nerves building as he thought of what was to come. Once the meat was cooked he watched the cook set about it with a set of knives. The choicest slices were placed on a platter to one side and Cynwrig's interest increased when he saw how carefully the trays were being set out, realising they were meant for Huw the Fat. A jug of cooled ale from the stone-lined pits in the basement was placed on one of the trays as a well-dressed servant entered the kitchen.

'Is it ready?' asked the newcomer.

'Almost, Master Lewis,' said the cook, addressing D'Avranches' personal manservant, and turning to call out across the kitchen: 'Where's the bread?'

'Coming,' called a familiar voice and Guy appeared with a tray of three loaves. Carefully, the cook inspected and smelled all three before selecting the best and casting his eye over the platters for the last time.

'Right,' he said to the manservant, 'take it up. The rest of you, back to your stations, we've got a hundred men to feed.'

Two kitchen servants picked up the trays and followed Master Lewis out of the kitchen but as the last one ducked out of the doorway, Guy stuck out a foot and tripped him up, sending the bread and wine flying across the floor.

Everyone in the kitchen turned to see the commotion. For a few seconds, Cynwrig was just as shocked as the others but suddenly realised this was the opportunity he and Guy had discussed. Quickly, he retrieved another goblet and while everyone's attention was diverted, poured in the contents of the poison vial.

'What's going on?' roared the cook, waddling over from the far part of the kitchen.

Guy turned to face the intimidating man with a look of horror on his face.

'Master Cook,' he said, 'my apologies, I was in too much haste to return to the ovens. He fell over my feet. Here, let me help.' He crouched to help the dazed servant but the cook lashed out in exasperation.

'Leave him,' he shouted, 'just get me some fresh bread and wine and quick about it.'

'I'll do it myself,' said the manservant in anger, striding to the table to pick up a loaf and without a second thought, accepted the fresh goblet of wine from Cynwrig. The cook arranged the replaced items on the tray and without wasting any more time, sent the three servants on their way.

'Back to work,' he roared, 'and as for you, Master Baker, I'll deal with you later.'

The kitchen returned to normal and Cynwrig returned to the sluices. Within moments, Guy entered and spoke under his breath.

'Did you do it?' he whispered.

'Yes,' replied Cynwrig, 'as soon as he drinks his wine, he'll be dead within moments.'

'Then we have to get you out of here,' said Guy. 'The first thing they will think of is poison and you are the obvious suspect. Finish that rack and make your way outside. Wait in the stables near the gate towers, I can get you through the gate but after that, you're on your own.'

Minutes later Cynwrig was heading for the door when one of the women called after him.

'And where do you think you are going, young man? There's yet plenty of work to do.'

'Latrine,' said Cynwrig, 'all that ale at the spit needs a new home.'

'Then make haste for there are rabbits to gut when you get back.'

Cynwrig left the kitchens and made his way to the door of the keep, passing the guards with no problem. They were more concerned with people getting in than getting out.

———

Huw the Fat sat in his favourite chair by the window, looking out across the bailey and over the palisade toward the distant roofs of Chester town. His manservant entered the room followed by the two kitchen hands bearing the trays of food. They placed the trays on the larger table against the wall before leaving again without acknowledgement.

'My lord, the food is here,' said the manservant.

'Bring it over,' said Huw without taking his eyes from the courtyard.

The servant brought a plate of pork and some bread along with the goblet of wine, placing it on the smaller table alongside the earl.

'Lewis,' said Huw, placing a handful of meat into his mouth, 'who is that man there? I have never seen him before.'

Lewis peered over the Earl's shoulder, watching a stranger cross the bailey and disappearing into the stables.

'I think it is the new servant, my lord. I saw him in the kitchens just a few moments ago.'

'And who hired him?' asked Huw, through a mouthful of pork.

'I would assume the cook,' said Lewis, 'for no one is engaged without his say.'

'Ordinarily yes, but I saw the cook this very morning and he did not say anything about new staff.'

'Perhaps he forgot.'

'Hmm,' acknowledged Huw as he took a bite of the bread. Lewis turned away but was stopped by the earl. 'Even so,' he continued as he swallowed a chunk of meat, 'why is he allowed to wander so freely and what business does he have in the stables?'

'A very good question, my lord,' said Lewis, 'new starters are usually confined to the kitchens for the first few months. Even then they are not allowed to wander the castle at will.'

Huw stared at the back of the retreating man for a few more seconds before turning his attention to the drink on the table. He picked up the goblet and placed it to his lips before pausing and looking up to the servant.

'Do you think he had any access to my meal?'

'Unlikely, my lord. It is usually prepared by the cook himself.'

'"Unlikely" is not a very strong assurance.'

'I cannot guarantee it, my lord. There was a commotion in the kitchens just before we picked up the meal. Some had to be replaced.'

'Why?' asked Huw.

'One of the servants tripped and dropped his tray. We had to get fresh meat and pour fresh wine.'

Huw placed the goblet slowly back down on the table.

'Who poured the wine?' he asked coldly.

'I'm not sure,' stuttered the servant, 'it all happened so quickly.'

Huw's attention turned back to the goblet and picking it up, he handed it over to the servant.

'Here,' he said, 'you drink it.'

'My lord?' started Lewis.

'Drink it,' ordered Huw, 'all of it.'

Nervously, the servant picked up the goblet and after the slightest of pauses, drank the vessel dry.

Silence fell and Huw's eyes narrowed as he stared intently at the servant.

'See,' said Lewis, 'your worries were in vain.'

'I had to be certain,' said Huw. 'Now go and get me fresh wine but oversee it yourself. While you are there, bring me more information on the new servant. I don't like unknown staff within these walls.'

'As you wish, my lord,' said the servant, and he left the room to descend to the kitchens.

<hr />

Over half an hour had passed before Huw grew impatient and summoned the guard outside his door. The day outside had become dark and the lanterns needed lighting.

'Where is that fool Lewis?' he demanded. 'I have a great thirst about me.'

'My lord,' replied the guard, 'I have terrible news. Lewis fell down the stairs and is now dead.'

Huw stared at the guard in shock.

'Do you want me to bring you fresh wine?' asked the guard.

'No,' said Huw, 'I will go myself. Where is Lewis's body now?'

'In the basement.'

Huw struggled to his feet and walked towards the door.

'Show me where he fell,' he said and followed the soldier down the stairs.

'We found him here, my lord,' said the soldier and pointed to where a maid was scrubbing the floor.

'Blood?' asked Huw.

'No, my lord, puke. He was seen to be retching as he descended and then emptied the contents of his stomach onto the stairs before falling.'

'Take me to him.'

They made their way over to the stair leading to the basement and descended the few steps into the candlelit room. A priest was praying over the body and a few of the other servants knelt in prayer beside him.

'Out of the way,' barked Huw. He approached the body. 'Where're his clothes?'

'Over here, my lord,' stuttered one of the girls, indicating a basket. 'I will wash them and have him redressed for his burial.'

Huw picked up the jerkin, noting it was still wet with blood and puke. He lifted it up to his nose and breathed deeply before handing it over to the priest.

'What does that smell of to you?'

The priest sniffed nervously before looking at the earl.

'I'm not sure, my lord, perhaps vermin?'

'Exactly,' said Huw, 'dead mice to be exact. Do you know what that is?'

The priest shook his head.

'Hemlock,' said Huw. 'This man was poisoned by the wine intended for me.' He turned to the guard at his side. 'Lock down the castle, we have an assassin amongst us.'

Throughout the night, guards searched everywhere for Cynwrig and it was only when dawn was breaking when they found his escape route. A message was sent to Huw the Fat and within the hour, he made his way down the steps of the motte and walked across the bailey. On the way he met Alan Beauchamp, the knight who controlled the castle on Huw's behalf.

'So he has escaped,' snapped Huw.

'It would seem so, my lord,' said Beauchamp.

'Show me,' said Huw, following the knight up the slope to the top of the palisade.

'Here,' said the knight, pointing at one of the sharpened logs that made the outer defences. Huw looked over the wall and saw a chain of leather bridles fastened together to make a semblance of a ladder. Down below, the filth-filled moat sent its stench heavenward and Huw stepped back quickly.

'He must have stolen the bridles last night,' said the knight, 'and in the confusion, managed to get up here unseen. After that it was just a case of climbing down and wading through the filth.'

'Very astute of you,' growled Huw. 'Who was on duty up here last night?'

'Those men are being held in one of the halls,' said Beauchamp. 'I expect you want them punished.'

'You expect right,' said Huw. 'I was nearly killed last night and because some of my own men were less than vigilant, the would-be assassin has escaped. Have the sergeant in charge whipped, fifty lashes. The rest of the men to receive twenty-five each.'

'Yes, my lord,' said Beauchamp, and he turned to walk away.

'Wait,' said Huw, 'I haven't finished. I have lain awake for most of the night, fearful for my life. I am now going to my bed and expect no interruptions. Start those punishments immediately and let them know that if I hear even one of them cry out, I will place every one of them on the gallows. Understood?'

'Understood,' said the knight. He watched as Huw made his way back up to the keep. When the earl was out of earshot, he turned to call to one of the guards.

'Sergeant!'

'Yes, my lord?'

'How many men are in detention?'

'Six, my lord.'

'Then bring them out immediately and prepare them for the lash. Make up six gags so their cries are muffled. Let's not give this tyrant any more fuel for his temper than he already has.'

Cynwrig lay perfectly still. For the last twenty hours, he had been in hiding, knowing full well that if he was found, there would be no mercy. He hoped fervently that the bridles he had left hanging over the palisade would be accepted as evidence of his successful escape, as at the last moment, he had scorned the opportunity, choosing instead to stay within the boundaries of the castle. The choice was not one taken lightly but he had overheard someone shouting that the earl's manservant had been poisoned and that could mean only one thing: D'Avranches was still alive.

Cynwrig knew that to stay probably meant certain death but he had set out to avenge the deaths of his family, and having come this far, could not turn back now.

Quickly, he had abandoned his makeshift ladder on the palisade and taking advantage of the confusion, managed to return to the kitchens unseen before hiding in the garderobe. Eventually the commotion died down within the keep and he crept up the stairwell towards Huw's quarters.

The guard was absent due to the demands of the search in and around the stables so hardly believing his luck, Cynwrig crept into the earl's bedchamber and hid himself away. All he needed now was Huw the Fat.

———— ‿ ————

Huw made his way back up the steps of the motte before stopping off in the kitchens.

'My lord,' said the cook, making his way over, 'we were not expecting you.'

'Obviously,' said the earl, watching as all the servants doubled the effort each was putting into their tasks. 'Now you take heed, Master Cook, I am going to my bed but tonight I want a large bowl of fresh potage and a jug of watered wine. Make it yourself and allow no other hands anywhere near it on pain of death.'

'Yes, my lord,' said the cook.

'In addition,' said the earl, 'it seems the assassin was given a position in these kitchens without my approval. I want the name of the person responsible. If you do not furnish me with a name by the time I wake up then I will pick one at random to be punished as an example to all the staff. That could be you, cook, so think well.'

'As you wish, my lord,' said the cook, and he watched the earl make his way to the stairs leading up to his quarters.

———— ‿ ————

Cynwrig's eyes snapped open as he heard the door to the bedroom being opened. Silently he cursed himself for having fallen asleep while waiting. He held his breath, waiting for the shouts that would announce his capture, but all he could hear was the sound of a servant lighting candles around the room.

'Is there anything else?' asked a voice.

Cynwrig almost gasped aloud when he heard the earl answer less than a few paces away from his hiding place.

'No, that will be all.'

'Then I will return to collect your platters when you have finished your meal this evening,' said the unseen voice.

Cynwrig breathed a silent sigh of relief when he heard the servant leave and the door close behind him. Better still was the satisfying turn of a key in a lock as D'Avranches locked himself in, no doubt still concerned about how close he had come to death.

Cynwrig lay in the dusty darkness beneath the earl's bed, waiting for the man he hated more than anything else in life to settle down. He heard the sound of the giant man discarding his clothes and saw some of the garments land on the floor within arm's reach. Finally, the earl sat on the bed and Cynwrig flinched when the frame sagged under D'Avranches's heavy weight, stopping just inches above his face. For the next few minutes, the earl tossed and turned as he tried to get comfortable, before finally settling down to sleep.

Cynwrig waited in the darkness, not quite sure what to do next. If he tried to crawl out from beneath the bed, then the earl would possibly hear him and call for help before any damage could be done. So Cynwrig had to wait until his target was asleep. He didn't have to wait long before the sounds of rhythmic snoring echoed gently around the room, and after waiting a few more minutes to be sure, Cynwrig inched his way from beneath the bed.

Moments later he stood beside the sleeping form of Huw the Fat, and stared down with hatred in his heart. Slowly, he drew the knife secreted in his boot and leaned forward, holding the blade less than an inch above the sleeping man's heart. But just as he lifted the knife, the earl opened his eyes.

Cynwrig froze in fear and for a long moment the two men stared at each other in the candlelight. Huw reacted first, his eyes narrowing and his face contorting with anger.

'Who are you?' he growled. 'And what are you doing in my chamber?'

Before Cynwrig could answer, the earl spied the knife in his hand and threw back the covers. 'Assassin,' he wheezed as he struggled from his bed and Cynwrig knew he had no option but to attack. Without a second thought he launched himself at the obese earl, knocking him backward onto the bed, and though his target was twice his weight, his momentum and strength carried him forward. Huw struggled valiantly, using what was left of his skills from when he was a knight many years earlier but Cynwrig punched him hard in the mouth before placing his blade against his victim's throat.

Huw knew instantly he had been bettered and stopped struggling.

'*Who are you?*' he gasped. 'What do you want?'

Cynwrig didn't answer, but just stared into the cold eyes of the man who had murdered his family.

'If you are naught but an assassin,' continued Huw, 'then get on with it, for it is a lower trade than that of a swine herd and you will be judged before God.'

'I am no assassin,' said Cynwrig, 'I am a mere man who seeks justice for a deed most foul, and you, Earl D'Avranches, take liberties with deciding who will and won't be judged before our Lord.'

'You talk in riddles, stranger,' said Huw, 'but if you don't get off me right now, I swear my torturers will make you scream for a hundred days, begging for death.'

'Death holds no fear for me, D'Avranches,' said Cynwrig, 'and if I am to die, it will not be in your torture chambers.' He used his other hand to pull a vial from his pocket and held it up before the earl. 'Do you see? Even if your soldiers come, it will be this that ends my life, not you.'

'You are the man who tried to poison me,' gasped Huw, 'the one who hid in the stables.'

'The very same,' said Cynwrig, 'and I am here to finish the task.'

With a fierce thrust, Cynwrig's blade cut deep into Huw the Fat's voluminous flesh, sending fountains of blood spurting in all directions.

'Goodbye, D'Avranches,' said Cynwrig quietly, 'I hope you rot in hell.'

Several hours later, life had almost returned to normality in the castle. The whipped soldiers were being attended by an apothecary in their barracks and the usual patrols rode back and forth through the gates after their usual forays into the surrounding towns and villages, keeping control of the population. Guy had his father's cart reloaded with empty ale barrels and rode out of the castle gates to return to the village.

The sun was lowering in the west as the cook finally made his way up the stairs with the earl's food and he knocked several times before opening the door and letting himself in.

The room was quite dark with no candles lit so as he walked towards the table, he didn't see the corpse of the earl at his feet and he tripped over the body, sending the tray and its contents across the chamber floor.

'My lord,' he shouted, seeing the shape in the darkness, 'are you all right?' He crawled to the body and reached out his hand before crying out in horror as it sunk into a pool of sticky blood. 'Oh, sweet Jesus,' he gasped, getting to his feet. He ran quickly to the top of the stairs, calling wildly for the guards.

Within moments, several soldiers came running into the room, one of them carrying a flaming torch.

'I found him like this,' spluttered the cook, 'I swear.'

The soldier with the torch leaned forward and everyone gasped at the pool of blood around the earl's head.

'His throat's been cut,' said the soldier, 'while we were running around the bailey looking for the assassin, he must have been up here all the time.' He looked around at his comrades, all staring in horror at the scene before them. The Earl of Chester was dead at last, murdered in his own quarters.

———

Down in the village, Guy pulled on the reins of the horse team as he reached the rear of the tavern. His father came out to meet him and looked up with concern in his eyes.

'Guy,' he said with relief, 'you have returned.'

His son climbed down from the cart and tied the horses' reins to the hitching rail.

'Well,' said Beatty, 'did you do it?'

Guy shook his head.

'D'Avranches realised his food was poisoned,' he replied, 'and metes out punishment as we speak. I fear it is only a matter of time before our involvement is suspected. We have to get away from here.'

'What about Cynwrig?'

'I don't know where he is,' said Guy. 'It seems like he escaped into the night and is probably back in Wales by now.'

'No,' said Beatty, 'that cannot be. He seemed like an honest man. There's no way he would leave us to face this alone, especially as he hasn't paid us yet.'

'We cannot expect any payment,' said Guy, 'the earl is not dead.'

'Oh, yes, he is,' said a muffled voice and both men turned in shock as one of the barrels was pushed to one side, revealing a hidden man in the centre.

'Cynwrig,' gasped Guy, 'how did you get in there?'

'I have been here since this afternoon,' said Cynwrig, 'hoping someone would be bringing these empty casks for refilling.'

'But I thought you climbed down the palisade last night.'

'I was going to,' said Cynwrig as he climbed down from the cart, 'but I heard that the earl was still alive and such was the confusion amongst the guards, I took the opportunity to sneak back into the keep. In the dark, I managed to get to Huw's bedchamber without being seen. I hid under the bed until earlier and then . . .'

Beatty and Guy stared at the blood-sodden Cynwrig, needing no further explanation.

'Let's just say that my family have been avenged,' said Cynwrig, 'but you are right, you have to get away.' He reached into his jerkin and retrieved the leather purse. 'Here's the money, as promised. Do with it what you will but I suggest you get as far away from here as you can.'

'What about you?' asked Guy.

'As soon as I can get my horse saddled I will ride away with all haste. With luck I can be back amongst the hills of Wales before nightfall.'

'Will we see you again?' asked Beatty.

'I think not,' said Cynwrig. 'I have carried the burden of revenge within me for many years but now it is done, I have a different path to tread.'

'Then fare ye well, my friend,' said Beatty.

'And you,' said Cynwrig, but one last thing 'Do you know of any man in Chester known as Tom the Horse?'

'I do,' said Guy. 'I have shared ale with him on many occasions. He works on a farm not far from here.'

'Can you give him something for me?' asked Cynwrig.

'Of course.'

Cynwrig flicked a gold coin through the air.

'Give him this,' he said, 'and tell him it's for a handful of oats he once gave a starving man. He will understand.' And without another word, Cynwrig turned towards the stable where his horse was waiting.

Windsor Castle

April 7th, AD 1102

Nesta stood at the window of her solar, looking out over the rooftops of Windsor. Her mind was whirling with the events of the past few weeks and though at first she had refused to believe the physicians, her body now confirmed something she had suspected for a long time. She was pregnant with Henry's child.

Her hand crept unconsciously to her belly, as if needing reassurance that this was really happening for though she wasn't averse to the idea, they had been careful to avoid any pregnancy, so as not to cause complications in their relationship. Alas, it now seemed it had all been in vain and though Nesta knew it meant the future was uncertain, deep inside she felt a warm happiness from the knowledge that she was going to be a mother.

She turned away from the window and walked over to sit at the table. All morning she had wondered how to tell the king she was pregnant with his child and had finally decided to send him a confidential letter. She picked up the quill pen and stared at the blank parchment before dipping the point in the ink and starting to write.

An hour or so later, Carla arrived with afternoon refreshments just as Nesta was applying a wax seal to the document.

'Carla,' said Nesta, 'your timing is impeccable. I have just finished a letter for the king. Can you arrange for it to be sent with the next batch of dispatches?'

'Of course, my lady,' said Carla.

'It is for his eyes only,' said Nesta. 'Ensure the messenger relays that information when handing over the document.'

'I will,' said the servant.

'Good,' said Nesta, 'now please sit down. I have some important news to share.'

—— ⌣ ——

Ten days later, Nesta sat embroidering a small tapestry by the light of several candles. Her mood was happy as although Henry had still not replied, the realisation she was going to be a mother became stronger by the day. A knock came at the door and even though she was not expecting anyone, she placed her embroidery to one side and looked over, hoping it was a message from Henry announcing his imminent arrival.

'Come in,' she said, and she smiled as her personal maid entered the room.

'My lady,' said the servant, 'I have just received some worrying news from Westminster. The queen is coming here on the morrow.'

'The queen?' gasped Nesta, getting up from her chair. 'Matilda is coming here?'

'She is, my lady, and I have been instructed to prepare chambers in the main keep.'

'Why is she coming to Windsor?' asked Nesta. 'I don't understand.'

'That's the thing, my lady, she has stated she wants a private audience with you at noon tomorrow.'

Nesta sat back in the chair, staring into the fire.

'I have never spoken a word to the queen,' she said slowly. I know she is aware of me, for it was agreed with Henry but apparently I was never seen as a problem to her. What could possibly bring her to Windsor?'

Carla shook her head.

'I have no idea, my lady,' she said, 'but I wanted to tell you as soon as I found out.'

'Thank you,' said Nesta, 'that will be all.'

'As you wish, my lady,' said Carla and she left Nesta alone in her room.

***

The following morning dragged for the Welsh princess. She had watched from her window as the royal wagon train entered through the upper gate and saw the queen enter the keep on the top of the hill.

Halfway through the morning, Carla arrived to make sure Nesta was dressed appropriately and soon they were walking across the courtyard, Nesta's mind racing as to the reason the queen had come across from London to see her.

'My lady,' said Carla as they paused before the reception hall in the keep, 'I have heard the queen is a dangerous woman. That combined with your temper is a recipe for upset. I beseech thee that whatever her reasons for summoning you here, please make every effort to remain calm.'

'I know of the queen's reputation,' said Nesta, 'and have no reason to cause her upset. Indeed, it is in my interests to make sure our relationship is as amicable as possible.' Her hand crept to her belly again.

Carla turned to the guard on the door. 'Princess Nesta is ready,' she said, 'please announce her.'

'There is no need to be announced,' said the guard dismissively, 'the queen is waiting. Please go in.'

⌣

Nesta stepped through the door and heard it close behind her. In the middle of the room, Matilda sat motionless in an ornately carved chair, waiting patiently for her visitor. Nesta had never seen Matilda close up and was surprised to see she was a lot older than herself and very attractive. At either side of the queen stood two elegantly dressed ladies-in-waiting, staring haughtily at the Welsh princess. A few paces in front of the queen's chair was a hard stool and a simple side table, obviously placed there for Nesta's convenience.

'Majesty,' said Nesta curtseying low, 'you wanted to see me.'

'Indeed,' said the queen getting up from her chair.

Nesta waited nervously as the queen walked over to stand before her. Matilda looked her up and down before walking slowly around her guest, taking in every detail she could about the woman she had never met. Nesta stayed motionless, waiting to be addressed until finally, Matilda returned to her chair and turned to address her ladies-in-waiting.

'Leave us,' she said, and the servants curtsied before leaving the two royal women alone in the room.

'So,' said Matilda coldly, 'you are the seductress who has captured my husband's heart.'

'My lady,' said Nesta, 'I don't understand—'

'Sit down, Princess Nesta,' said Matilda. She sipped on a goblet of honeyed water as she waited for Nesta to make herself as comfortable as possible on the stool.

'Please, join me,' said the queen with a forced smile, indicating another goblet on the table next to Nesta. Nesta did not particularly want to partake in any refreshment, but her throat was dry through nerves and anticipation. Fearing she may not be able to speak, she gratefully acknowledged the offer and picked up the goblet, noting that though it was beautifully carved, it was made from wood and nowhere near the value of the one in Matilda's hand. Someone had obviously gone to great lengths to ensure Nesta was reminded her station was far beneath that of a queen.

'You know full well what I am talking about, Princess Nesta,' continued Matilda, 'for there has been an unspoken agreement between us since before I married Henry. We may not share conversations but as we both know, we share the king's affections.'

'I thought this situation was agreeable to you,' replied Nesta.

'Agreeable? No. A necessary part of my station? Perhaps. The thing is,' she continued, placing her goblet back on a side table, 'I am not stupid enough to believe I can solely command my husband's attentions, especially in the bedchamber, for such is the way of kings. I am fully aware he holds a deep affection for you, but no more so than several other women I could name.'

Nesta slowly lowered her own goblet to the table, the drink still untasted.

'I don't understand,' she said.

'Oh, come on,' said the queen, 'surely you didn't think you were the only one?'

When Nesta didn't answer, the queen let out a short laugh.

'Well, this is indeed a revelation,' she continued. 'Nesta, I'm sorry to be the one to break such news but you are just one of many. Oh, I'm sure you are one of his favourites, after all, you are a very beautiful woman, but still, it was very naïve of you to think a king of England keeps his affections to just two women.'

Nesta stared right through the queen, not knowing what to say.

'Anyway,' continued the queen, 'I digress. The reason I am here is to discuss the bastard child in your womb.'

Nesta gasped in shock. Nobody else knew she was pregnant except Carla, and the servant would never betray her, she was sure of that.

'Oh, don't look so surprised,' said the queen, throwing a rolled parchment on the table. 'Surely you didn't think the king opened his own letters?'

Nesta recognised the document as the one she had sent the king days earlier.

'It was marked personal,' said Nesta quietly, 'and was for his eyes only.'

'No doubt it was,' said Matilda, 'but he is a busy man, and not just in the beds of the court ladies.'

'Why exactly are you here?' snapped Nesta.

'Ah, there it is,' said Matilda, sitting back in the chair, 'the short temper you are apparently famed for.'

'I can assure you this is not a temper, Majesty, just frustration. You have come a long way to speak to me and I would wager it is not just to destroy my love of your husband, for if it is, I can assure you it will not work. Even if these stories are true, I cannot deny my feelings.'

'I was worried you would say that,' said the queen, 'but you are correct, I have not come here for something as trivial as the king's lust. I am here to tell you that you will be leaving Windsor within the month.'

Nesta's eyes narrowed in confusion and she shook her head.

'I don't understand,' she said, 'is the king sending me away?'

'Oh, no,' said Matilda, 'you will leave of your own free will and what is more, before you go you will tell my husband that you no longer love him and never want to see him again.'

'Why would I do that?'

'Nesta,' said Matilda, 'let me be frank with you. You are not the only pregnant one in this room.'

Nesta stared at the queen and her eyes travelled downward toward Matilda's belly.

'I may not show yet,' said Matilda, 'but I can assure you I am also with child. Obviously, the king is delighted, as am I. At least, I was until I found out you too were carrying the king's baby; assuming of course, it is actually his.'

'Of course it is,' snapped Nesta. 'I have lain with no other man.'

'Well, in that case, you can understand my consternation. Both of us will give the king a child in the next few months and if we both have boys, then mine will become heir to the throne while yours will be a minor inconvenience. However, there is a potential problem. If I have a girl and you have a son, then Henry will pay your child far more attention than it deserves and even if I have a male child in the future, by then Henry may have grown far too close to yours, even perhaps favouring him in matters of succession.'

'But any son of mine could never be king.'

'These are troubled times, Nesta, who knows what is possible? Especially as a son of an English king and a Welsh princess could have the potential to unite both countries.'

'Why is that a bad thing?'

'Because it would mean that a future child of mine is denied the throne,' said the queen, 'and that, my pretty little Welsh princess, is never going to happen. So, you must tell the king that you no longer care for him.'

'I don't understand, why not just let me leave?'

'Because if you just disappear, he will come after you. I know he is coming here in a few days so I want you to make him believe you no longer have feelings for him. That way, you will be no more than a mere memory in a few months' time and the route to succession will be clear.'

'And the baby?'

'Henry will find out soon enough but by then, you will be far away and distance has a way of cooling the ardour.'

'I can't do it to him,' said Nesta looking down at the floor.

'You can and you will,' said Matilda. 'For your own sake, and for that of your child.'

Nesta's head snapped upward.

'My child?' she said. 'What do you mean, *my child*?'

'You heard me,' said Matilda, 'like I said, these are troubled times and you live alone here in Windsor, a dangerous place in a time of war between your country and mine. Anything could happen to you. You could fall down the stairs, or be poisoned by bad food. You could even be murdered in your sleep by some unknown assassin loyal to the English throne. The possibilities are endless.'

'Are you threatening me?' gasped Nesta.

'Nesta,' said Matilda, ignoring her question, 'my position as queen puts me in contact with many people. Some are indeed delightful but as you can imagine, some are, shall we say, not so nice and they have access to others who are downright despicable.'

'What is your point?'

'I have a very inquisitive mind, Nesta, and oft listen to tales from the castle guards, men hardened by warfare who have witnessed death and torture in all their forms. I find their tales of slaughter and suffering strangely fascinating. Sick, I know, but that is the way it is. Now, these men have sworn allegiance to the king and by default, me. That means any instruction I give will be carried out without question.'

'The knights of this castle are good men,' replied Nesta, 'and despite their loyalty, even they may baulk at taking the life of a royal without judgement from the king.'

'Perhaps so,' said the queen, 'but like I said earlier, if you were to suffer an unexplained accident, then I would be duty-bound to take Henry's child into our protective custody. After that, who knows what could happen? Of course, I would do all I could to look after the brat but I can't be everywhere and it would be awful if it were to be abducted and end up in some torture chamber or whore house. I hear they pay good coin for children of both sexes these days.'

'*You wouldn't*,' gasped Nesta standing up from her chair. 'What sort of woman threatens an unborn child while carrying her own in her womb?'

'Threatens?' said the queen with a sickly smile. 'I don't recall making a threat. I was just pointing out the horrible possibilities that could befall a mother or child without a chaperone.'

'N-no,' stuttered Nesta, taking a step backward. 'You cannot do this. Henry will never allow it.'

The queen stood up and stared at the distraught princess.

'Ah, Henry,' said the queen. 'I wondered when you would invoke my husband's name. It would be such a shame if he were to hear your assumptions. After all, it is so unfortunate when family members argue. Talking about family, how is your mother these days?'

'My mother,' asked Nesta. 'Why do you mention her?'

'No real reason, it just occurred to me that she lives quite alone, with naught but a few guards to protect her. Even in that quaint castle of yours, it would be such an easy task for brigands to break in and rape her before putting her to the sword. Anyway, let's hope that never happens.' Her smile disappeared and she stared at Nesta with cold eyes and a colder heart. 'Henry will not know of this conversation,' she growled, 'do I make myself clear?'

'Yes,' whispered Nesta, her mind spinning with the shock of the veiled threats.

'Good, then this audience is over. You are dismissed.'

⌣

Three days later, Nesta sat in a chair before her own hearth as Henry stared down at her in shock. They had been talking for an hour and finally she had plucked up the courage to tell him she wanted to break the relationship. From the moment she had left Matilda, there had been no doubt in Nesta's mind about her decision. Though she loved the king, she must protect her child.

'But I don't understand,' he said for the third time, the confusion and devastation clear upon his face. 'What has brought on this change of heart?'

'People change, Henry,' said Nesta, without looking up, 'and sometimes it is better to kill something quickly than let it die a slow and painful death.'

'This is ridiculous,' snapped Henry, 'and I will hear no more of it.' He turned to walk towards the door.

'Wait,' shouted Nesta, standing up to address him.

Henry stopped but did not turn around.

'You want to know the reasons,' said Nesta, 'but I cannot tell you because I don't know them myself. All I know is you hardly ever come here any more and when you do, my heart no longer flutters.' The lie bit at her throat. 'The flame that used to burn so brightly in my heart is a mere ember and if truth be told, I no longer lay awake at night, yearning to hear your horse galloping through the gates.'

Henry turned to face her.

'Is that what this is about?' he asked. 'The fact that matters of court take up so much time.'

'Not just that,' said Nesta, taking a step forward and touching his arm. 'I am still fond of you, Henry, and will always be so, but fondness is not the basis of a relationship, especially with a king. Can't you see I want so much more?'

'Nesta,' replied the king, 'even if we do this, you know I cannot let you go back to Wales. At least not yet.'

'I know,' said Nesta releasing her hold, 'but I hear the rebellion is weakening and hopefully, one day soon, your resolve will weaken enough to let me go home.'

For an age Henry stared at the beautiful woman before reaching out and gently wiping a tear from her cheek.

'Are you sure about this?' he asked softly.

'I am,' she said, her voice cracking under the strain.

Henry lifted her hand and kissed it gently.

'If this is what you truly desire, my love, then despite the blade within my heart, I will honour your wishes. Goodbye, my love. I will not return.'

Without another word he turned and left and as the outside door slammed behind him, Nesta collapsed to the floor to let her tears pour.

Oswestry Castle

May 15th, AD 1102

Lord Goronwy stared down at the charts upon his table, documents he and his officers had been poring over for the last few hours, assessing the strengths of their defences along the border with England. Alongside him stood the man who advised him on all things fiscal, Meirion Goch. Around them were the formidable walls of Oswestry Castle, an intimidating fortress made from the stoutest oak surrounded by deep ditches and a secondary palisade constantly manned by archers, a necessary precaution against the English enemy.

Less than a day's ride away stood the English castle of Hen Domen, another impressive fortress, though this time occupied by a mixture of Flemish and Norman troops under the command of Robert of Belleme, the third earl of Shrewsbury and the nephew of Hugh Montgomery. To have an enemy fortress so close was a constant threat and a permanent reminder of why Goronwy and his command would always stay on constant alert.

'If we petition Prince Cadwgan,' said Goronwy, 'perhaps he could release a unit of cavalry to watch over the southern bridge.

That way we would always have advance notice of any insurgence from Belleme's men.'

'But you already have men-at-arms in the village,' said Meirion Goch. 'Why waste valuable funds when that approach is already covered?'

'Infantry will not last long against any cavalry assault,' said Goronwy, 'and if the bridge falls the road is open to Belleme.'

'With respect, my lord,' replied Meirion, 'unless you put an unaffordable number of horsemen at the bridge, I would suggest that any enemy advance would only be delayed, not stopped.'

'Granted, but at least one or more could gallop here with all haste and give us advance warning.'

'I understand, my lord, but in that case, can I respectfully suggest that you place two horsemen on the ridge above the bridge, tasked only with reporting back should there be any sign of enemy advance. In addition, I would withdraw all infantry with immediate effect to within these walls where their skills will be better used should we come under siege.'

'I cannot leave the town undefended, Meirion. What would become of the people?'

'I would suggest they have a better chance without the men-at-arms.'

'How?'

'Should Belleme decide to advance, and is confronted by our soldiers in the village, surely he will be more inclined to kill the people. If, however, he is allowed peaceful passage, he may well allow them to live.'

'We can't be sure of that.'

'No, but put yourself in his place – if the villagers are allowed to live then he can impose a tithe of supplies for his army.'

'A fair point,' said Goronwy, 'but why do I suspect there is a financial side to your reasoning?'

'My lord, yes, we will save funds by not engaging the cavalry of Cadwgan, but is that not why you engaged me? Warfare is your strength, financial matters are mine. If I can save you a single silver penny with my advice, then that is an extra penny to be spent elsewhere, somewhere it is needed.'

Goronwy looked back down at the table and was about to respond when a knock came upon the door.

'Enter,' called one of the officers.

'My lord,' said the guard as he entered the room, 'there is a rider at the gate seeking an audience.'

'Can't you see we are busy?' replied Goronwy. 'Send him away.'

'My lord, he says he has business to put your way and is willing to pay a fair price.'

At the mention of money, Meirion Goch's head shot up and he stared at the guard. 'Wait, what business does he require?'

'I know not, my lord, he said it is not for the ears of someone like me.'

Meirion looked across at Goronwy. 'Perhaps I should go and speak to this man. It is probably a waste of time but in the circumstances, every coin we can add to our treasury is welcome.'

'Agreed,' said Goronwy and he turned back to the charts on the table as Meirion followed the guard down the steps.

———

A few minutes later he stood in the bailey before a well-built young man wearing a cloak over his chainmail and holding the reins of a pure white horse. The visitor had a shock of curly black hair that hung down past his shoulders and a ruddy complexion that boasted of a life lived in the open air.

'Greetings, stranger,' said Meirion as he approached. 'I understand you have a proposition for the Lord Goronwy.'

'I do,' said the rider, 'but would talk to the lord himself. Is he not here?'

'He is but engaged on other business. I will hear you on his behalf and relay the details back to him.'

'I was instructed to speak to Goronwy himself,' said the rider, 'and to no other.'

'In that case, our business is concluded,' said Meirion. 'Fare ye well.'

'Wait,' said the rider as Meirion turned away. 'This is too important to end in such a manner. Who are you and what is your role?'

'My name is not important but suffice to say I am empowered to make decisions on my lord's behalf. So state your business or leave; I have matters to attend to.'

The rider hesitated but realised he had no choice. 'My name is Osian and I represent my master, Darren ap Morlais, a trader established in Builth.'

'I am aware of Morlais, and have had the opportunity to trade with him in the past. He supplies my master's kitchens with beef, at extortionate prices if I recall correctly.'

'I have no say in the matters of commerce,' said Osian, 'but have been tasked with a far more important role.'

'Which is?'

'A month ago, my men and I were entrusted with escorting a team of drovers and fifty head of cattle to Rhuddlan, there to sell them on behalf of my master. Once done we were to return with all haste and deliver the purse to Morlais. Unfortunately, there was an illness in Rhuddlan and my men fell afoul of the ague.'

Meirion took a small step backward as the man continued.

'Fear not, we are well recovered but our number is cut by over half.'

'Why is this of interest to my master?'

'Because there is a band of brigands hereabouts who have come to hear of our task and seek to relieve us of our master's money. Ordinarily this would not be a concern but we are now only four in number and the purse becomes a burden too great to carry.'

'And why is that?'

'We still have two days to travel to get to Builth yet I fear we will be attacked before we get there.'

'Can you not ride a different direction?'

'We could, but our master's instructions were clear. We were to return no later than the full moon on pain of punishment. It seems he has an important deal to close and needs the coins.'

'Such is often the way of commerce,' said Meirion. 'So, what do you want of me?'

'I request a mounted guard for the next two days, until we can link up with our fellows in Builth. After that we will be safe and your men can return here.'

Meirion nodded sagely as his mind worked furiously.

'And what is in it for me?'

'The good will of my master,' said Osian. 'I will ensure he hears of your aid and he will be in your debt.'

'Good will does not feed my horses, Osian of Builth,' said Meirion, 'for that I need coin. Make me an offer and I will see what we can do, but without such an agreement, I cannot help.'

'But surely, having a trader as important as Morlais as an ally will benefit you in the long term?'

'Perhaps, but times are hard now. Tell me, what is the value of this purse?'

'I am not at liberty to divulge that information.'

'Yet you want me to risk the lives of my men to save it? I would suggest you are not in a position to make such statements.'

Osian thought for a moment before answering.

'We carry five thousand silver pennies,' he said eventually.

Meirion swallowed hard – it was a fortune to be carrying around in a dangerous country. No wonder the man was worried.

'That is a lot of money,' he said, 'surely cattle do not demand such a price?'

'It is also repayment of a debt,' said Osian. 'That is why he sent me and my men as guards.'

Again Meirion thought furiously. This was an opportunity he could not afford to miss.

'I'll tell you what I will do,' he said eventually, 'I will provide ten armed men for two days, the best I have. In return I want a payment of two hundred pennies.'

'Two hundred,' gasped Osian, 'you are a brigand worse than those who roam the forests.'

'No worse than your master,' said Meirion. 'Business is business and I have something you need. Two hundred is the price, take it or leave it.'

'Your price is extortionate,' said Osian, 'but you have me at a disadvantage. Without cavalry, we are dead men.'

'Then the answer is obvious,' said Meirion, 'I suggest you take my offer before the price increases.'

For a few moments, Osian glared at Meirion. But he knew he had no choice.

'Agreed,' he said. 'Ten mounted men for two days.'

'Good,' replied Meirion. 'Name the place and they will be there by dawn.'

'There is a farm an hour's ride west of here at the head of a rocky valley.'

'I know it,' said Meirion.

'We have secured lodgings in their barn and will be moving out at dawn. Have your men meet us there and I will hand over the price to your representative.'

'Agreed,' said Meirion, and he waited as the man mounted his horse. Within moments the sound of the horse riding out across the wooden bridge echoed around the bailey and Meirion watched as the guards closed the giant gates.

'My lord,' said a soldier, 'do you want me to muster ten men ready for the journey?'

'No,' said Meirion eventually, 'summon thirty.'

'But I thought—'

'These are difficult times, my friend,' said Meirion, 'and five thousand pennies is too good a prize to ignore. Assemble the men as soon as you can.'

'You intend to take it all?'

'I do.'

'And what about those four men escorting the money?'

'Alas, they cannot be allowed to return to Builth to tell their tale or our credit will be worth nothing.'

'You talk of murder.'

'I talk of business,' said Meirion, 'it's nothing personal.'

The following morning, three of the riders from Builth were saddling their horses, ready to continue their ride home.

'Any sign of them yet?' asked one.

'Not yet,' said Osian, walking over to check his own horse.

'Do you think they will come?'

'Yes,' said Osian, 'Goronwy's man was keen to earn the price negotiated.'

The last checks were made before all four led their steeds from the barn and into the crisp morning air. No sooner had they cleared the building when the riders stopped and stared at the sight before them.

'Osian,' said a voice, 'well met.'

Osian looked up at the man upon a horse.

'You,' he said, 'I forget your name.'

'That's because I never gave it to you,' said Meirion.

Osian looked around, seeing about thirty riders on the field.

'Why have you brought so many men?' he asked, 'the deal was for ten only. I cannot pay for more.'

'There is no extra charge,' said Meirion, 'in fact, I have had second thoughts about the deal.'

'What do you mean?'

'These are hard times, Master Osian, and money is in short supply. That purse you guard is better off in my hands than yours.'

Osian shook his head as the realisation sunk in.

'No,' he said, 'this coin belongs to Morlais. To take it from me would be an act of brigandry.'

'I prefer to call it a "consequence of war",' replied Meirion.

'Call it what you will but I will not hand over this purse,' growled Osian. He drew his sword.

'I thought you would say that.' Meirion sighed and turned to the man at his side. 'Sergeant, order your archers to cut them down.'

'I wouldn't do that if I was you,' said Osian with a grin.

'And why not?' asked Meirion.

'Because of them,' said Osian, pointing up the hill behind Meirion.

Meirion turned around and stared in astonishment at the line of armed men emerging from the trees.

'Brigands,' gasped Meirion.

'Those men do indeed seek a prize, Master Meirion, though it is not any coinage you or I may possess.'

Meirion turned and stared at Osian.

'I never told you my name,' he said, his eyes narrowing.

'Oh, I know who you are,' said Osian. 'I have known for many weeks. Now, if you want to live, I suggest you ride up the hill and join my men immediately.'

'*Your men?*' gasped Meirion. 'All this was just an elaborate trap to deceive me?'

'No more deceitful than the trap you attempted to set upon me,' said Osian. 'The difference is, we outnumber you ten to one.'

Meirion looked around and knew Osian was correct. There was no way he and his men would survive a fight.'

'What do you want of me?' asked Meirion.

'Me? Nothing. But there is someone else who wants to speak to you. Now get moving or we kill ten of your men.'

'If you do this,' said Meirion, 'Goronwy will hunt you down like a rabid dog.'

'A risk I am willing to take,' said Osian. 'Now, tell your men to discard their weapons or see the air filled with willow.'

Meirion knew there was nothing he could do and turned to face his men.

'Do as he says,' he shouted.

'And your side-arms,' said Osian.

Swords and knives followed before the soldiers were ordered to retreat back down to the barn. Two of Osian's men rode over and escorted Meirion up to the treeline as Osian turned to address the men from the castle.

'You men will march out of this valley on foot. Once you have gone we will leave this place and nobody needs die. If there is any suggestion of trickery, make no mistake I will remove his head and leave it on a spike. Now go, and don't turn back until dark.'

'You will hang for this,' shouted a sergeant. But he backed off when a crossbow bolt embedded itself into a tree trunk at his side.

'You heard him,' shouted the archer from above, 'be gone.'

The soldiers from Oswestry Castle wound their way slowly down the valley. When they were several hundred paces away, each man on the treeline returned to their horses and was soon galloping through the hills to a place of safety. Once the sun was high in the sky, the pace eased and soon the party stopped to water their horses. Meirion scowled as one of the brigands offered him a water skin but accepted it anyway, such was his thirst.

'Listen,' he whispered, after he had drunk his fill, 'if you let me go, I will make you richer than your wildest dreams.'

'No, thank you,' said the guard, retrieving the water skin, 'my master wouldn't like that.'

'So what?' snapped Meirion. 'You will be a rich man and can be hundreds of miles away in days.'

'I'd rather stay poor and honest than rich and treacherous,' said the man.

'Then you are a stupid man,' said Meirion, 'you could live the life of a lord but instead seek the life of a brigand.'

'Brigand?' said the man, his eyes widening with interest. 'Is that what Osian told you?'

Meirion stared at the guard, his own eyes narrowing in confusion.

'Actually, he didn't but I assumed—'

'Then you assumed wrong,' said a strong voice behind him and Meirion spun around to face a man wearing an ornate cloak.

'*You,*' he gasped in dismay.

'Hello, Meirion Goch,' replied Gruffydd ap Cynan. 'It's been a long time.'

The riders were almost halfway back to Ynys Mon when they finally stopped to make camp for the night. Gruffydd was confident they hadn't been followed but still posted a circle of guards to prevent any surprise attack in the night. Soon there were several campfires burning in the darkness and men talked quietly amongst themselves as they huddled around the flames boiling water for the broth that made up the staple diets of men on campaign.

Meirion Goch sat tied to a tree, shivering in the cold when Gruffydd approached and squatted in front of his prisoner.

'What do you want?' spat Meirion. 'For if you expect me to beg for my life then you are sadly mistaken.'

'I don't expect you to beg,' said Gruffydd, taking a bite from a piece of bread he had brought with him. 'I did enough begging from the bottom of that well for both of us. Though little good did it do me.'

'You survived, didn't you? It couldn't have been that bad.'

'Oh trust me, it was,' said Gruffydd.

'Yet still you lived.'

'I did, for though I stayed in that shaft for many years, soaked in my own filth amongst the rotting flesh of those I once called comrades, one thing kept me alive – the thought that I would one day see your scheming face again.'

'You won't get away with this, Gruffydd. King you may be but not even a monarch can murder a noble without inviting retribution. Once word of this gets out Goronwy will petition all the other lords to rise against you.'

'Against me? What possible cause could he have to ride against the house of Gwynedd?'

Meirion stared at Gruffydd, knowing the king was right. At no time did any of the men back in the ambush reveal any colours. The tale that would be carried back to Goronwy would be one of a band of brigands and any effort made by Goronwy to find Meirion would be spent on a fruitless quest. Nobody would suspect a fellow king almost fifty leagues away.

'So you've thought of it all,' said Meirion. 'You must be very proud of yourself.'

'Oh, I am,' said Gruffydd, 'though I haven't quite decided how to get rid of you yet.'

'Just get it over with,' snarled Meirion.

'Don't tempt me, Meirion, for I would like nothing more than to plunge my blade into your black heart right now. But that is too good a death for someone as treacherous as you. I need to think of something more appropriate and I have all the time in the world.'

Two weeks later, Meirion Goch hung in fetters from a wall in the basement of a manor house on Ynys Mon. He had been there for several days and despite his chains, he had been treated fairly well, receiving both food and water in ample amounts.

The situation gave Meirion hope that there was a chance he would still live, for why treat a prisoner so well if you only meant to kill him? It was a waste of rations.

Finally, the door at the top of the stairway opened and he heard two men descending into his temporary prison. The jailer lit torches in the holders on the walls and Meirion squinted to recognise the second person with the jailer.

'Gruffydd,' he said at last, 'you have come in person.'

For a few moments both men stared at each other, but it was Meirion who broke the silence.

'So,' he said, 'what is it to be, Gruffydd, the noose or do you have the mettle to bloody your own hands?'

'Oh, I have no problem sticking you like a pig,' said Gruffydd, 'so don't tempt me.'

'You could let me go,' suggested Meirion.

'And why in God's name would I do that?'

'Because I am far too valuable an asset to ignore.'

'In what way?'

'I know everything there is to know about Goronwy's treasury and with my help, you could get your hands on it without a single drop of blood being spilled. What's more, we could do it in a way so he would never suspect your involvement.'

'Goronwy is penniless,' said Gruffydd, 'and even struggles to pay the men who defend his walls.'

'He thinks he is,' said Meirion Goch, 'but I have secreted away a vast part of his fortune without him knowing.'

'And how did you manage that?'

'By increasing the tax burden on the commoners but only paying the normal amount into Goronwy's treasury. It is amazing how quickly it builds up. Now, after almost ten years the hidden pile is bigger than his total worth.'

'So, you are saying that not only have you tricked the man who has given you food and shelter since you left the employ of Huw the Fat, but you also took the bread from the peoples' mouths, your fellow countrymen who often don't know where the next meal is coming from?'

'Times are hard, Gruffydd, and every man must do what he can to survive. Some farm sheep, others rent out their sword arms. Me, I use my wits and live off the stupidity of others. This is the gift God granted me and who am I to deny him his vision?'

'Don't bring God into this conversation,' growled Gruffydd, 'for I believe your master is no less than Satan himself.'

'No, you're wrong,' said Meirion. 'I was given this ability so I could help others in need, people like yourself.'

'I need nothing that you have to offer,' said Gruffydd.

'Really?' asked Meirion. 'What king does not need a healthy treasury?'

'I need a treasury born of honest taxation, not from denying children the most basic of food.'

'Then you are a weak king,' snarled Meirion, 'and will lose your crown quicker than you regained it. No wonder you were so easy to trick all those years ago – you do not have the sense that God gave you. Stop being a weakling, Gruffydd, and embrace the opportunity I offer. With me at your side you can be a powerful ruler, as was Trahern all those years ago.'

'Trahern is now dead,' said Gruffydd. 'I defeated him at the battle of Mynydd Carn.'

'Defeated by you?' Meirion laughed. 'Whose hand was it that administered the poison on that last night? It wasn't you who killed Trahern, Gruffydd, but me. I am the strong one, and I am the killer of kings.'

Both men fell silent as Meirion's last words sunk in.

'And therein lies the problem,' said Gruffydd eventually. 'You killed Trahern, betrayed me to Huw the Fat and now offer me Lord Goronwy's treasury behind his back. You are more poisonous than any potion, Meirion Goch, and there is no place for you in this world.'

'You count yourself as higher than other men,' snarled Meirion, 'yet are no better than the lowest serf.'

'I have never claimed moral superiority,' said Gruffydd, 'but do what I can to be honourable in all of my actions.'

'Honour,' sneered Meirion, 'you have no understanding of the word. Where was the honour when Rhys ap Tewdwr fell at Brycheniog? Did you not swear after Mynydd Carn to always be there for the man who came to your aid?'

'What has that to do with this?' asked Gruffydd.

'Tewdwr and his men were helpless at Brycheniog, and slaughtered for the want of a hundred men or so from fellow Welshmen.

Where was your honour then, Gruffydd, when the one man responsible for you being alive today needed your help?'

'You know where I was,' growled Gruffydd, 'at the bottom of that stinking hole in Chester, praying to God I would see another day.'

'You think that excuses you? What about your estate, your comrades, your family? They surely knew about your oath and yet they too stayed away. The responsibility rests on your shoulders.'

'There was nothing I could do,' said Gruffydd, 'I did not learn of Tewdwr's fate until I was freed by Cynwrig the Tall.'

'Perhaps not,' said Meirion, 'but the stain on your family's name is still there and will never be forgotten. Unless, of course, you let me live.'

Gruffydd turned to stare at Meirion, his eyes narrowing in mistrust.

'What do you mean?'

'What if I was to give you something worth more than Goronwy's treasury, something which could restore your family's honour?'

'I'm listening,' said Gruffydd.

'What was the one thing Tewdwr wanted more than anything else in this world, the one thing that was to elude him even unto death?'

'Stop this jousting, Meirion, and tell me what it is you have to say, or this conversation is over.'

'His eldest son,' said Meirion, staring deep into the king's eyes. 'Hywel ap Rhys was taken by Caradog when Gwent attacked Deheubarth, and despite every effort from Tewdwr and his allies, no sign of him was ever found.'

'Hywel is probably long dead,' said Gruffydd, 'no man would survive over twenty years in captivity.'

'Why not?' asked Meirion, 'did you not survive twelve years yourself, and if you are to be believed, your conditions were probably far worse than any Tewdwr's son would have endured.'

'I still think it is unlikely.'

'Well, think what you like but I know that he is alive and also where he is being kept.'

'How can you be so sure?'

'Because I have had cause to talk to him on several occasions. If you let me live, I will reveal his whereabouts and you can do whatever it is you have to do to gain his freedom. Imagine that, Gruffydd, the chance to return a long-lost son and heir to the family of the man who was there when you needed him. Surely no man, whether serf or king, ever had a more noble cause.'

'How do I know you are telling the truth?' asked Gruffydd. 'I have already fallen for your vile trickery once and there will not be a second time.'

'If you swear before God that you will let me live should I be proved correct, then I am happy to stay in captivity until such time as you find out for yourself. Of course, these need to be removed,' he glanced down at his manacles, 'but apart from that all I need is your word as a king.'

'And if you speak false?'

'Then you can still have me killed without remorse. There's nothing for you to lose, Gruffydd, except perhaps a few days of your time.'

'I don't know,' said Gruffydd, 'you are as slippery as an eel, Meirion, and the devil himself speaks through you.'

'I see your reluctance,' said Meirion, 'but ask yourself this: what if I speak truly? Isn't the chance to honour Tewdwr's death too good to miss?'

Gruffydd stared at his prisoner for an age while he considered his options. Finally, he took a deep breath and nodded.

'Tell me what you know, Meirion Goch, and I swear before God that if your knowledge proves to be true then I will let you live.'

Meirion looked over at the jailer who nodded silently, acknowledging that he was a witness to the oath.

'So be it, Gruffydd,' said Meirion, 'in that case, listen very carefully.'

The Island of Ynys Mon

March 28th, AD 1103

The last of the snow had already gone and the morning sun was warm upon the skin. Spring was in the air and all around the manor, birdsong filled the air. The manor had been rebuilt in stone, and Gwynedd was slowly returning to normal after so many years of warfare. Even the new English king, Henry, had sent missives of peace to Gruffydd and though there were still tensions between the English throne and Gruffydd, since the death of Huw the Fat, relationships had become far more civilised.

Geoffrey Miller, the stable hand, had come to work at the manor when his father had died during the winter, leaving the fourteen-year-old boy an orphan. Gruffydd had found him curled up in a stable one morning and rather than have him beaten and sent away, had offered him food and a bed space amongst the hay in return for a fair day's work. The offer had been gratefully accepted and Geoffrey had settled down to be a hard worker and a quick learner, soon becoming a valued member of the stable staff.

It was on one warm spring evening when Geoffrey was exercising a lame horse that he looked up to see the lady of the manor running from the house.

'Gwenllian,' shouted Angharad as she ran. 'Where are you?'

When there was no reply, Angharad walked swiftly up to the stable hand.

'Geoffrey,' she said, 'is Gwenllian in the stables?'

'No, my lady,' said the stable boy, 'the last I saw of her she was fighting with Cadwallon.'

'Oh, that girl will be the death of me,' said Angharad as she turned back the way she had come.

'What's the matter?' asked a voice and Angharad turned to see her husband trotting his horse through the courtyard gate.

'Gruffydd,' exclaimed Angharad, 'I wasn't expecting you for another day or so.'

'Hmm, not quite the welcome I was expecting,' said Gruffydd, 'perhaps I should return whence I came and come back in a few days. The welcome may be a bit warmer.'

'I'm sorry,' said Angharad, with a forced smile, 'it's just that Gwenllian has disappeared again, and it looks like she and Cadwallon have been fighting.'

'Fret not, my love,' said Gruffydd with a smile, 'she won't have gone far.'

'I know,' said Angharad running her hand through her hair in frustration, 'but it's like this every day. If she's not fighting her brothers she is off exploring the forests or riding her horse. Yesterday I found her swimming in the river.'

'She is certainly a free spirit,' said Gruffydd.

'Free spirit?' exclaimed Angharad. 'The girl was naked and the boys from the village were spying from the bushes. She is a little girl, Gruffydd, and should be playing with a dolly in front of the hearth, not climbing trees and learning how to fire a bow.'

'You go inside,' said Gruffydd calmly, 'I'll go and see if I can find her.'

Angharad gave her husband her most annoyed glare but turned to go back inside the house, secretly glad he had turned up. Gwenllian was certainly a handful, and though Angharad loved her dearly, her daughter was a daddy's girl, responding to Gruffydd far better than she did her mother.

⌣

As soon as Angharad had gone, Gruffydd turned to the stable hand.

'Geoffrey, gather the rest of the staff and the dogs, it seems we are going on a hunt.'

'Again?' Geoffrey laughed.

'It seems so,' said Gruffydd, 'and hopefully this time we can find her before it gets dark.'

'As you wish, my lord,' said the stable hand. As he walked away, Gruffydd's youngest son came around the corner of the house, his nose swollen and signs of blood upon his jerkin.

'Cadwallon,' said Gruffydd, 'have you seen your sister?'

'She's in the back paddock,' snapped the boy as he brushed past his father without acknowledging it was the first time he had seen him in over a week.

'What happened to your face?' called Gruffydd.

'I fell over,' shouted Cadwallon as he disappeared into the house.

Gruffydd gave Geoffrey a knowing smile.

'Don't bother with the search party,' he said, 'it seems she is safe.'

'And in fine form,' suggested Geoffrey.

'Indeed.' Gruffydd sighed, staring after his injured son. 'The truth is, I'm not sure if I am happy she is so independent, or worried that she often betters her brothers in matters of conflict.'

'I'll stable your horse,' said Geoffrey, and he took the reins from the king.

Gruffydd walked around the manor house and over to the rear paddock, expecting to see his daughter sitting in her favourite place. But he was surprised to find the bench beneath the oak empty. For a few seconds he looked around in concern but soon relaxed when he saw his daughter in the distance, riding a pony around the perimeter of the field at full gallop, her waist-length blonde hair billowing out behind her, matching the mane of the golden horse beneath.

Gruffydd watched as she circled the field, waiting until she turned to return past the oak and he waved as she approached, indicating for her to stop.

'Father,' said Gwenllian breathlessly as the horse stopped alongside him.

'My task proved easier than I thought,' said Gruffydd, 'so I made all haste to return to the place I am happiest.'

Gwenllian slipped from the horse to run over to her father. Gruffydd knelt and embraced his daughter but breathed a deep sigh of disappointment as he looked at her horse over her shoulder.

'Gwenllian,' he said, 'what have I told you about riding bareback?'

'I know,' said Gwenllian, her voice lowering at her father's admonishment, 'but it wasn't planned as such. I came out here to sit on the bench and Honey just came over to see me. It was as if she was asking me to ride her so I did.'

'And what about Cadwallon?' he asked. 'Do you know anything about what happened to his face?'

'He fell over?' suggested Gwenllian.

'If you say so,' said Gruffydd. He didn't press for more detail. The one thing he loved above anything else about all his children was the way they each stuck up for each other and never betrayed their siblings to their parents, no matter who was at fault. Gruffydd secretly hoped that the loyalty displayed at this early age would remain as strong throughout their lives.

'Come,' he said, 'let Honey go back out to pasture. Your mother is looking for you and is annoyed you have disappeared yet again.'

'What does she want?' asked Gwenllian. 'For if it is yet another bath I swear I will run away right now and never come back.'

'No, I suspect it is something less traumatic.' Gruffydd laughed. 'Like the evening meal.'

'Oh,' said Gwenllian. 'I am rather hungry.'

'Good,' said Gruffydd, 'but let me give you some fatherly advice. Unless you want your mother and Adele to scrub you with horsehair, I suggest you wash that mud off your face before you approach their table.'

Gwenllian, flashed her father a beautiful smile, and ran to the nearby horse trough to wash the grime from her face.

Gruffydd waited as she carried out the task and contemplated what the future may hold for his daughter. Even at six years old she was beautiful beyond compare. She could better any boy her own age in a fist fight and only suffered the boring embroidery lessons from her mother on the promise that the afternoons could be spent learning the arts of swords and bows with her brothers.

Despite Gwenllian's age, the king had already received many expressions of interest regarding marriage when she came of age. But each messenger was sent packing with the threat of a beating should they ever broach the subject again.

'What am I to do with you, my girl?' Gruffydd sighed to himself as she wiped her face on the hem of her dress.

As if she had heard him, Gwenllian threw him another glorious smile before skipping across to take his hand.

'Ready to eat?' he asked.

'Yes,' she said, 'can I have a tankard of ale?'

'You're pushing your luck now, girl!' Gruffydd laughed and swept her up into his arms.

Later that evening, Gruffydd and Angharad sat at the window, looking out at the lightning bolts illuminating the night sky. The four children were abed and Adele had retired for the evening.

'I'm glad you are back,' said Angharad across the table.

'Me too,' said Gruffydd, sipping on his warmed wine, 'though I have to admit, it may not be for as long as you may like.'

Angharad sat back in her chair, a look of controlled anger on her face.

'Gruffydd,' she said, 'it seems you are away more than you are at home these days. The children grow up in your absence and need the steady hand of their father.'

'I know,' said Gruffydd, 'but the demands of kingship are great. No matter what I do, there is always another pressing matter to attend. Surely you accept this?'

'I do,' said Angharad, 'but why do you have to travel away so much? Surely those with issues that need your attention can come here. After all, you are only one man.'

'I agree,' said Gruffydd, 'and after this next task I swear I will try to stay at Aberffraw much more than I have recently.'

'I hope so.' Angharad sighed. 'We have been through so much these past few years, it is not unthinkable to imagine we could spend some time together.'

'And we will, my love,' said Gruffydd.

Angharad sipped on her own wine before continuing.

'So,' she said, 'where do your responsibilities take you this time?'

Gruffydd stared at his wife before putting down his goblet.

'My love,' he said, 'I'm afraid I cannot share the task, too much is at stake.'

'You said that last time,' said Angharad. 'What is so important that you cannot share it with your wife? Do you not trust me?'

'Of course I do, and I promise that this will be the last time, but there is something I must do that must remain in the strictest secrecy.'

'And you think I will tell someone?'

'Of course not, but if you should slip up and someone over-hears you, lives could be at risk.'

Angharad placed her goblet on the table between them.

'Then tell me this,' she said, 'is there killing involved?'

'If everything goes to plan,' said Gruffydd, 'then hopefully no one will be hurt. But that is why it must remain a secret. Besides, you would only worry if you knew. Just be gratified that it is a noble task I set before myself and if I am successful, then you will be very proud.'

'When are you going?'

'In a month or so. It will take that time to make the necessary preparations.'

Angharad stood up and started to walk across the room.

'Where are you going?' he asked.

'To my bedchamber,' she said.

'But the night is yet young.'

'Indeed it is, but if you are going away again so soon, we need to make every moment we have together count. Coming?'

Gruffydd recognised the wicked smile and stood up to take her outstretched hand.

'Of course,' he said and followed his wife to her bed.

Dinefwr Castle

April 22nd, AD 1105

In Deheubarth, life had improved for Gwladus ferch Rhiwallon. In the five years since she had killed Merriweather, the people of Dinefwr had repaired the main structure of the castle overlooking the valley and those local lords who had been loyal to her husband had paid her a combined allowance large enough to maintain a respectable household. In addition, although the manor house at Carew was in disrepair, the lands were quite extensive and she retained ownership of all the estate. She was as comfortable as could be expected in the circumstances, but her heart was still heavy and it was on stormy nights such as the one currently raging outside the castle walls when the memories hurt the most.

Her husband was long dead and though she missed him terribly, it was the absence of her children that still caused her heart to ache. Hywel was still missing, Tarw was growing into a fine young man in Ireland and Nesta, well she hadn't heard from her daughter in several years and she could only assume she had at last settled down at the royal court.

The storm was easing when someone knocked loudly on the doors of the main hall. Gwladus looked over to Emma, who was sitting in a chair before the fireplace darning a blanket.

'I wonder who that could be at this hour?' said Gwladus, standing up from her own chair.

'It always makes me nervous when people call during the hours of darkness,' said Emma, standing up and retrieving an oil lamp from the table. 'I'll go and see.' She approached the door and called out loudly. 'Who is there?'

'Marcus Freeman,' replied a voice. 'I need to speak to the queen.'

Emma glanced over at Gwladus who nodded her agreement. The servant slid back the two large bolts and stood back as the castle steward walked into the heat of the hall.

'Here,' said Emma, 'let me take your cloak.'

The ex-soldier handed over the sodden garment and walked over to face the queen.

'Majesty,' he said, with a slight nod of the head, 'please accept my apologies for the lateness of the hour.'

'You are always welcome, Marcus Freeman,' said Gwladus with a smile. 'Come closer to the fire and dry your clothes.'

Marcus did as he was told and for a few minutes, exchanged pleasantries with the queen.

'So,' said the queen eventually, as Emma handed over a tankard of warmed ale, 'what makes you knock on these doors so late at night?'

'My lady,' said Marcus, 'I have ridden all day to bring you grave news. There is an English army encamped beneath the castle walls at Carmarthen and it seems they intend to make their way south towards Kidwelly.'

'An English column?' said Gwladus, her brow lowering with concern. 'Why wasn't I made aware of this before? Surely the king of Powys would have sent word of any such force coming through his lands?'

'It seems they did not come from the east, my lady,' said Marcus, 'but landed a great fleet at Pembroke to reinforce the garrison. Within days they had marched inland and stopped at Carmarthen to reinforce the castle.'

'Why have they done that?' asked Gwladus. 'Do you think there is going to be a campaign in Deheubarth?'

'I think not,' said Marcus, 'for in truth we offer little threat and would fall before them should they decide to wage war against those of us who are left. However, I made enquiries before I left Carmarthen and the rumour is that King Henry has ordered that a fortress be built at Kidwelly as soon as possible to guard the coastal routes to Pembroke. It looks like he has selected a location near the Gwendraeth river and the column may be intended to protect the builders from any uprising during construction.'

Gwladus sat back down in her chair and stared into the fire.

'Another English castle within a day's ride of Dinefwr,' she said quietly, 'it seems we will soon be surrounded by such things.'

'My lady,' said Marcus, 'there is more. I also heard that whilst the main army will be headed for Kidwelly, a smaller column has already set out with Dinefwr as its destination.'

Gwladus' head turned quickly at the news.

'Here?' she gasped. 'What possible reason could they have to come to Dinefwr?'

'I know not, my lady.'

'But we offer no threat?'

'You and I know that,' said Marcus, 'but perhaps they need to see for themselves. After all, you are still a Welsh queen and as such could provide a rallying call to any potential rebellion.'

'My days of warfare are behind me, Marcus. All I want now is to rule what is left in Dinefwr in peace.'

'I understand,' said Marcus, 'and if I had an army of note I would ride out to block their path but alas, those days are also far behind me.'

'Fret not, Marcus.' Gwladus sighed. 'For in truth there is little we can do. Let them come and just hope that their purpose is peaceful. When do you think they will be here?'

'They travel slowly,' said Marcus, 'and I passed their overnight camp a few hours ago. I reckon they will be here by midday tomorrow.'

'At least that gives us some time,' said Gwladus. 'Have the garrison stand to and ensure our stores are as full as they can be.'

'You intend to close the gates against them?'

'I do,' said Gwladus. 'Once we have established that they come in peace then I will gladly welcome them as guests but until we know that is their intention, then I see no reason to offer them Dinefwr on a platter. If they want to take this castle by force then they will have to fight their way in. We may be light on numbers, Marcus, but the defences are sound and the men are stout of heart. Lock it down, my friend; remind us of how it used to be.'

For what was left of the night the castle was a hive of activity. All stocks of arrows were drawn from the armoury and located around the battlements while barrel after barrel of water was brought from the river and used to top up the cisterns within the castle walls. Riders were sent out to the local farms and despite the pouring rain, by mid-morning the following day the castle stores had been enhanced by dozens of chickens, several pigs as well as a small herd of sheep and several barrels of dried fish. Finally, any civilians who wanted to seek the protection of the castle were welcomed through the gates and by the time the English column appeared on the horizon, the drawbridge was up, the portcullises down and every man stood on the battlements, their hearts racing with anticipation.

‘Here they come,’ said Marcus, wiping the rain from his face. Gwladus stepped up alongside him and watched the riders approach as she pulled her own hood closer about her.

‘Marcus,’ she said as the four riders approached, ‘look at the two standards, they’re not the same.’

Marcus stared at the flags carried by two of the riders. The first was red in colour, emblazoned with two golden lions, one above the other, each with a raised paw. Marcus immediately recognised it as the flag of King Henry, adopted from the colours of William the Conqueror. But the other standard made the steward look at his queen in confusion.

‘A single golden lion, rampant on a field of blood,’ she said quietly. She turned to face Marcus. ‘I don’t understand,’ she said, ‘why are they carrying the colours of Deheubarth?’

‘I don’t know,’ said Marcus, ‘but take care, my queen, it could be a trick to make you open the gates.’

‘Well, we are about to find out,’ replied Gwladus as she looked down from the battlements at the cloaked riders come to a stop, their progress halted by a stake-filled moat.

‘Who goes there?’ shouted Marcus. ‘State your names and your business.’

One of the riders rode forward and removed his hood. He looked up through the pouring rain, his head protected by a chain-mail coif.

‘My name is Godwin of Bristol,’ said the messenger, ‘and I am here on behalf of Gerald of Windsor, Lord of Pembroke by Henry’s grace.’

'And what is it that the great Gerald wants of us,' asked Marcus, 'that needs the support of a strong army?'

The messenger glanced back towards the column on the far side of the river.

'The soldiers are there as escort only,' said the messenger, 'and as you can see they have held back so as not to offer concern.'

'Then what is your business?'

'My master embarks on a building programme,' said the messenger. 'You have probably heard that there is to be a castle built on the banks of the river in Kidwelly. But in the meantime, he seeks shelter for his lady from the ravages of the Welsh weather.'

'But why seek shelter here? I understand Pembroke Castle is far better suited to the life of a lady.'

'My mistress has expressed a preference to visit this castle,' said the messenger.

'What is your lady's name?' asked Gwladus, stepping closer to the perimeter wall.

'Alas, I am not at liberty to say, for if your hospitality is denied us, then it is better for all if it was never known she was here. If you let us in, perhaps we can discuss this in more comfortable circumstances.'

'What do you think?' asked Gwladus, turning to Marcus.

'It could be a trick,' he said, 'just to get inside the castle.'

'Yet the army holds off,' said the queen. 'What possible problem could four men cause us?'

'Very little, I suppose but this situation is so strange, my hackles are raised with fear of treachery.'

'Sometimes we have to take a risk,' said Gwladus, 'and I would see no lady taking shelter under a tent in these conditions. Allow them in, Marcus, for if they tell the truth then bloodshed is easily avoided. I will receive them in the hall.'

'As you wish,' said Marcus. As Gwladus returned to the main building, he had the drawbridge lowered.

———— ‿ ————

Several minutes later the visitors' horses had been led away and the riders walked out of the pouring rain into the warm hall.

'Please remove your cloaks,' said Gwladus, 'and I will have warm food provided, unless of course you want to get back to bring your master's lady as soon as possible.'

'I don't think that will be necessary,' said the first messenger.

'Why not?'

'Because,' said the second person, removing her hood, 'I am already here.'

Gwladus stared in shock and her hand flew to her mouth in astonishment as she recognised the beautiful young woman beneath the cape.

'I don't believe it,' gasped Gwladus, 'can it be true?'

'Indeed it is,' said Nesta with a wide smile. 'I've come home.'

Gwladus threw herself into her daughter's arms, sobbing with happiness and relief. For an age, both women held each other until finally, Gwladus released her embrace and stood back at arm's length.

'Nesta,' she said, 'I wasn't expecting you. You look so well. Why didn't you let me know you were coming and what is all this about you being married to Gerald of Windsor?'

'I am not married to Gerald, mother, at least not yet. I know you have a multitude of questions and I will answer every one but for now, do you mind if we just send for my wagon and my servants?'

'Of course,' said Gwladus and she turned to the man who had accompanied Nesta to the castle.

'Sir Godwin,' said Gwladus, 'may I thank you from the bottom of my heart for bringing my daughter home.'

'The doing was not mine, my lady, for as I explained, my master is engaged on the business of castle building in Kidwelly and the lady Nesta asked to be brought here as soon as possible. Now we know she is safe and will be well looked after, the rest of the column can join Gerald at the river Gwendraeth.'

'Oh, she will be more than well looked after,' said Gwladus smiling at her daughter. 'Have her things sent over and leave the rest to me.'

'As you wish,' said Godwin, and he turned to say his goodbyes to Nesta.

'I shall pass news of this to Sir Gerald,' he said, 'and I'm sure he will pay a visit shortly. In the meantime, fare ye well, my lady.'

'Thank you, Sir Godwin,' said Nesta, 'travel safely.'

When he had gone, Gwladus called Emma and instructed her to prepare a guest room for her daughter.

'You need to get out of those wet clothes,' said Gwladus. 'Unfortunately, my dresses are far too big and would not do you justice. I know that Emma has a nice dress you could borrow, unless of course you think that would be beneath you?'

'Of course not.' Nesta laughed. 'And besides, my cart will be here soon enough. Let me go and change and then we can talk.'

'I'd like that,' said Gwladus quietly as Nesta followed Emma out of the hall.

'Well,' said Marcus, from the doorway, 'that was unexpected.'

'It was,' said Gwladus, 'and I have a thousand questions.'

'I wager you do,' said Marcus, 'one of which has to be, how come she is betrothed to an English lord who has waged war across Deheubarth for so many years?'

'I'm just as intrigued as you, Marcus,' said Gwladus as she turned to face him, 'the last time I saw her, I thought she was destined to marry a prince.'

⌣

Half an hour later, Nesta was talking to Emma in the hall when Marcus put his head around the door and announced that her cart had arrived. Nesta grinned wildly and turned to her mother.

'Come,' she said, 'there is someone I want you to meet.'

Both women stepped out into the bailey and walked over to the cart. The man in charge of the horse team had already descended and walked around to help a woman down from the back of the covered cart.

'Mother, this is Tom,' said Nesta as she approached, 'and he is the groom in charge of my horses.'

'My lady,' acknowledged Tom with a nod of his head.

'And this is Jayne,' said Nesta, waiting as the servant turned and curtsied.

'And I assume you are Nesta's maid?' queried Gwladus as Nesta reached past Jayne to retrieve something from the cart.

'Oh no, my lady,' said Jayne, 'I am a mere nurse maid.'

Gwladus stared at the servant for a few seconds, struggling to take in the implications but finally turned when Nesta gently called her name.

'Mother,' said her daughter holding a three-year-old toddler in her arms, 'meet Henry Fitzroy, son of the king.'

'I don't understand,' said Gwladus, confusion written all over her face, 'why do you have the king's son here?'

'Because I am his mother,' said Nesta with a smile, 'this beautiful little boy is your grandson.'

———

Several hours later, Nesta walked back into the hall and settled down into a chair in front of the fire.

'He's fast asleep,' she said.

'At last,' said Gwladus from the other chair, 'I am completely worn out. I had forgotten how tiring little boys can be.'

'He is just excited,' said Nesta,' the trip from London was never-ending for him and he had little chance to play.'

'Your brothers were the same,' said Gwladus with a smile, 'always on the go and even with a manor full of servants, I was constantly on edge wondering what they were up to.'

'I remember,' said Nesta, 'and I so wanted to be with them but was forced to be schooled in the ways of a lady.'

'I don't recall it quite like that.' Gwladus laughed. 'Though what instruction we managed to impart seems to have had an effect. You have turned into a beautiful woman, Nesta, and young Henry seems to be a wonderful little boy.'

'Do you see them at all?' asked Nesta, changing the subject.

'Who?'

'My brothers.'

The smile waned on Gwladus's face and she leaned forward to throw another log onto the already roaring fire.

'No,' she said eventually, 'though not a day goes by without them being in my thoughts.'

'Do you have news of them?'

'I know Tarw is doing really well in Ireland,' said Gwladus. 'We write often and I have received letters from King Murcat telling me your brother is turning into a fine young warrior.'

'I am glad,' said Nesta. 'Does he ever think of coming home?'

'Apparently it is all Murcat can do to stop him leaving immediately.' Gwladus laughed. 'I would love to see him again but alas, the time is not right and his life would be at risk should it be known he has returned. So, I have told him to stay and complete his training. It is safer that way.'

'And what about Hywel?'

Gwladus paused again and took a deep breath before turning to face her daughter with a forced smile on her face.

'I fear he has gone, Nesta,' she said, reaching out to take her daughter's hand in hers. 'All I can hope for now is that he died a painless death.'

'You don't know that,' said Nesta, 'you *can't* know that.'

'I have to,' said Gwladus, 'else I would wither away in grief, imagining the hell he must be living in, in some dungeon. At least by thinking he is dead, I can go on with my life and carry on with what I do.'

'And what is that?' asked Nesta.

'Representing the people of Dinefwr against the worst of the English brutalities.'

'But you are just one woman.'

'I know, but my weakness has become my strength. The English see me as harmless and let me live here unhindered. In fact, they see me as an asset because I preach the virtues of peace to our people and encourage them not to turn against their masters.'

'Why do you do that?'

'Because in return I have the ear of the English and can sometimes garner leniency on the people's behalf. Without such intervention then trust me, the citizens of Dinefwr would suffer far more than they do now. At least this way, they have a reason to get through each day.'

An awkward silence fell until finally Gwladus took a deep breath and the smile returned to her face.

'Anyway,' she said, 'enough about me, you must tell me everything that has happened to you.'

'There's a lot to tell,' said Nesta.

'Then start at the beginning,' said Gwladus, 'the night is long
before us but we have wood aplenty for the fire. First of all, tell me
about the boy's father. When I left I thought you two may have a
future together.'

Nesta looked into the flames and thought for a while before
answering.

'I loved him mother, I really did. For a few years we had everything and I couldn't be happier. The years when his brother was
king were amongst the happiest I have ever seen. We spent time
together, shared tables at banquets – he even took me out on hunts,
teaching me the art of the bow, though if truth be told I never really
acquired any skill. Still, we were seen around the court as a couple
and I was happier than I have ever been. We even talked of marriage
but alas it was never to be.'

'What happened?'

'After Henry was crowned king, I thought I would be his queen
but the political pressure from the bishops proved too much and I
had to settle for being his consort while he was married to Matilda
of Scotland.'

Gwladus took her daughter's hand again.

'And what did Matilda think of the situation?'

'She was not happy but accepted it as the way of things. That is,
until she found out I was with child. The queen came to my quarters one day and made it clear I was to leave Windsor immediately.
If I refused, she said she would arrange for my baby to be killed at
the first opportunity.'

'She threatened the heir to the throne?'

'That's just it,' said Nesta, 'he would never be the heir, he would
be born out of wedlock.'

'Many such children have gone on to become king.'

'And that is what worried her. She was concerned that when her own baby was born, the king may have already formed an unbreakable bond with our child and make him the heir. In Matilda's mind she thought that if she could get both of us out of his life then the way would be left clear for any of her offspring. She made it clear that not only did I have to leave, but also that I had to let him think I had fallen out of love with him, a task I found heartbreaking.'

'Yet one you carried out?'

'What else could I do? As much as I loved Henry, I could not risk my unborn baby, so for his sake I did as she asked.'

'And Henry was happy with this?'

'At first no, but I was persistent and eventually he accepted my protestations. I thought that he would simply allow me to leave but he is a good man and when he saw I was serious, he contacted Gerald of Windsor to arrange a marriage.'

Gwladus sat back in shock. 'Gerald was still unwed?'

'He was married once but his wife died. Before I knew it, I was promised to him by the king.'

'How did you feel about that?'

'What could I do? To turn him down would reveal my lie and my baby would be in danger. I had to go through with it and though I tried to come home, Gerald was caught up in the intrigues of court and after some false accusations by a fellow noble, was removed from his station. For a long time we were forced to stay at his family's manor near Windsor and while his protestations were being considered by the king, we were allowed little communication with the outside world.'

'I wrote to you, Nesta,' said Gwladus, 'but when I never received a reply, thought the messenger may have suffered an accident or perhaps you were too busy to reply.'

'I received no letters, Mother,' said Nesta, 'and I wanted to write to you, I really did. But Gerald was being closely watched and if anyone had suspected he was sending messages out, especially into Wales, then there could have been serious repercussions, for him and me. Besides, I didn't want to worry you.'

'How could being a grandmother worry me?'

'Because you would want to visit and we could not allow that to happen. Between the false accusations against Gerald and Matilda's threat to my child, it was better to keep a low presence in society. For the past two years Gerald has been busy clearing his name and he has now been reinstated by Henry, but we have never wed. Perhaps there will now be time to contemplate such matters.'

'Does he treat you well?'

'Gerald treats us both well, Mother, and when I found out we were to live in the castle at Pembroke, I knew we would be close to you so couldn't be happier.'

'That is indeed a gift,' said Gwladus, 'and though I am sorry about your heartache, I am also happy to have you home.'

'Well,' said Nesta, 'there is so much more to tell but I am exhausted after the journey and if you don't mind, would seek the comfort of my bed.'

'Of course I don't mind,' said Gwladus. 'You go on and we will talk again on the morrow.'

Nesta kissed her mother on the cheek and retired to her bed while Gwladus stayed in the hall just staring into the fire. It had been an emotional day and a strange turn of events, but fate had brought her daughter home once more and though she was ecstatic to have Nesta back, the queen's mind was already racing with what other possibilities it may bring.

The following few months were amongst the happiest Gwladus could remember. Gerald married Nesta and Gwladus presented the estate at Carew to them both as a dowry. Life took on a semblance of normality for the family until one evening, when Nesta had come to visit her mother at Dinefwr, both women were once more in the hall talking quietly while young Henry was asleep on a bed of nearby furs.

'I used to do this all the time when you were a child,' said Gwladus, drawing a brush through Nesta's long black hair, 'it used to make you relax and get sleepy.'

'It still does,' replied Nesta quietly, enjoying the closeness with her mother, 'and is one of the many things I missed when I was away.'

'Does your maid not brush your hair?'

'Of course, but there is nothing like a mother's touch,' said Nesta and she closed her eyes to enjoy the sensation even more.

'Nesta,' said Gwladus eventually, 'I understand the building goes well at Kidwelly.'

'It would seem so,' said Nesta, 'the workers have already dug the ditch and erected a palisade. As soon as they put up some dwellings then I expect Gerald will leave the rest of the arrangements to his seconds. He has his own concerns waiting for him at Pembroke but already he talks of rebuilding the castle at Carew. Wherever we end up, it will be good for my son to settle down on a more permanent basis.'

'You could stay here,' said Gwladus, 'we have the room.'

'As much as I love the idea,' said Nesta, 'Gerald is my husband and my place is at his side.'

'Do you love him?'

Nesta stayed quiet for a while before answering.

'I'm not sure "love" is the right word,' she said eventually. 'I am certainly fond of him and my feelings grow stronger every day.'

'What about him, does he love you?'

'I think we are both wary of our feelings to each other. Our marriage was not undertaken in normal circumstances and he knows I once had feelings for Henry, but I do believe he cares deeply for me.'

'Then that is all you can ask,' said Gwladus. She continued brushing her daughter's hair before the tone in her voice changed slightly and Nesta's eyes opened in anticipation of the question that was obviously coming.

'Nesta?'

'Yes, Mother.'

'I have a favour to ask, one which I have no right to request but nevertheless, needs to be voiced.'

'Go on.'

Gwladus put down the brush and drew up a small chair in front of her daughter. Taking both of her daughter's hands in hers, she looked deep into Nesta's eyes and took a deep breath.

'Nesta,' she continued. 'You know how much I love having you here; it has changed my life. But I think your presence here could be the start of something even greater.'

'In what way?'

'After your father died, our family name almost disappeared from the memories of the nobles of Wales. Indeed, when I was in London with you, there were none of our line even this side of the border. When I returned, I found to my horror that we had been written off as a family of note and many thought that our lineage had come to an end. Obviously, I was aghast and spent many months travelling around the manors of those we once called friends and, over time, rebuilt our name. Of course, to claim any sort of status I had to have a suitable residence and being bereft of funds had no option but to return here, even though it was a shadow of its former self.'

'It looks fine now,' said Nesta.

290

'Indeed, but for a long time the palisade was in pieces and only one building was weatherproof. Slowly we made improvements, mostly due to the generosity of the people of Dinefwr, and eventually it became what you see around you now.'

'What is your point, Mother?'

'My point is, our situation seems to be improving. I have the ear of the local nobles, our castle is once more respectable and now you are the wife of Gerald, there are few who will challenge our resurgence due to the family ties. Oh, I'm not saying that we can once more rule Deheubarth but as two families tied by marriage, I see no reason why one day we cannot rule over a kingdom that was once as mighty as any in Wales.'

'Gerald would never share Deheubarth,' said Nesta, 'besides, he is only an extension of the king's power and does not hold the authority you allude to.'

'I understand,' said Gwladus, 'and expect no such thing, but he already allows us to manage our own affairs with regard to Dinefwr and I see no reason why he would not make that arrangement a formality, allowing us to become a minor kingdom subservient to Henry right here in Deheubarth.'

'You would settle for being a client kingdom?'

'Why not? The days of huge kingdoms are ending as surely as night follows day. The way of the world is changing, Nesta, and we either change with it or die out.'

'So what is it you want from me?' asked Nesta. 'If truth be told, even if I broached this subject with Gerald, I can't see him arguing your case before the king. Why would Henry yield the tiniest of control when he already holds the whole of Deheubarth in his fist?'

'You are right,' said Gwladus, 'for at the moment, we have nothing to offer and in his eyes we are mere women. But if Dinefwr became unified again and offered influence, no matter how small, then perhaps he would be more likely to listen.'

'And how do you propose to do that?'

'By reinstating a male figurehead at the head of this house. I have already sent word to Ireland and asked your brother to return with all haste.'

'You have asked Tarw to return?' gasped Nesta. 'Surely you realise you are placing his life in danger? As the sole heir of the Tewdwr line, Henry will see him as a threat and could order his demise.'

'Tarw is a grown man, Nesta, and in our communications has oft repeated his yearning to take up his father's mantle. All we needed was the right opportunity and your marriage to Gerald delivers just that.'

'You still haven't said what it is you want of me,' said Nesta.

Gwladus took a deep breath and stared at her daughter before answering.

'Even if Tarw returns,' she said eventually, 'he will need someone alongside him he can trust.' She paused and returned her daughter's stare before revealing her request. 'Nesta,' she said, 'I know it will be difficult and may take you some time, but if you have any love left inside your soul, I entreat you, I beg you – to find out if Hywel is still alive.'

Pembroke Castle

September 19th, AD 1105

Despite assurances she would do her best, over two months passed before Nesta broached the subject of Hywel with her husband. She had returned to Pembroke Castle with Gerald and her son and though the subject was never far from her mind, the time never seemed right. Eventually the matters of court took up less of her husband's time and she plucked up the courage to broach the subject.

'Jayne,' she said to the nursemaid, 'would you take Henry for his afternoon nap? I would have some private time with my husband.'

'Of course,' said Jayne, and she took the toddler by the hand, leading him out of the hall.

'This sounds intriguing,' said Gerald with a smile. 'Am I in trouble?'

'Of course not,' said Nesta, 'you never do anything wrong so I should scold you.'

'Perhaps I am just too clever in hiding my indiscretions.' Gerald laughed. 'And you just have not caught me yet.'

'If that is the case, then keep doing what it is you do for I am happy with the way things are.'

'Really, Nesta?'

'Of course,' said Nesta, 'do you doubt me?'

'No, but I am always aware that I was not your first choice and at the back of my mind, I can't help but wonder if and when the convenience may wear off.'

'Put such thoughts to the back of your mind, my love,' said Nesta, taking his hand. 'Yes, the circumstances were less than ideal but that was a long time ago. Our life together gets better by the day and I feel as if the sun is finally breaking through on a cloudy day.'

'Then you are truly happy?'

Nesta hesitated before replying. 'Yes, of course I am.'

'Nesta,' said Gerald, 'your eyes do not reflect your words. What concerns you?'

'I would rather not say,' said Nesta, 'for it is unfair to take advantage of your station for matters of family.'

'Is your mother well?'

'She is,' said Nesta, 'but while I was at Dinefwr, she shared a problem that now lays upon me like the greatest weight.'

Gerald took Nesta's hand and led her to a window seat.

'Come,' he said, 'sit beside me and share your burden. Perhaps it is one I can make lighter.'

'I wouldn't think so,' said Nesta, 'for it is a situation caused over twenty years ago.' As he listened patiently, Nesta went on to explain how Hywel had been taken prisoner as a boy and how her mother still fretted for his safety.

'Twenty years is a long time,' said Gerald, 'what makes you think he is still alive?'

'Because there are often rumours about an imprisoned Welsh prince of Deheubarth being held captive and passed around between the nobles of the marches.'

'Why would they do that?'

'Who knows? Perhaps they see him as some sort of guarantee against a potential uprising. I know it's probably a coincidence but

Tarw is the only other surviving heir to the Tewdwr estate and he is in Ireland. If the rumours of this prisoner are true, and I believe they are, then it has to be Hywel. Every night my mother cries herself to sleep and if I could arrange for her to see he is safe then she would grow old a happy woman.'

'So you want me to try to have him released?'

'Not necessarily. I know your name will have to be kept out of this but you have contacts and if you could just find out where he is, then perhaps I could petition his captors on behalf of my family.'

'Do you think that would do any good?'

'I don't know but I have to try, if only for the sake of my mother.'

Gerald stood up and walked around the room before returning to kneel before the sitting Nesta.

'Look,' he said, 'I can't promise anything and I doubt the rumours are true but if it puts your mind at rest, then I will do what I can to find out. Tomorrow I will send messages to all the barons of the marches and ask if they know anything about your brother. If he is alive, then I should know in a matter of weeks.'

Nesta didn't answer but just smiled and leaned forward to kiss him on the cheek.

'Thank you,' she said simply, 'you are a truly kind man.'

———⁀———

Over in Dinefwr Castle, Gwladus stood at the gates alongside Marcus, waiting for the two distant riders to get closer. As they neared, her heart raced even faster and though she knew it was unladylike to display such emotion before the castle staff, eventually she could hold back no longer and ran across the drawbridge and down the track to the valley. A few hundred paces away, one of the two men dismounted and passed the reins of his horse to his comrade.

'Connor,' he said, 'take these,' as he stepped forward to run towards the queen. Within moments, Gwladus threw herself into his strong arms, hugging him as tightly as her fragile frame would allow.

'I can't believe it,' gasped Gwladus as she released his hold and held him at arm's length, 'for so many years I have been without my children and now within months, two have returned home.' She looked up at her son, no longer a boy but a rugged young man, a head taller than his mother. His shoulder-length hair was tied back from his face and his chin was clean-shaven. His eyes were deep and thoughtful while his features were well defined and handsome.

'You have grown into a handsome young man,' she said. 'It looks like Murcat has brought you up well.'

'It is good to see you, Mother,' said Tarw. 'When I received your letter I knew I had no other option but to come.'

'Does anyone else know you are here?'

'Only King Murcat. He gave me the funds to make this journey and sends his best wishes.' He looked around. 'Where's Nesta?'

'She has returned to Pembroke with her husband but will send word soon. Come, let us retire to the castle and you can rest after your journey.'

'Perhaps for a day or so,' said Tarw, 'but then I need to see about getting Hywel released.'

Gwladus's smile faltered slightly and Tarw noticed her expression.

'Mother, what's wrong? Is Hywel all right?'

'Yes. I mean, I think so,' said Gwladus.

'What do you mean, you think so? Your letter said you knew where he was.'

'And I will do soon,' said Gwladus, 'your sister will send word any day now.'

'But I thought—'

'Enough talk,' said Gwladus, 'let's get back and I will explain further. As soon as I knew you were coming I had your old room prepared. You and your comrade must be exhausted.'

Tarw nodded silently and as Connor walked behind with the two horses, Gwladus linked arms with the son she hadn't seen in many years, to walk back to Dinefwr Castle.

The following day saw Tarw and his mother walking alongside the river in the valley. The day was pleasant and the bird calls echoed from the trees along the escarpment. Gwladus again had her arm through her son's and they talked quietly as they went.

'I'd forgotten how beautiful this place is,' said Tarw looking around the valley. 'It's been such a long time.'

'Too long,' said Gwladus, 'and I would have contacted you sooner but the management of our estate has taken far too much of our time. Indeed, it is only now Nesta has returned that it once more challenges the majesty it once held.'

'It's pointless dwelling in the past, Mother,' said Tarw. 'I'm here now.'

'How long can you stay?'

'There is no limit,' said Tarw, 'my lands in Ireland are well looked after and I have no family tying me back there.'

Gwladus smiled. 'Perchance you could stay,' she said. 'The times have changed and I reckon there is a possibility that the English may grant us part of what we once held.'

'Let's not get ahead of ourselves,' said Tarw. 'My journey here was initially made for one purpose, and that was to find Hywel. Your letter said that you knew he was alive, please tell me that is so.'

'I'm sure he is,' said Gwladus, 'for oft I hear the rumours of a jailed prince and it can only be your brother.'

'Yet you know not where he is held?'

'Not yet, but Nesta has asked her husband to make representations on our behalf.'

'I believe you have done this on many occasions with little effect. What makes you think he will succeed where you have failed?'

'Many reasons,' said Gwladus. 'A long time has passed and many who hated us with such a vengeance have either moved on or are dead. Those that are left are at least as old as me and there is only so long that a person can hold a grudge. Besides, Gerald is a powerful noble and has the ear of Henry himself. It will benefit no one to withhold information from a king's man, so hopefully we will hear something soon.'

'Even if we do, what then?'

'Well, I'm not sure but perhaps we can ask Gerald to use his influence to get your brother released.'

'You are putting a lot of faith in this Englishman.'

'I care only for your brother, Tarw, and if I have to use Nesta's husband to get him released, then so be it.'

'Is that fair on Nesta?'

'Nesta will do as she is told, it is in all our interests.'

'And what if Gerald can't help?'

'We'll have to worry about that if it happens, until then we must hope for the best.' Gwladus stopped and looked at her son. 'This is the closest we have ever been, Tarw. If God is with us then what is left of this family can soon be back together.'

'Mother,' said Tarw gently, 'do not confuse my questioning with reluctance. I am just as determined to see my brother walk in freedom as you, but it is important I know of all the facts. Only by doing so can I then plan out whatever needs to be done.'

'So you already have an idea of what may be needed?'

'Not yet, Mother, but I swear this before God: I will do whatever it takes to bring my brother home.'

Pembroke Castle

October 3rd, AD 1105

'Nesta,' said a voice quietly, 'Nesta, wake up!'

Nesta opened her eyes, and blinked in confusion. The room was still dark and there was no sign of dawn's first light through the shuttered windows. Above she could see the face of her husband illuminated in the light of the solitary candle in his hand.

'Gerald,' she said, 'it's still dark, is there a problem?'

'Get yourself dressed,' said Gerald, 'you should come with me.'

Nesta sat up and reached for her robe before walking over to check the sleeping form of her son in the nearby bed.

'He is fine,' said Gerald, 'but hurry, there is someone you need to meet.'

'At this hour?'

'All will be revealed, come.' He led the way from her bedchamber and down the stairs to the lesser hall where they received visitors during the day. As they entered, Nesta recognised one of Gerald's men alongside a man she had never seen before.

'Who's that?' she asked.

'We are about to find out,' said Gerald as he strode across the hall to greet the two men.

'Sir Godwin,' he said as he neared the two men, 'I had a message you had returned. It is good to see you again.'

'And you, my lord,' said Godwin, reaching out to take Gerald's wrist in friendship before turning to face Nesta. 'My lady, please forgive the lateness of the hour but I thought you would want to hear from this man as soon as we arrived.'

'I'm sure there is good reason,' said Nesta.

'Indeed there is,' said Godwin, 'this man is called Ivor and he hails from Brycheniog.'

The older man bowed slightly towards Nesta. His face was weathered and the few teeth he had left in his mouth were broken through mistreatment and rot.

'My lady,' he said, his voice as rough as the coarsest file.

'Good day, Master Ivor,' said Nesta, 'or should I say good morning? What can I do for you?'

'I have news that may be of interest to you, my lady,' said the man, 'news about your brother.'

Nesta stared at the man, waiting for him to continue but as he started to speak again he started to cough and doubled over in pain as globules of blood spattered on the flagstones. Nesta ran over and put her arms around him, guiding him to a chair as her husband ran to fetch a jug of water from a nearby table.

'What's the matter with him?' asked Gerald, handing over the water.

'He is dying,' said Godwin, 'and has little time left amongst us.'

'Where did you find him?'

'I didn't, he found me. I was staying in lodgings in Builth when he approached. He had heard I was making enquiries about your lady's brother and said he had information.'

'And is it of use?'

'I know not, he wouldn't say.'

'Why not?'

'He has certain demands.'

Gerald sneered. 'If he thinks he can wrest a single penny from me then he is sadly mistaken.'

'Worry not, my lord,' said Godwin, 'his requests are simple, just a warm room to see out his final days and the chance to eat like a king before he dies.'

'Is that all?'

'Modest demands to you and I, but they mean the world to a man such as he. I'm sure we will be able to accommodate him.'

'Only if his news is of value,' said Gerald, 'otherwise the only place he will be dining is with the pigs. Anyway, the state he is in, I doubt he will see out the night.'

'Thank you,' spluttered the man, sitting back in the chair. For a few moments he closed his eyes and breathed deeply, trying to catch his breath. Nesta wiped the spittle from his chin with a linen handkerchief before lifting a mug of honeyed water to his lips.

He sipped gently before pushing her hand away.

'My lady,' he said, 'your kindness is most welcome but these lips have not tasted wine for many a day. Perhaps I could entreat you to spare me a drop.'

'Of course,' said Nesta. She looked over at her husband in expectation.

'What?' asked Gerald.

'Could you please get me some wine,' she hissed, 'and make sure it is warm.'

'Do I look like a servant?' asked Gerald in exasperation.

'Gerald, *please*,' entreated Nesta. 'There is usually some left in the kitchens, but hurry.'

'I'll go,' said Godwin with a smile, 'you stay here.'

'No, I'll get it.' Gerald sighed. 'You go and wake some of the servants, it looks like this could be a long night.'

'Bring some food while you are there,' called Nesta as he left the hall, 'it looks like this poor wretch hasn't eaten in a month.'

As the men went their separate ways, Nesta returned her attention to the old man.

'Just relax,' she said, 'you will have your drink in just a few moments. Is there anything else I can get you, a soft blanket perhaps?'

'I already partake of luxury just sitting in front of this fire,' said the man weakly. His head turned and he looked around the walls, each draped with rich tapestries depicting the life of the privileged. 'So, this is how the lords and ladies live.'

'Have you never been in a castle before, Ivor?'

'Oh yes, my lady, for the past ten years I have lived in one of the greatest of them all but alas, my status was not one of honoured guest.'

'What do you mean?'

'I was little more than a slave,' said Ivor, 'dragged from my rat-infested cell only to undertake the most menial of tasks not fit for even the lowest of the servants.'

'What sort of tasks?'

'It varied. Sometimes we just carried rocks from the quarries or turned the treadmills for the mills, often walking within the wheels for days without rest. Sometimes, when the weather was so hot the smell from the latrines made the ladies gag, we were sent into the cess pits with leather buckets to empty them, burying the filth away from the castle. Often we were chest deep and I saw many men die from infection.'

'Oh my God,' gasped Nesta, her hand flying to her mouth in disgust. 'That sounds horrible.'

'It was,' said Ivor, 'and I saw one man deliberately drown himself in the filth such was his desperation.'

Nesta shook her head in disbelief.

'How could someone treat anyone so badly?' she asked. 'Surely it is inhuman.'

'It is, but they did not see us as human so it mattered not. Only the strongest survived but even the stoutest oak will eventually fall and now it is my turn to meet my God.'

'Ivor,' said Nesta, 'I am so sorry to hear your tale and I promise I will do whatever I can to make your last days as comfortable as possible. But you came here with information for me so please, put me out of my misery.' She took a breath. 'Does my brother still live?'

Ivor stared at Nesta for what seemed an age before giving her the answer she so desperately needed to hear.

'Yes, my lady, he is alive.'

———⌣———

When Gerald returned with the food and wine, Nesta pulled up another chair and waited patiently as Ivor savoured the luxuries.

'Warm pork,' he said, pieces of meat falling from his full mouth as he spoke, 'I had forgotten how nice it is.' Without waiting for an answer, he lifted the goblet and emptied it in one go before holding it up for a refill.

'There will be plenty of time for more,' said Nesta, 'for as much as you can drink. But first you must tell me of Hywel.'

Ivor's face fell as he realised he would have to wait but after swallowing the last of the meat, he leaned forward and started his tale.

'Ten years ago,' he said, 'I was at the battle of Brycheniog.'

'My father was there,' interrupted Nesta. 'Rhys ap Tewdwr.'

'He was your father?' asked Ivor in surprise. 'I never knew. Of course, I never had chance to speak to him for I was a mere pikeman, but I hear he was a good man. Anyway, as you know we were defeated that day and many of us were taken into captivity. Some were hanged, mainly the officers and the sergeants, but us foot soldiers were put to work doing the jobs the English hated doing for themselves. Sometimes we were sold on to other manors and I saw four different masters before ending up at the place where I have been these past few years.'

'And where was that exactly?' asked Gerald.

'Hen Domen Castle in Montgomery,' said Ivor. 'A more devilish place you can never imagine.'

'Is my brother there?' asked Nesta.

'He is,' said Ivor, 'or at least he was a month ago.'

'What do you mean?'

'The last time I saw your brother he was dragging me off a cart to bury me alive.'

For a few moments, the room fell silent. Then Nesta cleared her throat and started to speak again.

'I'm sorry,' she said, 'I don't understand. Why would he bury you alive?'

'Because I was dead,' said Ivor, 'or at least they thought I was. You see, there were ten of us in my cell and for some reason, they forgot about us for several days. Either that or they couldn't be bothered to answer our pleas. Whatever the reason, we were left to die of thirst until eventually I was the only one left. I managed to stay alive by licking the moisture off the stone walls, and I caught a rat to eat. But just as I thought I would surely die, someone must have remembered about us and opened the door. The smell must have been horrendous for them, for all around me the corpses of my cellmates were rotting in the heat and none of the guards would come in. Instead, they sent in another working party and they were told to bury us in the forest so as not to spread disease.'

'Your brother was one of those who came into the cell,' he continued, 'and when he saw I was still alive, he bade me stay still, as if I was truly dead. He threw me on the cart with the rest of the corpses, knowing that at least one of us had a chance to escape. When we were clear of the castle, the other prisoners dragged the bodies off the cart and when they buried the corpses, he made sure I was on top with enough room between the bodies to breathe.'

'How did you get out?'

'The graves were never deep, my lady, and oft we were called to those where the wolves had dug up the bodies. When the burial detail returned to the castle, it was easy to push my way out. After that I just wandered around, stealing from farms and living like an animal until I reached Builth. It was there I overheard someone talking about our friend here and his interest in a missing prince.'

'And it was definitely my brother?'

'Yes, for we mocked him for it. A prince of Tewdwr working amongst the destitute. Oh, how we laughed.'

'What happened to him?'

'After they buried the corpses, they went back into the castle.'

'But why didn't he run when he had the chance?'

'The prisoners are in no fit state to run, my lady; they can hardly walk. I am only alive today by the grace of God and the generosity of your brother.'

'So he is still there?'

'The last I saw of him he was, but he was no stronger than a babe and you could see the bones beneath his skin. If you want to get him out, I suggest you will have to move fast.'

Nesta saw the glance between Gerald and Godwin.

'What's the matter?' she asked, turning to face her husband. 'You seem concerned.'

'Nesta,' said Gerald, 'of all the castles where your brother could have been incarcerated, Hen Domen is probably the worst.'

'Why?' asked Nesta.

'Because the castellan there is a knight called Belleme, a soulless man who hates the Welsh with a vengeance. If Hywel is there, then there is no way he will ever be freed unless, of course, you have a king's ransom to bargain with.'

'You don't know that,' said Nesta, 'and besides, if you speak to him he may see sense.'

'It is pointless,' said Gerald, 'my word will hold no sway.'

'Why not?' asked Nesta.

'Because despite our common allegiance to Henry, we once fought on different sides and I humiliated Belleme in battle. He would give anything to see me dead and would never grant any plea I made.'

Ivor reached for the wine jug as the conversation continued.

'Gerald,' said Nesta, 'please scour your mind for a resolution, we can't come this far just to be turned away at the last moment by something as minor as the character of one man. You heard what Ivor said, my brother suffers a hell no man should endure. There must be something we can do.'

'My hands are tied, Nesta,' said Gerald, 'Belleme is also a king's man and has no reason to bend to my will. If your brother was anywhere else then perhaps I could do something but as it is, there is nothing more I can do.'

'But, Gerald—'

'Nesta,' snapped Gerald. 'I have done everything I can and fulfilled my promise to you. Let it go!'

Nesta turned back to Ivor.

'Perhaps you can tell me a little more about my brother?'

'There's not much to tell,' said Ivor. 'He was very quiet and seemed like a good man. He kept himself to himself and though he also suffered, he often helped those even more destitute than himself.'

'In what way?'

'Oh, simple things like tending injuries or sharing what little food he had.'

'He sounds very kind.'

'He was, and despite his station, never played on his royal blood to garner favour.'

'Do you know what kept him going after all these years?'

'The thought that one day his family would come for him. He never doubted that he would be remembered and every night he would dream of his childhood.'

Tears rolled down Nesta's face as she listened to the old man, her heart breaking with the thought of Hywel's never-ending wait. She turned to face Gerald, her voice rising in anger.

'We have to do something, Gerald,' she said through her tears. 'I can't just leave him to rot.'

'You could rescue him.' said Ivor unexpectedly.

All heads turned to stare at the old man.

'And how do you propose we do that?' asked Gerald eventually. 'Hen Domen is one of the most heavily defended castles in Wales and their garrison is strong and well trained.'

'You forget, my lord,' said Ivor, 'that I lived there for ten years and know their routines better than any man; at least, the routines of their prisoners.'

'Continue,' said Gerald.

'The prisoners are often let out to cart away the waste of the castle or work in the forests on behalf of the castellan. I know where they go and when they go. Of course, they are well guarded but there may be an opportunity to rescue the prince while he is outside the castle walls.'

Godwin looked across at Gerald.

'My lord,' he said, 'any attempt at rescue would need the involvement of armed men and if we were to be found out then it could be seen as treason, especially as it will be seen as giving succour to an enemy of the crown. If found guilty you could be executed for activity against the king.'

'Henry would never execute Gerald,' said Nesta, 'he is far too important.'

'As is Belleme,' said Godwin. 'The last thing that Henry needs right now is nobles fighting nobles and besides, Belleme occupies one of the most strategically important areas in the marches. Henry just can't afford to upset him.'

'Then we are no further forward,' said Gerald. 'I'm sorry, Nesta, but this conversation is over.' Without another word he turned and left the hall, closely followed by Godwin.

'So that's it,' said Nesta quietly, 'there is nothing we can do.'

'Do you not know of any other man who can undertake this task on your behalf?' asked Ivor.

'There is Tarw,' said Nesta, 'but he is only one man and I can't risk losing another brother.'

'Is he not also a prince?'

'In name, yes, but he holds no lands in Wales.'

'What about elsewhere?'

'I believe he has interests in Ireland. But how does that help?'

'Because if those interests have value then your answer is obvious. Any man can hire an army, my lady, and I know exactly where you can find one.'

⌣

Two days later, Nesta was back at Dinefwr castle, talking to Gwladus and Tarw, relaying everything Ivor had said.

'And you think he is telling the truth?' asked Gwladus.

'I do,' said Nesta, 'he may be destitute but he seems like an honest man. Besides, he fought for our father at Brycheniog and is loyal to our name.'

'Where is he now?'

'He is being looked after by the castle staff in Pembroke. I have given him a room within the keep and he is being feted as an honoured guest.'

'What does Gerald think of that?'

'It concerns him not for it is obvious the man will soon be dead. Ivor weakens by the day, but at least I can make those last days as comfortable as possible.'

'So what else did he have to say?'

'He has told me of the routines of the work parties,' said Nesta. 'Unfortunately, the parties are usually in sight of the castle walls, but that may not be as much of a problem as it sounds.'

'We are talking about Hen Domen here,' said Tarw. 'Even I know about Belleme – there is no way he will just sit back and allow us to take any men from beneath his walls, even if they are mere serfs.'

'He will if he is distracted elsewhere.'

'In what way?'

'What if there was to be an unexpected assault on the castle walls from an unknown enemy. A force strong enough to have him lock down the castle while he evaluates the threat. In the confusion he will be unconcerned about a couple of worthless prisoners and we can affect their rescue whilst his attentions are elsewhere.'

'It could work,' said Tarw, 'but we have no such army.'

'No, but Ivor told me about a young rebel in the north who oft fights for money and glory.'

'And who is this man?'

'His name is Owain ap Cadwgan.'

'Owain.' Gwladus laughed. 'That blackguard is the source of frustration for both sides.'

'You know of this man?' asked Tarw.

'Everyone in Wales knows him. He is a scoundrel of the highest order, breaking hearts and robbing merchants on an equal basis.'

'I take it he is a ladies' man?' asked Nesta.

'In every sense of the word,' said Gwladus, 'it is said he is as pretty as a picture with speech as smooth as honey. Not many women can resist his charms and many a husband has had cause to chase him from their wife's bed.'

'I dislike him already,' said Nesta.

'Since he set out upon this path, even his father, Prince Cadwgan, has disowned him,' continued Gwladus, 'such is his notoriety. He now makes his living relieving travellers of their purses and selling his services to any who can pay.'

'How big is his army?' asked Tarw.

'It is irrelevant.' Gwladus sighed. 'We cannot use him'

'How big is his army?' asked Tarw again.

'It is said to be over a hundred strong, manned with young men of a similar ilk. A band of irresponsible brigands only interested in the moment, living and dying in the search for adventure.'

'Tarw,' said Nesta, seeing the expression on her brother's face. 'You cannot be seriously considering this.'

'Why not? It sounds perfect. They already suffer from a bad reputation so will worry not about being found out and besides – this was your idea.'

'Yes, but that was before I found out that the man was little more than a good-for-nothing knave.'

'Don't forget, we are talking about our brother's life here, and whether this Owain is godly or the son of Satan himself matters not. If he can help us rescue Hywel, then I say we should make all haste to make contact.'

Nesta looked at her mother and silence fell for a few moments.

'Well?' said Tarw. 'Are we going to do this or not?'

Gwladus sighed deeply before nodding her head in agreement.

'Nesta?' asked Tarw.

'For Hywel's sake,' she said.

'Then it is agreed,' said Tarw, 'all we need to do now is raise funds. What do we have between us?'

'I have nothing to speak of,' said Gwladus, 'but the king of Gwent is a close friend. Perhaps he would consider affording me a loan, especially if I use this castle as surety.'

'Dinefwr!' gasped Nesta. 'But this is our home – we should never put it at risk.'

'Without Hywel it is nothing more than a pile of wood and stone,' said Gwladus, 'and I would burn it in an instant to see Hywel for just one more day.'

'Then that is what we should do,' said Tarw. 'I can raise some from King Murcat. He treats me as a son so I think he will be generous in his funding.'

'That just leaves me,' said Nesta. 'I have no money but I have accumulated a healthy collection of jewellery from my time with Henry. I can throw that into the purse if needs be.'

'What will Gerald think?'

'There is no need for him to know about any of this,' said Nesta, 'and besides, what husband would enjoy the sight of his wife draped in jewellery from another man?'

'Then we are done,' said Tarw. 'I will return to Ireland immediately and should be back within ten days.' He turned to his mother. 'How long do you need?'

'A few days, no more,' replied Gwladus. 'By the time you return I will have the money ready.'

'As will I,' said Nesta.

'There is one more thing to consider,' said Gwladus.

'And that is?'

'When we gather our own men to ride with Owain, I want to go along.'

'*You?*' gasped Tarw. 'With respect, Mother, you no longer have your youth and I see no reason to subject you to the risk.'

'I may be getting old, Tarw, but I can still ride as well as any man. If we find Hywel, I want to be there at his side from day one. I refuse to waste even a moment more than I have to.'

'But—'

'This is not up for debate, Tarw, I will be at your side whether you like it or not.'

'As will I,' said Nesta suddenly.

'Nesta, you have a child,' said Gwladus, 'and a husband. There is no need for you to be there.'

'On the contrary, during my stay at Windsor I often watched the apothecary amidst his duties and have garnered a knowledge of medicines. If Hywel is ill, I may be able to ease his pain.'

'Gerald will never allow it,' said Tarw.

'You leave Gerald to me,' said Nesta. 'Now, shall we set out upon our respective tasks? For every moment we waste is an extra moment my brother spends in that hellish place.'

'So be it,' said Tarw eventually. He took his mother's hands in his. 'We are getting closer, Mother, and though it may be dangerous, if everything goes to plan, Hywel could be back within these walls before the month is out.'

'Please God,' said Gwladus, 'let it be so.'

Hen Domen Castle

September 23rd, AD 1105

A soldier sat against a tree, his helmet lying alongside him along with his coif. Across the clearing, several more soldiers sat in a circle, playing dice in the afternoon sun. In the distance, a lone sentry stood at the edge of the cemetery, always on the lookout for any threat from the Welsh.

In the opposite direction, a group of ten emaciated prisoners struggled to wield heavy picks and shovels as they tried to break through the rocky ground of the makeshift cemetery.

'Put some effort into it,' yelled one of the soldiers, 'or you'll feel the bite of the lash.'

The prisoners increased their feeble efforts, desperate not to become victims of the guard's whip. Each had the scars upon their backs as evidence of the brutality but in their weakened state, and with little flesh left on their bones, they knew even the lightest of blows would cut straight through to the bone and when that happened, few survived. The soldier turned to his comrade.

'I hate this task,' he said, 'why can't we just throw the dead in the bloody moat. That's what we used to do.'

'It's because Belleme's latest wench complains about the stench,' said the other man, 'and anyway, have you seen the state of them? Every one is riddled with disease. If I had my way I'd throw the lot of them into that bloody grave and be done with them, dead or not.'

'Nah,' said the first soldier, 'if we did that, who would empty the latrines? Knowing our luck we'd end up doing it. At least out here we get to sit down for a while. Even Sergeant Carter seems less harsh away from the castle.'

'There is that,' said his comrade as he picked up a nearby rock to throw at the sweating prisoners.

'Hurry up,' he shouted as the missile bounced off one of the men's heads, 'your friends there will be rotted away by the time you finish and will enter hell no more than skeletons.'

The rest of the soldiers laughed and seeing the discomfort the thrown rock had caused, searched around for missiles of their own, keen to join in the fun.

'Look at those bastards,' whispered Owain ap Cadwgan from his hiding place on the nearby hill. 'I'd love to cut the throats of every one, given the chance.'

'I know how you feel,' replied Tarw, 'but don't forget, the whole point is to rescue my brother. If we can do that without inflicting any casualties, then Belleme may decide not to pursue us. If we kill any of his men, they will be after us like wolves on the scent of a kill.'

'Which one is your brother?' asked Owain, staring at the prisoners.

'I know not,' said Tarw, 'I have never met him.'

'Then how do you know which man to take?'

'We will take them all,' said Tarw.

'They will slow us down.'

'They are all Welshmen, Owain, and my conscience says no man deserves the fate they endure. I could no more leave them here than my brother.'

'I understand,' said Owain. 'So, are you ready?'

'As ready as we'll ever be,' said Tarw, 'you take your men around to the far hill and do what we agreed. As soon as we hear the signal, we'll make our move.'

'Good luck,' said Owain, and he crawled back into the undergrowth.

Tarw watched him go. The young man was several years his junior but already had the confidence of a king. His fair shoulder-length hair was lightened further by the sun making him undoubtedly attractive to women and giving him a gentle aura. But according to his men, his appearance belied his abilities and many told of how he had beaten many men in combat.

At first, Tarw found it hard to believe but quickly saw the change in Owain's manner when the talk was of fighting. His eyes seemed to glaze and an excitement burned in his speech, as if war was the meaning of everything. Tarw had no doubt that one day the young man would meet a bloody end – he just hoped that today was not that day.

———⌄———

In the cemetery, Hywel swung the pick downward once more, seeing the point only just break the surface, such was the weakness in his arms. Despite the pain, he repeated the action mindlessly, lifting his tired arms time and time again, relentlessly continuing the feeble strikes knowing that eventually, they would add up. For too long he had been a prisoner of the English and had long ago learned that to survive, you just had to do what they said, no matter how pointless it all seemed. Since he had been abducted as a child he had known no other life except that of a prisoner and though there had been some easier times, this latest captor was the worst he had ever known. The body that had toughened after many years of hard labour was wasting away through malnutrition and he knew he had little time left.

'Take a break for water,' shouted the sergeant in charge of the guards. The prisoners shuffled slowly over to the cart bearing the barrel of water.

Hywel picked up a wooden bowl from beside the barrel and dipped it in the water before turning to carry it carefully over to a tree where the other prisoners were already sitting. One of the soldiers nudged his comrade.

'Look at Sergeant Carter,' he said. 'I suspect he's going to have some fun with the prisoners.'

Sure enough, the soldier walked towards the water barrel, a sneer upon his face.

'Wait,' he called and walked over to Hywel.

"My lord,' gasped Hywel, expecting the worst, 'my thirst is great, please let me drink.'

'Oh come on, Welshman,' said Carter coldly, 'I'm not so bad that I would deny a thirsty man his water.'

'Thank you, my lord,' said Hywel but before he could turn away, Carter cleared his throat and spat into the bowl, much to the amusement of the other soldiers.

'Sorry about that,' said Carter, 'it was an accident.'

'Can I refresh my bowl?' asked Hywel quietly, already knowing the answer.

'Sorry.' The soldier sighed, with a smirk. 'You know the rules. One bowl of water per man. If I was to give you a second bowl, what message would that send out? Before long, the rest of the prisoners will want more and that will never do.'

Hywel stared at the globule of phlegm in his water before lifting his eyes slowly to stare at the sergeant.

'Of course, you could tip it out,' said Carter.

Without taking his eyes from his captor, Hywel lifted the bowl to his mouth and drank the water down, complete with spit. The rest of the soldiers burst into laughter at the sound of their comrade's roar of disgust.

'Get away from me, you disgusting pig,' shouted Carter and he shoved Hywel in the back, sending him sprawling into the mud. Hywel lay there for a few moments, waiting for the soldier to walk away before dragging himself to his feet and joining his fellow prisoners.

'If I thought I had enough strength to choke that bastard I would gladly take a blade as a consequence,' growled one of the men as Hywel flopped down beside him.

'Disperse such thoughts, Lloyd,' said Hywel, 'even combined we are no match for any one of them.'

'I know,' replied Lloyd, 'but the thought that one day an opportunity will arise keeps me going.'

'Every day that passes sees us weaker and weaker.' Hywel sighed. 'Perhaps all we can hope for now is a painless death and a Christian burial.'

'A false hope,' said Lloyd, 'they'll just plant us like our friends there,' he indicated the three dead men on the cart, 'and waste no fancy words on the likes of us.'

'I have said a prayer over every grave I have dug,' said Hywel, 'and there have been many.'

'I've never heard you,' said Lloyd.

'I say it in my mind,' said Hywel, 'but God needs no spoken word to hear our prayers. As far as I am concerned, every man I helped bury has had a Christian burial.'

For a few moments there was silence until Lloyd spoke quietly again.

'If I die before you, will you pray for me?'

Hywel nodded.

'And if you go first,' said Lloyd, 'I will do the same.'

'That may be sooner than we think,' said Hywel. 'I have had many masters, some brutal, but this one has no equal. We are nothing in his eyes and that makes him stand out. At least the others saw us as having some benefit but with Belleme, we don't exist and the guards are allowed to work us to death.'

Lloyd stared across at the soldiers sat in a circle, each laughing raucously at an unheard joke while helping themselves to potage from a communal pot on a small fire. The prisoners stared in silence knowing they would get nothing.

'Do you think we may get some food tonight?' asked Lloyd quietly.

Hywel was about to answer when the sound of a horn echoed around the hills and all heads looked up in confusion. Across the clearing, the soldiers got to their feet and looked nervously towards the treeline.

'What is it?' asked one of the soldiers.

'Pick up your weapons,' shouted Sergeant Carter. 'Get the prisoners on their feet. Plant those corpses quickly and we can get out of here.'

'The grave is only half dug,' came a response.

'It will have to do. Throw them in and cover them up. Something doesn't feel right.'

In the treeline, Tarw and Connor had also heard the horn, and their hearts raced with anticipation.

'Ready?' asked Tarw.

'Aye,' replied Connor.

'Right, let's do this. Just as we planned, you cut them off, and leave the rest to me.'

Without another word, Connor turned his horse and rode away through the undergrowth, closely followed by twenty horsemen.

Tarw watched him go and when he could see his comrade was in position, took a deep breath before urging his horse forward out of the trees and down the grassy slope towards the cemetery.

Around the other side of the castle, the guard upon one of the towers above the gatehouse had also heard the horn and peered intensely over towards the distant treeline.

'What is it?' shouted the captain of the guard, breathing heavily after climbing the ladder up to the tower. 'Can you see anything?'

'Not yet,' said the soldier, 'it may be a hunting horn.'

'Perhaps,' said the captain, his eyes narrowing as he stared across the open space. As they watched, the horn sounded again and the captain's eyes widened in shock, staring in horror at the sight unravelling before him.

'Captain,' shouted the guard, 'what do you want me to do?'

The captain glanced at the soldier before turning to shout down into the castle bailey.

'*Shut the gates!*' he roared. 'Stand to the garrison, we are under attack!'

Across the clearing, the once still treeline had sprung into life as dozens of riders burst out from the trees and galloped towards the fortress, each brandishing swords or spears in an obvious display of aggression. The captain looked into the fortress again, gratified to see the bailey swarming with men as they ran to the palisades. As he watched he heard the giant gates slam shut and the hefty locking bars slide into place.

'*Archers*,' roared the Captain, 'to your stations. Someone get me the castellan.'

Moments later a young man climbed up the ladder, an English knight by the name of Broadwick.

'Where is Belleme?' asked the captain as the knight joined him.

'He left for London a few days ago,' said Broadwick.

'Why wasn't I told?'

'You are told what you need to be told. I command in his place so brief me. What is the situation?'

The captain pointed over the palisade at the line of riders along the forest edge.

'They appeared a few moments ago and rode as if to assault our walls only to turn away at the last moment.'

'Have you responded?'

'Our archers are deploying as we speak and the garrison has been deployed, but the attackers are out of range.'

The knight looked over at the lines of attackers near the trees.

'They show no colours,' he said.

'Brigands,' spat the captain, 'hoping to catch us unawares, no doubt.'

The knight's experienced eye scanned the enemy lines and beyond.

'Where are their foot soldiers?' he asked.

'I have seen none,' said the captain.

'Does that not seem odd to you?'

'In what way?'

'Who would try to take a castle with cavalry only?'

'Perhaps they hoped to breach our gate before we had time to lock down.'

'No,' said the knight, 'even the most stupid of men would see such an idea foolish. Something else is going on here.' For several minutes both men watched the enemy lines as they just rode back and forth, brandishing their weapons. Along the parapets of the castle, men raced into position, waiting to repel any assault that may come.

'Something isn't right,' said the knight, 'it seems to me they have no intention of attacking. They just posture for our attention.'

'Why would they do that?'

'I don't know, unless it is a diversion.'

'All the walls are strongly manned,' said the captain, 'if this is a diversionary tactic, it will not find us wanting.'

'Unless,' said the knight, 'the castle is not their target.'

'What do you mean?'

Broadwick suddenly turned and faced the captain.

'What patrols do we have outside of the walls?'

'None,' said the captain, 'except, of course, those guarding the burial detail.'

'The prisoners are outside?'

'Yes, my lord. They are on burial duty and are guarded by ten men. But why would they be of any interest to a band of brigands?'

'Is Hywel Tewdwr amongst them?'

'Who?'

'The one who has been here longer than you or I.'

'I assume so but—'

Without waiting for the captain to finish his sentence, Broadwick turned and shouted down to the bailey.

'*Cavalry to the stables*,' he roared. 'Look to your steeds, prepare to move.'

'What's going on?' asked the captain. 'You can't go out there for the sake of a bunch of prisoners, you could be slaughtered. Let them go.'

'One of those prisoners is a prince of Deheubarth,' snapped Broadwick, 'I suspect that our attention is being captivated while attempts are made to free him. If that is the case, they need to be stopped. The last thing we need in Wales is a pretender to the throne free amongst the enemy. Prepare to open the gates, Captain, let's see if these brigands have the mettle they proclaim.'

———

Back at the graveyard, a voice rang out, causing prisoners and guards alike to turn in alarm.

'To your guard, men,' shouted Sergeant Carter, 'it looks like we have a visitor.'

Across the clearing Tarw rode slowly towards the soldiers. His sword was sheathed and despite his racing heart, his manner was relaxed. Sergeant Carter stepped forward to meet the rider, holding up his hand to stop him in his tracks.

'Stop right there, stranger,' he called, 'state your business.'

Tarw reined in his horse and stared over at the soldier and his armed men.

'Sheath your sword, my friend,' he called, 'there is no need for bloodshed here. My business is minor and easily resolved.'

'Then share it,' said the soldier.

'I want you to release those men into my custody,' said Tarw. 'Do that and I will leave you to continue your business unharmed.'

The soldier gasped in astonishment. 'These scum are the property of Lord Belleme,' he said, 'and you have no right to demand their release. Now be gone before you feel our steel.'

'I was afraid you were going to say that,' said Tarw, 'so I have put some arrangements in place for your own safety.'

'You talk in riddles,' said the soldier, 'and are but a single man. I suggest you ride away before you occupy one of the graves beneath my feet.'

'Then look behind you,' said Tarw, 'and you will see the meaning of my words.'

The soldiers turned and saw a line of twenty cavalry forming up behind them, cutting off their escape route to the castle.

'Those are my men,' continued Tarw, 'and as long as you don't do anything stupid, they will remain at a distance. Of course, if you try anything foolish then trust me, you will get a far closer view of the steel they carry.'

'You are making a mistake, stranger,' shouted Carter. 'Why risk your lives for the sake of such filth?'

'Slaves are slaves,' said Tarw, 'and I suspect with a bit of fattening up, they will bring a good price in the tin mines.'

'So you are no more than a brigand, dealing in the sale of flesh?'

'Don't judge me, Englishman,' said Tarw, 'for I suspect they will live a little longer in my employ than yours. Now, make your decision for we intend to leave this place with those prisoners. Whether we leave you behind dead or alive is up to you.'

Back at the castle, Broadwick strode over to his horse and vaulted straight up onto its back. He took his helmet from his squire and fastened the strap below his chin before turning to his men.

'When we ride out,' he shouted, 'deploy immediately into line abreast and upon my command, take the attack straight to them. Worry not about their number for they look untrained and ill equipped. However, should they withdraw, do not follow them into the treeline. When they are gone, muster on my location and follow my lead, we have a more important quest than to chase brigands all day. Ready?'

'*Aye, my lord*,' roared the men.

'Then draw swords,' shouted Broadwick, 'and prepare to move. Captain of the guard, open the gates.'

'Here they come,' shouted Owain as the gates slowly swung open. 'Remember, don't face them in a standing fight, just hit and run. Keep them tied up for as long as you can but though it's been a while since we polished our blades with English blood, do not waste your lives needlessly.' He drew his sword and held it high. 'The life of a Welsh prince is at stake here, not to mention a hefty purse. Be fearless in deed and shrewd in thought. Upon my command, *advance!*'

The makeshift army rode forward to face the rapidly deploying English defenders and before the enemy had chance to organise properly, drove their horses into full gallop, forcing Broadwick's men immediately onto the defensive. On the palisades the archers were taken by surprise and before they could bring their bows to bear, the Welsh attackers were amongst the English and too difficult to target.

'Hold your fire,' shouted the captain of the guard and he watched helplessly as the battle unfolded.

Down below the fight was short and brutal. The movement was frantic with horses galloping in all directions and though Broadwick's men were well trained, the Welsh attackers never stopped long enough to engage one on one, driving their mounts through the melee to slash at any passing enemy.

'*To me*,' roared Broadwick, and he gathered his cavalry around him, daring the enemy to come at them head on. But Owain was far too clever to be drawn in, pulling back his own forces to the treeline.

'What now?' asked one of his men.

'Now we wait,' said Owain breathlessly. 'The element of surprise has gone so if he decides to charge we will withdraw. But every second he hesitates gives Tarw time to free the prisoners. This Englishman cannot risk leaving the field until he has dealt with us so we still have the upper hand.'

Across the field, Broadwick had already come to the same conclusion and thought furiously.

'He is stalling for time,' he shouted to another knight, 'and that is something we do not have.' He thought for a few moments more before making a decision. 'Sir John, we can wait no more. Upon my command you will engage them head on with a view to engaging them in pitched battle or driving them into the trees. Whichever they choose, ensure they are fully engaged. In the meantime, I will take ten men to the cemetery and relieve the soldiers there. Agreed?'

'Aye, my lord,' shouted the other knight.

'Good, upon my command, *advance!*'

'Owain, what are your orders?' shouted a voice as the English horses thundered towards the treeline. 'Do we flee or fight?'

'We have done enough,' shouted Owain, 'retreat into cover. Keep moving and rendezvous at Three River Junction. Move!'

As one, the attackers turned their horses and melted into the trees, their diversionary tactic complete.

Across the valley, Broadwick and his men galloped towards the cemetery. Within moments they turned into the copse and immediately saw the aftermath of Tarw's visit. Ten men were tied against the trees but they weren't the prisoners – they were the guards.

Ten Leagues West of Oswestry Castle

September 24th, AD 1105

Nesta and Gwladus lay on mats of sheepskin in the back of an abandoned barn. The building stank but it had a sound roof and the wind was kept at bay by stout walls.

Outside, five men loyal to Gwladus stood guard at the perimeter while another five slept under their waxed cloaks, taking their turn to rest from their duties. Gwladus stirred as the hinges creaked and someone put their head around the door.

'My lady,' said a voice quietly, 'I think they are on the way back.'

Gwladus sat up immediately and wiped the tiredness from her eyes. Across the small room, Nesta woke and also sat up.

'What is it?' she whispered.

'I think Tarw is returning,' said Gwladus. 'Come, we should get dressed immediately.'

Both women donned their shoes and wrapped themselves in their warm capes before leaving the hut and joining Marcus outside.

'Where are they?' asked Gwladus quietly, painfully aware they were in the heart of English-held territory.

'A rider came in a few moments ago,' said Marcus. 'He said the main column is close behind and should be here by dawn.'

'Do they have Hywel with them?'

'We don't know, my lady,' said Marcus. 'There are some prisoners but their names are unknown. Their flight from Hen Domen has been frantic with no chance of discourse. The English pursued them but were lost in the night. When our people arrive we must get ready to move immediately.'

'Understood,' said Gwladus, 'but add fuel to the campfire so I can warm up some soup. Our people, whether prisoner or rescuer will no doubt need something to eat.'

'Yes, my lady,' said Marcus.

Gwladus turned to Nesta.

'Well, we have come a long way,' she said. 'In the next few hours we will know if your brother is alive or dead.'

'He must be alive,' said Nesta, 'to come so far to be denied is an outcome too painful to contemplate.'

'There are now other issues to consider,' said Gwladus, 'for if they are being pursued, we need to consider your safety.'

'Just mine?' Nesta laughed.

'I am growing old, Nesta,' said Gwladus, 'while you have your whole life ahead of you. You are also mother to a beautiful boy and cannot be risked. In fact, I am surprised Gerald let you come at all.'

'He didn't,' said Nesta.

Gwladus's head spun around to face her daughter.

'What do you mean, he didn't? You said he gave his blessing.'

'I had to say that or you would have denied me the opportunity,' replied Nesta, 'and I am just as concerned about Hywel as you. If he died here while I was safe in a castle on the other side of the country then I would never have forgiven myself.'

'So where does Gerald think you are?'

'In Dinefwr, with you.'

Gwladus shook her head and sighed deeply. Although she was frustrated with her daughter she could understand her reasoning.

'What's done is done,' said Gwladus eventually, 'what we need to do now is concentrate on Hywel. Come – help me with the soup. He may be here sooner than we think.'

Several leagues away, a line of horsemen walked their horses carefully through the darkness. In amongst them, the prisoners sat huddled on the back of a cart, not sure what was happening or who their rescuers were. Their hands and feet were also tied and for all they knew, they were just swapping one master for another.

The lead rider held up his hand and the message was passed from man to man, halting the column in its tracks.

'What's the matter?' asked Connor, walking up beside Tarw.

'I thought I heard something,' said Tarw.

Connor looked around nervously. The English had been on their trail through the forests for most of the day but he thought they had been lost in the darkness.

'We have to keep going,' said Connor. 'To wait plays into their hands.'

Tarw nodded and the column started to move once more.

Hywel opened his eyes in confusion. The rocking of the cart had sent him into a fitful sleep, and though he shivered in the coldness of the night the day had tired him out completely. He looked down, feeling someone undoing the ties around his feet, and realising at the same time that his hands were free.

'Lloyd,' he hissed, recognising his friend, 'what are you doing?'

'I've managed to untie my bonds,' whispered Lloyd looking around the cart. 'You too are now free, so we can slip over the side and hide in the forest.'

'Why?' asked Hywel.

'We don't know where we are being taken,' whispered Lloyd, 'for all we know it could be someplace worse.'

'Why would they go to so much trouble to rescue us only to place us in captivity again?

'You heard our rescuer back at the cemetery,' replied Lloyd, 'he made it clear he was a slave trader. And anyway, what sort of rescuer ties the hands and feet of those they have rescued?'

'Perhaps to ensure we stay put,' said Hywel, 'our flight has been manic and to lose their prize in the darkness would be an avoidable loss.'

'Exactly,' said Lloyd, 'and I refuse to see out the rest of my days as no more than a wretch, rotting at the end of a chain.' Lloyd grabbed the sides of Hywel's face, forcing him to return the stare. 'You listen to me,' he whispered, 'you have spent almost a lifetime in captivity, hoping against hope that your family would come. You have cheated death more often than any man deserves and witnessed brutality beyond comprehension. This is your chance, Hywel. Leave with me now and you may even live long enough to see them again. It could be the last chance you ever get.'

'I wouldn't know how to survive out there,' said Hywel, looking over the side of the rocking cart.

'Leave that to me,' said Lloyd, 'I think I know where we are and know of several farms close to here. If we can make it to one of those, we have a chance.'

'And if we die?'

'Then we do so as free men,' said Lloyd. He paused before continuing. 'This could be your last chance to live a semblance of a good life. I am going with or without you, Hywel, so what is it to be – captivity or freedom?'

For what seemed an age Hywel stared at the man he had called friend for several years before nodding in the dark.

'Go ahead,' he said eventually, 'I'm right behind you.'

*

'Mother, they're here,' said Nesta, as the column rode up to the shepherd's hut.

Gwladus put the ladle back into the pot on the fire and stood up, brushing the hair from her face. Both women walked over to the column and as Nesta hugged Tarw, Gwladus walked straight past and over to the wagon, staring in confusion at the group of tethered men in the back. The frightened look in the eyes of the emaciated men was both haunting and sickening, and Gwladus looked over at Tarw as he approached.

'Have you said anything?' she asked.

'Not yet,' he said, 'we had to concentrate on getting away.'

'Which one is he?' she asked looking again at the cowering men.

'I don't know,' said Tarw, 'but we are about to find out.' He turned to the prisoners and spoke calmly. 'You men, listen very carefully. We mean you no harm. Once we get you from this cart you will be untied and well looked after. We have food and fresh clothing waiting and we will do what we can to tend to your wounds. With immediate effect you are free men, but there is something we need to know. Which one of you is known as Hywel ap Tewdwr?'

For an age nobody replied and Gwladus stepped closer.

'There is no need to be afraid,' she said, 'you are all safe. But we need to know. Where is the one called Hywel?'

Again they only received the hollow stare in return.

'Do any of you speak?' asked Nesta.

'We are prisoners, not imbeciles,' growled one of the men, 'we do not know the answer.'

Gwladus turned to face Tarw. 'Did you get them all?'

'I did,' said Tarw, 'I swear.'

'Then he must be already dead,' said Nesta coldly.

'Wait,' said Tarw and he pulled back the tarpaulin that covered most of the men. 'We placed ten men on this cart, now there are only eight. Where are the other two?'

'I told you,' said the prisoner again, 'they are not here. They escaped from their bonds a few leagues back and left us here to face whatever fate you have in store for us.'

'What were their names?' snapped Tarw. 'The ones that escaped.'

'I don't know,' said the man.

'You must know,' shouted Tarw, 'you were imprisoned with them.'

'*I do not know!*' shouted the man. 'We were always kept separate except during the work details and everyone kept to themselves. People died so often it was pointless making comrades, it was easier that way. The two who ran were the exception. They had been there the longest and had formed an alliance, one which obviously excluded us.'

'Describe them,' said Tarw. 'Was there anything about them that made them stand out?'

'Yes,' sneered another one of the prisoners, 'one of them was mad.'

'What do you mean?'

'Gone in the head,' said the prisoner tapping his temple, 'suffered from delusions.'

'Why do you say that?' asked Nesta, stepping forward.

'What does it matter?' asked Tarw with a deep sigh.

'*Everything matters!*' shouted Nesta. She turned back to the prisoner. 'Tell me, why do you think he was mad?'

'Because at night he would cry out in his sleep,' said the prisoner.

'Many men suffer nightmares,' said Nesta.

'Yes, but these were different.'

'Why?'

'Because in his dreams, he thought he was a prince.'

Nesta's mouth dropped open and Tarw stared at the prisoner in shock.

'He's talking about Hywel,' said Tarw, turning to face Gwladus. 'Did you hear him, Mother? Hywel is alive.'

'In the name of Jesus,' gasped Nesta, 'he must have thought he was swapping one captor for another and made his escape. I can't believe we came so close just to lose him yet again.'

Tarw turned towards Gwladus, who had tears running down her face.

'Mother, are you all right?'

Gwladus nodded and wiped her eyes before responding.

'See that these men are looked after,' she said, 'and arrange some fresh horses.'

'Why?' asked Tarw.

'Dawn is almost upon us,' said Gwladus, 'and we can follow their tracks. In their state, they can't have got far.'

'You are not coming with me,' said Tarw. 'Belleme's men could still be on our trail and it may be dangerous.'

'I am running out of time, Tarw,' said Gwladus, 'I feel my body weaken by the day and I am not going to forego the chance to see my son again, no matter how fleeting the moment.'

Tarw stared at his mother and knew she was deadly serious.

'So be it,' he said eventually. 'Connor, you stay here with Nesta. In the morning, head for Deheubarth with the prisoners, but take the lesser routes. Wait for us in Builth. Marcus, you will join the queen and me in our quest; the rest of the men will escort the column. Bring two spare horses for Hywel and his comrade. With a bit of luck, we can catch them up by mid-morning and re-join the rest of you before nightfall tomorrow.'

Marcus turned away to his task as Nesta approached her mother.

'Mother, let me come, I may be needed.'

'Not this time,' said Gwladus, 'you have a son to think of and the chance of capture or death is now very real. You stay with the column and look after the prisoners – they are in a terrible state.' She paused before taking her daughter's hands in hers. 'Worry not, Nesta, for if Hywel is still alive, I swear I will see he returns to Dinefwr.'

'I'm sure you will, Mother,' said Nesta. 'Bring him home.'

The Marshlands

September 25th, AD 1105

'Lloyd, wake up!' hissed Hywel, kneeling up to peer over the wall that had sheltered them from the wind over the last few hours of the night.

'What's the matter?' asked Lloyd, instantly awake.

'Horsemen,' whispered Hywel, 'a lot of them.'

Lloyd scrambled to his knees and looked up at the nearby hill. Sure enough, a patrol of at least twenty horsemen were descending from the forest, heading for the river at the bottom of the valley.

'Can you see their colours?' asked Lloyd.

'Yes,' groaned Hywel, 'they are Belleme's men. It seems our freedom is going to be even shorter than I had thought.'

'Not necessarily,' said Lloyd, looking down into the valley below them. 'That water down there is the southern river of Powys. Belleme's reach only extends as far as the river and no more. If we can make the bridge, we will be in safe territory.'

'Since when did Belleme's men respect borders?'

'It was agreed between Lord Goronwy and Belleme,' said Lloyd. 'To cross it would be seen as an act of invasion and could cause conflict – something Henry frowns upon at the moment.'

'There's only an incursion if someone is there to see it,' said Hywel. 'All his men will do is ride us down and return across the river immediately.'

'Not if there are witnesses,' said Lloyd. He pointed to the far side of the river where three horsemen were riding slowly along the bank.

'We'll never make it,' said Hywel, 'the bridge is too far.'

'If we stay here we are dead anyway,' said Lloyd, 'and I'm not giving up now.' Without another word he got to his feet and crouching low, turned to sprint down the slope as fast as his weakened frame would allow. For a moment, Hywel was shocked. But realising he had no other option, he struggled to his feet and followed his comrade down the hill.

On the other side of the river, Tarw stared down at the ground, desperate to find some trace of the trail he had lost just a few hours earlier.

'Are you sure they would have come this way?' asked Gwladus.

'It's obvious they would head northward,' said Tarw, his eyes never leaving the ground, 'and this is the best chance to pick up their trail again. At some point they would have to cross this river.'

'My lord,' shouted Marcus, 'look there.'

'What do you see?' asked Gwladus, lifting her hand to shade her eyes from the morning sun.

'Two men running down the far slope,' said Marcus, 'could they be our quarry?'

'It is too much of a coincidence not to be,' said Tarw. 'Come on, let's go and see.'

All three riders kicked their horses and trotted along the bank towards the point where the men would reach the river.

'Look,' shouted Marcus again and he pointed further up the hill where a column of mounted men had also seen the escapees.

'They must be Belleme's men,' shouted Tarw, 'come on!' He urged his horse to a gallop, desperate to reach the fugitives before the English. In front, the two men realised they could not reach the bridge and hurled themselves from the bank into the fast-flowing river.

'Faster!' shouted Tarw as the flow carried the two men further downstream. But moments later, his horse lurched on the uneven ground, sending him hurtling to the floor.

'Master Tarw,' called Marcus reining in his horse. 'Are you all right?'

'Leave me,' shouted Tarw struggling to his feet, 'go with my mother.'

As the soldier turned his horse to ride after Gwladus, Tarw started to follow on foot, running as fast as his damaged leg would allow.

Broadwick and his men galloped their horses along the far bank before coming to a halt and dismounting further downstream.

'Give me a crossbow!' roared the knight.

One of the archers handed him a loaded weapon. Broadwick aimed carefully at the nearest of the men as the current drew them closer. After a few breaths to steady his breathing he squeezed the trigger and the bolt flew through the air before thudding into one of the escapee's backs.

Instantly, the wounded man screamed in agony and his head flew back as the water around him turned red. Within seconds he stopped trying to swim and sunk beneath the water, his arms floundering uselessly against the strong current.

Gwladus urged her horse to greater speed. In front of her, the second prisoner had reached the near bank but struggled to stand in the shallows, his strength gone from fighting the river.

'My lady, wait,' shouted Marcus as the queen reined in her horse and slid from the saddle, but there was no stopping her and she ran to the bank to help the struggling man. Marcus spurred his horse to greater effort and as he neared, he could see the knight on the far bank placing a second bolt into the crossbow. Gwladus ran down the riverbank and ploughed into the river, desperate to reach the lone survivor.

'*Hold your fire!*' Marcus screamed to the bowman, but Broadwick ignored the call and lifted the crossbow to his shoulder, taking careful aim at his quarry.

'No,' shouted Marcus as he heard the crossbow fire. He watched in horror as the bolt sped across the water towards its target. The man in the water had already turned to face the English, as if to greet his fate but before the bolt could thud home, Gwladus threw herself forward, enveloping him in her arms and forcing them both back down into the river.

Marcus jumped into the water and helped to drag the queen to the bank. Her arms were still tightly clamped around the exhausted man and as they reached the shallows, Marcus could see the water was beginning to turn red. One of them had been hit. He looked across the river and roared at the bowman.

'Hold, your fire,' he screamed. 'In God's name this woman is a queen and you risk the ire of the nation should this man die.'

Broadwick looked across as the three people in the river were joined by a fourth, a man limping heavily.

'You interfere in the affairs of King Henry, strangers,' shouted Broadwick, 'but there is no need for any of you to die. Step away from my prisoner and I will conclude my business.'

'No,' shouted Marcus as Tarw joined him in the water, 'we will not. This man may be the son of a king and as such does not deserve to die in such circumstance. Call off your men or I swear we will turn the weight of an entire nation upon your heads.'

'My lord,' said one of the men beside Broadwick, 'he speaks sense. To kill a prince outside of the field of battle invites not just the wrath of a country but also the ire of our own king. Surely he would not have us commit murder in his name?'

'Leave the matters of court to me, sergeant,' snarled Broadwick. 'Trust me, the king's interests are better served if both of those prisoners are dead.'

'But what of the consequences? If you kill him, these people could lay spark to the fires of rebellion. We have been through too many years of bloodshed to reignite those flames.'

'For that to happen,' said Broadwick, 'there must be survivors to relate the tale.' He looked at his sergeant, their eyes meeting as both considered the implications. Finally, the sergeant turned to the rest of the crossbow men, now descended from their horses.

'Load your weapons,' he called, 'and take aim upon those in the water.'

Without any thought of dissent, all the remaining crossbow men did as they were told and stepped up to stand alongside their sergeant, each aiming carefully at one of the four targets in the river.

'Upon my command!' shouted Broadwick.

'My lord,' shouted a voice before he could give the order to fire, 'look – up on the hill.'

Broadwick turned and to his horror saw hundreds of riders galloping down the slope towards them.

'And there,' shouted another voice, and Broadwick turned to see hundreds more galloping along the far riverbank towards the fugitives.

Nervously, the crossbow men lowered their weapons and watched the two armies descend upon the river. Within moments horsemen formed a defensive line between the English and their intended victims.

'Whose banner do they ride under?' asked one of the soldiers.

'I'm not sure,' said one of the sergeants, 'but I think we are about to find out.' As they watched, two riders rode through the massed ranks of cavalry. One was obviously a man of importance upon a magnificent steed and wearing a tabard over his chainmail hauberk, bearing the same colours as those upon the standard.

'Who speaks for you?' roared the man in the tabard.

'I am he,' replied Broadwick stepping forward, 'and who is it who interferes with the business of the king?'

'I'm Lord Goronwy of Powys,' replied the other knight, 'and demand to know why you are set about killing innocents on my land.'

'That man is no innocent,' said Broadwick pointing at the prisoner being helped from the river, 'he is a fugitive from the law.'

'Whose law?' asked Goronwy.

'Henry's law,' shouted Broadwick, 'and as such I demand his return immediately.'

'Our treaty clearly states that Henry's jurisdiction ends at this river,' said Goronwy, 'and as such, the fate of these people now lays in my hands.'

'Three you can keep,' shouted Broadwick, 'but the prisoner amongst them belongs to the throne of England, and I demand his return in the name of the king.'

'I do not recognise the king's law on this side of the river,' roared Goronwy, 'and what is more, I demand you leave this valley forthwith before I forget where we are and have my army cut you down as the murderer you clearly are.'

Broadwick was seething, but despite his anger he knew he had been bettered. If he raised the ire of the two kings opposite, he and his men would be dead in moments. Without another word he turned away and mounted his horse. Finally, he turned back and faced the two armies.

'You haven't heard the last of this, Goronwy,' he roared. 'Henry will make you pay with blood for your insubordination.'

'For the sake of a mere prisoner, Sir Knight?' shouted Goronwy. 'I very much doubt it. Now be gone before I lose my patience.'

Broadwick and his men turned away and headed back to Hen Domen. Goronwy watched them go before riding to where his soldiers had formed a circle around those they had just rescued. He dismounted and pushed his way through before looking at the scene before him. To one side, an emaciated man was sat with a blanket over his shoulders while Tarw knelt at the side of Gwladus. Goronwy's heart sank as he saw the woman's dress was sodden with blood.

'How is she?' he asked no one in particular.

One of the soldiers looked up and shook his head.

'The bolt passed straight through, my lord, but she has lost a lot of blood. I fear she has only moments to live.'

Goronwy walked over and kneeled beside Gwladus.

'Who are you, good lady?' he asked. 'And what awful events have brought you to this fate?'

'Her name,' snapped Tarw, 'is Gwladus ap Rhiwallon, wife of Rhys ap Tewdwr and once queen of all Deheubarth.'

Goronwy turned to stare at Tarw in shock.

'This is the wife of Tewdwr?' he gasped.

'Yes,' said Tarw, 'and a purer soul has never walked God's earth. She took an arrow in the back to save a man, even though she didn't know whether or not he was her son.'

Goronwy looked over at the emaciated prisoner. His mind working furiously as he realised the implications and he turned back to Tarw.

'If that is Gwladus, who are you?'

'I am her youngest son, Gruffydd ap Rhys, otherwise known as Tarw, prince of Deheubarth.'

Goronwy stared in astonishment. 'God moves in mysterious ways,' he said quietly, staring down at the dying woman.

'It seems that God is a cruel master,' hissed Tarw, fighting back the tears. 'Why would he send an army to help save my brother only to take my mother in his stead? What sort of God plays such tricks?'

'Don't judge the Lord, Tarw, lest you be judged yourself.'

'Let him do what he must,' said Tarw, 'for I have no time for him this day.'

'I only wish I had arrived sooner,' said Goronwy. 'A few moments earlier and they would both have lived.'

'The fault is not yours,' said Tarw without taking his gaze from his mother's face. 'It was the result of a tyranny we Welsh have put up with for far too long, and one that I swear I will one day bring to an end.'

'There is fire in your words, Tarw,' said Goronwy, 'but now is not the time or the place. Look to your mother and see that her last moments are blessed with the love of her family.'

Tarw saw the queen's eyes flicker open.

'Mother,' he said quietly, 'lie still, the pain will be less.'

'Bring him to me,' she whispered.

'Mother, I know not if it is him,' said Tarw, 'he could be anyone.'

'Bring him to me,' she said again, her words hardly audible.

Behind Tarw, Marcus marched over to the prisoner and dragged him to his feet, pulling his face close to his.

'Now you listen to me,' he hissed, spittle splashing on the prisoner's face. 'That woman over there is dying. She saved your life hoping you are the son she hasn't seen for many years. There is no time to establish the truth so you will go over there and make her last moments on this earth as happy as they can be, even if you have to lie. Understood?'

The man nodded and turned away, walking slowly to where Gwladus lay. He dropped to his knees and took her hands in his.

'Mother,' he said quietly, after a glance over at Tarw, 'I am here.'

'Hywel?' asked Gwladus, her eyes opening again and struggling to focus on the face above her. 'Is it really you?'

'Yes,' said the man, 'I am here for you. We are together again.'

Gwladus breathed deeply several times before speaking.

'If it is truly you, my son,' she said then answer me this. 'What is the name of the only other woman who loved you as a child? Tell me truthfully and I will go to my God with a pleasure greater than I have ever known.'

Behind them Marcus stepped forward to intervene but was restrained by Goronwy. 'Leave him,' he said.

The fugitive started shaking and tears rolled down his face at the sight of the dying woman. Tarw looked at the sobbing man, unsure if the emotion was real or as a result of the suffering he had endured in his life. Their eyes met for a mere moment and instantly, Tarw knew the truth.

'Tell her,' Tarw said.

'Nesta,' whispered the man through his sobs, his hand reaching out to stroke his mother's hair. 'Her name was Nesta ferch Rhys and she was my beautiful little sister.' His body shuddered with grief as the memories came flooding back. As he cried, Gwladus used the last of her strength to lift her arms and embrace him.

'It's all right, Hywel,' she said gently, 'your mother's here. You are safe now.'

And as Hywel ap Rhys collapsed into his mother's arms, Gwladus ferch Rhiwallon died from her wounds, knowing that both her remaining sons were by her side at last.

The Outskirts of Brycheniog

October 10th, AD 1105

Goronwy rode over to Tarw, reining in his horse beside that of the southern prince. His army had escorted them southward through brigand-held territory and had eventually caught up with Nesta and the wagon the previous day. They had camped overnight near a local village and after finding a priest, took the opportunity to bury Gwladus in the cemetery of a nearby church.

'This is as far as we go, Tarw,' said Goronwy. 'From here on, the princes are loyal to Wales and your journey should be event free. Not even Belleme will pursue you this far south. With good fortune and fair weather you should be back in Dinefwr Castle within a few days.'

'Thank you, my lord,' said Tarw, 'your protection was much appreciated.'

'How is your sister?'

'Surprisingly strong,' said Tarw. 'I'm sure that deep inside she grieves in her own way but outwardly she is just concerned about Hywel.'

'Perhaps that is a good thing,' said Goronwy, 'and in time, the grief will come. So what lies before you now?'

'First we have to make my brother well again,' replied Tarw. 'Believe it or not, I have never met him in the flesh and we have a lot to catch up on.'

'I think he will recover well,' said Goronwy, 'but take your time for his injuries are of the mind as well as the flesh.'

'I know,' said Tarw, 'and my sister will ensure he has the best of care.'

'And what of you, will you return to Ireland?'

'I don't know yet. My head says I should for I have a good life there but my heart burns to stay in Wales and fight for that which is lost.'

'That is a lifetime's commitment,' said Goronwy, 'and a decision that should not be taken lightly.'

'Did you know my father?' asked Tarw.

'Alas no,' said Goronwy, 'though I am told he was a good man.'

'Yet he left no enduring legacy.'

'Let the memory of what he did at Mynydd Carn be his legacy,' said Goronwy, 'for that day, alongside Gruffydd and against overwhelming odds he stopped Wales becoming absorbed into the English nation. No man can claim a better memorial.'

'So are you going home?' asked Tarw.

'I am. Though there be treaties in place with the king, the Marcher lords are just as dangerous as ever. Besides, I need to report back to Gruffydd about what has taken place these past few days.'

'Then travel safely,' said Tarw, 'and one day, when my kingdom is restored, I will repay this debt a thousand-fold.'

The following day, the column rode through Brycheniog, heading westward towards Deheubarth. Hywel lay in the back of the cart, tended by Nesta while Marcus rode alongside Tarw and Connor. As they neared a bridge, their path was blocked by a single rider.

Tarw held up his hand and the rest of the column drew to a halt.

'And who may that be?' asked Connor.

'I don't know,' said Tarw. 'Go ahead and find out.'

Connor urged his horse forward and talked to the lone rider before coming back to speak to Tarw.

'It's one of Owain's men from the assault on Hen Domen,' said Connor. 'He says Owain hopes that everything went as expected but now waits upon his purse.'

'A fair expectation,' said Tarw. 'Where is Owain now?'

'There,' said Connor and he pointed up the nearby hill where a solitary man was sat upon a log.

'Why does he have to be so dramatic?' Tarw sighed. 'That man really annoys me sometimes.'

'Who?' asked Nesta, walking over from the back of the cart to see what the delay was.

'Owain ap Cadwgan,' said Tarw. 'He has the personality of a snake, the morals of a rat and the cunning of a fox. What women see in him I'll never know.'

'What does he want?'

'He seeks the cost of his involvement,' said Tarw, 'and in truth, Hywel would not be here without Owain's aid.'

'Then we should pay him the agreed cost. Where is the purse?'

'In the strong box in the cart. Bring it to me and I will pay the man.'

'No,' said Nesta slowly, 'let me be the one to hand over the blood money. I am intrigued to see what man causes so many women to fall at his feet.

Tarw looked at Nesta and then up at Owain before returning his gaze to his sister.

'I don't see why not,' he said with a grin, 'it would be good to see the man meet his match. Marcus, go with her, you never know, he may just need protection from my sister, methinks he has never met a woman as strong-willed as she.'

Nesta returned to the wagon and brought a satchel of money from the strong box before borrowing a horse from one of the soldiers.

'Come on then,' she said, 'the quicker we pay our debt the quicker we can get Hywel home.'

'Marcus Freeman,' said Owain as the man walked up the hill to meet him, 'we meet again. And who is this beauty at your side?'

'Greetings, Owain,' said Marcus, 'this is Nesta ferch Rhys, the sister of the man we released from Hen Domen.'

'Lady Nesta,' said Owain getting to his feet and taking her hand. 'It is an honour to meet you. Please accept my deepest con-dolences about your departed mother.'

'Thank you,' said Nesta withdrawing her hand. 'She was indeed a special lady.'

'I never had the pleasure of knowing her,' said Owain. For a few moments there was silence between them until finally Nesta spoke.

'So, I believe we have some business to conclude?'

'We do,' said Owain, 'but before we continue, I feel obliged to make my feelings clear.'

'In what way?'

'I had heard rumours about your incredible beauty,' replied Owain, 'but I pity the man who told me for he was obviously blind. You are far more beautiful than even he described. Had I known then perhaps I would have made an effort to meet you sooner.'

'Thank you,' said Nesta, 'but I have come here to pay a debt, not to listen to a scoundrel with words sweeter than the honey of a bee.'

'Ordinarily I would see that as a challenge,' said Owain, 'but there is something about you I have never seen before.'

'And what is that may I ask?'

'I have no idea,' said Owain, 'only to say I am enchanted.'

'Then un-enchant yourself,' said Nesta holding out the satchel, 'and take what you have earned.'

'How much is in there?' asked Owain.

'The full amount,' said Nesta, 'we are an honourable family and pay what is promised.'

'If I recall, the price was more than a minor lord would see in an entire lifetime.'

'Almost a king's ransom,' said Nesta. 'Now do you want it or not?'

Owain stared at Nesta and she felt his eyes burning into hers. For the first time she could see how attractive he really was and the confidence of his manner made her breath harder to draw.

'Well?' she asked.

'I'll tell you what,' said Owain, 'I'll make you a deal. You give me a single kiss and you can take that money back to your family.'

'*What?*' gasped Nesta, lowering her arm. 'There is a fortune in this bag. Why would you give it up for such a small thing?'

'Money I can get,' said Owain. 'A kiss from someone as beautiful as you is a far more precious award.'

'This is nonsense,' said Nesta. 'I am a married woman. What makes you think I would kiss you?'

'Because I suspect your family could use the money,' said Owain, 'and in return, all I ask is one simple kiss. Surely your husband would forgive you that.'

Nesta stared at the man, her pulse racing. His eyes still pierced deep into her soul and she could feel herself blushing.

'Well?' he said as she wavered.

'You are right,' she said eventually, 'my family needs this money more than you could ever know, and yes, my husband would forgive me, for he has forgiven much worse. But it is not about him, or my family, it is not even about you. This is about me and my self-respect.' She threw the satchel towards him and he caught it easily with one outstretched hand. 'So take your money, Owain ap Cadwgan,' she continued, 'and no, you will not be getting your kiss, today or any time in the future. I have a family to repair and a kingdom to rebuild.'

Without another word she turned away and made her way back down the hill, closely followed by Marcus.

'Travel safely, Lady Nesta.' Owain laughed. 'But know this. Before my days are over I will have that kiss, no matter how long it takes. And when I do, it will be with your blessing.'

'Ignore him,' said Marcus as they continued to walk.

'I am trying,' hissed Nesta, 'but he is so damn annoying.'

A few minutes later they reached the wagon and Tarw looked at his sister.

'Well,' he said, 'how did it go?'

'Just get us home,' snapped Nesta walking straight past him and climbing into the wagon. 'We have work to do.'

'What's wrong with her?' Tarw asked Marcus.

'I don't think it went quite as well as she had planned,' said Marcus, and with a laugh he spurred his horse forward to cross the bridge.

Back in the cart, Nesta tucked a blanket around the sleeping Hywel, but as the column resumed its journey she sneaked one last look up the hill, and was strangely disappointed to see the log empty. Owain had gone.

Dinefwr Castle

October 29th, AD 1105

Tarw walked slowly around the deserted bailey of the castle alongside
Marcus. Over at the gate, Connor waited patiently, holding the reins
of two horses, each loaded with enough rations for a week's travel.

'So,' said Marcus as they walked, 'you are going back to Ireland.'

'For now,' said Tarw. 'I have to sort out my affairs there but once
that is done, I will return and try to salvage what I can of our estates.'

'How long do you think that will take?'

'I don't know,' said Tarw, 'perhaps a couple of months, perhaps
a bit longer. But while I am away, I want you to run this place for
me. I have a little money left, enough for you to engage some staff
and run the estate until winter. Once that is gone, you will have to
earn a living some other way but this will always be your home.'

'A castle of my own.' Marcus laughed. 'Oh, how I've come on
in the world.'

Tarw smiled. 'My mother would have liked it,' he said, 'she was
very fond of you.'

'And I was fond of her,' said Marcus, 'and if truth be told, I was
always envious of your father for marrying the best-looking woman

in the south. I only regret that she never knew the affection I held for her.'

'I think she had a good idea,' said Tarw. 'Anyway, what news of Hywel?'

'I left Pembroke Castle just yesterday,' said Marcus, 'having spent a few days there with Nesta.'

'And?'

'Hywel recovers well and already gains fat about his bones. He suffers badly from nightmares but at least he is regaining his health.'

'That's good,' said Tarw, 'by the time I return, perhaps he will be well enough to ride alongside me and together we can rebuild what was once ours.'

'Tarw, there is something you should know,' said Marcus, stopping and looking at the prince.

'What is it?' asked Tarw. 'Your countenance concerns me.'

'Tarw, your brother was in a terrible state when he arrived at Pembroke.'

'I know,' said Tarw, 'and I am truly grateful to Gerald for taking him in.'

'Yes, but there is more,' said Marcus. 'Hywel has been mutilated and is not the man you think he is, nor can he ever be.'

'What do you mean, Marcus?' asked Tarw. 'Spit it out.'

'They castrated him, Tarw, when he was a boy.'

Tarw gasped and tilted his head back to look up at the sky in shock.

'I'm sorry,' continued Marcus, 'but I thought you should know.'

'Who else knows about this?' asked Tarw, straightening up and facing the steward.

'Apart from the physicians in Pembroke Castle, just you, Nesta and myself.'

'Then let's keep it that way,' said Tarw. 'In addition, send Nesta a message and tell her to keep his rescue a secret. No matter what his injuries, he will always be my brother and when I return, he will ride alongside me with head held high. But until then, he needs to lie low.'

'Understood,' said Marcus.

The two men completed their circuit of the bailey before returning to the horses.

'Well, old friend,' said Tarw, 'my time to leave is upon us. Look after the castle for me and keep one eye on my sister. She is a firebrand and more than capable of getting into trouble.'

'Nesta will be fine,' said Marcus, 'just worry about yourself.'

'In that case,' said Tarw as he climbed up into his saddle, 'fare ye well, Marcus. I will see you before the year is out.'

'Until next time,' said Marcus.

As Tarw rode out of Dinefwr, the empty castle echoed with the sound of receding horses' hooves. It would be a long time before it heard the like again.

At the other end of the country, two men rode silently side by side along a deserted road.

'Where are we going?' asked Meirion Goch for what seemed like the tenth time that day.

'Silence,' said Gruffydd, reining in his horse. 'I think this is the place.'

'Three years I have rotted in that dungeon,' continued Meirion, 'despite your sworn oath to set me free.'

'Indeed I swore such a thing,' said Gruffydd, 'though I believe the timing was never discussed. Anyway, compared to the suffering your treachery caused me, three years is nothing.'

'What's past, is past,' snapped Meirion, 'and you promised me my freedom.'

'I am a man of my word, Meirion, unlike you.' Gruffydd reached beneath his cloak and drawing a knife, leaned forward to cut Meirion's bonds.

Meirion rubbed his wrists to ease the stiffness.

'So,' he said, 'is this it?'

'It is,' said Gruffydd, 'you are a free man, as promised.'

'Then I will keep you no longer,' said Meirion, taking up his reins. 'I have a new life to build.'

'You do,' said Gruffydd, as the traitor rode away, 'though it remains to be seen how long that may last.'

Meirion stopped his horse and turned to face Gruffydd.

'What's that supposed to mean?'

'Not much,' said Gruffydd, 'but you should know the truth about what awaits you.'

'Explain,' growled Meirion.

'I promised you freedom, Meirion Goch, and gave you my word that I would not harm you. I have now delivered my promises in these matters, but I also have my honour to think of and was duty-bound to tell Lord Goronwy of how you robbed him for ten years, costing him money as well as the lives of many trusted men.'

'You told him that?'

'Why wouldn't I?'

'Because we had an agreement.'

'I recall nothing about keeping your vile tendencies secret,' said Gruffydd. 'In fact, I see it as fair retribution for all those years I was held in that stinking well.'

'I should have known,' spat Meirion. 'You are no better than me, Gruffydd.'

'On the contrary,' replied Gruffydd, 'a young man told me not so long ago that I should rule with my conscience. Well, know this, Meirion ap Goch – my conscience is clear.'

'You don't frighten me, Gruffydd!' shouted Meirion as the king rode away. 'I know these lands better than any and know what it takes to stay clear of trouble. I will be long gone before the hunt can begin.'

'Begin?' Gruffydd laughed over his shoulder. 'Oh, Meirion Goch look around you. It is already over.'

As Gruffydd galloped away, Meirion Goch looked over to the treeline and his heart sank as hundreds of men emerged. Behind him, more men appeared and both ends of the track were soon blocked off by cavalry. He was surrounded. At the head of the valley, Gruffydd rode up to Goronwy.

'He is yours to do with as you will, Goronwy,' said Gruffydd.

'My torturer is waiting, Gruffydd,' said Goronwy, 'and will make the traitor's pain last an eternity before the blessing of death falls upon him.'

Gruffydd nodded in silence before urging his horse northward once more. Behind him he heard Goronwy give the order.

'Deliver the traitor to the castle dungeons, there is someone there I want him to meet.'

Epilogue

The Palace of Aberffraw, November 15th, AD 1105

Gruffydd ap Cynan, King of Gwynedd, dropped onto the bench beneath the oak tree and reached for the hand of his wife. For a few seconds he stayed silent, enjoying the last of the autumn sun and catching his breath after the exertions of the last half an hour.

'Tired, my love?' asked Angharad with a smile.

'Those children will be the death of me,' he gasped. 'Where do they get their energy from?'

Angharad looked over at the four children running around the grass wielding their toy swords.

'They have the stamina of their father,' she said simply, 'a man who goes on and on, never knowing when he is beaten.' She squeezed his hand and looked at him lovingly. 'Are you home for good?'

'For as far as I can see,' said Gruffydd. 'The treaty is holding with Henry, Cadwgan is keeping peace in the marches and even his troublesome son, Owain, seems to be quiet at the moment.'

'Good,' said Angharad, snuggling in close to her husband. 'That means we get to have you all to ourselves for a while.'

'I don't know,' said Gruffydd. 'I may have to start a war just to get some respite from my children.'

Angharad nudged him with her elbow and continued to watch the children playing.

'Do you think they have a good future?' she asked eventually.

'I don't see why not,' said Gruffydd, 'they are royal born, live in relatively peaceful times and have a loving family about them. Whatever happens, I will ensure the boys have adequate training so whatever this world throws at them, they will be ready to meet it head on.'

'And our daughter?'

Gruffydd's head turned slightly and he stared at the eight-year-old girl. She had knocked her eldest brother down and now stood over him, pointing her wooden sword at his throat, demanding surrender.

'Gwenllian?' he said with a smile. 'Something tells me that she is going to be just fine.'

'You really think so?' asked Angharad. 'For not a day goes by without me worrying about her.'

'Trust me, my love,' said Gruffydd as Gwenllian raised her toy sword in the air and roared her victory. 'Something tells me that one day that girl is going to be one very special woman.'

Author's Note

The Rescue of Gruffydd ap Cynan

Estimates of the length of Gruffydd's imprisonment by Huw the Fat vary from eight to sixteen years. However, most sources agree that he was rescued from Chester by a man called Cynwrig the Tall who seized an opportunity and carried him to safety. Gruffydd fled to Ireland to recover from his long imprisonment before re-joining the struggle against the English, carrying out a guerrilla campaign before finally capturing Ynys Mon.

Gruffydd ap Rhys

Gruffydd ap Rhys (Tarw in our tale) was sent to Ireland for his own safety as a child, eventually returning to Wales as a young man to take part in the continued fight against the English. His tale becomes a very important part in the history of Wales, which is expanded upon in book three.

The Assault on Ynys Mon

Hugh Montgomery actually did face a Viking fleet on the shores of Anglesey (Ynys Mon) and it is said that he was cut down before the battle began by an arrow to the eye, shot by the king of the Vikings,

Magnus Barefoot. Gruffydd later went on to recapture the island before consolidating his rule across North Wales.

The Siege of Pembroke
Gerald of Windsor did actually defend Pembroke Castle against a Welsh army and it is very interesting to learn that he did indeed use cooked meat to taunt the besiegers, and tricked them into believing he was well armed by arranging a false letter to be intercepted. The ruse worked perfectly and the Welsh abandoned the siege, thinking the enemy was in a far better state than they actually were. It was a brilliant strategy and due to the important location of Pembroke Castle, possibly altered the course of Welsh history.
During the siege, up to 15 of Gerald's Knights deserted and made their escape by boat.

Nesta ferch Rhiwallon
Nesta did indeed attend the court of William II and had a passionate relationship with his brother Henry. She went on to have Henry's child before returning to Wales to become the wife of Gerald of Windsor, having been given the estate of Carew as part of her dowry.

The Death of William II
William the Second, or William Rufus as he was known, died after being hit by an arrow fired by Walter Tirel while hunting stags. Some say it was an accident while others say it was deliberate and a conspiracy with Henry who went on to rule as king. Whatever the truth, Tirel fled to France and never returned to England.

The Incarceration of Hywel ap Rhys
Hywel ap Rhys was a prisoner of the English for many, many years and was probably incarcerated in a fortress called Hen Domen.

Records vary as to whether he was released or escaped but most agree he was in a terrible state when he finally joined up with his brother, suffering from severe injuries as well as castration.

About the Author

Kevin Ashman is the author of fifteen novels, including the bestselling Roman Chronicles and highly ranked Medieval Sagas. Always pushing the boundaries, he found further success with the India Sommers Mysteries, as well as three other standalone projects, *Vampire, Savage Eden* and the dystopian horror story *The Last Citadel.* Kevin was born and raised in Wales and now writes full-time. He is married with four grown children and enjoys cycling, swimming and watching rugby. Current works include the highly anticipated Blood of Kings series, of which *A Wounded Realm* is the second instalment. Links to all Kevin's books can be found at www.KMAshman.co.uk.